A LITTLE JADED

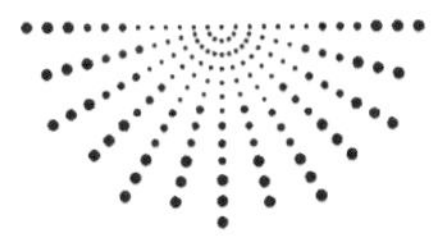

KELSIE RAE

TWISTY PINES PUBLISHING, LLC

CHAPTER ONE

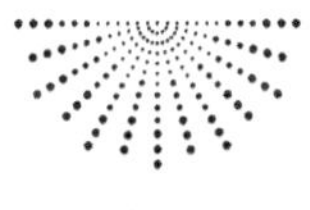

EVERETT

Adrenaline lingers in my veins as I slide my jeans on after my shower. The locker room buzzes with energy after our three-to-one win against the Grizzlies. It was a rough game, but since the Hawks came out on top, it was more than worth it. I roll my shoulders as the ache from a particularly brutal hit spreads up my neck and down my spine. Yeah. I'm gonna feel it even more tomorrow.

I've been playing hockey for as long as I can remember. My dad might not have played professionally like my uncle and my friends' families, but I'm still convinced it runs deep in my blood. Making me who I am while holding my future if I can maintain the willpower and determination to stay in top form.

"Good game, man," one of my teammates offers.

As I rub my white towel against my damp hair, I lift my chin and reply, "Thanks," when the heavy metal door bangs against the locker room's cinder block walls.

It's followed by someone yelling, "Ev!"

"What?" Cameron, another teammate, answers for me.

"Where's Everett?" the person demands.

It's Reeves.

My roommate. Teammate. And more recently, *friend*. Still holding onto my white towel, I button my jeans the rest of the way as Reeves looks around the corner and comes into view.

"What's up?" I ask.

"Come out here."

"Why?"

"Come on," he pushes.

Forgetting about my shirt still hanging in my locker, I stride closer. "What is it?"

"Remember our deal?" he asks. "There's a girl outside. She needs your help."

Aaaand, there goes the high I was riding from our win.

Yeah, I know exactly what my buddy's talking about, and it doesn't give me any warm fuzzies. Reeves and I have always been at odds with each other, and that's putting shit lightly. But after sticking my nose in his relationship with our best friend's little sister, I decided I owed him one, and he cashed in on it big time. How? By making me agree to take over his side gig for the next six months. Normally, I wouldn't complain about taking on a little something else, but when it involves fake dating girls under the guise of protecting them from their shitty boyfriends? Well, I've been less than enthusiastic about the whole thing. Don't get me wrong. I'm not a heartless bastard. But why can't they just... leave? Or, I dunno, maybe *not* date assholes in the first place?

Damn, maybe I am heartless.

It's not that I don't care—I do. But when I'm already busy keeping track of my baby sister and her friends on campus or calling my dad to make sure my mom's okay, it's...exhausting. Having one more person rely on me feels like it might be the straw that breaks the camel's back. But what the hell do I know?

Reeling in my annoyance, I throttle the towel in my hand. "Fuck, man. I don't have time—"

"And I don't give a shit." Reeves grabs my arm and shoves me out the door to the arena's main hallway. Then, he scans the premises with an urgency I'm not used to. Reeves doesn't give a shit about anything or any*one* except his girlfriend, Dylan. Or at least, it's the persona he leads everyone to believe. Over the last few months, I've caught glimpses of the real guy and learned his heart's bigger than any of us ever gave him credit for. But right now, something has him on edge, and I don't like it.

When his attention lands on the back of a small-framed girl in a black jacket, he repeats, "Come on," to me while jogging toward her at the end of the hall and calling out, "Hey, wait up!"

Her body freezes, and she slowly turns to face him. "Look, I'm sorry I bothered you—"

"You didn't bother me," he argues. Glancing over his shoulder, he gives me a look telling me to hurry the hell up.

I grumble under my breath but pick up the pace, wishing I'd thought to slip on my sneakers before rushing out. Who knows when the last time these floors were actually cleaned.

Gross.

When I reach them, my muscles lock as I take in the strange girl. Long, dark brown hair. Highlights. She's pretty. And *small.* Hell, she barely reaches my shoulder. Sunglasses cover her eyes, and I want to push them away so I can see what color they are. I don't really care, but having them covered when we're indoors causes warning bells to ring in my head. It feels like she's hiding something, and if Reeves' response is anything to go by, I'd say she is.

"This is Everett," Reeves adds, introducing me to her. "And you are...?"

He doesn't know her.

Interesting.

A beat of silence follows until she finally answers. "I'm Raine."

"Everett, Raine. Raine, Everett," Reeves repeats.

Raine. If she wasn't such a dark cloud on my day, I'd say it's pretty. Guess it's fitting, considering the circumstances.

"Hello, Raine," I mutter. My greeting is tight and forced and makes me sound like a dick, but I can't help myself.

What the fuck does Reeves expect me to do? Shake her hand and ask where her boyfriend is so I can beat the shit out of him? This is ridiculous. I don't fake date girls. I don't fake anything. This has always been Reeves' department, and he expects me to jump right in with both feet?

No, thank you.

Remembering the manners my mother spent years teaching me, I reach my hand out for Raine to shake, but she only stares at it. Like it's a snake. One ready to strike at any second. It makes me feel like more of a dick.

"Raine," Reeves interrupts, "Everett can help you with your...issue."

"Issue." A quiet scoff echoes past her lips, surprising me. "So that's what we're calling him."

Him.

The asshole.

Great.

"Look, I gotta go." Reeves takes a step backward, adding, "But, uh, you two chat. Figure shit out. And, Ev? If you need anything, let me know." He turns on his heel and jogs toward the opposite end of the hall where his girlfriend waits, though I have no idea how long Dylan's been standing there. She gives him a quick hug, and they disappear from view.

Leaving me alone with a girl I should have nothing to do with.

Fucking promises.

What the hell are we supposed to do now?

Scratching the scruff along my jaw, I tilt my head. "So, uh, I don't exactly know how this works."

Her gaze darts from left to right as she curls in on herself. "Neither do I."

"Do you…wanna talk about it, or…?"

The girl scoffs again. "You know what?" She starts to turn away. "You're off the hook. I changed my mind."

"Wait." I reach for her arm, but she flinches away from me. And fuck, it hurts. The way her body tenses up. The way she assumes I'll harm her. I don't even know her. Lifting my hands in surrender, I rush out, "I won't touch you, all right? Just…wait for two seconds."

She scowls but stays in place, studying me. "Why?"

It's a good question. I shift on my bare feet, squeezing the back of my neck as I fight the urge to turn around and let us go our separate ways, even if it would confirm my asshole status.

"I don't know?" I answer honestly. "Because"—I wave my hand toward her—"I promised my friend I'd step in if someone wanted to hire him since he's now in a relationship, and you obviously need…*help*."

Another scoff escapes her as her eyes drop to gaze at the floor, and she shifts from one foot to the other. "Obviously."

"What, it's not obvious?" I push. "You're wearing sunglasses inside."

As if only now remembering she's wearing them, her dainty fingers skate against the dark frames, but she doesn't take them off. "Maybe I don't want the world to see what a fist can do when provoked."

"Yeah, well, you're not fooling anyone, so maybe you should give the disguise a break."

She nods, though I don't know if it's for me or if she's trying to convince herself it's a good idea. To give the disguise a break. To not cover up the damage some asshole left on her. Regardless, her hands tremble as she slips the glasses off and folds them. Lifting her chin, her forest-green eyes hit mine and almost knock me on my ass as soon as our gazes lock. But the fire in them does me in. The anger. Determination. It's almost enough to distract me from the purple and black bruising along her cheekbone and the blood-red veins tainting the white surrounding her left iris.

"Fuck," I breathe out.

As if my words are a lash, she forces a smile and unfolds her glasses again, avoiding my gaze. "And this is why I keep the glasses on."

I reach for her, hesitating at the last second to keep from touching her and scaring her all over again while feeling like I'm moving in circles. Like *we're* moving in circles. I don't know this girl, but whoever she is, she's like a scared little mouse, and if I don't tread lightly, I have a feeling she'll bolt.

She stares at my half-outstretched hand the same way she did when I offered it to shake during our introduction. Then, slowly, her gaze trails along my bare torso—fuck, I forgot to put a shirt on when Reeves dragged me out here—until her eyes reach mine. "I don't want your pity."

"What *do* you want?"

"From you?" She slides her glasses back on. "Nothing."

"Then why come in the first place?" I demand. I shouldn't be offended, but dammit, I kind of am. When she stays quiet, I push. "What? I'm not good enough to help you, but Reeves is?"

"This wouldn't have been Reeves' first rodeo. Not if the rumors are true."

I move closer to her. "And you think it's mine?"

"By the look on your face? I'm gonna go with yes, this would be your first time helping someone in my situation.

I'm not stupid enough to risk pissing off my boyfriend even more than I already have by being here."

"Yet you're stupid enough to date him in the first place, am I right?" Regret clogs my throat as soon as the words roll off my tongue, but it's too late.

Her sharp inhale lingers in the otherwise silent corridor as she glares at me. And I'm surprised by the girl's tenacity.

"Fuck. You."

The words slam into my chest, leaving a heavy dose of shame in their wake. I shouldn't have said it. What the hell is my problem? Moving in front of her, I block her escape and rush out, "Look, I'm sorry—"

Heavy footsteps echo off the walls, breaking the building tension and distracting us both. Raine glances over her shoulder, searching for the culprit. The way her body tenses, the way she looks like a ghost is chasing her, gets to me and pisses me the fuck off.

"I have to go," she whispers.

"Wait!"

"I *can't.*" She scurries down the hall like the little mouse I pegged her for, disappears around the corner, and cuts off the heavy footsteps heading my direction.

I should be grateful. For the get-out-of-jail-free card. For the chance to wash my hands of this entire thing and go back to the locker room to celebrate today's win with the rest of the team. Instead, I stand here. In the middle of the empty hallway. Waiting. For what, I'm not sure. But I can't walk away. Can't get my feet to move.

"Where the fuck have you been?" a low voice growls.

"I was looking for you," Raine answers. There's a tremor in her voice, and, dammit, it urges me forward.

I have a feeling I'll regret this.

CHAPTER TWO

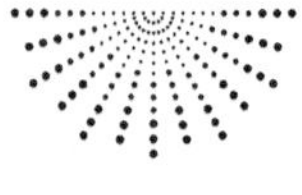

RAINE

There are bad ideas, and then there is *this* bad idea. Reaching out to a guy I've never met and asking him for what? Protection? I'd laugh if it wasn't so pathetic. *What was I thinking?*

So. Damn. Stupid.

I pull my arms a little closer around me, rushing toward the familiar gait, hoping to keep Drake's frustration in check, though I doubt it'll work. Not after today's loss. It looks like the honeymoon phase after he decked me a couple of nights ago is about to end. It's a pity. If the Grizzlies had won, I'd probably have a solid few days until Drake's asshole side decided to make another appearance.

Why am I not surprised?

It's funny. How easy it is to judge a person from the outside without seeing the intricate details weaving together to make them who they are. Make their situation the way it is. I know how ridiculous it seems for me to stay with Drake after he hit me. The reminder makes my stomach churn, but I shove it aside and quicken my steps.

In the beginning, he was charming. Charismatic. We met at a coffee shop, and he asked for my number. There were no red flags. No warning bells. Only a passionate hockey player with something to prove. And for a while? I was his main goal. Winning me over. Making me fall for him. With roses and kisses and back massages and takeout. It was perfect. *He* was perfect.

It wasn't until months later, after we moved in together, that I started catching glimpses of who he really was beneath his carefully constructed facade.

At first, it was nothing more than a few asshole comments here and there. Then, an empty threat or a rough shove. Still screwed up, don't get me wrong, but easy to overlook. Easy to justify when I was so used to the flowers and the presents and the easy compliments. Eventually, a girl from my work started noticing the bruises along my wrist, and after my first black eye—ever—she told me about a guy from her school.

Reeves. No first name. I didn't even believe it was a real name until the announcer's voice boomed it from the speakers as the hockey players took the ice earlier today. Regardless, he got Lilah out of a bind not so long ago, and she figured I could use the help, too.

Part of me didn't want to bother. The other part? Well, can you blame me for being curious?

Yeah. I really am an idiot.

As soon as Everett walked out of the locker room, I realized this stupid plan was a mistake. A big, fat mistake I'll probably pay dearly for since I wasn't waiting outside the visitors' locker room like Drake ordered me to. Okay, ordered is probably the wrong word. Begged is more like it. He's been walking on eggshells since he hit me. Like he's afraid I'll try to bolt. Like he knows he screwed up but isn't sure exactly how much or if I have the ovaries to finally leave him.

If I wasn't so terrified he'd track me down—or worse—I would.

Wouldn't I?

Maybe I am a coward.

Tucking my chin to my chest, I pick up my pace. My body feels like it's been injected with carbonation. Like I'm fizzing and shaken and could burst at any second as I round the corner to the next hall, and my heels dig into the cement floor.

"Where the fuck have you been?" Drake growls.

"I was looking for you."

"Don't give me that shit," he spits. "I told you to wait by the men's locker room."

"I thought I was." I peek behind me, then look back at Drake. "I've never been to this rink. I got turned around a—"

His biting grasp on my bicep cuts my words off as I choke on my whimper.

"Fuck." He lets me go as if I've burned him. "Baby, I'm sorry."

"It's fine." It isn't, but I don't know what else to say. I rub away the residual ache from his angry grasp, unsure what to do or where to go.

"It's just..." Slowly, he lifts his hand and cups my cheek, letting his thumb slip beneath my sunglasses as he carefully caresses the bruise he knows is hidden there. "After the other day, I was worried you left."

The other day.

As in, when he knocked me on my ass with a solid right hook.

Refusing to flinch from his touch, I murmur, "I promised I wouldn't go anywhere, remember?"

He nods. "That's my girl."

His girl.

My stomach twists.

"Hey, you okay?" someone demands from behind me.

Shit.

"Raine, you okay?" Everett prods.

Whatever compliance I managed to siphon from Drake dissipates as he drops his hand. "You know him?" His voice is deathly cold, leaving a chill on my skin.

Ignoring Everett, my eyes plead with Drake, though I doubt he notices, thanks to my sunglasses. "Drake—"

"Raine," Everett interrupts. "Are. You. Okay?"

Bringing us nose to nose, Drake ignores Everett and grits out, "He knows *you*." The darkness in his eyes burns a hole in the pit of my stomach until he stands up straight, as if only now remembering his white knight act we both know is a lie.

But the lie isn't for me.

It's for Everett.

And it makes me hate Drake even more.

I don't know Everett. Not personally, anyway. I've seen him once or twice when Drake's team played LAU, but otherwise, I don't know anything about him. To say I was freaking flabbergasted when Reeves disappeared into the locker room only to drag his replacement out? His *shirtless* replacement? Well, let's just say my libido's been on the fritz for a while now, yet all it took was ten seconds in Everett's vicinity to know the girl's still alive and well, no thanks to my boyfriend.

Hooking his arm over my shoulder, Drake asks, "So, how long have you known my girlfriend?"

"He doesn't," I start.

"About three months," Everett lies.

"Three months?" Drake repeats thoughtfully. He bends down, moving into my line of sight again. "You hear that, Raine? Three months."

"He's lying," I argue. "We met a few minutes ago. I was looking for the men's locker room, ran into him, and asked for directions."

"Just met, huh?" Lifting his head again, he turns to Everett. "You lyin', man?"

Everett shakes his head. "What's there to lie about?"

Drake's full lips flatten as he studies Everett. I wonder if he notices how attractive the guy is. If he can practically taste Everett's pheromones the way I can. The way every girl in the vicinity could if they were in my position. If they were a few feet away from a hockey god like Everett. Yeah. I might not have met Everett until today, but I've heard plenty, thanks to Drake's late-night ramblings. Drake is competitive with everyone. People with actual talent? Drake's a goner. I have no doubt if I did wind up dating someone like Everett and Drake found out, he'd be… I don't even want to know.

It's strange, though. Seeing them side by side. Where Drake is all brawn, Everett's more toned. Leaner, maybe. His legs are longer, too, even though they're matched for height, making Drake look almost imbalanced with how long his torso is. Regardless, it only makes their staredown more tangible. More intimidating. Where Drake's hair is cropped short in a buzz, Everett's is longer on the sides. More black, less brown. Straighter, too. Everett's jaw is sharper, his nose less crooked. I've never minded Drake's nose. It's been broken so many times I used to find it charming. The thought is laughable now. Or it would be if I wasn't so worried a fight's about to break out.

The question is, does Drake believe me or Everett? Does he really think I'd sneak around behind his back? Especially for three months? Before he hit me, I'd say no. Not a chance. Since then? Well, things have been precarious at best.

As if Drake can read my mind, his focus snaps to me, then back to Everett. "Look, here's the truth. I'm in a bad mood after today's game, you know? After those bullshit calls, and—"

Everett's scoff cuts him off.

Drake moves closer to Everett, and my adrenaline spikes.

Way to piss off the bull, Everett.

I know this side of Drake. The hotheaded side. The let's-go-out-back-and-sort-this-shit-out-like-men side. The macho-man, pound-your-fists-against-your-chest side. The short fuse side. Granted, Drake's always had a short fuse, but after a loss like tonight? Let's just say I know he's already close to the edge. All he needs is a little push, and I really don't want Everett to be the one to tip him over.

"Drake, let's go home," I offer.

He lifts his hand behind his back, showing me his palm and warning me to stay out of this, but doesn't bother facing me. Instead, his entire focus is on Everett and only Everett. "You think you won fair and square?"

"I think the refs did their job to make it a fair game, yeah."

"And I think you should stay the fuck away from my girl."

"Maybe she doesn't want to be your girl anymore," Everett argues.

Shit.

Read the room, you idiot!

A knot forms in my stomach, and my breathing grows shallow because Everett has no idea what he just said or how badly I might pay the consequences for it. If he honestly thinks he's helping me right now, he's even more dense than I thought. It confirms my decision to leave him out of this. If only he'd take the hint.

Nostrils flaring, Drake steps even closer, crowding Everett in the nearly empty hallway. "And maybe you have no fuckin' clue what you're talking about."

"And maybe you should back the hell up and remember where you are," Everett snaps, refusing to back down or cower under Drake's scrutiny. It's impressive. Or it would be if I wasn't so scared right now.

The testosterone floating in the air burns my throat as I breathe it in, my eyes darting from Drake to Everett and back again. They're nose to nose. Chest to chest. Everett has a little less weight than Drake, but it's close. Really close. If I didn't personally know the power behind Drake's punch, I'd think there was a chance for Everett to walk away the victor, but I'm not stupid. Drake isn't afraid to fight dirty. He isn't afraid of anything. Anything except me abandoning him.

I should get someone. One of Everett's teammates, maybe? I don't really know, but standing here with my hands at my sides makes me feel helpless. Useless.

A door opens at the end of the hall. The hinges creak, and the heavy metal slams against cinderblock, followed by loud laughter. It's Everett's teammates. They're coming this way.

Drake tilts his head, registering the footsteps growing closer as he continues glaring at Everett.

What are you going to do, Drake? I want to ask but keep my mouth shut. This is LAU's stomping ground. Not Drake's. Not mine. And if things go south, I have no doubt Everett's teammates will happily jump in to defend their center. Drake has to know this.

Doesn't he?

"See you around, dipshit," Drake finally growls. He steps back and pins me with his stare. "Raine. I'll see you at home. Right?"

I nod, too stunned to speak.

Satisfied, he leaves, taking the last of the oxygen with him as I rest my back against the wall and watch him go.

When the exit door slams closed, letting us know we're finally alone, I breathe in deep, only for it to catch in my throat as a lineup of LAU players round the corner.

"Hey, man," one of them greets Everett. "You comin' to SeaBird?"

"I'll meet you there," Everett offers.

His friends spot me, and one of them grins. "Oh. Hey."

"Hi," I mumble.

The guy turns to Everett but tilts his head toward me. "Who's this?"

"I'm no one," I interject.

With a slight smirk, he turns back to me. "Hello, *No One.* I'm Griffin." He offers me his hand. "Griffin Thorne. Nice to meet you."

Griffin Thorne. I'd recognize the name anywhere. The guy's practically hockey royalty, thanks to his dad, Colt Thorne. The infamous player holds multiple records during his time in the NHL, and if ESPN is correct, Griffin's right on track to follow in his dad's footsteps.

Drake hates the guy. Well, technically, he hates most of LAU's lineup, including Everett and Reeves, but Griffin didn't go unscathed during Drake's constant rants, either. Something about his dad playing with Griffin's dad in college and screwing up his career in the NHL, but what do I know? Yet, here's Griffin. Being nothing but a gentleman.

Everett frowns as I take his friend's hand and shake it once. "Nice to meet you, too."

"Wanna come to SeaBird with us?" Griffin prods.

I'd laugh if the offer wasn't so ludicrous. Drake would kill me if I was seen hanging out with the enemy. Well, *enemies.* And since I'm already on thin ice, I think I'll pass.

"Can't," I give him a one-shouldered shrug. "Sorry."

"No worries. Maybe next time." He lifts his chin at Everett once more. "See you there." He tucks his hands into his front pockets and moseys out the door while the rest of his entourage follow behind.

Once we're alone again, I fold my arms and keep my chin

tucked as I head toward the exit, anxious to get the hell out of here.

"Wait," Everett calls.

My feet stop moving as if they have a mind of their own, and I hate it. With a deep breath, I face Everett again. "What do you want?"

"Are you okay?"

A pathetic laugh escapes me as I stare up at the ceiling. "Why did you do it?"

"Do what?"

"Why did you lie to him?"

Him.

I can't even say my boyfriend's name without feeling nauseated. What does that say about me?

With a sigh, Everett says, "If we're gonna be fake dating—"

My choked laugh interrupts him. "We're not faking anything."

"You're the one who approached me, remember?"

"No, I approached Reeves out of stupid curiosity. I turned *you* down," I clarify. "Why did you tell him we've known each other for three months? Do you have any idea how pissed he is now?"

"I was trying to help!"

"How?" I snap. "By making it look like I was sneaking around behind his back?" My laugh is maniacal at best as I shove my hair away from my face and start toward the exit.

He blocks my path. "I was trying to build a foundation for our fake relationship."

"There is no fake relationship!"

I swear I can taste his exasperation as he scrubs his hand over his face. "Take the sunglasses off, Raine."

"Once was enough, thanks."

"You need me," he pushes.

"I don't need anyone."

"Your black eye says otherwise."

I shake my head and step toward the exit again before he grabs my arm, stopping my retreat. But it isn't rough. It's surprisingly gentle. I haven't been touched gently in a long time. It's weird and strange and kind of makes me want to cry as I stare at his long fingers engulfing my wrist.

"Do you really live with him?" he murmurs.

"What?"

"He said, 'I'll see you at home,'" Everett reminds me. "Do you really live with him?"

My eyelids close, and I give him a single nod.

"Fuck, Raine," he rasps. It's quiet. Defeated, almost. "What am I supposed to do now?"

"You aren't supposed to do anything."

"Guess I can't help myself." He lets me go and runs his hand over his dark, straight hair. "Tell me what I can do."

Isn't that the million-dollar question? I wish I had the answer. One to erase my relationship with Drake altogether so I wouldn't have to deal with the inevitable fallout. And trust me, I tried. To end the relationship without a fallout. And look where it got me. A black eye. A tracking app. And a threat the size of Texas if I ever try to leave Drake again.

Wetting my bottom lip, I fold my arms and rock back on my heels. "You can forget you ever met me."

"Easier said than done."

"Yeah, well, you seem like a pretty"—I scan him up and down, my focus landing for a beat too long on his bare chest, and I step back to put space between us—"*savvy* guy. I'm sure you'll figure something out."

CHAPTER THREE

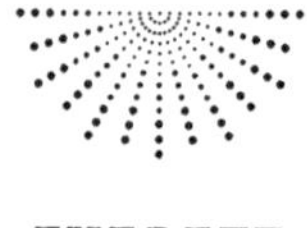

EVERETT

"So, who's the girl?" Griffin asks. He's my roommate, teammate, and best friend. Hell, we might not be blood, but we're practically brothers, along with our other friends, Maverick and Archer—before he passed away.

Our moms were all roommates in college and raised all of us like siblings until my family moved away when I was in high school. Even then, we'd come to visit. And when it was time to apply to colleges, LAU was the first on all of our lists despite each of us being drafted during our senior years of high school. Now, here we are, playing in our last season at LAU until graduation in the spring. Well, all of us but Mav and Arch. Fuck, I still can't believe he's gone. Archer was our rock both on and off the ice, and Mav was always the wild card who knew how to carry his weight and bring results. Regardless, the team has worked hard to find our footing since Archer's passing and Maverick's early retirement from the game, thanks to his recent heart transplant. With any luck, my plans with Griffin will work out, and we'll play for the NHL like we've been dreaming about since we were kids. Fuck, it's crazy how time flies.

"Not gonna tell me who the girl is?" Griffin prods, bringing me back to the present.

"I don't know what you're talking about," I mutter as I glance around the open bar. People shuffle around us, ordering drinks, dancing to the live band on stage, flirting and talking and taking turns stopping by our booth to congratulate us on the win. I should bask in it, but I'm too exhausted to care. Too distracted to pay attention to it all.

"Ah, come on," Griffin pushes. "She was looking for Reeves, right?"

My head falls, and I stare at the amber liquid in my glass, running my fingers along the outside of it as the same image of forest green surrounded by bruising assaults me. What kind of asshole hits a girl? And not only hits a girl but hits a girl hard enough to leave a mark, let alone burst a blood vessel in her eye? Fucking prick.

"Ev?" Griffin prods.

"She needed help with her boyfriend."

"And since Reeves is dating my baby sister, you got stuck with her," he assumes.

"Doesn't look like it." I shove aside the image of her black eye and look at my best friend again. "She turned me down when I offered to help."

With a low laugh, Griffin brings the beer bottle to his lips. "Man, that's gotta sting. Being rejected for a job you don't even want."

"You know the asshole from the game?" I ask. "Forty-six?"

Griff nods. "Haitt, right?"

The name alone makes me want to throttle my drink. "He's her boyfriend."

His brows hitch. "The asshole who kept taking cheap shots?"

"Yeah."

Settling into SeaBird's booth, Griff frowns. "Fuck."

"Yeah," I repeat.

"No wonder she was looking for Reeves. You couldn't pry a stick from the asshole's cold, dead fingers. You really think he'd ever want to let go of a girl who looks like she does?"

I scowl at my best friend, and he quirks his brow.

"What? You don't think she's pretty?"

"She's a job."

"Nah. She's not even that." He points the neck of his beer bottle toward me. "She refused to hire you, remember?"

He's right, but I don't back down. "She needs my help."

"Yeah, well. What are you gonna do about it?" He leans closer, resting his elbows on the table separating us. "Do you even know her last name? How to get ahold of her? Anything?"

I've thought about it since she walked away at the rink, but I don't have anything to go on. Only a pair of forest-green eyes, long brown hair, and a name. Raine. It's unique, but I doubt it's enough information to get me anywhere.

"Ev?" Griffin prods.

With a slow shake of my head, I answer, "Nah. I don't know how to reach her." I take a sip of my beer, sitting it back on the table when the solution hits me. "But I do know how to get ahold of Haitt."

My best friend's eyes widen. "You sure it's a good idea?"

No.

But not doing anything feels even more wrong.

Jaw clenched, I tell him, "She needs help. I know she does."

With a sigh, he scratches along his jaw and shifts in his seat. "I'm sure she does, but..."

"What is it?" I demand.

He stays quiet and stares at his half-empty drink, probably debating on whether or not he wants to answer me when we both know I'm already amped up from the arena. When his gaze flicks to mine, I realize he has more balls than I give him credit for because he isn't backing down.

"Listen," he starts, "I know you've always had a God complex, but maybe it's best for you to sit this one out."

Sit this one out? He didn't see the bruises. Didn't see the fire in her eyes or how she flinched when I reached for her. And he expects me to do nothing? To let her fend for herself? To leave her alone with an asshole like Drake?

"I'm not going to—"

"If she refused to hire you, what makes you think she's okay with you using her abusive boyfriend to track her down?" he argues. "It might make things worse for her."

Fuck. He's right. If Drake finds out I'm using him to track down his girlfriend before I have a chance to protect her, he might take it out on Raine. It's the last thing either of us wants. But not doing anything feels about as pleasant as having my balls dipped in a vat of acid. So where the hell does it leave me?

Without a word, I down the rest of my drink and set the empty bottle on the table in front of us. It doesn't drown out the voice inside my head or the image of what was beneath Raine's sunglasses.

I've gotta do something.

I have to.

CHAPTER FOUR

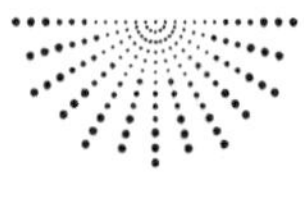

EVERETT

I lasted four days. Four days until I couldn't take it anymore, and I started putting out some feelers before caving and asking my little sister to do some internet sleuthing.

Drake Haitt is the son of Sue Haitt and Bradley Ackerman, though they were never married. His dad played for some league in Canada and was known for being a hothead. Like father, like son. He knocked Sue up on one of his visits to the US. Based on an interview from a couple of years ago, I'm gonna go out on a limb and say his relationship with his dad is less than perfect. His mom passed away about six months ago, and ever since, he's been even more of an ass on the ice.

Drake signed with the Springfield Titans during his senior year of high school and has been dating Raine Anders for almost two years. Raine works at a tattoo shop named Eternal and is under an apprenticeship with Lucian Boone, though most of the time, she answers the phone.

I turn my ignition off and climb out of the vehicle, heading into the gray brick building. Despite the dim lighting, the tattoo shop is busy. Rock music blasts from the speakers, and the large room is layered with half-walls, creating a maze and an ounce of privacy for the customers receiving tattoos. No Raine, though. Or at least not that I can see from the front of the building.

Dammit. I half expected her to be at the reception desk, but it's occupied by a pretty blonde in a black tank top with a phone pinned between her ear and shoulder as she types at the computer.

What now?

Hands tucked into my pockets, I rock back on my heels, not ready to give up and leave.

When the pretty blonde sees me, she smiles and hangs up the phone. "Hi. How can I help you?"

"I'm looking for Raine," I reply. "Is she working tonight?"

The blonde nods. "You're in luck. I'm covering the phone while she takes her break. I think she's creating some sketches, though. She's right back there." The blonde points to her left toward a cubicle space in the back.

Rising onto the balls of my feet, I look for the same small-framed woman from the game but only catch a glimpse of brown hair hunched over something. "Mind if I go and talk with her?"

The blonde lifts a fully-tatted shoulder. "Sure thing."

"Thanks."

As I make my way toward Raine, I spot the crown of her head above the half-wall again. Her hair is pulled into a high ponytail, wisps of brown frame her face, and her black T-shirt hugs her curves. No sunglasses this time. The bruise around her eye is either covered with makeup or starting to fade. It's probably a combination. No new damage, at least. That's something.

Pen in hand, she swirls the tip over paper, her mouth lifting as she focuses on whatever she's drawing. She's prettier than I remember. Less guarded. Like she's lost in her own head. Her problems finally on the backburner, unlike the first time we met.

As if she can feel my stare, she looks up and freezes.

"Hello again," I greet her.

"You."

"Me," I return dryly.

She looks around the parlor, then turns back to me. "What are you doing here?"

"I came to check on you."

"I don't need anyone checking on me."

"Your fading black eye says otherwise."

Lips bunched, she stands from the swivel chair she was straddling, grabs the sleeve of my jacket, and tugs me to the empty seat. It almost reminds me of a chair you'd find in a dental office. Once I'm seated, she lets me go and drops her voice low. "Look, I know you're trying to be thoughtful and everything, but really, you're coming off as an arrogant ass, so I think it's best if I handle this on my own. You need to leave."

"Look, I'm sorry for how I acted—"

"I don't care, okay? It doesn't matter anyway, but if anyone sees you—"

"Will you let me finish?" I snap. "I'm trying to apologize."

"I don't need your apology. I need you to leave."

"Yeah, well, I'm not lea—"

"This isn't about you," she seethes, collapsing into the chair across from mine. "Lockwood Heights is a small town. They're all about their hockey, and they're all about supporting LAU, right?"

I nod, confused. "Yeah?"

"Well, Cedar Springs is the same way. Grover University might be the underdog in this region, but we're equally as passionate, and I have no doubt there's already buzz about seeing one of LAU's best players less than a mile from the Grizzlies' campus. Do you hear what I'm saying?"

"You're saying it's only a matter of time until word gets out that I'm here."

"Exactly. And that you're talking to me." She takes a deep breath. "I should've never come to see you or Reeves, all right? It was a huge lapse in judgment on my part, but if you really want to help me, you need to leave me alone. Drake is a jealous guy, and thanks to your bullshit lie, he's already suspicious that I'm cheating on him. Oh, and let's not forget how our apartment is literally across the street, and one of Drake's favorite pastimes is popping in to say he's missed me, so please, just…go."

The green of her eyes is practically glowing as she stares at me. Pleads with me. Begs me to let her fend for herself when we both know exactly where it's gotten her. I want to ask so many questions, but mainly? I want to ask why she can't walk away from him. Why she can't leave. Why she's deciding to stay when it's clearly a terrible idea. But voicing any of my questions aloud feels pointless because it's obvious she doesn't want to hear them.

Resigned, I murmur, "Can I use your pen?"

She frowns. "What?"

"Your pen," I repeat. "And a piece of paper."

With a huff, she grabs the pen and pad of paper she'd been using and hands them to me. My eyes widen as I take in the sketch she's creating. Thin blue lines. On-point shading. It's a tree. Twisted limbs. Molting branches. Sunlight cutting through and casting shadows between the bare patches. It's fucking insane.

Glancing up at her, I ask, "You drew this?"

She glances down at the paper, then back to me. "It's only a sketch."

I look down at the drawing again and shake my head. "Only a sketch, my ass. This is really good, Raine."

"You're easily impressed."

"Bullshit," I argue. "This is incredible."

She peeks at the work of art on the paper again, then lifts a shoulder.

"Why do you use a pen?" I prod. "You know, instead of a pencil or whatever."

"It takes away the pressure of being perfect," she explains before a frown mars her lips. Like she just remembered she's annoyed with me or something. "You need to leave."

Right.

I scribble my number beneath the kickass tree, then hand everything back to her. I stand and tug at the end of my jacket, smoothing it. "I know you don't want my help, but if you ever need anything, and I mean anything, call or text me. I'll be there."

I weave my way to the front of the tattoo parlor and walk out the door without a backward glance.

CHAPTER FIVE

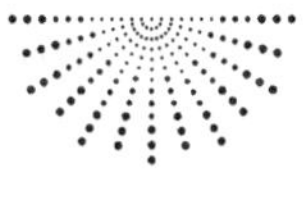

RAINE

I plugged Everett's number into my phone, replacing the contact information I had for my gynecologist. It's stupid, but I didn't know what else to do. It's not like I could save it under his name. Not without poking the bear. The only reason Drake didn't entirely lose his shit after Everett's bold-faced lie at the LAU arena about us having a relationship for the past three months is because I don't have a passcode on my phone, and he checks it on occasion. If he finds Everett's name in my contacts now, he'll never let it go. My body feels heavy as I take the stairs toward my apartment while my wary thoughts go haywire at the possibility of someone reaching out to Drake and telling him about Everett's visit.

I wasn't kidding when I told Everett Cedar Springs is a small town. My only hope is no one saw me talking with him and relayed their findings. It's not like Drake has eyes and ears everywhere, waiting to catch me doing something I shouldn't. But even so, lying to Drake is always dangerous. Lying about something like this when the wounds are still fresh? It's practically begging for an explosion.

As I push the door open, I find Drake relaxing on the couch with his feet on the coffee table. ESPN plays on the television screen, and a bag of chips rests on the cushion beside him.

"Hey," I call out, hoping he can't hear the tremor in my voice.

Drake glances over the back of the gray couch. "Hey."

I head toward him and sit on the arm of the sofa. "How's the game?"

"Two to one." He presses the mute button on the remote.

I want to squirm from his full attention but keep my expression blank, unsure what to say or do or...anything. Does he know? Has anyone told him about Everett's visit? Did he see him walk in or out of Eternal?

"I got you flowers," he murmurs.

"You did?"

"Yeah. Chocolates, too." He smiles. "They're on the counter."

"Oh." Sure enough, a dozen red roses are in a glass vase next to a box of chocolates. It'd be a sweet gesture if I didn't know what love-bombing is. The irony isn't lost on me. How I know all the signs, yet I'm *still* here. My family would be so ashamed.

"You're not going to say thank you?" he challenges.

Turning back to Drake, I force a smile. "Thank you."

"You're welcome." He brings my hand to his lips and kisses the back of it. "I also figured out how you can make it up to me."

It.

There are so many *its* in the world. Nailing down which one he's referring to is hard, so I keep my fake smile firmly in place. "Oh?"

"Yeah." He grabs my knee. "There's a party tomorrow. I want you to go with me."

My brows dip. "A party?"

"Yeah. I think it'll be good for us to get out. Maybe have some fun. Reconnect." His grasp on my fingers tightens. It isn't uncomfortable. Honestly, it's almost sweet, and my pathetic heart flutters at the memory of how things used to be. Before his mom died. Before his dad started coming around again. Before his possessiveness became overwhelming, and I couldn't justify the red flags anymore. I'm not stupid. I know how abusive relationships work. I know it's a slippery slope, and I know if they hit you once, they'll hit you again.

Why'd you have to hit me, Drake?

Granted, he hit me because I was trying to break up with him, so it's not like things were perfect until the incident. But still. Before, I felt like I could end things if I could scrounge up the courage to leave despite the inconveniences accompanying said decision. And yes, I know how ridiculous it sounds. Convenience has kept me here for so long it's laughable. Well, convenience and empathy and memories of when things were better, along with the hope they could be better again if I simply...waited. Joke's on me, I guess. I'm so ingrained in every piece of his life that I really shouldn't have been surprised when he refused to let me go. When he not only threw a fit but hit me, then threatened to kill himself if I even thought about leaving him again. The reminder makes it hard to breathe. Hard to keep my fake smile in place as I stare at his hand engulfing mine. I glance at the flowers again and let out a soft breath, forcing my lungs to work.

Why'd you have to get me flowers, Drake? Why'd you have to make me second-guess everything? Again. Flowers don't exactly fix it all. But he's trying. I was terrified about what would happen after my first encounter with Everett and his bold-faced lie. Instead of ripping my head off, Drake told me he trusted me. It was...strange. Seeing a glimpse of the man I fell for. But instead of finding it comforting, it's dizzying trying to keep up with him and his mood swings. Like if I'm patient enough, he'll come back. Drake will come back. My Drake. Not this stranger I sleep next to.

"What do you think?" he prods. "You said you love me, remember?"

"I do."

"Good. I love you, too. Fuck, I'd die without you, Raine. You know I would."

"I know," I whisper.

"I know you do." He smiles and kisses my hand again when my phone rings in my purse.

As if it's personally offended him, Drake scowls at my purse hanging off my shoulder. "Who is it?"

"I don't know." My nerves kick up a notch until I remember I never gave Everett my number. I only have his. It's fine. "Let me check." Slowly, I open my purse and find my phone.

"Who is it?" he demands again without even giving me a chance to read the name on the screen.

A familiar picture greets me. Weathered face. Tan skin. Crinkles around his eyes. It feels like it's been forever since I've seen him and my mom. Penelope, my older sister, moved away when she got married a few years ago, and Dodger, my older brother, is busy touring the country with his band. But my parents? They don't live very far away, yet I haven't really seen them in…a few months now? How is that even possible? Shame licks at my gut, and I suck my lips between my teeth as I stare at the photo.

"Raine?" Drake demands.

"It's my dad."

"Of course it is." He chuckles darkly. "He always calls at the worst fuckin' times." Unmuting the television, he turns back to the game and grabs a chip from the bag while I sit on the arm of the couch and send the call to voicemail. I shouldn't. I've avoided him for too long, but the idea of facing him, of showing him who his little girl turned into and all of the shitty decisions she's made despite his and my mom's awesome parenting, let alone the consequences which could follow if they found out about everything?

No, thank you. Not until I can figure out how to get out of this.

I let out a slow, unsteady breath, stand, tuck my phone into my back pocket, and wipe my sweaty palms against my jeans. "I'm going to shower. I'll be out in a few."

"Uh-huh."

CHAPTER SIX

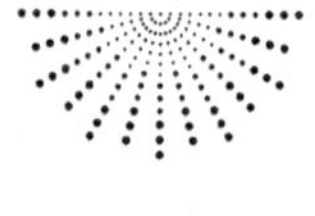

RAINE

Cars line both sides of the street as Drake finds a place to park. We're in a neighborhood. A random neighborhood so far outside of Cedar Springs's city limits it's not even funny. Drake invited four of his friends to join us, though they drove separately, leaving me as the lone girl. It isn't the first time, but knowing we're deep in Lockwood Heights territory doesn't exactly leave me feeling relaxed. Not after the last time I was here. Not after Everett tracked me down at work and offered to help me. Not when I know how much Drake hates LAU and everything about its small town.

So, what are we doing here?

"Come on." Drake pushes the driver's side door open, climbs out, and rolls his shoulders in his black T-shirt and leather jacket while staring at the house in front of us. It's a duplex. A really big, duplex. With red brick, cream stucco, huge windows, and a large tree out front. One side is dark, and there's a huge dumpster out front, making me wonder if it's being renovated or something. The other side? It's practically spilling over with bodies despite the cold temperature.

The door might as well be propped open with how many people move from outside to inside and back again. The blinds are all open, and the windows are glowing, giving everyone on the street front-row seats to dancing, laughing, and cups raised in the air.

Yeah. This is definitely where the party is.

Slipping his arm around my waist, Drake guides me up the driveway, and his friends meet us at the front porch, each of them flanking his sides as we step over the threshold. Why does this feel like a test? Something lodges in my esophagus, and I wipe my sweaty palms on my thighs.

Something is up. Something is definitely up.

I peek at Drake.

What game are you playing?

No one notices when we enter. Why should they? It's a party. A huge party, packed to the gills. So why am I freaking out right now?

"Johnny, get us some drinks," Drake orders. Johnny St. James. The Grizzlies' center.

Slipping through the crowd, Johnny heads toward the back of the house without a word. This place is nice. And big. A set of stairs hugs the right wall, and a family room takes up the majority of the left. A kitchen is tucked in the back, while a hallway hides behind the stairs. White walls. Tall ceilings. The scents of cheap beer and fancy perfume permeate the air.

When I'm bumped from behind, I run into Drake's back, and he turns around, glaring at whoever's behind me. "Watch it." His attention catches on something else, and he grins, turning his amused stare to me. "Dance with me."

Curious about what turned his frown upside down, I start to look behind me, but he grabs my wrist and drags me toward the makeshift dance floor in the middle of the family room without asking for my permission. Most of the furniture is pressed against the walls, leaving space in the middle of the floor for dancing, but all I do is stand here and look around. The music's so loud it's hard to think straight, let alone keep up with Drake's mood swings. He hates dancing. Always has. And parties? Yeah, he's all about a good party, thanks to his access to free alcohol, but why here? Why Lockwood Heights? Something doesn't add up.

"Come on," Drake urges. Grabbing my hips, he yanks me against him, grinding into my ass like he's already had three drinks and is hoping to get laid. I can't tell if it feels forced because I feel as stiff as a board or if it's because he's actually being forceful. I guess that's what happens when the person you're supposed to trust—to love—hurts you, shredding your trust into a billion tiny pieces, then expecting them to be glued back together after a single apology and a couple dozen roses.

Okay, a single apology is a stretch. Drake has apologized for hitting me at least a dozen times since the incident.

God, even the word incident leaves a sour taste in my mouth.

He hit me.

My boyfriend *hit* me.

And here I am, pretending like I can let it go. Like he deserves for me to let it go. For me to sweep it under the rug like all the shitty things he's said and the times he's grabbed me too roughly or shoved me out of anger. Whether it's at me, or a shitty grade, or a bad game. It doesn't matter. I've always been the one to deal with the fallout and pick up the pieces. Giving him an out. A justification.

It's why I finally swallowed my pride, scrounged up some courage, and tried to break up with him. Why I tried to end things. And what did he do? He blocked the exit, refusing to let me go. And when I tried to scoot past, he sucker punched me, then threatened to do a lot more if I ever attempted to leave him again. And the truth is, I believe it. I don't doubt him when he says he'll do anything to keep me all for himself.

How did I get here?

"Come on, baby," Drake rasps against my ear. "Loosen up."

Loosen up? The guy expects me to be loose around him after he's hit me? Is he really this delusional? And why is he being so pushy and acting so strange? I'm missing something. I know I am. But if I don't play along, if I don't dance, I'll never figure out what it is. Closing my eyes, I let the rhythm of the song blasting through the house roll over me and force my body to move with the beat when Drake's grasp on my waist tightens, and my eyes pop back open.

That's when I see him. Everett. He's standing on the side of the room, watching me. Watching Drake's hands as they trail down my body. Watching how my hips sway and the way Drake's lips move against my ear as if he's whispering sweet words instead of sharp orders.

"Why are you so frigid, baby?" He grabs my waist. "Loosen up."

It makes me feel…dirty.

Turning around, I slide my hands along Drake's chest and loop my arms around his neck, urging him closer when all I really want to do is push him away. "I need to use the restroom."

"Nah."

"I'm serious, Drake," I argue. "I won't be long, I promise."

He pulls back slightly, his dark gaze narrowing. "Fine. Be back in five, or I'll come looking."

Of course, he will.

With a nod, I step away. He lets me go, but I can feel his focus on me as I weave between the throngs of people and find the hallway I hope leads to a bathroom. Before I can make it, a familiar face appears, and my breath stalls.

"*No one?*"

It's Griffin. The guy from the arena and the ESPN specials.

My brows bunch at his question. "What?"

"You introduced yourself as *no one* when we met," he reminds me with a smile.

"Oh. Uh, my name's Raine."

"Nice to see you again, Raine," Griffin returns. "Does Ev know you're here?"

Glancing behind me, I gulp. "Probably."

He nods. "What are you doing here?"

"My boyfriend brought me."

His amusement falls, and he looks behind me, taking in the family room and kitchen. "Any chance he's here to pick a fight?"

"I'd say the odds aren't small," I muse.

A low curse slips past his lips as Griffin scans the party again. "Great." Looking back at me, he adds, "Maybe stay here for a few."

"Probably a good idea," I reply. "Where's the bathroom?"

He hooks his thumb toward the closed door on my left, then heads to the main area, leaving me alone. It's probably for the best. If Drake caught me talking to Griff, it would give him a reason to go off. But maybe it's the point? There's no way he didn't know who this house belongs to. Add to the fact he brought his hockey friends with him, and the pieces are finally clicking into place.

Here, I thought I'd gotten off scot-free from the arena altercation. Joke's on me, I guess.

My hand trembles as I knock on the bathroom door, anxious for a hiding place. Instead, I'm greeted with, "One sec." Resting my back against the wall, I pull my phone out and bring up Everett's contact information as I wait. I can't decide if I should message him and apologize for coming to his house when I had no idea he lived here or if Griffin's taking care of all of it and I need to hide away for the foreseeable future.

Or, you know, indefinitely.

What was Drake thinking? Is it because he found out Everett infringed on his territory, so he feels like he has a right to infringe on Everett's?

What the hell am I thinking? This isn't *West Side Story*. There aren't territories at all.

Are there?

As the door opens, another familiar face appears, and his brows tug. "Raine?"

I tilt my head up and nearly choke on my breath. "Reeves?"

Seriously? Can I not catch a break?

"Give us a minute," a low voice growls behind me. I peek over my shoulder and find an indecipherable Everett behind me. He looks good tonight. Dark hair pushed away from his face. Same chiseled jaw I remember. Black T-shirt. Low slung jeans. Full lips. Blue eyes demanding my full attention. They're so…astute? So bright, yet dark at the same time. It's confusing, and makes him even harder to read than the last time we spoke, which I'm pretty sure is just my luck, considering the circumstances.

Ignoring me, Reeves addresses his friend. "Thought you said she didn't want to hire you anymore."

"Apparently, I got under her boyfriend's skin without the contract," Everett answers dryly.

"Is he here?" Reeves asks over the top of my head like I'm not sandwiched between them. It kind of makes me want to throat punch the guy.

Giving Reeves a slow nod, Everett squeezes the back of his neck. "And he brought four buddies."

"Damn." With a low whistle, Reeves looks at me again. "He must be really possessive of you."

"Maybe this isn't about me," I lie.

"And maybe you're full of shit." Reeves starts to slip past me but stops at the last second. "Take it from someone who's been down this road a time or two. Playing by his rules won't get you any farther in life, and it won't prevent the fallout, either."

"Who says there's a fallout?" I challenge.

"You came to me for a reason, Raine," he reminds me.

He's right. I did. But admitting it out loud feels like I'm caving. Like I'm giving in. Like my life really is spinning out of control and there's nothing I can do to stop it. I lift my chin higher, holding his knowing stare. "Maybe I was curious."

"Nah," Reeves tsks. "Fear led you to me. And fear is holding you back from trusting my buddy enough to let him help you."

"I…" I fumble for a response, but he walks away before I can muster any actual words. Shaking my head, I step into the bathroom, anxious for an escape, when the heat of a body follows and the click of the lock rings throughout the small space.

Twisting around, I scowl at a surprisingly stoic Everett "What are you doing?"

"I could ask you the same question."

"He told me he wanted me to come to a party," I explain. "He never said it was yours."

"He's trying to prove you're his."

I open my mouth to argue but close it quickly. Seriously, what is wrong with my brain today?

"Not gonna deny it?" he challenges.

"My relationship with Drake is complicated."

He scoffs. "He hits you."

"*Hit*," I argue. "Singular. It happened *one* time."

Another angry scoff rumbles through his chest. "That's how you justify it?"

Blinking back tears, I shake my head back and forth. "I'm not trying to justify—"

"It's exactly what you're trying to do."

"You don't get it!" I snap.

"What's there to get, Raine?" Everett prowls closer until my back hits the wall behind me with a quiet thud. He doesn't stop until we're chest to chest. Eye to…nipples. My heart thuds faster and faster, making me feel like the walls are closing in as I gulp thickly.

Sensing my spiral, Everett's eyes narrow, and he growls, "What's wrong?"

He's taller than I realized. Hotter, too. Literally. I can feel his heat branding me as he pins me to the wall.

Breathe, I remind myself, forcing my gaze to meet his.

"Seriously, what's wrong?" he asks.

"You're scaring me," I whisper.

He jerks back and lifts his hands in defense. "Fuck, I'm sorry." He drops his hands and looks around the room. "I'm not gonna hurt you."

"Only corner me in a bathroom, right?"

"So now *I'm* the bad guy?" he volleys back. "Me? Not the guy you were grinding against in my family room?"

"I already told you my relationship with Drake is complicated."

"It's not *that* complicated." He inches forward again, but I realize it isn't to try to intimidate me. He's just…passionate. And confused. Honestly, he's not the only one.

Why does he care, anyway?

"He hit you," he pushes. "No one should *ever* hit you. And here you are, defending him."

"I'm not—"

His minty breath hits my cheeks as he bends closer. "You are."

The same warmth from his body seeps through my top as he towers over me, but for some reason I can't explain, I'm not really scared, even when I know I should be.

Why am I not scared?

Peeking up at him, I take in his icy blue eyes. They aren't filled with anger. Frustration, sure. But not anger. Determination, maybe? Stubbornness, definitely. But they lack the unhinged, wild look I've grown accustomed to, and I hate how I notice the difference. How I compare him with Drake. How, when I told him I was scared, he immediately backed down, ashamed I would even consider the possibility of him touching me—hurting me. And even though I most definitely don't know him well enough to make this assessment, something pulls at me. I don't think he would hurt me. Not physically, anyway.

"Let. Me. Help. You," Everett demands. Despite the fact it isn't posed as a question, I can tell it is. Hell, it's a plea—one I desperately want to accept. But at what cost? So far, all he's done is make my life more difficult, so why do I want to trust him? Why do I want to ask for his help? Am I really this pathetic?

Sucking my lips between my teeth, I murmur, "I don't want to drag you into this. I don't want to drag anyone into this. I just want to pretend—"

The door rattles like thunder, and I jump at the sound.

"Raine!" *Thud. Thud. Thud.* Drake slams his fists against the door. "Times up!" *Thud. Thud. Thud.* "Told you I'd come looking! Open up!"

I squeeze my eyes shut and let out a soft breath but don't move a muscle. "I need to go."

"Stay here," Everett whispers.

"You don't know me."

"I don't need to know you to understand whatever's going on between you and the fuckwad pounding on my door is a bad idea."

"*This* is a bad idea," I argue.

"Stay. Here."

I shake my head, ignoring how my blood boils at his stubbornness. "Hide behind the shower curtain. I'll slip out, and he'll never know."

"Not gonna hide in my own house, Raine," Everett warns.

"Open the goddamn door!" Drake booms.

I flinch at the harshness in his voice and another heavy dose of frustration flashes in Everett's soft blue eyes. He pushes off from the wall and yanks the door open.

It happens so fast I don't even have a chance to register what's going on until Drake comes into view. My jaw drops, and panic blooms in my chest as his attention shifts from surprise to confusion to full-blown rage.

"What the fuck?" Drake shoves Everett, but the guy barely budges.

Lifting his hands in the air, Everett says, "We were just talking."

In an instant, Drake swings at Everett's face. Everett dodges it at the last second, then lands a hard punch against Drake's jaw. His head whirls to the side. It only takes a moment for Drake to recover, and he's returning a cross-jab combo of his own. Footsteps echo from the main area of the house as the two brawl in the doorway, blocking my escape while giving me a front-row seat to a spectacle I want no part of. With my back pressed against the wall, I cover my mouth, frozen. Fucking frozen. I don't know what to do. I don't know what to say. I don't know where to go. I—

Do something!

"Stop!" I yell. "Both of you! Stop!" I try moving closer but jump back when Everett stumbles a few steps toward me after a particularly brutal hit. He immediately takes the offensive again and barrels toward my boyfriend. "Drake! Nothing happened! I swear, nothing happened! Please—"

From the open door, Griffin jumps into the chaos, taking an elbow to the jaw before dealing a nasty right hook to Drake while simultaneously placing himself in the center of the fight as Everett winds up for another hit. Two more strangers follow Griffin's lead and drag Drake away from Everett as Griffin turns around and reaches for my impulsive savior, pushing him back from going for another round with the enemy.

Red faced and chest heaving, Everett glares at my boyfriend. I have no doubt if Everett had his way, Drake would be swallowed by an inferno and burned alive, never to be seen again. To be fair, I'm pretty sure the sentiment is mutual with the way Drake is staring daggers at the guy who had me pinned to a wall not too long ago. The question is, who will drop their little staring contest first?

"Raine!" Drake finally booms. Blood trickles from the corner of his mouth, but he doesn't bother wiping it away. He also doesn't bother looking at me as he continues his little staredown with his newly gained nemesis. It's like I'm a dog. Like I'm an object. *His* object. It makes me sick. But now isn't the time to stand up to him, even if this is the final straw. The last reminder I'll ever need about what an asshole he really is. I knew it already, but...

"Raine," Drake warns. It's quieter and even more lethal.

Forcing my legs to move, I walk closer to him but hesitate when I'm within reach.

"Get in the car," he growls.

I want to get out of here. I want to disappear. I want to rewind the last six months and make so many different decisions. But I can't. I can't erase the fact I'm here or how I'm in the middle of a bathroom with more eyes on me than I ever want. Each of them judging. Each of them assuming. Each of them making things so much worse for me.

Drake's eyebrows pull low as he finally steals his attention from Everett and glares at me, letting the blood from the corner of his mouth paint his sneer. "Now, Raine."

"Raine," Everett calls from my periphery.

My body freezes as I meet his gaze for a split second. Then, I slip out of the door.

CHAPTER SEVEN

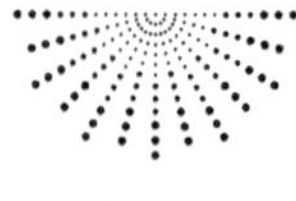

RAINE

My eyes trail to his bloodied knuckles as Drake throttles the steering wheel like he's wishing it was Everett's neck. It's quiet. Nothing but the roaring engine and the whooshing of my racing heart pounding in my ears. I can't do this anymore. Can't sweep this under the rug or brush it aside. I can't.

I'll pack my things tonight, then sneak out once he falls asleep. He can't stay awake forever. I just need to survive the drive. I'll figure out the rest once I'm…anywhere else. Everything will be fine.

Everything. Will be. Fine.

He hasn't said a word.

Not a single word since we left the party.

It isn't helping my nerves.

He's stewing. Probably making up what he thinks he saw or weaving together an alternate reality, painting me as the villain.

I know I should've stayed at Everett's house. I'm not stupid. But everything I own—my clothes, my toiletries, my sketchbooks—is in the apartment. And I have a feeling after tonight, Drake won't let me retrieve my things without a fight. And a battle with Drake is always a nasty affair. One I really don't want to tackle if I can help it.

Way to go, Raine. Procrastinate more. It won't blow up in your face at all.

I scoot a little further down in my seat, attempting to make myself smaller.

While Drake was busy having an all-out brawl in the bathroom and hallway, his buddies were having their own fight in the family room. I can't decide if Drake's pissed at me or if he's mad at his friends for not having his back when he needed them.

That's a lie.

Of course, he's pissed at me.

I can feel it. The rage. The way it clings to him. Radiates off him. Like a scorching heat. Like a blazing fire. One I can feel down to my bones.

"You gonna tell me what the fuck that was about?" Drake finally snarls.

I tuck my hair behind my ear and face him fully. "Drake, I promise—"

My head swings to the side, and stars explode behind my eyelids.

Shit.

The hit was so fast I didn't even see it coming. Slowly, I lift my hand and touch the side of my face. I feel like I took a baseball bat to the mouth.

"I can't lose you, you dumb slut," he spits.

I'd laugh at the contradiction of his words if my lip wasn't throbbing. You can't lose me, but I'm a dumb slut? Does he even hear himself? This isn't the guy I fell for. It isn't the guy I moved in with. This is…this is a fucking asshole.

Pressing my fingers to my tender skin, I wince and look down at my crimson stained fingertips.

I'm bleeding.

The realization makes me want to cry. Or maybe it's the pain from being backhanded. At this point, who the hell knows? It's like a sick, twisted game of deja vu. A replay of the last nightmare I've relived for weeks. I'm both livid and shocked, yet not surprised at all. It's confusing and dizzying and disappointing and rage inducing. I want to cry. I want to laugh. I want to fucking scream.

How is this even happening?

Forcing myself to stay calm, I whisper, "You promised you wouldn't hit me again."

"And you promised you'd never leave me!"

I blink back my tears. "I didn't leave—"

"Did you let him touch you?"

I stay quiet. The light reflects off my fingertips, show-casing the blood clinging to them as I carefully lick my bottom lip. It stings. And throbs. So much so, I can feel my heartbeat in it. It feels like it's three times the size it should be.

How did I get here? How did *we* get here? This can't be happening. Who is this man? How could he do this to me? How could he do this to anyone, but especially me? He's supposed to love me and cherish me and treat me like a princess. My heart cracks even more as I stare at the crimson staining my fingertips. Like a carousel, memories of us together flash through my mind. The first time we met. When he slipped me his number. Our first kiss. The first time he said he loved me. When he bought me flowers on my birthday. When he asked me to move in with him. When we made love. They all swirl together, every moment, every memory, until each and every one is painted with a sour stroke of regret, leaving a bitter tang in my mouth.

Then again, maybe it's the blood.

"Don't. Fucking. Ignore me," he yells.

My bottom lip quivers, and I blink the burn behind my eyes away. "No, I didn't let him touch me."

"And I'm supposed to believe you?"

"And I'm supposed to believe *you*?" I spit, dropping my hand to my lap and turning to face him fully again. "You promised you wouldn't hit me again!"

The crunching of gravel beneath our tires hits my ears, and I nearly bash my head against the glass as he yanks the steering wheel to one side, swerving onto the side of the road.

"Get out," he growls.

I look out the pitch-black window, then back to Drake. "Are you serious?"

"You don't want me to hit you again, right?" he counters. "Get out of the car. You can fucking walk home."

"Drake—"

"You always said if we're fighting, and I can't control my anger, I should walk away."

Now, *he listens?*

I'd laugh if I didn't feel like I was talking to a fucking toddler.

"It's the middle of the night." I wave my hand toward the dark passenger window as if to showcase my point while choking back tears. "And I have no idea where I am."

"Maybe you'll think twice before you wind up in a room with a locked door and a guy who isn't me."

"Who are you?" I cry.

Face twisting with rage, he warns, "I'm your worst motherfucking nightmare if you don't get out of this fucking car right now."

"Why'd you take me there in the first place?" I demand. "If you were so hellbent on keeping me away from him—"

"Get out of the fucking car!" he screams.

Spittle hits my cheeks, and I jerk back. The look in his

eyes terrifies me. Like he's gone. The man I fell in love with. No. This man is nothing but a stranger. An animal, even. Like he could kill me in this moment, and honestly? A small part of me wouldn't even be surprised if he tried. He's too far gone. This is too far gone. Our relationship. Our trust in each other. It's obliterated, and there's no going back. There's no pretending this didn't happen. No writing it off as a one-time thing. No justifying it.

Do. Not. Justify. This.

Blindly, I reach for the door handle, my hands trembling, and climb out of the passenger side on shaky legs. Without even waiting for me to close the door behind me, he peels onto the road, the tires squealing as they search for traction on the black pavement.

Is this man serious?

A numb tingle spreads across my body, and I shake my head, convinced I'm hallucinating or in shock or...hell, maybe I have a concussion at this point because my brain is struggling to process what the hell just happened and how I wound up on the side of the road at one o'clock in the morning at least twenty minutes from home. It's cold. It's quiet. It's foreign. It's...scary. I take in my surroundings, unsure what to do or who to call. There's nothing but inky blackness all around me. No street lights. No signs. No buildings. Nothing but Drake's fading brake lights.

As they're swallowed by darkness, I wrap my coat tighter around me and try to hold my tears at bay.

What the hell am I supposed to do now?

CHAPTER EIGHT

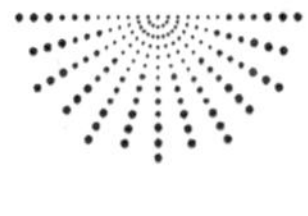

EVERETT

We cleared the house out after the fight. Not that we had to. Everyone would've stayed all night if we'd let them. Honestly, the fight only amplified the original energy in the house. Like a heavy dose of adrenaline was injected into everyone's veins—everyone's but mine—and they were ready for the next round. There was a brawl in the family room, too. Drake's friends got into it with Reeves and a few of my other teammates.

Assholes.

Pressing the bag of frozen peas to my jaw, I stretch my legs out on the couch as exhaustion spreads through me. I can't erase the image of Raine walking away. The way she got in the car without a word. Not like a coward. Like a survivor. It's messing with my head.

The cushion dips beside me when Griffin takes a seat and rests his forearms on his knees. "Any idea what that was about?"

"I'll tell you what it was about," Reeves interjects from the kitchen. "It was about a possessive motherfucker who didn't like you being locked in the bathroom with his girlfriend. Is she or is she not your client?"

Scrubbing my hand over my face, I mutter, "Not."

"Why not?" Griffin asks.

"Because she's scared," Reeves answers for me. "I've seen it too many times. She got cold feet and figured hiring help wasn't worth rocking the boat."

"Okay, then why'd he come here if she isn't working with Ev?" Griff questions. "Or was it her idea?"

I shake my head. "She didn't know this was our place."

Rounding the center island, Reeves steps over a broken lamp and sits on the sofa opposite ours. "So, it was his idea. Why'd he come here, Ev?"

I exhale slowly. "I went to see her a few days ago."

"What do you mean you went to see her?" Reeves demands.

"At her job," I clarify. "She works at a tattoo shop, and I stopped by."

Kicking his feet up on the coffee table separating us, Reeves laces his fingers behind his head. "How'd you find out where she works if she never hired you?"

It's a good question, one I don't want to answer, but I have a feeling the guys won't drop it until I do.

"I wanted to give Raine my number in case she needs anything," I admit.

Exchanging a look with Reeves, Griffin points out, "You didn't exactly answer him."

"Fine. I did some digging. Used Drake's name. Recruited Finley's online stalking and figured out where Raine works."

"Should've known it was your baby sister who helped," Griff grumbles under his breath.

Leaning closer, Reeves prods, "Do you think Raine told Drake you came to see her?"

I shake my head. "I doubt it. She was pretty adamant I

leave, but she did mention how Cedar Springs is a small town and word would get around I was there."

"So he knew you were sniffing around, and he decided to return the favor," Griffin acknowledges, motioning to the broken glass littering the floor from tonight's fight. "Well, look how it all turned out."

"Yeah, I'm gonna go with not good," Reeves says with a laugh. "Your parents are gonna kill you guys if you don't clean up the place."

"You're the one who wanted to throw a party," I remind him.

"And it definitely didn't disappoint." He flexes his hand. "Haven't been in a fight like that since before Dylan." Snapping his fingers, his grin widens. "Actually, since Homecoming. Man, I bet Drake's feeling your fists right about now. I know I did when I was in his shoes."

I almost crack a smile at the memory, grateful I was able to work shit out with Reeves and come out the other side as actual friends instead of the fake bullshit we'd endured since he flaked before last season's playoffs, and we lost.

My phone rings. I frown when I pull it out of my front pocket. The number's unknown. Curious, I slide my thumb across the screen and answer. "Hello?"

A soft sniffle cuts through the silence, and I cock my head, waiting.

"Everett?"

I sit up a little straighter, ignoring my friends' curious stares. "Raine?"

"Yeah." She breathes deep. "It's me."

She sounds like shit.

"Where are you?" I demand.

"Honestly?" A quiet, bitter laugh echoes through my cell. "I have no idea. I'm on the side of a back road somewhere between your house and mine."

What the hell?

"Can you share your location?" I ask.

"Uh, yeah."

Her pause makes me sit up even straighter.

"Yeah, I think I can," she whispers.

I wish I knew her better. Could read her better. Because right now, I feel like I'm in the dark, and after everything that happened tonight, it leaves me even more on edge.

"I just shared my location," she breathes out.

"Good."

"Dude, what's wrong?" Griffin interrupts.

My gaze cuts to him, and I shake my head, silently telling him to stay quiet.

"Are you okay?" I ask into the receiver.

"Uh, I mean, yeah? I guess?" She sniffles again. "Honestly, I don't even know."

"Do I need to bring backup?" I demand as I get straight to the point and fish my keys from my front pocket.

She hesitates. "No. No, I'm all alone."

"Got it." I toss the defrosted bag of peas on the coffee table. "Stay here. I got this," I add to Reeves and Griffin, then I'm out the door in a flash. "I'm coming, all right? Stay with me, Raine."

"Okay."

I KEEP THE CALL CONNECTED THROUGH MY BLUETOOTH, BUT we don't talk. Not sure there's much to say anyway. The asshole drove her into the middle of fucking nowhere, then left her on the side of the road. Who does that?

Fucking prick.

When a silhouette greets me fifteen minutes later, I let out the oxygen I'd been holding while Raine covers her face with her phone-free hand, shielding the bright lights from blinding her.

"It's me," I murmur, ending the call and pulling up beside her on the side of the road.

Without a word, she opens the passenger door and climbs in, folding her arms and using her hair as a shield to hide her from my view. She looks so small. I hate how she won't look at me. Not like I've earned her trust or anything, but her silence is suffocating. I want to know what happened. How she wound up out here all alone. What he did. What they said. It's none of my business, but I can't stop the questions from filtering through me. One after the other. Leaving me on pins and needles as I squeeze the steering wheel. Taking a deep breath, I force my muscles to relax.

Giving her the side-eye, I finally ask, "You okay?"

What little light from the dashboard makes her green eyes practically glow as they flick toward me for the shortest of seconds before she looks out the passenger window, avoiding me at all costs.

"I didn't know who else to call."

Where's her family? Her friends? Is she seriously all alone? I can think of a dozen people I could call if I needed someone, so what's this girl's backstory? And why do I even care?

I don't know her. I don't know anything about her. The only reason I know her last name is because I did some light stalking, and even that's flimsy at best. But getting any answers out of her feels like a moot point. At least for right now. Still, I can't stop staring. Even then, she doesn't look at me. Doesn't do anything but stare out the passenger window, probably wishing she could disappear.

"Seatbelt," I remind her.

Her shaky breath greets me, and she reaches for the buckle, sliding it across her body and clicking it into place.

That's when I see it. The glimpse of her face. The swollen lip. The red cheek. The light from the dashboard acts like a flashlight, highlighting her bruised complexion.

He hit her again.

Mother. Fucker.

Without thinking, I shove the car into park and reach for her. It's like silk. Her hair. Gently, I push it away from her face and inspect the damage. It's starting to clot. Her bottom lip. But the flesh is still swollen and angry, proving it was quite the hit. My blood boils as I drag my thumb along the edge of her mouth, imagining all the ways I could kill him. All the ways I could inflict pain the same way he's clearly done to her.

Slowly, Raine reaches up and grasps my wrist. My attention snaps from her cut to her pleading gaze.

"Please stop," she begs.

"Stop what?" I growl.

"Stop looking at me like this. I don't…I don't want your pity. I don't even really know you."

"How many times?"

A divot forms between her brows. "What?"

"How many times has he touched you like this?"

Her eyelids fall. "Ev…"

"Answer the question."

"Twice. Like this," she clarifies, staring back at me with a glint of resentment. "Before then it was asshole comments and a random shove or rough grab, you know? Still unacceptable, but…"

"But easy to write off?" I finish for her.

She shakes her head. "I guess I was the frog."

"What?"

"You know, the frog in the boiling water." My frown deepens as her tongue darts out between her lips, and she winces. "Where the frog is put in a pot of boiling water, and it hops right out. But if it's put in cold water, and the temperature is increased slowly, the frog doesn't even notice and winds up dead."

"I'm familiar with the metaphor," I mutter.

"Of course you are," she says with a pathetic laugh. Truth be told, it sounds a hell of a lot more like a whimper, but I keep the thought to myself as she adds, "I never thought this would happen. Never thought I'd be the girl in an abusive relationship. And I wasn't. Not for a long time. I thought I knew better, you know? I thought I knew the signs. The red flags. And I did, but…it's so easy to ignore them or write them off like you said, or…"

Unshed tears make her eyes glassy as she presses her fingers to her lips.

"Then Drake kept putting off meeting my family, and I moved in with him, and then his mom died, and he became super clingy and more controlling, and I thought…it's because he cares. Because he's afraid of being alone again or…you know."

She blinks, and a tear rolls down her cheek. Angrily, she wipes it away. Like it's a weakness. A glimpse behind the strong front she's putting on. It makes me want to kill him even more.

Oblivious to my frustration, she sniffs and continues. "But, uh, then I tried to end things with him, and he hit me, and I lost my shit, and he promised it wouldn't happen again, and I reached out to Reeves and met you, and…I guess the rest is history."

"Why'd you go with him tonight?" I ask. "After the fight."

The same silence swallows my words. Or maybe it amplifies them. Turning them into something more. Something heavier.

She plays with her fingers in her lap, refusing to look at me. "Because it wasn't your job to protect me. It *still* isn't your job to protect me," she whispers, though I'm not sure if the words are meant for me. "You don't even know me."

It isn't the first time she's pointed out how we're practically strangers. She's right, though. I don't know her. But I don't need to. Not to know she deserves more than being treated like shit. Besides, I have a sister, and if some asshole was treating her the way Raine's clearly been treated, I'd lose my shit. Fuck, I'd kill him.

And for the first time since Reeves suggested I help him out, I actually want to. I want to help. I want to save her. Even if it backfires. Even if it blows up in my face. The idea of walking away. Of letting Drake touch Raine again. It's unacceptable. All of it is.

"Come on." I rub my thumb along her cheek, realizing how smooth her skin is. Then, I drop my hand and grab the steering wheel. "Let's get you home."

"I can't go ho—" Her words die on her tongue as I make a U-turn and head back to my place.

I wait for her protest, but she stays quiet. Part of me wants to ask if she'd like me to take her to her parents or something. A friend. A distant cousin. But the other part? I guess I already know the answer. If she had someone else, she would've called them.

Instead? She called me. And she might only be a favor to Reeves, but dammit, I'm grateful.

Now she has someone.

She has me.

At least for a little while.

CHAPTER NINE

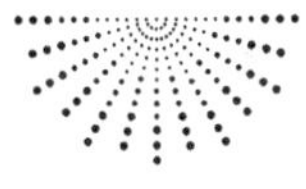

RAINE

I'm exhausted. Like bone tired, never-want-to-open-my-eyes-again, exhausted. After restricting Drake's access to track my location through my phone, I rested my temple against the cold passenger window and haven't moved since. When Everett pulls up to his house, the front door is closed, and the porch light is on. People no longer litter the driveway, and the blinds are closed. If I didn't know any better, I'd say it isn't the same house.

The garage door lifts a second later, and Everett drives inside, cuts the ignition off, and turns to me in his seat. "You okay?"

"You've already asked me that question," I point out.

He nods and, without another word, climbs out of the car. Honestly, it's surprising how he isn't forcing me to talk about something I don't want to. If it was Drake? We would've gotten into a fight, and he would've accused me of shutting him out or hiding something, when really? I just want the quiet. The moment to process my thoughts without needing to justify them to another person. Is it so wrong? Then again, it doesn't matter. Drake isn't here, and if I never face him again, it'll still be too soon. At least I don't have to worry about walking on eggshells anymore. It has to count for something, doesn't it?

When I realize Everett's waiting for me by the hood, I force my body to move, climb out of the car, and keep my jacket pulled snug around me as I meet Everett by the headlights. Satisfied, he heads inside. I follow without a word.

It's quiet. Either everyone's asleep or hiding in their rooms, but I appreciate it. The quiet.

"Do you want to shower?" Everett murmurs.

When I don't answer right away, he glances over his shoulder at me, and I nod. "Actually, yeah. A shower would be great."

"Follow me." He guides me toward the same bathroom we hid in earlier tonight on the main floor and pushes the door open. "Fresh towels are in the cabinet. I'll leave a change of clothes on my bed in the room across the hall."

"I can wear these," I offer.

Road salt stains the bottom half of my jeans, and he stares at the discolored fabric. "Would you feel better if I borrowed some of my sister's clothes for you?" he asks.

"You have a sister?"

His mouth lifts with the ghost of a smile. "Yeah. Her name's Finley. You'll meet her tomorrow."

Panic sparks inside of me. "Oh, I don't—"

"She lives here," he explains. "At least until the contractor finishes renovating her place next door. Pretty sure she'll track you down herself if I don't introduce you in the morning."

If I had my car, I'd plan to sneak out before anyone wakes up, but since it's not an option, I guess I have no choice. Meeting Everett's family wasn't part of the plan when I called him. But now the ball's already rolling, so I'm not sure what else I can do to stop it. It's not like I can tell him no, either.

Forcing a smile, I fold my arms. "Okay, then. Uh, don't worry about the clothes, though. Or at least, not your sister's. I feel weird borrowing a stranger's things."

"Then it looks like you're stuck with mine." He grabs the door handle and closes the bathroom door, cutting me off from him without giving me a chance to argue. As I stare at the solid piece of wood for at least thirty seconds, the night crashes into me along with all its messy implications.

What do I do now?

Rocking back on my heels, I fold my arms and catch my reflection in the mirror. I look awful. Stringy hair. Smudged makeup. Swollen lip. Blocking out the sight, I undress and turn on the faucet, making sure the stream of water is as scalding as possible in hopes of burning away the consequences of tonight. But I'm not stupid enough to believe it'll work.

My shower is quick because even though the hot water feels like heaven on my muscles, I'm desperate for a bed, so I barely give myself any time to enjoy it. I want nothing more than to go to bed and pretend tonight never happened.

After wrapping a towel around me, I open the door and find a neatly folded black T-shirt and black boxers waiting for me on a small side table. It most definitely wasn't there when I entered the bathroom. Everett must've carried it from the family room so the clothes wouldn't be sitting on the floor while I showered. My lips twitch at his thoughtfulness —or aversion to germs. Regardless, I pick the clothes up, dress, and wrap my wet hair in the towel. When I force myself to take one final look in the mirror, I frown. Yup. There's definitely a cut along my bottom lip, and I'm more swollen than I expected. Leaning closer to my reflection, I gently touch the wound and wince, letting out a soft, resigned breath.

I can't believe he hit me. Twice. Then again, maybe I can

believe it. A tiger doesn't change his stripes no matter how well he camouflages himself. And damn, he was quite the expert at camouflaging in the beginning.

Sleep, I remind myself. Everything will look better in the morning. It has to.

Tearing my attention from the mirror, I square my shoulders and flick the light off. The floor creaks softly beneath my feet as I tiptoe to the room across the hall and push the bedroom door open. A gray pillowcase is in Everett's hands, and he slips it over the bare pillow on the twin bed.

"I changed the sheets." He glances at me again and frowns as he sets the pillow on the newly made bed. Rounding the edge of the mattress, he grabs something from his nightstand, offers it to me. When I don't take the ointment, he untwists the cap and moves closer. Gently, he lifts my head, giving him a better look at my split lip. An undercurrent of frustration heats his icy blue gaze.

"Gonna fuckin' kill him," he says under his breath. Squirting a small dab of the ointment on his pointer finger, he spreads it along my cut. As he dabs at my lip, a hiss slips through my clenched teeth.

"Shit. Sorry," he apologizes.

Sorry.

Up until this point, I was starting to wonder if apologies were even possible coming from the opposite sex. Guess I stand corrected.

I stay quiet and stare at the LAU logo above Everett's heart on his T-shirt. I can feel his breath against my forehead. Peeking up at him, I confirm my assumption. Yup. He's close. Really close. Standing over me. Looking sexy as sin with a furrowed brow as he stares at the damage from Drake's hand.

It's…strange. Instead of feeling trapped by being so close to him, I feel…protected. Safe, almost. And honestly? I can't decide whether or not I'm all right with it. With us being this close. With him looking at me like this. With pity, sure, but curiosity, too. Or maybe I'm imagining it. Maybe I want to imagine it. What it would be like to have someone care. Not that he does. He doesn't know me. He knows nothing about me. In his eyes, I'm nothing but a victim.

I should remember that.

I let his icy gaze hold mine for one more heartbeat. I clear my throat and drop my chin an inch. It isn't much, but it's enough. Enough to remind him he's still touching me despite having already dabbed on whatever magic medicine he had hiding in his nightstand. As if only now realizing the same thing, he lets me go and steps back.

"Didn't, uh, didn't peg you for a twin bed kind of guy," I note, anxious to change the subject.

He barely looks at the two beds on opposite sides of the room. "I share the room with Griff."

"Oh." I frown, confirming both beds are as empty as I initially assumed. "Where's Griff sleeping?"

"On the couch."

"I could—"

"I know," Everett interrupts. "And Griff knows, too. He doesn't mind, though. After your phone call, he assumed I'd bring you back here to crash for the night, and I wouldn't want to let you out of my sight."

I tilt my head in question as I register his comment, convinced I misheard him. "Y-you don't want to let me out of your sight?"

His attention drops to my lips. "You should get some rest. Do you mind if I sleep in Griff's bed?"

"This one's yours?" I point to the bed closer to the window. The one he recently finished remaking.

He nods.

"Did you change Griffin's sheets, too?"

He nods again.

"You know, you could've saved yourself some time and only changed Griff's." I pause. "Actually, I should probably still sleep in his bed, and you should sleep in yours. Then you'll only have to change one set of sheets tomorrow."

"Just get in the bed," he orders gruffly.

I don't move. "Why?"

Squeezing the back of his neck, his frustration palpable, he grumbles, "So you'll sleep in a stranger's bed, but you don't want to borrow their clothes?"

I open my mouth to argue but close it quickly. He makes a good point.

"Just…get some sleep." He climbs into Griffin's bed, turns on his side, and gives me his back while my feet stay planted on the ground. I can't help it. I'm speechless. And confused.

What the hell?

"'Night, Raine," Everett mumbles.

It's a hint. A nudge. A gentle push telling me I should get moving and go to bed. Then again, he's right. I should. I'm absolutely exhausted. So much so, I may or may not be hallucinating since the last five minutes make almost zero sense, and so does Everett's surliness.

Flicking the light off, I head to his bed and slip beneath the crisp sheets. It smells like detergent. I don't know why I'm disappointed, but a small part of me is. I'm not sure what else I expected.

His cologne. That's what I was expecting.

Biting back my groan, I roll onto my back and stare at the ceiling. "Goodnight, Everett."

CHAPTER TEN

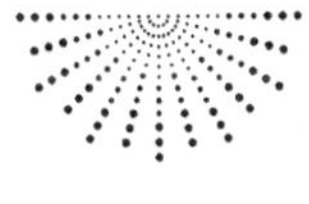

RAINE

With a yawn, I cover my mouth and roll onto my side. It's morning. It has to be. Light filters in around the blinds while voices seep beneath the closed bedroom door. As my brain tries to register where I am and what I'm doing here, I rub at the corner of my eye, then sit up, letting the wrinkled sheets fall to my lap. Memories of last night flood my senses as I smack my parched lips together, wincing in discomfort.

Right. The party. The fight. The drive home. The hit to the face. The shower.

I blink the sleep from my eyes and look around the room. Everett's bed is empty. Er, Griffin's bed? It doesn't matter. He's gone. Something squeezes in my stomach, and I slip out of the covers, finding the ointment from last night resting on the nightstand along with a bright orange sticky note.

Put this on your lip. It'll help it heal so it doesn't split again. I went to the gym with the guys. Be back soon. Don't leave. - Everett

He left me a note?

He left me a note.

My fingers trace his blocky, masculine handwriting

before I set the Post-It back on the nightstand and apply the ointment to my lip. It doesn't sting as much this time, but my nose still wrinkles when I run my finger along the damage, realizing how swollen I am. Yeah. This isn't going away any time soon.

Great.

The ground is cold against my bare feet as I pad toward the dresser closest to the window, finding my clothes folded neatly on top of the wood surface. Everett must've done it. Searching the pocket of my jeans, I open my phone, and my heart lodges itself in my throat.

One hundred and two missed calls. Seventy-one voice-mails. Ninety-seven texts. Pretty sure Drake broke his all-time record.

Hands shaking, I set my phone back on my clothes, refusing to read any of his messages. He must be furious.

Not your problem, Raine.

With a deep breath, I force myself to keep the phone where it is, turn around, and tiptoe toward the hallway. The voices are a little louder now, and when I round the corner to the kitchen, my heels dig into the ground.

"Oh. Hi," a girl greets me. Her hair is long and dark, and even though her eyes are a few shades grayer than Everett's baby blues, I have no doubt she's Everett's sister. His *little* sister, if I had to guess. The girl's short and curvy and beautiful. She strides toward me and offers her hand. "I'm Finley. Nice to meet you."

Accepting her hand, I shake it once. "Raine. Hi."

"Hi," she repeats. "This is Dylan." She motions to a gorgeous blonde with black-framed glasses and a bowl of Reese's Puffs cereal at the kitchen table, then points to the strawberry-blonde bombshell beside her. "And this is Ophelia."

"Or Lia," Ophelia adds. "Nice to meet you."

I give her a small wave. "You, too."

"Do you want any coffee?" she asks.

"Uh…"

"Take a seat, I'll grab you some," Finley interjects. "Do you like sugar or cream?"

"Uh, both, please," I reply, sitting across from the girls I've literally never seen in my entire life. Scratch that. My gaze narrows as I study Dylan carefully. "Do I know you?"

"I'm pretty sure we saw each other after the Hawks game when you came looking for my boyfriend." When I blanch, she laughs. "Dude, you're totally fine. Don't stress."

"I didn't know he was unavailable."

"Don't worry. I know why you were looking for him," she replies carefully. "Speaking of which…" Her attention drops to my swollen mouth. "How are you feeling?"

My tongue drags against the damage on instinct, and I flinch then gently rub my lips together as if it'll hide the evidence from last night. "I'm, uh, I'm fine. Thanks."

They're not idiots. They know I'm far from fine, but the girls have enough social prowess not to call me out for my bullshit. It makes me like them even more.

"So, tell us about yourself," Ophelia says while Finley continues rummaging through the kitchen cabinets. "Where are you from?"

"I grew up right outside Lockwood Heights and moved to Cedar Springs a little while ago," I answer.

"Are you going to school at Grove University?"

I shake my head. "No, I'm actually apprenticing at a tattoo studio."

Ophelia's eyes widen. "Seriously? Don't tell my boyfriend, but I've been dying to get a tattoo."

"You should check out my dad's work. He's amazing."

"Aww, is he the one teaching you?" Dylan asks.

I shake my head. "Actually, no. I thought about it, but…I

kind of felt guilty, I guess. Like it would make me a nepo baby or something."

A nepo baby is someone who becomes famous by riding on their parents' coattails. Usually, it's directed toward actors or celebrities, but considering my circumstances and who my dad is, the term still fits. Drake's words come back to me from when I first mentioned my interest in working at my dad's tattoo shop, Etch 'N' Ink. He scoffed, saying I was better than a free pass, suggesting I check out the tattoo parlor across the street from our apartment to see if anyone would be willing to work with me. By some miracle, Lucian took me on as an apprentice, and I haven't looked back.

"Working with your dad wouldn't make you a nepo baby," Dylan argues. "And even if it did, only your talent will get you clients. Not your dad's."

"Dylan's right," Ophelia agrees. "And if I actually decide to take the plunge, I'll be happy to be your first client."

Steam swirls in the air as Finley sets a mug in front of me, then leans her hip against the edge of the table. "Speaking of first clients, tell us what you think about my brother because he is clearly smitten."

"Smitten?" Dylan scoffs. "What are we? From the fifteenth century?"

"Hey, there's nothing wrong with being smitten," Finley argues. "I want to be smitten, and I sure as shit want the guy I end up with to be smitten, too."

"You're saying Drew isn't smitten?" Ophelia pipes up, though I have no idea who she's talking about.

"My boyfriend's plenty smitten," Finley argues.

Ah. Drew's the boyfriend. Got it.

"And we aren't talking about me and Drew," Finley adds, "we're talking about our new friend, Raine"—she waves her hand toward me—"and my big brother. So?" She bats her lashes at me, not so patiently waiting for my response.

I'm not sure what she expects me to say. Everett's... Everett. I don't know him. Not really. I know he plays hockey. I know he's good. I know he has a little sister who's a bit pushy but nice. I know he's protective. And I know he's kind because only a kind person would leave their house in the middle of the night to pick up a stranger on the side of the road and offer them a place to sleep with no questions asked. Okay, technically, he did ask a question or two, but—

"Hmm?" Finley prods.

With a shrug, I offer, "Your brother's really...nice."

"And?"

I tug on the hem of...yup, I'm still wearing Everett's shirt in the middle of his kitchen while surrounded by his sister and her friends. *Perfect.* I stop fidgeting with the soft cotton and clear my throat. "I don't know what else you want me to say."

"Are you guys like...officially fake dating, or...whatever?" Ophelia asks.

"Uh..." I shrug again, surprised by how much they know and how bold they are. I can't decide if I'm impressed or offended, but I'm not sure it matters. Their friend and brother is helping me. Helping me more than he knows, and likely, more than he wants to. "We haven't really talked about it," I hedge.

"Well, after the chaos from last night, I'd say you probably should be officially faking dating. At least until your ex gets bored or something," Finley offers.

My brows pull as I take a sip of my coffee. Drake? Bored? Yeah, I don't see that happening, which means I'm screwed. How the hell am I going to get out of this? And the fact she said ex? As in...it's over? Hardly. He hit me, then kicked me out of his car. That's it. Which means this mess is far from being cleaned up.

"What is it?" Ophelia prods.

"Hmm?" I ask.

"You're making a face."

Setting my mug back on the table, I lick my bottom lip and wince. "It's…well, you said ex."

"Yeah?" Finley answers.

"We haven't officially broken up."

The girls exchange glances, each of them grimacing. "Well, shit."

I laugh. "My thoughts exactly."

"Has he tried contacting you yet?"

I nod, thinking back to my phone still resting on the dresser in Everett's room. "Only about three—no, four— hundred times."

Ophelia's eyes pop. "Four hundred times? Are you serious?"

"Yeah. I should probably turn it off."

I start to stand, but Ophelia stops me. "Girl, four hundred is like a major red flag."

"Yeah, so is hitting her," Finley quips.

"Finley!" Dylan scolds.

"I'm just saying," Finley defends, looking at me again. "I hope you break up with him with a text. He doesn't deserve an actual phone call, and I wouldn't be face-to-face with him *ever* after the way he hurt you last night."

She's right. How am I supposed to see him again? How am I supposed to break things off? The first time ended with a major blow up and an extra bottle of foundation. Now, with Everett involved? Drake will kill me.

I rub at my tired eyes when the door from the garage opens. One half-naked hockey player after another enters the kitchen. Muscles upon muscles. Tan skin. Low slung joggers. My lips part, and my jaw threatens to unhinge.

I gulp and stare into the caramel liquid in my cup, blind-sided by all the gorgeous male specimens walking into the room. Don't get me wrong. I've seen plenty of half-naked hockey players in my life, and maybe it's because I haven't finished my cup of coffee or something, but these guys? They're something else entirely. From the corner of my eye, I catch Reeves dipping low and kissing Dylan's cheek across from me as a guy scoots beside him and bends closer to kiss Ophelia. My pulse stalls as soon as I recognize him. He must feel my gaze because his attention snaps to me, and his brows wrinkle.

"Bo?" he asks.

"Uh." I gulp again. "Hey, Mav."

"What the hell are you doin' here?"

CHAPTER ELEVEN

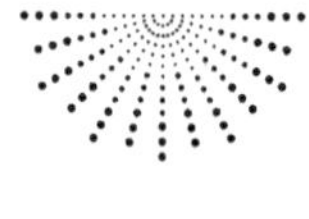

RAINE

I feel like the world is spinning. Like I might literally vomit as the room turns into a tomb. No one moves. No one even seems to be breathing. Instead, they just… stare at me.

"I'm sorry, who's Bo?" Ophelia finally asks.

Mav glances at his girlfriend, then back to me. "This is Bo. Bo's my what? Second? Third cousin?"

"Technically, we aren't related," I rush out. "My dad was roommates with his uncle a couple decades ago. And I'm, uh, I'm so sorry I didn't make it to the funeral. Really, I am." I swallow the acid in my throat. "How are you? How are… things?"

"I thought your name was Raine," Everett growls from the edge of the room. It's not like I didn't notice when he first walked in. The guy's freaking gorgeous, but I was a little distracted, thanks to the family connection that could screw everything up if he decides to open his mouth to my parents.

Ignoring the panicked butterflies in my lower stomach, I argue, "Raine is my real name."

"Her family calls her Bo," Maverick informs him.

"Hold up," Finley interjects. "One, that's adorable. And two, why Bo?"

Mav scrubs his hand over his face. "I don't know? Her mom had a miscarriage before Raine, and since Raine was her rainbow baby…"

"Ah, like after the storm," Finley realizes. "A *rainbow*. Okay, that's so cute!"

"My mom says the pregnancy was super rough," I add. "She puked the entire time. Had to have an I.V. to keep liquids down. It was a whole…thing. So, my dad started calling me Rainbow when I was in the womb to help remind her things would get better. Then Rainbow turned to Bo without the *w*, and it kind of stuck, even though my first name is Raine." I turn to Everett, praying he can see my sincerity.

If he does, he doesn't show it. Nope. This man's emotions are officially on lockdown.

"Did you know Maverick's my roommate?" he demands.

I shake my head. "If I did, I wouldn't be here."

"Why?" Maverick crosses his arms over his bare chest. There's a scar on it close to six inches long, reaching from his collarbone to the bottom of his sternum, thanks to his heart transplant, or at least it's what I heard down the pipeline. And the funeral I apologized for missing? It was his twin brother's. Archer. The two were always inseparable, and the fact Maverick has Archer's heart? It's…well, I guess it shows how twisted fate can be sometimes.

And so is the fact that I'm here. In his kitchen. When I'd rather be anywhere else. Especially if there's any possibility of him relaying my experience with Drake to anyone who might pass the information along to my family.

Dipping my chin, I stare at the table in front of me, then start to stand. "I should go."

"Stay," Reeves orders.

I plop back down in my seat and chew on the edge of my thumb. This is bad. Really bad, actually. How do I get out of here?

"How'd you sleep?" Reeves asks me.

I drop my hand back to my lap and force myself to stop fidgeting. "I, uh, good, I guess."

Reeves eyes gleam, and he smacks Maverick's shoulder. "And how'd you sleep? I almost forgot last night was your first one home since the surgery."

"I slept good," Mav answers.

"*We* slept good," Ophelia clarifies with a smirk. It pulls a low laugh from Maverick as he leans in for another kiss.

I can't help the jealousy flaring in my chest. He's so sweet with her. His hand on the back of her neck as he rubs slow circles. The way she smiles up at him like he hung the moon.

It's love. Pure. Unrestrained. Love.

And I'm so happy for him. He deserves it more than anyone.

However, it also makes me feel like I'm most definitely intruding, so I stare at my hands instead, fighting their trembling.

"Mav," Reeves orders.

Maverick turns to him and quirks his brow.

"Mind giving us a minute with your cousin?"

"Not related," I remind him.

Ignoring me, Mav nods to his friend and pulls Ophelia with him.

"Wait," I call.

Brows knitting, Maverick stares down at me.

"Can you…not say anything?" I plead.

"Who am I gonna tell, Raine?" He links his fingers with Ophelia's and gives her a smile. "Come on. Let's go shower."

"Ew." Finley's nose scrunches. "And on that note, I'm gonna be super subtle and change the subject. Everett?

Brother?" She searches the kitchen, and I do the same as Mav and Ophelia leave. He's leaning against the kitchen sink with his arms folded and his gaze solely focused on me.

"Our girl's asshole of an ex has been spamming her phone all night and this morning," Finley explains. "What are you gonna do about it?"

"Am I supposed to do something about it?" he challenges. His gaze stays locked with mine for the barest of seconds, then he looks at Reeves.

"Depends," Reeves answers. "Has Raine officially hired you yet?"

All eyes turn to me, and I tuck my hands beneath my thighs to keep from squirming. "We, uh, we haven't talked about it."

"Well, do you want to?" Finley prods.

Do I want to hire him? No. Do I want my entire relationship with Drake to be wiped from existence? Yes. One hundred percent yes. Do I want to be left alone and have a clean slate? Again, yes. Do I want everyone to stop staring at me and sticking their noses where they don't belong? Also, yes. But getting what I want feels pretty close to impossible lately, so I'm not sure what Finley—or anyone else, for that matter—expects me to say right now.

"I'm not entirely sure what I'd be hiring him to do," I admit.

Stealing Dylan's cereal, Reeves picks it up and shoves the spoon into his mouth, oblivious to the eyes pinning him in place like they did to me. He chews slowly as he sets the spoon back into the bowl.

"Ollie." Dylan drops her head back and looks up at Reeves standing behind her.

Is his first name Ollie? Huh. Who'd of thunk it.

"I think this is the part where you give Everett and Raine

a rundown of the process since you're the only one with experience on this front," she explains.

Reeves swallows the last bite of Reese's Puffs and clears his throat. "All right. Honestly, it's pretty straight forward. First, Raine needs to solemnly swear she is up to no good." He smirks at me. "Get it? Harry Potter?"

"I'm aware of the Marauder's Map," I volley back at him.

"See? I knew I liked you." He turns to Dylan. "I knew I liked her."

"Yeah, yeah, we all know you're a whore for Harry Potter. Now get to the point," she orders.

With a wink, Reeves gives me his full attention. "My point is, you need to commit to yourself and to everyone here that you'll never go back to your ex, or else this will wind up being a waste of everyone's time."

Part of me wants to be offended by his bluntness, but I can't. He's right. If I go back to Drake, last night and every-thing I do moving forward will be a waste of time. *Everyone's* time. And if they're willing to help me, I need to be all-in, too. Not that I wasn't before, but…

Running my tongue along my upper teeth, I admit, "I tried to break it off with Drake before he hit me, which only confirmed my decision to get away from him in the first place. Ever since then, I've been trying to figure out *how* to leave him without poking the bear or having him track me down, but it's been…difficult, I guess."

"We can help take care of that part," Reeves promises. "There are mainly three steps. First, you need to set yourself up to be done with him. No run-ins. No pop-ups. Nothing. Everett said you live with him?"

I nod.

"All right. First order of business." He rubs his hands together. "Collect your shit or say goodbye to whatever's at his place."

"Everything I own is in our apartment," I argue.

"Then it looks like you need to go get it."

My pulse gallops, and I let out a slow shuddered breath, feeling paralyzed at the prospect alone. I know it's necessary. I also know it's dangerous.

Pushing himself away from the center island, Everett grunts, "I'll go with you to grab your things."

My neck snaps toward him. "You don't have to—"

"Yeah, he does," Reeves interrupts. "After last night's shit show, you can kiss your alone time goodbye for the foreseeable future."

My shoulders hunch, but I don't argue. Honestly, I don't even want to. What does it say about me? What does it say about my relationship? If my parents knew…

"You need to block his number and vary your routine for the next little while, too," Reeves continues.

My brows tug. "Vary my routine?"

"We don't want to give him any opportunities to track you down. Not unless it's on our terms. Which reminds me, can I see your phone?" He offers his hand palm up, and I set my cell in it.

"What are you doing?" Everett demands.

"Checking for any hidden tracking apps," Reeves explains as his fingers fly across the screen. A few moments later, his mouth turns down at the corners. "Huh. Surprising."

"What is?" I ask.

He hands me my phone, and I take it. "None of the usual tracking apps are on it."

"What kind of tracking apps?"

"The ones stalking assholes like to download onto their victim's phones without their girlfriend's knowledge." He shrugs and steals another Reese's Puffs from Dylan's bowl, tossing it into his mouth. "The only ones on your cell are

Find My Friends and Life360, which you already disabled from sharing your location with him. Good girl."

"Watch it," Everett grumbles.

Reeves smirks. "Which brings me to step two. You need to prove you aren't isolated or alone and have someone on your side. Someone who has your back. Usually, with abusive motherfuckers like your boy, they try to isolate you, proving you don't have anyone but them. It's a way to lure you back because no one likes being lonely. I'd say family's a good avenue to try, and it is, but if your boy's known you for a while, he likely knows your family, too, which means he knows your relationships or lack thereof, depending on the client."

"What's your point?" I ask.

"My point is, you need to go out and party and show Drake you are most definitely not alone, and you aren't lonely."

"You mean fake date Everett," I clarify.

Reeves' mouth lifts. "Exactly."

"What if it pisses Drake off?"

"It should piss him off. You're his favorite toy, and not only were you taken away from him, you were also given to someone else to play with."

"Ollie," Dylan scolds.

Reeves lifts his hands in defense. "Just sayin' it like it is, Pickles."

"How long?" Everett murmurs. I can't tell if he's disappointed or resigned. If he wants this to happen, or if he wants me to leave him alone and never contact him again.

Scratching his jaw, Reeves answers, "Depends on the ex. I've helped girls for a few weeks. Others for a few months. The more you're seen together, the shorter the timeline. Usually, anyway."

"And with what little you know of Drake?" I ask.

"The fact he came here, attempting to prove you're his, only for it to blow up in his face means he's cocky. Arrogant. Even more so than the usual dickhead. If I had to guess, I'd say Drake will be a tough nut to crack."

"And what if he doesn't?" I question. "Crack?"

"Then we get the police involved."

"That isn't an option," I murmur.

"Why not?"

"Because I don't want my family to know I was dating Drake, and if I go to the police, it'll blow things out of proportion, and they'll find out, and…" I tuck my trembling hands beneath my thighs again, unsure what else to say.

"He beat the shit out of you," Everett growls. "I don't think calling the police is blowing anything out of proportion."

"I don't want to involve them," I repeat. "Please."

"What are you hiding?" Everett demands.

"Everett," Reeves warns. "Let it go."

Everett tosses his hands into the air. "This is bullshit!"

"Let. It. Go," Reeves pushes, setting down his empty bowl of cereal. "Besides, until things blow over with Dylan's investigation, it's probably best we all lay low, too."

I frown and turn to Dylan as Finley explains, "Reeves' dad is a dirty cop who planted cocaine in the back of his car, thinking it would ruin his NHL career, but Dylan decided to say it was hers, so it blew up in his face, and now there's an ongoing investigation."

"It's a whole…"—Dylan grimaces—"*thing.*"

"A *thing*," I repeat. "Got it."

Reeves smirks back at me and squeezes Dylan's shoulders. "At least you know you're in good company, right?"

I'd smile back at him if I didn't feel the anger emanating from the guy across the room. A vein throbs in Everett's forehead as he stares at me, but he keeps his lips pressed into a thin line when I finally meet his gaze. I know he wants to ask. I know he wants to push. I know he wants to make demands. To pry. To force the truth from my frozen vocal chords, even if it's the last thing he does.

But he doesn't. He simply…stares at me. Making me want to squirm. Making me want to spill all my secrets, no matter how pathetic they are.

"For now, we need to figure out where you'll be staying," Dylan points out.

She's right. If I can't go back to my place, where can I go?

Nibbling on the edge of my thumb, careful not to snag my bottom lip, I lift a shoulder, unsure what to say. "Like I said, I don't, uh, I don't want my parents to know I've been sharing my life with an abusive asshole."

"You can stay with us," Finley offers.

"Where?" Griffin challenges. His attention darts to me. "No offense."

With a laugh, I reply, "None taken."

"Seriously, though," Dylan starts. "My brother's right. I'm staying with Reeves. Mav and Lia are in his room. Griff is already sharing with Everett, and Finley isn't exactly a picnic to sleep next to."

"Hey!" She smacks her best friend on the shoulder. "Rude."

"I'm just sayin' you're a sleep talker," Dylan argues. "A really noisy one who likes to kick and steal the covers."

"Gee, thanks." Finley rolls her eyes but quickly sobers. "There's always Archer's room…"

The words are hushed. Tense. And laced with regret as soon as they're spoken, causing a haze of discomfort to fall on the room. And I hate that I put it there. Maybe not literally. I didn't suggest Archer's room as a potential refuge, but the only reason it was offered is because I have a shitty ex and no place to stay.

"I'll figure something out," I announce. "If I could maybe use the couch for a night or something, that'd be great. But even then—"

"I know where she can stay," Everett interrupts.

My head swivels toward him as Finley asks, "Where?"

"Yeah, where?" Dylan chimes in.

"The cabin."

Like the Fourth of July, Finley's eyes light up, and she claps her hands. "Yes! Why didn't I think of the cabin? It's perfect, and Mom and Dad left last week. Ohmygod, Raine, you're going to love it. It's secluded and gorgeous, and—wait. Your car has four-wheel drive, right?"

I grimace. "If I say no, does it ruin everything?"

Finley's head bobs. "One hundred percent, it does, yes."

"I'll drive you everywhere," Everett grunts from the sink. "Drake will recognize her car, anyway. It's best if she doesn't have it."

Silence follows.

And it isn't only me.

It's Reeves and Dylan and Finley. It's Griffin and the way he's looking at Everett. Like he grew a second head or something.

"You don't have to drive me anywhere," I murmur.

"Actually, he kind of does," Reeves interjects, interrupting our little staredown. "Buckle up, Raine, 'cause I'm gonna be honest with you. Whether or not you accept Everett's help, your world's about to be turned upside down for a while. I've done this a time or two, and considering the way Drake responded last night when you were trying to placate him before winding up at Everett's place instead of your apartment, I doubt he'll let you go easily. You're gonna want Everett around. In fact," he slaps Everett's shoulder, "consider him your shadow for the foreseeable future."

My shadow?

My eyes dart to Everett, and I push my hair away from my face, trying to keep my world from spinning out of control.

"What about my job or Everett's schooling or how much this is going to cost or—"

"Not gonna charge you for this," Everett grunts.

Reeves nods. "Yeah, we're not complete assholes. You need help. He's here to give it."

"You still didn't answer my question about schedules," I remind Reeves.

"We'll figure it out," Everett argues.

"How?"

"You can use my space in the garage to park your car since we won't be staying here."

"I haven't officially agreed yet," I say.

"What's there to agree to?" Everett's nostrils flare, and he pushes himself away from the counter. "Stop being so damn stubborn."

"Stop being so damn bossy, then," I snap before I press my lips together and dare to look up at him again for what somehow feels like the first and thousandth time all at once. New, but familiar, and with an intensity I'm already growing accustomed to. Pretty sure it's the one constant I've experienced over the last twenty-four hours. Everett's intensity. His chiseled jaw is locked. His arms are folded, making his muscles bulge. And his expression? It's unreadable.

"Aaaand, we're gonna go," Finley announces. Chair legs scrape against the hardwood floor as everyone stands, disappearing from the kitchen like a perfectly orchestrated magic act.

But the silence? It grows stronger and stronger with every passing second. I want to know what he's thinking. If he feels like I've been thrown into his lap without any say in the matter. If he feels like this entire situation is a waste of his time and he'd rather be anywhere else. If he feels like this is too much effort. Like *I'm* too much effort.

And maybe it's my own insecurities screaming at me, but I don't like it. The silence. The restraint in his gaze. The way he's looking at me so objectively. Like he's...detached. And why wouldn't he be? I came to Reeves for help. Not Everett. And sure, he's the one I called last night after Drake kicked me out of his car, but all he agreed to was one night. One night of help. Moving forward with Reeves' three step plan, let alone staying at his family's cabin for the foreseeable future? It's...a lot. It would be a lot for anyone, but for someone who's so unreadable and stoic, it's clearly more than he signed up for.

"Do you want me to go?" I finally ask, unable to take another second of silence.

"Stay."

I wipe my sweaty palms against my thighs until I remember all I'm wearing are his boxers and T-shirt. It makes me feel vulnerable. Seen.

"If I'm going to stay, I need you to stop looking at me like this."

"Like what?" he challenges.

"Like I'm a project or a...problem."

His footsteps are slow as he walks toward me, grabs the chair beside mine, and sits down. "I think we should have some rules."

I don't miss the way he doesn't acknowledge my assessment, but I give in anyway, letting him steer the conversation where he wants as long as it doesn't involve Mav or any of his family—*my* family.

Carefully, I ask, "What kind of rules?"

"For starters, you can't flinch anytime I try to touch you."

"I don't—"

He reaches for my face, and I shy away, causing his mouth

to twitch. "You do." Gently, he reaches for me again, and I force my body to stay still as he tucks a few strands of my hair behind my ear. Satisfied, he keeps his hand in place and nods. "Don't get me wrong. I get it. But if we're gonna convince your ex this is real, it needs to look real."

I nod.

"I'm gonna have to touch you," he repeats.

I nod again.

"And you're going to have to look like you like it." His icy blue eyes darken. "Like you want me to touch you."

I force my head to bob once more and gulp.

"I also need you to understand this isn't real."

Fighting the urge to roll my eyes, I answer, "Not a problem."

"You sure?"

I nod. "Trust me, after everything I've been through, I'm swearing off men altogether, but yes. I think I can handle a few fake touches."

"So if I do this…" He moves even closer until the smell of his musky sweat tickles my nostrils. He should stink. Every guy stinks after he works out. But Everett? I don't know what it is, and I don't know how I feel about it, but a not-so-small part of me wants to lean closer. To breathe him in.

Those icy blues shoot straight to my lower stomach as he dips his head, keeping his eyes on mine.

Is he going to kiss me? He wouldn't. There aren't any witnesses, and he just said this isn't real, but if that's the case—

His bottom lip grazes my top one, being careful not to brush against my still-healing split bottom lip. Heat floods to where he touches me, making my face feel hot and leaving me lightheaded as I force myself to stay still. To not pull away. Not because it's unpleasant, but because…because I'm curious. If this is how he kisses all his conquests, even his real ones. Soft. Controlled. Calculated. Pleasant, even. Hell, if I wasn't so jaded, I might even be interested in a guy like him. He's kind of surly, sure. But there's something about him. The way he watches me. All too aware of my every move. Every breath. Every—

He pulls away and drops his hand from my chin. "So you will let me touch you," he decides. "Good. Maybe we'll be able to pull this off after all."

A small part of me wants to call him an ass for kissing me under the guise of a test when there aren't any witnesses, but I bite my tongue.

Not. Real.

Right.

"What do I owe you?" I ask.

He scoffs. "Not making you pay for this."

"I want to."

"Not gonna happen," he repeats.

"What's in it for you?" I flinch back, surprised by my annoyance, until I realize I need an answer if I want this to work. "I only mean…if you won't let me pay you, what do you get out of this?"

"Who says I need to get anything out of it?"

"I don't know? Every guy on the planet?"

"Maybe I'm not like those guys."

He isn't. It took two minutes of being in his presence to figure out he's nothing like Drake or half the guys I've met in my life, most of them being Drake's friends, but I digress.

"Let's say we do it," I murmur. "Even if our entire relationship is fake, if we're going to make it look real, you can't be seen with other girls. Drake will see right through it."

"No girls. Got it."

"I'm serious. It was the one line Drake knew not to cross."

Everett scoffs. "Hitting you is one thing, but touching another girl is off limits?"

"Apparently," I reply dryly.

His mouth twitches, and he scratches his jaw. "Fine. No girls."

No girls. He says it so nonchalantly. Like I'm asking him to pick up some milk on his way home or something, when we both know asking a hockey star to be celibate for the foreseeable future isn't exactly an easy task, considering the puck bunnies who I have no doubt follow him around like little puppies during the season. Yet here he is, accepting it.

"It's not a problem for you?" I push. "Putting your life on hold to help me?"

His eyes darken a shade, making them appear more navy than sky blue as he studies me while keeping his thoughts to himself. Is he already second-guessing this ridiculous plan the same way I am? And that's coming from the girl who actually gets something out of this. Everett? He gets nothing. Nothing but a month or two of abstinence and likely a couple of right hooks as a consolation prize.

Yeah, this is a great idea.

"Why don't you want to tell your parents?" he finally asks.

I'd laugh at the ludicrousness of his question if I hadn't considered it a thousand times. It's so simple yet complicated that most days, the possibility of my family finding out makes me want to cry and curl up in a ball of shame when, if I just told them, it would eradicate most of my problems. It would also potentially create even more.

"Answer me," Everett pushes. "I won't do this unless you tell me the truth."

"You really want the truth?" I bite the edge of my black lacquered thumbnail and avoid his gaze. "It's because I feel stupid."

"Stupid?" He frowns and gives me a look making me feel like I've grown a second head or something.

"My parents taught me better than to spend time with

someone like Drake. Someone who's manipulative and controlling and possessive. The idea of giving my parents front-row seats to something like that makes me feel… stupid," I repeat. "And with how low my confidence already is considering the circumstances, I think keeping them in the dark is probably the one good decision I've made since I started dating Drake. Oh," I snap my fingers, "and let's not forget I've been treated with kid gloves ever since the moment I was conceived, remember?"

"What does that have to do with you keeping your family in the dark?"

"You're kidding, right?" I laugh. "After my mom's miscarriage and years of infertility until she finally wound up pregnant with me, I was basically deemed a miracle before I even had a heartbeat. Don't get me wrong. I'm happy to be alive and love my family more than you'll ever understand. But do you know how messed up it feels to simultaneously be put on a pedestal for existing and also treated like a frail princess in need of protection from…everything? And it's not only coming from my parents, either. If my older brother—who thinks he's untouchable, by the way—found out about what Drake's been doing to me, he would literally kill him, Everett. And no, I'm not just saying it. That is if my dad didn't pull the trigger first."

"Raine—"

"Do you really think I want my dad or my brother to wind up in jail all because I screwed up by falling in love with the wrong guy?" I scoff. "I can't let that happen. I can't."

"We won't let it happen," Everett interjects.

I fold my arms and lean back in my chair. "You're right. We won't. Because we all agreed I'm not going to the cops."

He's annoyed. I can see it. Feel it. The tension in his jaw. The vein in his forehead. If he's expecting me to cave, he's going to be sorely disappointed.

I hold his stare and ignore the swell of butterflies in my stomach.

"Not. Going. To. Happen," I push.

His eyes thin even more, and a grumbled sigh escapes him. "The cabin's up in the mountains. All it takes is one storm without four-wheel drive, and you're stuck for a week. That's why I'm gonna drive you everywhere until this shit is taken care of, especially since Drake knows your car, too. When you get a second, send me your schedule. I'll work it around my classes, practice, and games. We can figure it out as we go."

"Ev…"

"Do you go to school?"

I shake my head. "Just work at Eternal."

With a slow nod, he steps back, giving me room to breathe. "Do you feel safe at Eternal?"

My brows pull as I consider his question. "Why?"

"Because I can't hang around during your shifts. I have practice and school and—"

"I don't think Drake will do anything while I'm in the shop," I tell him. "He'd wait to get me alone."

"So as long as you wait inside after shifts, you should be good?"

"I think so, yes."

His chin dips again. "Let me pack my shit, then we'll grab your things."

My eyes pop. "I'm sorry…two things. One,"—I lift my forefinger into the air—"why do you need to pack? And two" —I add my middle finger—"You want to pick up my things right now?"

"One"—he mirrors me, lifting a finger into the air—"the cabin's a thirty-minute drive from town, and Reeves said you shouldn't be alone until we know Drake's finished being an asshole, so yeah. I'm moving in with you. And two,"—he lifts another finger, going toe to toe with me in the middle of his kitchen—"yes. We're gonna pick up your shit right now. Let's go."

"I don't know if it's a good idea," I hedge.

He tucks his hands into his pockets, rocks back on his heels, and turns toward the hallway. "And I don't give a shit. Come on."

CHAPTER TWELVE

EVERETT

She's curling in on herself. I can see it. Feel it. The heavy dose of anxiety. The fear. Of her boyfriend. Of the unknown. Of...me?

I glance at her from the corner of my eye and crush the steering wheel with more force as we drive down the highway toward Cedar Springs. The trees whir past us, blurring into different shades of brown and gray. The leaves have long since fallen, and winter's right around the corner. Fuck, it's already here, and it's the only reason I agreed to drive Raine everywhere in the first place. I can't stop thinking about our earlier conversation.

That isn't a problem for you? Putting your life on hold for me?

I've been putting my dating life on hold long before Raine stumbled into my life. Sure, I've had some casual hookups and shit, but anything real has always felt out of place in my life. Family. School. Hockey. A relationship's never been on my radar because I haven't had time for it to be on my radar. With everything in my life, I live by one rule. When I'm all-in, I'm all-in. And I've never found a girl worth being all-in for. It's why I'm okay putting off any potential hookups with random girls for the woman beside me. Because right now? Now, I'm all-in to help her escape the shitstorm she's been tossed into without a life raft. I think it's why my friends went quiet in the kitchen. Why they looked at me with hesitation. Knowing if I agreed to this, everything else would be put on the back burner until I saw it through, which is what I'm doing. Seeing it through. Even if I'd rather be anywhere else. After seeing the bruises on her face, I've been all-in, and I won't rest until Drake's out of her life for good.

"Take the next exit," Raine whispers between gnawing on the edge of her thumb and staring blankly out the passenger window.

Flicking on my blinker, I merge into the far right lane and take the exit. It's dirtier here. More urban, maybe. Less of a small town like Lockwood Heights. We rarely come up this way. There's no need. But still, it makes me curious. About the girl beside me. Who she is and where she's from. The girl's been nothing but a vault, and I don't know why.

"Turn left at the light," she murmurs.

I do as I'm told.

"It's the gray building," she adds.

A minute later, I pull into the parking lot, and she directs me around the back. When I find a parking spot near a set of stairs, I cut the engine and wait. Raine's lips part with a deep breath, and she stares up at the building. But she doesn't move. Doesn't reach for the handle to climb out of the car. She merely sits there.

"Do you think he's home?" I ask. I considered bringing up his whereabouts before we left. Then, I decided he shouldn't have the power to choose when we swing by to grab her things. It isn't up to him. It's up to Raine. Well, and me, but it's beside the point.

With a soft shake of her head, Raine continues gazing at the building. "He should be in class, but we have a video on our doorbell, so he'll know we're here as soon as we approach the front door." She hesitates and presses her lips together. "Maybe you should stay in the car."

"Not gonna happen, Raine."

Tearing her attention from the looming building in front of us, she turns to me. "I don't want to rock the boat."

"Not rocking the boat is how you got here in the first place," I remind her.

Her head falls forward, and she takes a deep breath. "Right."

Part of me wants to ask if she's having second thoughts. If she's wasting my time. If she's going to go back to him. If she's really done. The other part?

I bite my tongue and turn toward the driver's side door, preparing to get this shit over with. "Come on."

"What if he comes home?" she whispers.

Letting go of the door handle, I face her again. "You really think he'll do something while I'm here?"

"I think he's terrified of losing me," she counters.

"Why?" I grimace. "Don't get me wrong. You're beautiful, but there are a lot of fish in the sea, right?"

Her quiet laugh surprises me as she tucks her hair behind her ear. "Normally, I'd agree with you."

"But?" I challenge.

"But Drake's been through a lot with me."

"Like what?"

"Like losing his mom. Like opening up about his dad and the childhood he had. He might put on a strong front or whatever, but I know him better than anyone." She hesitates. "I think when you've experienced a lot with a person, it's easy to cling to them and convince yourself they're your life raft, you know? And without them, you can't stay afloat."

"Do you believe that?" I ask. "Do you believe you can't stay afloat without Drake?"

"I think…" Her brows dip. "I think he's been dragging me down for a long time, and I thought if I could kick hard enough, if I could…learn to be a better swimmer, we'd be okay, but apparently, I kind of suck."

With a bark of laughter, I twist the keyring around my forefinger and catch the keys in my palm. "You suck for not being able to keep two heads above water when one's clearly been nothing but dead weight?" I shake my head. "Raine, you aren't invincible."

"Says the guy who's willingly faking like he's in a relationship with a girl to protect her from an asshole ex," she points out. "Why do you do it?"

I shrug. "I owed Reeves a favor."

"A favor," she repeats.

"Yeah."

Her chin lowers slightly, and I swear I can see something click behind her eyes, but I don't know what it is. "I'll be sure to keep that in mind. We should, uh, we should get going."

I watch as she climbs out of the car and folds her arms, keeping in her body heat as she stares at her feet and walks toward the building. Forcing myself to follow, we make our way up the steps to the second floor, and she digs her keys from her purse. Her hands are trembling. Fuck, her whole body is shaking. It's barely noticeable, and if I hadn't been paying such close attention to her since picking her up on the side of the road, I doubt I would've noticed. But now? Now, I see it. The way he affects her. The way she shuts down. The way I was given a glimpse of the girl she was before dating Drake when we went head-to-head in the kitchen, yet now, she's nothing but a shell, and it's all because of him.

As Raine attempts to slide the key into the lock, I look at the camera and lift my chin, well aware Drake will see this. Whether it's right now, or later when he replays the footage, he'll know I was here. He'll know I'm the one Raine called. The one she asked for help. The one who shared his bed with her and took care of her.

Good.

Fuck you, Drake.

When I realize Raine's struggling with the lock, I look down. Her hands are still shaking. Placing mine on top of hers, I slowly twist the key, and she peeks up at me, her brows pinching into the tiniest of frowns.

Remembering Reeves' guidance from earlier and his insistence we make our relationship look real, I slip my other hand around Raine's hourglass waist. Warm. Small. Her stomach tightens against my palm and her breath hitches, but she doesn't elbow me in the gut like I half-expected, so I'll call this a win as long as she doesn't blow our cover.

"What are you doing?" she whispers.

"Breathe." I lean closer like earlier in the kitchen. "I won't let him hurt you. Not anymore."

Surprise hits her pretty green eyes until a glint of awareness follows.

Yeah. She knows he's watching, too.

"I know you won't." She leans into my embrace, forcing her muscles to relax against me. "Thanks for last night."

"Thanks for trusting me enough to call."

"Thanks for coming today, too."

"Thanks for asking me," I volley back with a smirk, hinting I can play this game all day.

She lets out a breathless laugh. "Thanks for *almost* making me forget what we're doing here."

Twisting her around, I let her back hit the front door and step closer. Her breath hitches again as I press my front to hers, knowing Drake won't be able to see us anymore. But it's almost better this way. Let his imagination drive him insane.

"And what are we doing here?" I challenge.

Another breath catches in her throat before she presses her hands to my chest and smiles up at me. "Getting my things, remember?"

"Right." My smirk widens. "Because you're leaving your asshole of an ex."

Her throat tightens with a gulp and I swear I see a flash of fear hit her eyes. It makes my grin falter for an instant until I force it back into place. I hate that I might not be the one to put the fear in her pretty green eyes, but I'm still the one calling Drake an asshole and poking the bear. I'm also the one giving her the opportunity to do the same. She doesn't get it though. She deserves this moment, no matter how small it is in the scheme of things. The opportunity to take back a sliver of the confidence he beat out of her.

Don't be afraid of him, I want to tell her, but I keep my mouth shut, knowing Drake can hear us now.

"Yes," she finally whispers. "I'm finally leaving my asshole of an ex." Her chest expands on a cleansing breath. "And I'm never coming back."

Genuine relief and pride fill my chest as I stare down at her. I don't know Raine. Not really. But I do know that if Finley was in this position, I'd expect her to give two giant middle fingers to her ex as she ended things. While Raine might not be able to break up with Drake face-to-face, she's stood up to him now, letting him know she's leaving and never coming back.

Remembering the facade we're still putting on, I murmur, "That's my girl," praying the words don't sound as forced as they feel as they roll off my tongue. "Now, come on. Let's grab your things so we can get out of here." I reach around her waist, turn the key still lodged in the lock, and slowly push the door open while making sure Raine doesn't lose her footing in the process. The hinges squeak in protest, and Raine turns around, opening it the rest of the way, letting us both inside.

It's messy.

Not average messy. More like a grown-ass toddler threw a fit without caring about the wreckage, and fuck me, it's everywhere. Pillows are knocked off the couch. One of the kitchen chairs is on its side. Glass litters the floor, along with a dozen wilted roses and a puddle of water staining the transition from tile to carpet in the small kitchen and family room. A shattered mirror clings to a single nail still pinning it to the wall, and I'm pretty sure if I breathe on it wrong, it'll clatter to the ground. The clothes and shoes are the biggest mess, though.

Shit is everywhere, and if I had to guess, most of it belongs to Raine.

My attention flicks to her. Molars grinding, she scans the apartment, then marches toward a broken picture frame on the wall. Pieces of paper lie on the ground. She wipes beneath her nose with the arm of her jacket, then bends down and scoops up different items of clothing. Jackets. Shoes. Shirts. Jeans. She's pissed. She has every right to be. But whatever fear she was drowning in when we walked in here has morphed into something angrier. Something more fierce.

Reaching for the edge of the front door, I close it behind us. "You okay?" I ask quietly.

"This is Drake's way of being a dick." She huffs, dropping the collected clothes onto the coffee table, and gathers more scattered items from the kitchen. "He's probably hoping it'll give him more time to corner me when I decide to come grab my things. Doesn't mean he had to rip up my art, though," she mutters under her breath. "Sonofabitch."

Striding toward the broken frame, I bend down and pick up the ripped pieces of paper. None of them are much bigger than a coin, but whatever it was, it meant something to her. Like pieces of a puzzle, I'm given a tiny glimpse of the entire drawing. Is it a…dandelion? A bouquet of dandelions? I tilt my head and try to line up a few of the pieces in my palm.

"Leave it," Raine murmurs behind me. "We should hurry."

Avoiding the broken glass, I pick up the rest of the pieces and push them into my pocket, kicking my ass into gear. I gather anything looking like it belongs to a girl, adding the pink sweats and matching hoodie to the pile on the coffee table with the various shit Raine already set aside when a bright red thong catches my attention on the back of the worn gray couch. An image of what it would look like on Raine flashes through my mind, and I freeze. The girl's so guarded, I half-expected her to be a boyshorts-only type of girl. Nothing wrong with boyshorts, mind you. Fuck, a girl like Raine could pull off anything. But a thong? A red thong? My eyes wander to the owner in question and drift back to the scrap of fabric.

"Is there a—*oh*." With red cheeks, Raine snags the thong from the top cushion and tucks it into her pocket.

"You good?" I ask.

"You can wait outside."

"I can help—"

"I've got this. Go."

Like I'm the plague, she avoids me, keeping a wide berth between us as she heads to the kitchen, clearly dismissing me.

"Nothing wrong with red," I point out.

Her gaze narrows, and she folds her arms. "Didn't say there was."

"Good, because there isn't." I snag a black heel from the ground and toss it onto the growing pile of clothes when my attention catches on a neon yellow lacy bra. "Wouldn't have pegged you for this color, though."

Her head pops above the kitchen counter and she follows my gaze. Her nose wrinkles. "You can leave it."

"Not a fan of yellow?" I ask.

"It was a…" Her lips purse. "*Gift.*"

"Got it." I leave the bra where it is and get back to work, trying to create order in a sea of chaos.

It's strange. Being here. In her space. Being given a glimpse of who Raine is outside of what she's told me, which, now that I think about it, is basically nothing. And maybe I should keep it that way. Keep the distance. The walls. After the shit she's been through, she's smart to have them. But being here. Seeing the damage and the little things making up the girl I barely know only piques my curiosity.

Like a busy little bee, she buzzes around the room, then disappears down the hall, returning with a well-used Grove University Grizzlies duffle bag. I doubt everything will fit, but it's a start. Silently, I help her fill it until the zipper threatens to give out if I dare shove anything else inside.

"Is this everything?" I ask.

She lifts a shoulder and scans the apartment. "Yeah. Yeah, I guess it is."

"You don't own any of the furniture?" I prod.

"He can keep it. The sooner I get out of here, the better."

With a nod, I hook the strap of her duffle bag over my shoulder, pressing my hand to her lower back, ready to get the hell out of dodge.

"I can carry it," she argues.

"I think you've carried enough shit on your own, don't you think?" I push her toward the door, and by some miracle, she lets me.

CHAPTER THIRTEEN

RAINE

When Everett called his parents' home a cabin, I assumed he meant the term figuratively. And maybe he did, but one thing's for sure. Wherever Everett's taking me, he wasn't kidding about the thirty-minute drive or the fact it's far from civilization. We already stopped at the grocery store, and now the back of Everett's truck is packed with food, my duffle bag, and Everett's suitcase. Icy water clings to the pine trees lining the winding road as we drive up the mountain. It's colder up here than in the valley, but the pavement is still clear.

"You know, I'm pretty sure my car can make it up here," I murmur.

"Pretty sure you've never been in a snowstorm up here," he counters.

"I've been in a snowstorm."

"Up *here*," he repeats, emphasizing the word as he pulls off the main road and onto a muddied dirt one.

"And what makes snowstorms up here so special?"

"When I was a kid, Fin and I would play outside all the time. When a storm hit, the snow would come down so fast I couldn't even see my hand in front of me. So, yeah. Storms up here are something else."

I peek over at him, surprised. By the softness in his voice. The glimpse into his childhood. The lack of gruffness I've grown accustomed to.

"You came up here a lot when you were kids?" I ask.

"We lived up here."

"In the woods?"

"My parents like the quiet."

My mouth twitches. "I'm sorry. Have they met your little sister?"

He laughs dryly. "Yeah, she's somethin' else, but I think my parents blame my half-sisters for it."

"Half-sisters?" I shouldn't pry, but I can't help it. This is the most we've spoken…ever, and even if I have a feeling he's only opening up to distract me from my shitty day, I want to take advantage. Besides, I could use the distraction. A moment out of the spotlight for once.

"I have two half-sisters from my dad's previous marriage. Hazel and Miley," Everett explains. "They're both almost twenty years older than me and Fin, so when Fin was born, they basically treated her like their own personal dress-up doll."

"Not you?"

A faint smile graces his lips. "There's a photo or two of my sister dressed up when she was a baby that I'm convinced is really me, but no one will fess up to it."

My nose crinkles as I hide my laugh behind my hand. "You're joking."

"Definitely not joking."

I shouldn't find this as hilarious as I do. Especially after the week I've had. But the image of the sexy, alpha hockey player next to me in girl's clothes is pretty much the funniest thing I've ever heard. It takes everything inside of me to keep from asking for a copy of the evidence.

As if he can sense my amusement, he gives me the side-eye. "Glad someone finds my childhood torture entertaining."

I drop my hand to my lap and give in, showcasing my giant grin as I imagine a baby Everett in pink ruffles and bows. "At least you don't remember the trauma, right? It's gotta count for something."

"Not sure repressing memories is any healthier, Raine," he jokes.

"Good point." He's right. It isn't. I had a good childhood. A great childhood, actually. But even then, I know what it's like to want to forget certain events. I drag my tongue against my swollen lip and turn back to the passenger window.

"Not too much farther," he adds.

"You know, you're lucky I trust you," I point out.

"You trust me?"

"I have to, don't I?" I glance at him again. "I'm pretty sure you could kill me up here, and no one would know."

"Quite a morbid thought," he muses.

"Doesn't make it less true. It is pretty, though."

I lean a little closer to the windshield, taking in the gorgeous forest surrounding us as he drives around the bend. And leaves my jaw practically hanging off its hinges.

It's beautiful. Absolutely beautiful and so picturesque I can almost believe I've died and gone to heaven.

"This is your childhood home?" I ask, refusing to look at Ev, let alone blink in case I miss a single detail of the landscape. The leaves have all fallen from the trees, but the ground is wet, and the massive log cabin tucked between two hills and a valley for a backyard looks like it was placed here by God himself. I bet it's beautiful in winter. Covered in a blanket of snow. And summer? I can only imagine how lush and green the foliage must get in contrast to the blue sky. I roll down the window and breathe deeply. The air is fresh. Clean. Earthy.

It's perfect.

Everett pushes a button on his car, and the garage door rumbles to life in front of us. "This is it."

I roll the window up as he pulls inside, cuts the ignition off, and leads me into the house.

To say it's gorgeous would be an enormous understatement. It's as beautiful inside as it is outside. The kitchen is masculine yet homey, with dark green cabinets, maple-colored floors, and white walls. There's a huge stone fireplace in the family room on the opposite side of the open floor plan, too, along with a large leather sectional I can't wait to melt into. Pictures line the walls, and if there was a definition of a picture-perfect family, this would be it. A mom. A dad. An older brother. A little girl. Smiling faces and a warmth you can feel through the photograph. My fingers itch to reach out and touch it, but I keep my hands tucked into the crooks of my elbows as I study a young Everett in his hockey gear. He must've just won something because his grin is contagious, and I catch my lips lifting.

"That's us," Everett explains beside me.

I tear my attention from the photograph and turn to him, searching his face for similarities to the boy in the picture. "You have your dad's eyes," I conclude.

"My mom says the same thing." He tilts his head toward the hallway. "Come on. I'll show you to your room."

Flicking the hall light on, he points toward the first door on the left, pushing it open. "This one's yours. Mine is on the right, and the bathroom is right..." He steps a little further down the hall, stopping at the next door on my side of the hall. "Here. Any questions?"

I shake my head. "Nope. I don't think so."

"Good. Do you want to settle in while I make some food?"

"You cook?"

"Is that a problem?"

"No, it's...um, I've never met a guy who cooks."

He squeezes the back of his neck, almost looking...shy? My pulse thrums a little faster, but I shove the feeling aside.

"My dad's the cook in the family and taught me how, along with Fin," he finally explains.

"That's...really cool," I admit.

"Don't be too impressed. You haven't tried any of my cooking yet." He rests his shoulder against the wall. "I bought stuff for lasagna, chicken noodle soup, and steaks with broccoli and mashed potatoes. What sounds good?"

"Uh..." I try to keep my surprise in check, but did he seriously say lasagna? And chicken noodle soup? *And* steak with broccoli and mashed potatoes? Drake couldn't make toast without burning it. Don't get me wrong. I was right beside Everett when he purchased the ingredients, but I guess I assumed he'd have me cook for him or something. The fact he's the one who planned to cook all along? It's...strange.

Tucking my thumbs into the back pockets of my jeans, I rock back on my heels. "Whatever you feel like cooking sounds great. Can I help with anything?"

"Nah, I'm good." He pushes himself away from the wall and starts toward the main area, calling over his shoulder, "I'll be in the kitchen."

"I'm not helpless, you know." I don't know why I say it, or maybe I do, but the idea of someone like Everett—someone who seems like he has every single piece of his life exactly where he wants it—waiting on me, and carrying my luggage, and driving me here, and making me dinner, and *not* assuming I'd be the one to cook for him tonight. It...it's messing with me.

He turns around and faces me again. "What?"

"I said I'm not helpless."

"I never said you were."

"Yeah, but you look at me like I am."

He frowns. "When have I—"

"At the rink when we first met," I argue. "And at the tattoo shop. And at the party. And when you picked me up on the side of the road." My tongue darts out, and I lick my bottom lip. "And when I couldn't make the lock work at my apartment."

"I stepped in because we're trying to make this look real to Drake."

"And your reason for insisting I not help you cook?" I challenge.

"I figured you might want a break."

"And maybe I feel like I could use a distraction," I point out. "My house is gone. My car is gone. I am solely relying on you, and now you're cooking me food? Homemade, yummy food when I've been living off cereal and takeout? It's...I don't know. I guess you can drop the boyfriend act when we're alone, okay?"

"Boyfriend act?"

"You said we're trying to make this look real," I remind him. "Well, no one's here to fake it for, so..."

"So you think I'm only offering to cook you a meal because it's what a good boyfriend would do?"

"Isn't it, though?" I push, well aware of how crazy I must sound. I'm not mad. I'm...well, I'm confused, dammit. He's the one who wanted to make it clear none of this is real, not me, so why is he being so...kind? Especially when we both know he isn't getting anything out of this. Hell, the only reason he's doing it in the first place is because he owes Reeves a favor. It might be smart for both of us to remember.

Unfortunately, I have a feeling all I've done is piss him off, and it makes me feel even smaller. I don't want to be a burden. I don't want to make him mad. But it doesn't matter what I want because I can feel his frustration as he scrubs his hand over his face and drops his arm to his side.

"Hey, Raine?"

My brows crinkle as I wait for him to spit out whatever he's going to say. When he doesn't, I give in. "Yes?"

"I'm craving lasagna, which takes a little while to make. Want to help me in the kitchen?"

I know what this is. It's an olive branch. A terribly veiled but desperately needed olive branch.

Drake never offered olive branches. Hell, pretty sure the asshole didn't believe in them. The reminder makes me want to cry, but I force it back.

"Sure," I murmur. "I'd love to."

As he leaves, my phone rings, and I pull it out, expecting to see Drake's name, but I find my boss's instead.

Sliding my thumb across the screen, I lift my phone to my ear and answer, "Hello?"

"Raine?"

"Hey, Lucian. What's up?"

"Just checkin' in. You all right?"

Like a bucket of ice water, dread washes over me. "W-why wouldn't I be? Am I scheduled for tonight? If I am, I didn't know."

"You're not on the schedule tonight," he tells me.

The pit in my stomach grows, and I press my hand to my abs, letting out a slow breath as I wait for him to say…something. To clarify why he's calling or what the problem is. When he stays quiet, I prod, "Okay?"

"Drake's been here."

"What?"

"He's been pestering Lana all afternoon. Asking for your schedule. When you'll be in again. Wanting access to your locker and shit."

My chin drops to my chest, and I squeeze my eyes shut. "Is he still there?"

There's a short pause before Lucian's low voice comes back on the line. "He's parked out front."

Of course, he is.

"We broke up," I admit. "Obviously, he isn't taking it well."

"Figured as much. You want me to call the cops?"

"No," I rush out. "No, it's fine."

"You sure?"

"Yeah, positive."

"What do you want me to tell him the next time he comes in?"

"Tell him I quit," I murmur.

"Raine..."

"I know," I whisper. "Thank you, Lucian. For giving me the job. For helping me out."

"Sure thing, Raine. You know I'd do anything for you, right?"

Even though he can't see me, I still bob my head up and down as I fight back tears. "I know." I sniff. "I know you would. But, I think it's going to take some time before Drake lets this go, and since he lives across the street from the shop, it's only a matter of time until he tries to corner me so we can talk, and I really don't want to talk, so..."

"So, this is it, huh?" he asks.

"Thanks, Lucian," I repeat. "I'm serious. I... Thank you."

"Anytime, darlin'. Want me to put some feelers out? See if there're any other shops with open apprenticeships?"

"No," I whisper. "No, it's fine."

"Too late. I already decided," he announces. "Talk soon."

The call goes dead before I can push him to explain what he meant. I let my hand fall to my side. It's over. My apprenticeship is over. It sucks. It really freaking sucks.

What the hell am I going to do now?

CHAPTER FOURTEEN

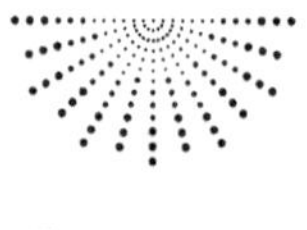

EVERETT

She looks cute in an apron.

She's also a terrible cook.

There's too much salt in the sauce. The noodles are far from al dente, and it took her twenty minutes to grate the cheese. Still. It might be the best lasagna I've made since cooking a batch in the kitchen with my dad as I watch Raine slide her fork into her mouth and take a bite. When the cheese hits her tongue, she practically moans.

"You like it?" I ask.

"This is incredible."

I nod, taking my own bite when her phone vibrates against the table.

It's been buzzing off and on since we started boiling the water for the noodles. Her muscles tense, and she pushes the mute button, grabbing her glass of wine and bringing it to her lips.

If I didn't know any better, I'd say this feels like a date.

Until her phone goes off again.

"Haven't blocked him yet, huh?" It isn't an accusation. It's an observation. One bothering me more than I'd like to admit. Reeves gave her rules for a reason, and I'm not one to waste my time.

"He's using his friends' phones," she counters.

My frustration triggers, and I stand up, reaching for her cell on the round table. Before she can stop me, it's in my hand as it vibrates with another message. There are at least a dozen of them. Some from the same number. Some from different ones. Her phone isn't password protected, so I can see everything. Part of me wonders if it's because he didn't trust her enough to let her have a lock. The other part doesn't want to know, in case my theory's correct. It'll only make me feel more sorry for her, and I have a feeling it's the last thing she wants.

As I sit my ass back down, another message pops up and I stare at the screen. It's a picture. I click on it, and the image expands. It's a screenshot of the security footage. My hands on her. Raine looking up at me. Her back pressed to my chest. Before I pushed her against the door. Before she labeled Drake as her ex and promised she'd never go back to their apartment. The footage is convincing, even if it's relatively innocent. The way I stare down at her. The way she stares up at me. All innocent and ripe for the picking. Wide eyes. Lips parted. Fuck. My hand threatens to crush the phone as a text follows.

555.321.4924

What the fuck is this?!

I'll tell you what this is, asshole. This is proof that Raine isn't your girl anymore.

"What's he saying?" Raine asks, interrupting my inner dialogue.

I glance up at her and force my grip to relax. "He sent a picture of us from your doorbell camera."

She nods but doesn't ask to see it when the phone buzzes

again. This time, it's a video message. Against my better judgment, I click on it, and a silhouette of a girl comes into view. It might be dark, but I can tell it's Raine. She's naked on a bed. Her head is thrown back, and she's moaning. The sound shoots straight to my cock until I register what I'm seeing. It's a sex tape. She's fucking someone. Scratch that. Someone was fucking her, and it doesn't take a genius to figure out who. My gut knots as I shut the phone off but don't give it back to her. I stare at my lasagna, but it's like it's tattooed in my mind. The image of Raine riding his cock.

She must've heard it. Recognized the sound of her writhing. Moaning. Begging.

Her phone vibrates against the table, but neither of us reaches for it.

"Did you know he filmed you?" I rasp. Jealousy licks up my spine and fucks with my head.

Her fork clinks against the edge of her plate. She picks up her napkin and crumples it in her hands. "Not when he was doing it."

"But you know he has the footage," I push.

"He has three videos. One of me sucking him off. One of us in our bedroom. And one of us in the shower."

Rage simmers beneath my skin, and I shake my head. "How could you let him—"

"You don't know Drake." She drops the napkin and pushes her half-finished plate further away from her. "And like I said, I didn't know he was filming, so maybe you should stop looking at me like you're disgusted to even be in the same room with me."

Her gaze drops to a knot in the wooden table, and she folds her arms, refusing to look at me. To make eye contact with me. To let me past those impenetrable walls.

But her shame and embarrassment practically waft off her with a vengeance. It's thick. Potent. Nauseating.

My own appetite vanishes as I stare at the girl across from me. "You're right," I concede. "I'm sorry."

"For what? Being a judgmental asshole? Even if I had let him film us together—which I didn't—it doesn't justify him sharing it."

"You're right," I repeat. "It doesn't. Nothing justifies this. And I'm not disgusted with you. I'm disgusted with him. Sharing a piece of yourself with someone you trust, then finding out they misused that trust—especially like this—is fucked up."

She scoffs. "You can say that again." Wiping at the corner of her eye while still refusing to look at me, she whispers, "And now, he's going to share it with even more people."

"*More?*" I growl.

"The one of me sucking him off?" she offers. "Yeah. He already shared it with his friends. Didn't even bother holding it over my head before he sent it. Look what my baby girl can do," she mocks, mimicking his voice. "Like I was something to show off, you know? How I could deep throat his cock like a good girl. And then, when I called him out for acting like a dick, he told me it was a joke, and I should stop overreacting." Her laugh is laced with resentment as she shakes her head back and forth. "The best part was when I showed up at his next game. You should've seen his teammates' faces. It took less than two seconds for me to realize they'd all seen it. Called me *good girl* for a solid month afterward like it was an inside joke or something." She forces a smile. "What a bunch of gentlemen, am I right?"

The phone buzzes against the table again, interrupting her. This time, it's a call.

I slide my thumb across the screen and bring it to my ear. "Hey, asshole."

Drake's voice echoes through the speaker after a short pause. "Let me talk to my girlfriend."

"Yeah, she's not your girlfriend anymore."

"Give her the phone," he seethes. "Now."

"You lost the right to talk to her the moment you hit her."

"Tell her if she doesn't come home, I'm gonna—"

"Careful," I warn. "If you finish your sentence with a threat, you'll regret it."

His laughter booms through the speaker. I pull it away from my ear briefly.

"You think you know her, man. You think you know me. But you have no fucking clue who you're dealing with. Raine is mine."

"Raine is Raine," I tell him calmly. "And if you don't stop calling her, we'll call the police."

"Everett," Raine whispers.

"Nah, I don't think you will," Drake interrupts, oblivious to Raine's protest. "Your friend group already has enough heat with the police, don't you think?"

My molars threaten to crack as I register his words. How the fuck does he know what's going on with our group and the police?

"Stay away from her," I warn.

"Yeah, I don't think so. See you around, Taylor."

The call goes dead, and my attention snaps to Raine. "*Now*, you need to call the police."

She pales and shakes her head. "I can't."

"Why not?"

"I already told you. I don't want to blow things out of proportion."

I slam my hand against the table. "This isn't blowing things out of proportion, Raine! He has videos of you he recorded without your permission!"

"You think I don't know that? You think I don't know I got mixed up with the wrong guy?"

"Then let me call the police."

"No."

"Why not?"

"Because then my parents will know!"

"Maybe you could use your parents' support right now," I growl. "Did you ever think of that?"

She wipes beneath her eye and shakes her head again, refusing to look at me as we go head-to-head. "You don't get it."

"Then explain it to me, Raine."

"I don't owe you anything."

"You're staying under my roof! You're—"

"Fine!" she snaps, pushing to her feet. "I'll leave!"

"I'm not asking you to leave," I spit. "I'm asking you to explain why you don't want your parents to know. Fuck, I'm begging you to! What's so wrong with your parents finding out about you dating an asshole like Drake?"

"I already told you—"

"Because you feel stupid," I say, recounting her words from before.

"Yes!" she yells. The fight seeps out of her, and she collapses back into her seat. "I feel so fucking stupid, Everett." Her breath hitches as she stares at her plate like she's refusing to look at me. Like she can't stomach it. "My parents are strong. They're resilient. My mom practically raised herself, and my dad one-hundred percent did. They warned me not to date assholes and to stand up for myself and to be confident and smart. Falling for Drake, dating him, and moving in with him was the opposite in every. Fucking. Way. So you'll have to excuse me for not wanting to look into my parents' eyes and only see disappointment, especially when they find out exactly who Drake's father is, all right?" She wipes at the corner of her eye, letting out a slow breath through pursed lips.

"Who is Drake's dad?" I ask.

Her lower lip trembles, and I know she let something slip she wasn't planning to share.

"Raine," I warn.

"His, uh, his dad is Bradley Ackerman."

I stay quiet, searching my memory for any association to the name but come up empty. "Am I supposed to know who he is?"

She shakes her head. "I don't know? Maybe not. He, uh, I think he went by Shorty or something? He went to LAU with Mav's mom. I don't know all the details, but my parents gave me the highlights as a word of caution, along with my mom's shitty experience, and why it's important to know who you're dating and what red flags to look for. Bradley dated Mia for a while but turned out to be a massive scumbag. Like father, like son, right?" Another pathetic laugh escapes her.

I sit back in my seat, blindsided. Not only with Drake's connection to Mia but also Raine's guilt over it. The urge to protect her. To justify her logic. It hits closer to home than I anticipate, and I clench my hands into fists on the table, forcing myself to stay in place instead of pulling her into me and comforting her. "You didn't know he would turn out like his dad."

"You're right. I didn't. But even if he turned out to be a saint like I hoped, it would still be a betrayal to my family."

"You don't know that."

"I do, though," she argues. "If my parents found out we were together, and I not only hid it from them but also completely stabbed Maverick's mom in the back by defending his offspring, they'd never forgive me."

"His dad doesn't make him who he is."

"It doesn't matter!" she yells. "Drake's just like him, and even when I knew what signs to watch for, I ignored them. I thought he was different. I thought I could change him." Her laugh is practically a whimper. "God, how stupid am I? I thought I could change him? Really?" She wipes beneath her eyes again as if her tears are nothing but a reminder of her weakness, and letting them fall will only solidify my view of her. It's like the girl's so used to bottling up her emotions—so used to being afraid of setting off the people around her—she doesn't know how to let them out. To let someone see the ugly side. The irony isn't lost on me as I take her in. All rosy cheeks and glassy eyes.

Still. Fucking. Gorgeous.

Even when she's unraveling at the seams.

"I did every stupid thing in the book," she whispers. "Every stupid thing I was ever warned not to do. And look where it got me. When I found out Drake's related to Mia's ex, I swept it under the rug. Pretended like I didn't know all the shit his dad put her through." Her gaze falls to her hands. "Not that it matters. I started noticing the similarities of what I was going through to the stories I heard from my own parents." She scoffs and wipes beneath her eyes once more, refusing to let me in despite airing her dirty laundry. "But I ignored them. Ignored all of it. And if they find out I was so fucking stupid to ignore his familial ties, let alone how it might hurt my family and what he was doing to me, I'll never…I'll never forgive myself. I'll never live it down. I just…I want it to go away. I want all of it to go away."

I lean back in my chair, studying her. Her sincerity. Her strength. Her stubbornness. She's an enigma. One I can't quite put my finger on. Part of me wants to point out how stupid it is to hide something like this from the only people she should rely on. The other part? I guess I get it. My family is great. They're nothing but supportive, but even the smallest fuck-ups feel larger than Everest whenever I think about my parents finding out. Yeah, Raine isn't the only one who holds herself to high standards. And the idea of letting the people I love most down when I don't reach said standards is a hard pill to swallow. Add in her family's connection to the guy, no matter how flimsy it is? It's gotta sting like a bitch. Besides, Aunt Mia and Uncle Henry have already been through enough. No need to poke around in their closet searching for skeletons.

"Okay," I finally cave. "No police. No parents. Promise."

She sniffs and gifts me a glimpse of those forest-green eyes from across the table. They're brighter than before. Or maybe it's the sheen of tears she's refusing to let fall highlighting the natural color. Or maybe it's my fault for finally looking—seeing—how bold and beautiful she really is.

"You're serious?" she whispers.

I nod.

The same tiny wobble hits her bottom lip, but she sucks it between her teeth, wincing when she's reminded it's still tender. "Thank you."

"Just…" I grab my fork from the table and cut off a giant square of cheese and noodles from my lasagna but stop short of shoving it in my mouth. "Don't make me regret it. What's your schedule for tomorrow?"

"Nothing, really. What's yours?"

"Practice in the morning."

"So, I'll…stay here, then?" she offers.

"I don't trust Drake enough to leave you alone."

A frown tugs at her pouty lips. "He doesn't know I'm here."

I want to laugh at her naivety but push the bite of food into my mouth while considering our options. Something about the phone call with Drake grates on me. His arrogance. His frustration. His determination. There's no way I can leave her by herself. The cabin has a security system, but even then, we're miles from civilization. The idea of leaving her up here by herself turns the lasagna in my mouth to ash.

She watches as I chew slowly then wipe the corner of my

mouth with a napkin. Placing it on my lap, I ask, "Do you want the girls to come here, or do you want to go to the duplex until I'm finished with practice?"

"I don't need a babysitter."

"Fine, I'll let the girls decide."

"Everett," she pleads.

Standing up, I grab my half-touched plate of lasagna and round the table toward her. "I won't cave on this."

"I'm not asking—"

"Yeah, it's exactly what you're doing." I tower over her, making sure she can feel my determination the same way I could feel Drake's through the fucking phone. "Drake isn't going anywhere. Not anytime soon. So, if we're leaving the police out of this like you want, you have to play by my rules. Do you understand?"

She cranes her head back a little further, giving me her full attention. "Yes, I understand."

"Good. The girls are coming here tomorrow, and you aren't going anywhere until I get back."

"Fine."

"Fine." I grab her dish, toss the uneaten lasagna into the garbage, and set the plates in the sink. Turning on the faucet, I mutter under my breath, "So she *can* listen," as I squirt some dish soap onto the plates, getting straight to work.

CHAPTER FIFTEEN

EVERETT

I dial Reeves' number, glancing over my shoulder to make sure I'm still alone. I debated for hours over whether I should make this call, but I can't shake it. This feeling. The pit of dread in my stomach. The knowledge of exactly how far south this situation can go if I don't play my cards right. The reminder of exactly who I'm dealing with and why I need to remember all of my interactions with Raine need to be nothing but professional if I want to walk away from this arrangement unscathed. If I want Raine to be able to walk away from this arrangement unscathed. Drake's connection to Aunt Mia's asshole ex doesn't make shit any easier, either. But I get why Raine doesn't want to tell people. I understand why she wants to sweep everything under the rug. And even though it's stupid, I agreed to help her do exactly that.

Hitching up my shoulders to protect my ears from the frigid wind, I rock back on my heels and wait for Reeves to answer.

"Hey, what's up?" he asks.

"Nothing."

A short pause follows, and I swear I can hear his confusion through the fucking speaker. "You good?"

"Uh, yeah." I clear my throat. "Just calling to see how long this shit usually takes."

"Trouble in paradise?" he quips.

My hand clutches my cell even harder. "Look, are you sure there isn't someone else who might be better at this?"

Another beat of silence hits, and I shift my phone to my opposite ear.

"What's the problem, man?" Reeves asks.

"I'm just saying," I scrub my hand over my face, "I'm not sure if I'm the right guy for this."

"Why?"

"Because he treated her like shit," I admit. "He's done things I would never even think about doing, and...and I dunno. I...I've been trying to keep my distance from Raine so I can keep things professional and shit, but..."

"But the situation isn't quite as black and white as you assumed?"

"Yeah. Yeah, I guess so." I sigh. "I'm used to taking care of everyone, you know? But Raine...the shit she's been through is...fuck." I look down at the ground and kick a stray pebble along the driveway. "She's different, and we're staying under the same roof, and this isn't real, and she's gotta be fucked up after everything, and...and I dunno, I don't...I'm not sure if this is a good idea."

"Have you heard from him?" Reeves questions.

"He called last night. Sent a video of Raine having sex with him. Raine wasn't even surprised. Said he filmed them without her permission in the past and threatened to send it to other people if she left." I pinch the bridge of my nose. "But since she doesn't want to call the cops, I feel like my hands are fucking tied, man. Like I'm drowning."

"If you feel like you're drowning, how do you think she feels?" he counters.

I lower my hand and sigh.

"You have three options. Hang her out to dry and be a dick. Lie low and wait for Drake to either make a move or grow bored enough to leave her alone. Or, we can try to lure him out. Throw a party, make sure he knows about it, then show you aren't going anywhere, and if he wants to keep bothering her, he'll have to go through you."

"The not going anywhere part is fucking with my head, Reeves," I remind him. "What if I mess this up? What if I'm not here when she needs me? What if, shit, I don't even know. A million scenarios keep playing through my head, and...and I'm fucking lost, man."

"Calm down, Everett. It's gonna be all right. I know your schedule's full, but Drake plays hockey, too. He's gonna be as busy as—"

"Not the fucking point." I shove my fingers through my hair and tug at the roots. "She needs...she needs help. She needs more than I can give."

"You're wrong, Ev," Reeves murmurs. "I've seen you with Fin and Dylan and Lia. How you're always looking out for them. Making sure they're safe."

"They're different," I argue.

"How?"

My mouth snaps shut, and I shake my head. I don't know. I don't know how they're different. I did, but the idea of someone filming Fin or Dylan or Lia. The idea of them being threatened by some asshole, let alone being on the other side of their fist? Rage licks through my veins. What if I lose control? What if I fucking kill him? Drake.

Reeves' gruff voice filters through the speakers and shuts my spiraling thoughts down.

"I wouldn't pass this off to you if I didn't think you could handle it. If I didn't know you had plenty to offer," he murmurs.

"I don't know about that."

"I do," Reeves answers. "Talk to Raine and see which route she wants to take. Maybe you aren't the only one feeling restless."

I nod even though he can't see me. "Sure thing."

"And, Ev?" he adds.

"Yeah?"

"It's all right to get attached. You won't hurt her."

Staring at the ground, I clear my throat again. "I'll let you know the game plan as soon as I can."

Then I push "end."

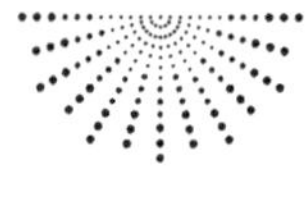

RAINE

With a groan, I roll toward the nightstand as my phone buzzes against the hard surface.

Buzz. Buzz.

I blink slowly, attempting to make my eyes work as I sit up straighter in my bed. I could ignore his call like I've done a hundred times in the past. Or, I could answer it.

Answer. It.

I slide my thumb across the screen, bring my cell to my ear, and croak, "Hello?"

"So she *is* alive."

My dad's grumbly voice wraps around me like a warm blanket, and I smile, shifting my phone to my other ear. "Hey, Dad."

"Hey, Rainbow."

"Hi," I repeat, though my voice is even more of a croak than anything else.

"Did I wake you?"

I clear my throat and try again. "Yeah, but I forgive you."

"Gee, thanks," he grunts. "How are you?"

"I'm good. You?"

"Could be better," he grunts. "Seems my youngest daughter is still avoiding me."

"I'm not—"

"Or she's shit at returning phone calls."

I lay back on my pillow and stare at the ceiling. "I believe I learned my hatred of phones from you."

"Yeah, yeah. So, how's the internship going?"

My nose wrinkles. "It's, uh, it's all right."

"Is it?" my dad pushes.

I frown, sensing the shift in his tone. "Uh, yeah? Why do you ask?"

"Because I just got an email from Lucian. Since when are you looking for a new mentor?"

Sitting up again, I press my back to the headboard and tug my knees to my chest. "Since, uh, recently?"

"I thought you liked Lucian," he grumbles. "Seems Lucian liked you."

"Yeah, he was a really good mentor."

"Yeah, I know he is. It's the only reason I didn't try to convince you to come to Etch 'N' Ink when you first showed interest in tattooing."

My shoulders fall, and I pinch the bridge of my nose. "Dad…"

"What's going on, Raine?"

"My apartment flooded, so I decided to find a new place, and the drive was too much—"

"You moved?" he growls.

"I, uh, yeah. It was a spur of the moment decision, but I didn't want to drive from Lockwood Heights to Cedar Springs everyday, so—"

"Bo," my dad prods. "What's this really about?"

Oh, what a loaded question. I pinch the bridge of my

nose, trying to come up with an answer not involving my abusive ex while also telling the truth or at least part of it.

"Dad…" My word hangs in the air, and I swallow thickly.

"Why didn't you call me?" he murmurs.

"I was too ashamed to tell you what happened," I admit. "And even now, I don't really want to…you know. I mean, who, uh, who lets their apartment flood, right?"

"I'm gonna take you on. Mentor you."

"Dad."

"I'm serious, Bo," he pushes. "It'll be good for me to step back from the gallery for a little while, anyway. I could use a break."

My mouth lifts. "Liar."

"I would never," he argues, but I can hear the amusement in his voice, and it eases the ache in my chest.

My dad's an artist. A big, burly, fully-tatted artist who started out in the tattoo industry until a few of his pieces were displayed in a gallery or two, then, just like that, he became a world-renowned creative whose paintings go for more money than most make in a lifetime, let alone a year. He hasn't worked in the tattoo shop he owns for over two decades, other than a quick pop-in here and there for his favorite clients. The idea of him stepping back from the gallery he opened with my mom a few years ago to mentor me is…a lot.

Thoughtful, sure. Intimidating, definitely. Unfair to every other starving artist out there? Yeah. One hundred percent.

"Dad," I sigh. "I can figure this out on my own, remember?"

"That's the beauty of family, though. Because of us, you don't have to," he reminds me. "Meet me at the shop at four, all right?"

"Daaaad."

"I'm serious."

"So am I," I push. "I don't want any handouts. If I'm going to make it in this business, I need to make it because of my talent, not because of who my dad is."

"I hear you, Bo," he rasps.

"Do you, though?"

"You want to make it on your own, and you will," he adds gently, "but there are a lot of shit artists out there, and if you're back in Lockwood Heights, it makes sense to come to Etch 'N' Ink. Come on. Do your dad a favor and stop being stubborn. Just this once, yeah?"

Nibbling on the edge of my thumb, I consider my options while hating how few there are at the moment. I'm a nobody. A big. Fat. Nobody. Even with Lucian's offer to help find me a new mentor, I'm stuck in the mountains for the foreseeable future, and asking Everett to drive me anywhere more than the bare minimum feels about as pleasant as having my toenails ripped out.

"Promise me you won't treat me any different than you would a regular apprentice."

His hesitation is louder than a blowhorn, and I pull my cell away from my ear, confirming he's still on the line. Yup. The call is still connected, which means I'm not the only one dealing with a curveball from this conversation.

Good.

Because if I'm honestly caving right now, then I need to know it isn't for nothing. And I need to know my super duper amazing—and super duper overprotective—family doesn't get caught in the crosshairs of my screwup.

"I'll see you at Etch 'N' Ink at four," my dad grunts. "And give me access to your location again so I can see where you are every once in a while. Don't think I didn't notice when you stopped sharing with me. And it's not because I'm stalking you, but because I care about you."

"Mm-hmm," I hum, though I know he sees right through it.

"That's my girl. I'll see you then."

"See you, Dad," I murmur when something catches my attention from the corner of my eye.

Resting his shoulder against the doorjamb, a shirtless Everett balances a plate in his hand.

I hang up the call and drop my phone onto my lap as I watch him carefully.

"How long were you eavesdropping?" I ask.

"Not too long." Pushing himself away from the door, he strides closer and offers me an omelet. It smells amazing. Bacon, sausage, red peppers, purple onion. A sprig of, honestly, I don't even know what herb it is, lies on top of the melted cheddar cheese, and my mouth waters.

"Did you make this?" I ask.

He nods. "Didn't know if you preferred sausage or bacon, but, uh…eat up. It's the most important meal of the day."

"Thanks." I take the plate, set it in my lap, and cut off a small bite with the fork he handed me, only to find a…I scoot the dark gray chunk from the omlet. Yup. It's a mushroom. I hate mushrooms.

"There a problem?" Everett asks.

"Nope." I push the stupid thing aside and cut off another bite, careful not to grab any mushroom with it before shoving it into my mouth. When my eyes nearly roll back into my head from the flavor explosion on my tastebuds, he asks, "You don't like mushrooms?"

"This is great," I point to my plate with the fork and go in for another bite while steering clear of the fungus bomb at the edge, praying he didn't dice any stray pieces into the fluffy egg mixture.

As he watches me chew, Everett tilts his head. "You don't

like mushrooms." It isn't a question this time, and I kind of hate how easily he reads me.

I stop mid-chew and hold his gaze, trying not to squirm.

"You can tell me you don't like mushrooms," he adds.

Swallowing the most delicious omelet I've ever tasted—sans mushrooms—I argue, "Seriously, they're great."

His fingers brush against mine as he steals the fork from my grasp and stabs the mushroom, bringing it to my lips. "Prove it."

My nose wrinkles, and he takes the bite for himself, chewing slowly as he holds my gaze, his own shining with curiosity. Once he swallows, he says, "You're allowed to have opinions."

"I know," I murmur.

"And you're allowed to tell me your opinions," he adds, though it's softer this time. I swear the low rasp of his voice is directly connected to the stupid organ in my chest as it picks up its pace.

"Here," he reaches for my plate, but I tug it back.

"I like it."

"I'll make you another one," he argues. "Without mushrooms."

"Seriously, Ev, I want this one."

"Stop trying to bullshit me."

"I'm not bullshitting you." I keep a firm grip on the plate, refusing to let him take it. "Seriously, I'm not."

He stops fighting me but doesn't let go of the dish, so I add, "I actually really like the flavor of mushrooms, but the texture messes with my head, and if I'm being completely honest, this is the best omelet I've ever tasted despite the fungus balls, so will you please let me finish it?"

His eyes fall to my mouth, but he lets go of the plate, and I take another bite of eggs, careful not to get any mushrooms with it.

"Do you need a ride somewhere?" he prods.

I cover my mouth so he can't see me chewing and answer, "Uh, yeah. Have you ever been to Etch 'N' Ink?"

He shakes his head.

After swallowing, I explain, "It's close to SeaBird. I need to be there at four."

"I'll be home in time to take you after practice and will hang out at the house until you're finished. Does that work?"

"I might be late," I argue.

"I can wait. Might wanna figure out what to do with your lip, though." His eyes trail over me one more time. "Girls are on their way."

"That isn't necessary."

"Don't go anywhere," he warns, pinching another mushroom between his fingers, popping it into his mouth, and sucking the edge of his thumb. His strong jaw flexes with every chew, and it's weirdly…hot. Watching him clean up my mess and eat the scraps off my plate. "I'll be home in a few hours." Then, he walks away.

And as I watch him leave, my brows pull.

How can someone be so mercurial? So helpful but combative at the same time. It's…dizzying. He's right about the lip, though. I touch the still-tender cut and frown. My dad's gonna kill me. But at least I'll die with a belly full of deliciousness. Seriously. I cut another bite off and pick it up, studying the cheese's string pull, perfectly tender vegetables, and bits of crumbled bacon folded into the fluffy egg.

Yeah, this man is…something else for sure.

"You have no idea how much I need this," Finley announces as soon as I unlock the front door.

I won't lie. I've been dreading this. Hanging out with girls

I barely know all because Everett's too stubborn to leave me alone. It's…annoying. Thoughtful but annoying. Then again, I can't decide if lining up a babysitter for me is the annoying part or if it's the fact he thinks I need one in the first place.

Drake doesn't know where I am. He has zero idea. And even if he did, the only thing he's more obsessed with than me is hockey. Since he has hockey practice every morning, there's no way he'd jeopardize his place on the bench by missing it to track me down. It also doesn't help that I've only had one interaction with these girls, and even though they were nothing but friendly, I'm still wary. They don't know me, and I sure as hell don't know them, so why are we being forced to hang out together under the guise of a weekend morning hang out when we all know they're only here to babysit me and hopefully keep Drake at bay.

Yeah, because these girls could stop him if he showed up on the doorstep. Then again, I guess there's safety in numbers? Honestly, at this point, I don't even know.

As Finley walks into the cabin like she owns the place—then again, I guess she does—Ophelia and Dylan trail behind, giving me smiles when they pass. Once everyone's inside, I lock the front door, take a deep breath, and follow them into the kitchen. They each have sacks hanging from their arms, and I tilt my head as they set them on the counter, rummage through the contents, and place things in the fridge.

"What are you guys doing?" I ask.

"We've decided we're vegging today," Ophelia informs me.

"Oh! I brought you something," Dylan adds.

She pulls a black and yellow gun from one of the sacks and tries to hand it to me, but I only stare at it. "I'm sorry?"

"It's a taser," she explains. "Reeves got one for each of us a little while ago. Thanks to his previous line of work—"

"And Everett's current one," Finley chimes in.

Dylan bats her friend away and offers me the taser again.

"Reeves figured it would help him sleep at night if he knew all of us were carrying one since there are a lot of creepers out there."

"Go figure you'd need it most," Finley quips. "And in case you're wondering, Dylan can confirm it definitely works."

Dylan rolls her eyes. "I shot Reeves *one* time."

"Yeah, and it was hilarious," Finley replies.

Jutting her bottom lip out, Dylan folds her arms. "You said you wouldn't make fun of me for it anymore, remember?"

Finley's grin widens. "To be fair, you're the one who brought it up."

"You know what?" Dylan huffs. "One of these days, I really am gonna get a frog so I can threaten you with it."

And just like that, the blood drains from Finley's face. "Don't. Even. Think about it."

Confused by the chilly shift in the air, I ask, "I'm sorry, what did I miss?"

"Finley's terrified of frogs," Ophelia informs me as she starts digging through the cabinets for...something.

"I'm sorry, but who isn't terrified of frogs?" Finley argues. "They're slimy and squishy and unpredictable and—"

"And the bane of Finley's existence." Dylan's Cheshire grin is contagious, but I bite mine back and dig my teeth into the insides of my cheeks as she turns to me and adds, "They're also the only leverage actually keeping Finley in check."

"Har, har," Finley grumbles under her breath. "At least my fear has merit. You and your aversion to anything pink and glittery is absolutely ridiculous."

"I won't crap my pants if I see something glittery," Dylan argues. "Unlike you and your—"

"Okay, enough fighting," Ophelia interrupts. She opens the freezer and rummages through the shelves. "Fin, do you think your parents stashed any of Grandma's famous cookie dough in here before they left?"

Finley scoffs. "You really think there's ever any leftovers of that gold?"

"But I'm craving it," Ophelia pouts.

"Can't you call and ask for the recipe?" I chime in before I'm pinned with three pairs of eyes. Squirming from their scrutiny, I tug at my long sleeves and fold my arms. "What? Is that not an option?"

With a disgruntled push, Ophelia closes the freezer door. "Sometimes I forget most people look at recipes like they shouldn't be held under lock and key."

"Yeah, and then there's our family," Finley quips. She pulls out a bag of Cheetos and sets it beside a bottle of Diet Coke. "Don't worry, though. I've helped my mom and grandma make those cookies a thousand times. I'm pretty sure I can remember the ratios."

Pointing her finger at Finley, Dylan says, "You better because after your fight with Drew last night, you deserve the chocolate fix more than anyone."

Finley folds her arms. "Who said I had a fight with Drew?"

"Come on. It doesn't take a genius to overhear you screaming in your room," argues Ophelia.

"I wasn't screaming," Finley defends. "I was…scolding. Loudly."

"Because that's what a boyfriend needs. A loud scolding from his girlfriend." Ophelia snorts. "Take it or leave it, but in my opinion, the only time a guy should make you scream is when you're riding his—"

"Lia!" Dylan squeals.

"Yeah, I feel like that's something I would say, not you." Finley tilts her head and rocks back on her heels, tapping her finger against her chin as she studies Ophelia. "I don't know if I should be offended or impressed. What do you think, Raine?"

"I think Ophelia's onto something," I admit.

"Yeah, Maverick's dick," Finley quips.

"Oh, shut up." Ophelia smacks her friend's shoulder, folds her arms, and turns to me. "You were saying, Raine?"

"I was saying that even though I think you make a good point, I'm not sure I'm the best person to give relationship advice, so…"

Finley laughs. "Good point. Speaking of which, how was your first night with my brother, anyway?"

"Fine." I shrug. "We made lasagna, then went to bed."

"Lasagna, huh?" Dylan smirks at her friends, sits at the granite island, and rests her chin in her hands. "Interesting."

"And why is it interesting?"

"Because lasagna's the big guns," Finley points out. "Did he let you help?"

I hesitate. "Why do I feel like this is a trick question?"

"Come on. Answer it," Dylan pushes.

My lips purse, but I give in anyway. "Yes?"

"Damn," Dylan sits back in her chair and folds her arms. "I'm impressed."

"Why?"

"Because my brother's hella controlling. If he let you help, it's because he wanted to be around you. Wanted to give you a glimpse of his world instead of keeping you at arm's length like he does with…basically everyone."

"I think you're reading too much into things," I decide.

"And I think you aren't reading into them enough. But don't worry. We're the queens of over-dissecting situations, so…maybe keep it in mind," Ophelia teases. "But first, I wanted to ask if you're okay with Maverick crashing our party since all the guys are at practice."

She isn't looking at Dylan or Finley. She's only looking at me. And I hate that I think I know why. "Why would I care?"

"Because you were kind of weird around him the last time you two were in the same room," Finley chimes in.

Pressing my lips together, I stay quiet. I could tell them the truth. I could also deflect. But for some reason, I like these girls. I like their banter. Their chaos. Their inside jokes and innocent teasing. It's a little pathetic to admit I don't have many friends who are girls. And the few I collected over the years all kind of fell off the face of the earth after I started dating Drake. Or maybe it was me who fell off the face of the earth. Regardless, it's nice. Nice joking about riding guys' dicks and tasing boyfriends by accident. It's nice opening up and chatting about…anything, really.

Finley pops the bag of Cheetos open and offers it to me. "You can fight it all you want, Rainey, but we *will* be friends one day."

"And friends talk," Dylan adds.

"Which means you should, too." Finley nudges the bag toward me again. "Come on. Give us a chance."

Reaching into the bag, I take a Cheeto and toss it into my mouth as Finley grins back at me like she just solved a cold case.

"Fine," I concede. "My family doesn't know I was dating Drake." I hesitate. "Okay, they knew I was dating someone, but they didn't know how serious we were or that we were living together or that he left me on the side of the road in the middle of the night—"

Finley scoffs. "Yeah, he's a real gentleman, that one."

"Exactly," I muse. "It's why I was acting weird around Mav. I didn't…I *don't* want him to tell them about… everything."

Ophelia reaches across the island and puts her hand on mine. "I think if Maverick's learned anything over the past year, it's the understanding that sometimes people keep things close to their chest for a reason, and it isn't fair to pry until they're ready." She leans closer. "But he's also learned how much easier it is to carry a burden with help than by yourself."

"Subtle," Finley notes dryly.

Ophelia ignores her. "I'm just saying…"

"Yeah, I know," I murmur.

"But for now, what do you say? Do you mind if he comes if he promises not to pry?"

"This isn't my house."

"Yeah, but it's your safe space," she argues. "At least for a little while, so you definitely have a say in who is and isn't allowed to walk through those doors."

A safe space.

I'd laugh if it wasn't so pathetic.

Since when is a stranger's house more safe than your own apartment? Oh, I know. When you're dealing with an asshole like Drake.

What's worse is knowing I made this bed all on my own. I'm the one who isolated myself. Like a frog in water, like I described to Everett, I took something for granted and replaced it with toxicity, and now I'm the one who boiled to death.

Okay, what a gross metaphor.

Doesn't mean it isn't fitting, though.

Still, I do believe Ophelia. And if she thinks Maverick won't say anything to his parents, I do, too.

With a deep breath, I announce, "Maverick's welcome whenever he wants." I hesitate. "But maybe don't invite his parents?"

The girls laugh, each sharing a knowing look as Dylan grabs some glasses from the cabinet and Ophelia reaches for the Diet Coke. "Don't worry, Raine. We love our parents and know they'd do anything for us, but we also know what it's like to make decisions they might not understand."

"And I know you might not know us very well," Dylan adds, "But we're good at keeping secrets."

"And we're good at having each others' backs, too," Ophelia murmurs.

"Thanks," I whisper.

"And now..." Finley pops a Cheeto into her mouth. "We veg."

IT'S A SOLID HOUR LATER WHEN THE FAMILIAR KNOCK OF knuckles against wood echoes through the house. With a grin, Ophelia jumps to her feet and practically skips toward the door, returning with Maverick a minute later.

I wasn't kidding when I said our families aren't very close. Or at least not compared to my dad and his roommates from college. But still. His mom is my dad's best friend's niece. It might be a smaller branch of the family tree, but it connects us nonetheless.

Please don't say anything.

My stomach knots as I peek over at him, offering a pathetic wave.

He lifts his chin in greeting, then plops down on the couch as Ophelia sits right next to him. Slipping off his shoes, he sets his feet on the coffee table and makes himself comfortable as *Game of Thrones* plays on the television. It was Dylan's choice. Apparently, Reeves has been begging her to watch the series for a while now, and they're already in season three. After giving me a quick recap that included a whiteboard and a very twisted family tree, we pushed play, stocked up on snacks, and got comfy on the couch. It's been nice.

Relaxing.

I haven't had a day like this in…I don't even know how long.

But what I like even more is Maverick's lack of interrogation. I've always known my cousin was a good guy, but he proved it all over again, and I kind of want to hug him for it.

"I'm gonna make some popcorn," he announces a little while later. "Do any of you want some?"

"I'll help you," I offer. Standing up, I wipe my sweaty palms against my leggings and follow him to the kitchen. It feels awkward and forced, but I don't see this conversation not having both feelings no matter how long I put this off, so I pull my big girl panties up and rip the whole thing off like a Band-Aid.

When I reach the kitchen, I tuck my hands into my elbows, and my lips scrunch on one side. I'm unsure what to do or say now that I'm actually standing here.

With a smirk, he glances at me. "Is this you helping?"

I clear my throat, grab a bowl from one of the cabinets, and hand it to him.

"Thanks." Plastic crinkles as he rips the popcorn open and sets the trifold bag into the microwave, slapping it closed and pressing the popcorn button. Turning back to me, he murmurs, "A little birdie told me I'm not allowed to pry."

"Yeah, well, the little birdie is very kind to stand up for me."

He smiles. "She's a goose. And geese can be pretty, uh," he scratches the scruff of his jaw, "overbearing sometimes."

My mouth lifts. "I can imagine. Speaking of overbearing…you've met my family, Mav. You really don't think my dad or brother would kill Drake if they found out about what he's been doing to me?"

His brows pull. "They love you."

"I know they do," I rush out. "And I know they'd do

anything for me, and I mean anything." I tug at the edge of my sleeves and squeeze them in my fists as I stare at the granite countertop. "But you know my dad, let alone Dodge."

He chuckles softly. "Yeah, your older brother's something else."

"He's insane, Mav."

"He's a rockstar, Bo," Mav counters. "Being a little unhinged comes with the job title, don't you think?"

"He thinks he's untouchable," I argue. "And he's impulsive, and—"

"And you think he'd do something stupid under the guise of protecting you."

I nod slowly. "Yeah. Yeah, I do. And when you factor in my dad and mom and Penelope, let alone Dodger's PR team, it…it would be a disaster."

He leans against the counter as if his strength is depleted, pinching the bridge of his nose. "I get it."

I pull back, surprised. "You do?"

"Yeah. I'm not saying you're right to keep them in the dark, but I get why you want to." He pulls me into his chest and rubs his hand along my spine. "Fuck, Bo."

I squeeze my eyes shut and lean into him.

"Your secret's safe with me. Besides, between my surgery and Archer's…" He gulps. "I think it's enough shit on our families' plates. If it gets worse, we have to tell them, though."

I nod. "Yeah. Yeah, I agree."

"Good. For now, we do whatever Reeves tells us to. Your safety is our first priority. Then it's everyone else's feelings and your brother's protection."

"Okay."

The beep of the microwave makes him sigh. "Grab the bowl."

"Okay," I repeat, handing the bowl to Maverick. He

empties the bag of popcorn into the glass, making me feel as light as the little puffed-up kernels covered in butter and salt.

He isn't going to say anything.

My family never has to know. And honestly, it's nice knowing I now have one less ax hanging over my head. One less thing to worry about.

Maybe I'll be able to get rid of a few more after all.

CHAPTER SEVENTEEN

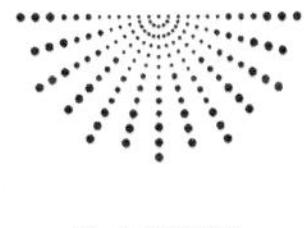

RAINE

Etch 'N' Ink is my home away from home. Maybe it shouldn't be, but it is. My mom started handling the books for the shop, and my dad took over the business after my older sister, Penelope, was born. My siblings and I spent more weekends hanging out in the breakroom and making friends with all the artists than we did at home watching Saturday morning cartoons.

It's probably one of the reasons why I fell in love with art in the first place. The scent of laundry detergent with an underlying wisp of weed is probably a weird smell to most people, but I love it. The laid back yet hardworking employees, the rock music, the Milo Anders original paintings hanging on the walls. It's home. And it's what was missing the entire time I worked under Lucian despite his friendliness. Class and grunge and sophistication and comfort. Honestly, I still don't know how my parents pulled off the balance, but they have.

I'm surprised how much I've missed it. For the last six months, I've been so enveloped in all things Drake I didn't realize how much I was pulling away from my life before Drake. Before I moved to Cedar Springs. Before he would scoff anytime my family would call or point out how he didn't have a family anymore, and without me, he'd be all alone, so I should be, too. Before his tantrums after a loss or his gropings when he'd have too much to drink. Yeah, I screwed up. Big time. Add it to the list, I guess. And I hate how it makes me feel guilty. Like I don't belong because it's been so long since I've been here. Since I've seen these people. My own dad included.

"Bo!" one of the artists calls from the back of the room. More people join in, moving toward me and pulling me into their own hugs until I'm the center of a Raine sandwich next to the front door.

"It's been forever, girl," Max says as he lets me go. A frown takes up his features as he stares at my lip. Shit. I did everything I could to cover the damage. I even asked the girls if they had any tips and tricks to help it look less...terrible. Finley called her half-sister who does makeup for a living, but there's only so much help she could offer over the phone and with what little supplies I had available on such short notice. Even then, I thought we did a pretty good job, but apparently, lots of ice, concealer, and Vaseline only got me so far. I hate it. The confusion in his eyes. The concern. The fucking horror.

When he opens his mouth to ask me about it, my dad appears from the breakroom and strides toward me with his arms wide open.

"There's my Rainbow—"

He stops short, and his brows tug at the center. Yup. He sees it, too. And instead of being confused, he's already jumped to his conclusion. I can see it by the way his eyes darken and his upper lip curls. I steel my shoulders, bracing for it.

"Max," my dad barks, though he doesn't take his eyes off me. "Get back to your station."

Max lifts his hands in defense but backs away, leaving me alone with my dad in the front of the shop.

Well, this isn't awkward at all.

Pretending to be oblivious, I say, "Hey, Dad."

"Was it Lucian?"

"What?" I shake my head and touch my bottom lip with my hand. "No, not even a little bit."

Reaching for me, my dad hugs me, then lets me go and lifts my chin, studying the damage in a way that's eerily similar to Everett's response. Well, other than the possibly wanting to kiss me part. Not that Everett wanted to kiss me or even thought about it, for that matter, but—

"Gonna tell me what happened?" my dad demands.

"Bar fight in Cedar Springs," I lie. It was the best one I could come up with since our phone call earlier. "Took an elbow to the mouth in all the commotion, but I'm fine." I grab his wrist and force him to lower his arm. "Promise."

His gaze narrows. "You sure?"

"Pretty positive, actually. It should go down in a few days, but if we could not make me feel like an alien with a bad lip injection until it goes away, that'd be great."

His mouth twitches, and he clears his throat. "Did you bring your notebook?"

I slip the weathered book from underneath my arm and offer it to him while trying to hide my surprise over the fact he actually dropped his interrogation for once. The guy's been overprotective since day one. The fact he bought my lie is a freaking miracle, but I'm not about to question it.

When he takes my notebook, he smiles. "That's my girl. Come on. We have a full afternoon."

"Already?" I ask.

"You doubt your old man's abilities to book a few

clients?" He tosses his arm around my shoulders and guides me to his cubicle without any further explanation. Then again, I guess he doesn't need one.

Sometimes, it blows my mind. How he can basically work whenever he wants, and with a simple post on his social media, he has clients champing at the bit to book an appointment with him. I should know better, though. The guy's talented, and his reputation is insane. It's…inspiring and hella intimidating, too. Honestly, it's one of the reasons why I was scared to work with him. Terrified of disappointing him. Of disappointing his coworkers or fans. Terrified of one of them pointing out how I'll never live up to my father's legacy when I'm already well-aware of it. The shadow he casts. The shoes I know I'll never fill.

But I guess it's life.

"Come on," he prods, leading me to his small desk tucked beside the vinyl adjustable chair he uses for clients. "Let's see what you've learned so far."

CHAPTER EIGHTEEN

EVERETT

She's late. It's the first time she's been late since she started last week. Things have been…quiet. Between school, hockey, and Raine working, we've barely even crossed paths other than our daily car rides and a few dinners here and there. Half the time, she scurries to her room as soon as her dishes are clean, but I haven't pushed her on it. Honestly, part of me is grateful. Call me a bastard, but I have a feeling if she opened up to me, I'd let her in, and with all her baggage, it's the last thing I need.

Yeah, I really am a bastard.

I stare at the entrance to Etch 'N' Ink when I cut off my car's ignition. The open sign above the door is dimmed, but lights are still on inside. I can see through the glass door. She's sweeping, mouthing the lyrics to whatever song is playing. Or maybe she's talking to herself. I don't know her well enough to say which possibility is more likely. She looks pretty, though. Dark hair braided over one shoulder. Messy. Chaotic. Like the storm she is. The black crop top and low-slung jeans showcase her lean stomach as she bends at the waist, sweeping under one of the black cabinets near the waiting area. Pretty sure my hand could reach from one hipbone to the next, covering her entirely. The thought hits out of nowhere, and I look down at my phone, making a mental note to get some food as soon as possible. Must be low blood sugar or something.

Yeah. That's what it is.

I had a game tonight. We lost. It sucked. Now, all I want to do is head home and lick my wounds in private. Easier said than done since I'm parked out front, waiting for Raine to finish her shift. Normally, I wouldn't mind waiting, but after tonight, I only want some good food, a hot shower, and my bed. As I continue watching through the glass, Raine nods at someone, rests the broom against the back wall, and disappears through a hall toward the back of the building.

When I catch myself staring at her swaying hips, I climb out of my car. I head inside, anxious to get home. A bell dings as I push the front door open, noting it's past closing time as I shove my keys into my front pocket. It's nice. Nicer than the other shop where she worked, though I didn't mind that one. This place has less graffiti, though. Smells better, too. Like it's cleaner, maybe. The walls are dark gray, with pictures scattered throughout. Some are black and white. Others have bold, vibrant colors. The images are so clear, most could pass for photographs.

Tilting my head, I study a particular piece. It's a dandelion. Some parts are still yellow. White seeds are speckled throughout. And fuck me. I swear I can feel the wind through the image as I stare at one of the smaller seeds. It looks like it could let go and be carried away at any second. Actually, it's…pretty sick.

"Hey," a gruff voice calls.

I tear my attention from the artwork. A guy with wavy hair stands next to the front desk. Streaks of white weave through the blonde strands pulled into a messy bun on top of his head, leaving his weathered face on full display. I can't tell if he looks happy or mad to see me here. With a Broken Vows T-shirt stretched across his body, he folds his arms, showcasing how built the guy really is. He might be older, but it's clear he hasn't let himself go.

"Welcome to Etch 'N' Ink," the stranger adds. "We're actually closing up, but you can make an appointment online, or if you'd prefer, I can help you schedule a time to come back another day."

"I'm okay, thanks."

He frowns.

"I'm here to give Raine a ride," I explain.

"A ride?" The stranger cocks his head. "You know my daughter?"

My eyes widen. "Raine's your daughter?"

"Yeah." Whatever warmth was in his eyes vanishes. It's replaced with cold calculation as he sizes me up. "Yeah, Raine's my daughter. Who are you?"

"I'm, uh…" I tug at the collar of my T-shirt.

"Are you her boyfriend?" he demands.

Well, shit. I don't know what she's told him. I don't know anything, actually, and lying to a guy like this feels like the wrong choice, but putting Raine in a bad spot doesn't feel great, either. She doesn't want her dad to know about Drake, and now that I've officially laid eyes on the bastard, I can't blame her for wanting to keep him in the dark. He doesn't exactly look like someone you'd want to mess with, and he *definitely* looks like someone who holds a grudge.

No, thank you.

Forcing a smile, I tear my attention from him and look at the empty hallway Raine disappeared through before I fucked up by walking in here. "Is she, uh, is she here?"

The guy's chuckle is low as he steps even closer. I could back down. I probably should back down. Instead, I stand my ground. He's taller than I guessed. Built like a tank. He might have a good twenty-five years on me—maybe more—but it's clear he's spent them in the weight room, probably in the boxing ring, too, with the way he carries himself.

"You there for the bar fight last week?" he demands.

Confused, my brows wrinkle, and Raine's dad laughs. He moves even closer and glares down at me like I'm nothing but the scum of the earth.

"Nah, I didn't think there was one, either." His upper lip curls. "What's your name?"

Where the hell is Raine?

Again, I glance toward where she disappeared. This would be a hell of a lot easier if I knew what I am and am *not* allowed to say to this guy.

"I'm sorry, but I think you're confused—"

"Name," he growls.

"Everett Taylor." My focus snaps from the hallway to the pissed-off father in front of me. "Nice to meet you. And you are?"

"I'm the last face you'll ever see if you fuckin' touch my daughter again. This isn't a warning. It's a promise. Now, get the fuck out of here." He shoves me, but I barely move. Not because the guy can't hold his own, but because I was waiting for it. Expecting it. Doesn't take a genius to figure out he's pegged me for Drake's outburst, and even though I'm itching to set the record straight, Raine asked me not to, and for some reason I can't explain, I don't want to let her down or betray what little trust she's given me since we first met.

Carefully, coolly, I clear my throat and reply, "I didn't touch your daughter, and I'm not going—"

He grabs my shirt, twists the fabric in his hands, and brings us nose-to-nose. It takes everything inside of me to keep my cool. To not fight back. To let him treat me like a rag doll when I'm already too close to the edge, thanks to tonight's loss and, well, his assumption I'd touch a single hair on his daughter's head. On *anyone's* head.

"You ever heard assuming shit makes an ass out of you and me?" I grit out, attempting to de-escalate the situation without airing Raine's dirty laundry.

His grip tightens on my shirt. "Nah, I think I'll take my chances."

"You have no idea what you're talking about," I warn him.

I should've waited in the car. Should've stayed as far away from here as possible. But I didn't know he was still here. She said she wanted to keep her parents in the dark, and here I am, talking to her dad, er, being talked *at* by her dad. The semantics don't really matter because Raine's gonna be pissed.

"Dad?"

Aaaand, there she is.

Raine's dad turns toward his daughter, lets my shirt go, and steps away from me. "Glad to finally meet your boyfriend."

My attention slides to Raine, and I wait to see what she says. How she handles this. Does he think I'm Drake? I hope not since I introduced myself as Everett. *Whoops.*

Her words from our argument the first night at the cabin come screaming to the front of my mind. Right. Drake never met Raine's family. If that isn't a red flag, I don't know what is.

What the hell am I supposed to do? What does she *want* me to do? She just saw her dad pushing me against the wall with my shirt fisted in his hand. She has to say something or defend me.

Doesn't she?

With a fake-ass smile, Raine moves closer to us, but even I can see the rigidity in her muscles. The way she looks like she's been blindsided—join the club, Raine—and left uneasy, trying to come up with a lie that doesn't create an even more tangled web than the one she's already made for herself. "Uh…"

"I'm sure your mom would love an introduction," the behemoth adds. "And Penny. And Dodge when he gets back from his tour. You should bring this guy to dinner next week."

"Everett's going out of town for an away game," she rushes out.

"Away game?"

She tucks some loose strands from her braid behind her ear, her gaze darting everywhere around the room. "H-he plays hockey, actually. He's really good, too."

"Yeah, I'm sure he is. Shame he'll be gone next week." Her dad doesn't even bother hiding his sarcasm. "Dodge will be home at the end of the month. You can bring your boy to his concert at SeaBird."

Raine opens her mouth to argue but closes it quickly, forcing herself to nod. "Uh, yeah. We'll have to look at our schedules, but that sounds…like a lot of fun."

"Good," he grunts. "Can't wait to hear all about the bar fight from last week, too."

Raine blanches, and I wait for her to defend me. Instead, all she chokes out is, "Sounds great."

Seriously? We're gonna ignore the part where he thinks I hit his daughter? Ignore how she walked in on him threatening my own fucking life and completely sweeping his not-so-subtle remark about her swollen lip under the rug like he wasn't insinuating I was the culprit behind it?

What. The actual. Fuck?

I turn my stare on Raine beside me and wait. For what? Honestly, at this point, I'm not even sure. I feel like I entered the Twilight Zone, and now, I'm just along for the bumpy-as-shit ride.

Raine must sense it, too. The tension. The assumptions. The haze of miscommunication twisting around us. Because she looks like she's about to puke.

"Raine," I prod.

Rocking back on her heels, she murmurs, "You're totally right. We, uh, we should probably get going, so…"

"*We?*" her dad challenges.

"Uh, yup. It's late, and…my boyfriend here is probably tired from his game, so…" She loops her arm through mine and rests her head on my shoulder. "It's, uh, it's best if we head out. Thanks for today, though."

"*We*," he repeats, as accusatory as before.

"Yup," Raine says, though this time she tacks on a smile as if it'll erase the fact she's about to walk out of this door with an *assumed* abusive boyfriend.

Seriously, at this point, I'm convinced the girl is *trying* to get my ass kicked by her old man. Still, I keep my head held high and tuck my hands into the front pockets of my jeans, attempting to look like I *don't* beat women on the weekends despite knowing it's exactly what Raine's dad has pegged me for.

"Well, don't let me keep you, I guess," he growls.

My brows hitch, but I stay quiet.

With another frigid look at me, he grunts, "Drive safe. Understand?"

Touch her again, and I'll hunt you down, is what he's really saying. Not with his mouth, but rather with his eyes. Honestly, I'm surprised I'm still standing at this point. This guy wants to rip me limb from limb, and if the roles were reversed, I would, too, so all I can do is dip my chin in response.

Yeah, old man. I hear you loud and clear.

"Night, Dad." An oblivious Raine lets me go to give him a quick side hug. Then, she rushes toward the back corner of the large room. Thanks to the half walls spread throughout, it's broken into small spaces. She reappears with her purse and a notebook tucked beneath her arm. Without looking up at me, she slips past and out the door like a bat out of hell, leaving me no choice but to follow.

What. The actual. Fuck?

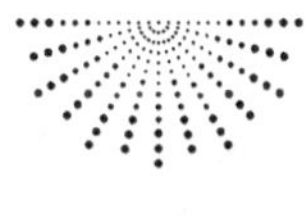

RAINE

The drive home is relatively quiet other than the music playing through the speakers. It's awkward and forced and I keep waiting for Everett to bite my head off for his run-in with my dad, but he hasn't said a word since we left Etch 'N' Ink.

I don't know what to say, though. I don't know how to fix this or how to apologize. I glance at Everett again, but his expression is locked tight. I can't get a read on it. Can't get a read on him.

If I was in the car with Drake, he would've already bitten my head off. And if not, I would've at least known what to anticipate from his silence. It was always so heavy. Tense. Charged. Like it was meant to make me uncomfortable. With Everett? I'm not sure what it means, and the unknown is... triggering.

What are you thinking, Everett Taylor?

When we pull up to the cabin, he enters the garage and turns off the car but doesn't reach for the door handle, so I don't either. A not-so-small part of me wants to escape to the safety of my room, where I can drown in my own silence without second-guessing its meaning or waiting for the other shoe to drop. Instead I only...sit here. I wish I could read his mind. I wish I knew what he's thinking or feeling or wanting from me.

"Thanks, uh, thanks again for the ride," I offer.

His nod is mechanical at best.

I pick at my nails, unsure what to say or do. Why hasn't he exploded yet?

Peeking over at him again, I realize I don't know the outcome of tonight's game. And, if I was still dating Drake, well, that would be a really, really big problem.

My stomach swells with unease, but I force my vocal cords to do their freaking job and ask, "So...how was the game?"

"We lost." Everett shrugs. "It sucked."

"Oh." I nod. Desperate to fill the silence, I add, "Do you want me to cook dinner or anything? Or...leave you alone for the rest of the night? Or...I don't know? Anything?"

He continues staring in front of him. "I'm good."

His hand still rests on the steering wheel. I wait for him to open the door and climb out of the car or to pull it into a fist or...I don't even know. "Okay, then?" My mouth feels like it's full of cotton balls. "I mean...I guess I just...don't really know what you want me to do right now."

His brows crease, and for the first time since we left Etch 'N' Ink, he looks at me. "What?"

"I mean, if you were Drake after a hard game, you'd be pissed, and you're acting...kind of pissed?" I hesitate and tilt my head, as if the new angle will give me a better assessment of the man behind the steering wheel. "But you said you're not hungry, so I can't exactly cook you dinner. And I can't give you a blow job. I mean, I can give you a blow job, but I'm not going to because we both agreed this is...purely platonic, but—"

He shoots me a look. "Do you always ramble when you're nervous?"

"Ramble or keep my mouth shut," I offer. "There is no in-between."

His nod is slow, but I swear I see his mouth twitch. Or maybe I imagine it because he still hasn't reached for the door handle, and his lack of...I don't even know what...is starting to make me feel like I'm a crazy person.

"Not mad we lost the game, Raine," he finally reveals.

"But you *are* mad," I assume.

He scrubs his hand over his face. "I don't know what I am, honestly."

My attention moves from his chiseled profile and I look down at my hands instead. "Oh."

"Confused, I guess," he admits.

Confused? What does he have to be confused about? After the weird conversation I walked in on between Everett and my dad, and now this awkward silence while we're parked in the garage, I'm pretty sure if anyone's allowed to feel confused, it's me.

As if he can hear my spiraling thoughts, he announces, "Your dad threatened to kill me for hurting you."

I pull back, surprised. Not by my dad's threat or that Everett's sour mood has something to do with their interaction, but because of the second part. The *hurting me* part.

"Hurting me?" I ask.

"He isn't stupid." Everett drags his calloused fingertips against the black stitching along the steering wheel. Slowly. Methodically. "I know you want to hope he is so you can get away with all the lying, but it's only gonna bite you in the ass."

With a slow blink, I try to catch up with the topic change, but I'm only left reeling. "I-I never said he was stupid."

"You're treating him like he is. Sweeping your split lip under the rug won't fly with him."

"I'm not sure how else you would've liked me to handle—"

His scoff cuts me off as he faces me fully. "You could've started by defending me instead of letting him think I hit you."

My jaw drops. "He doesn't think—"

"It's exactly what he thinks." He scrubs his face again, lets his heavy hand fall to his thigh, and rests his head against the headrest. "I'm still trying to figure out how he let you leave with me."

Now that he mentions it, it's a good question. One I don't fully understand, either. Why did my dad let me go with him? I mean, I'm an adult, so it's not like he can physically keep me locked up at Etch 'N' Ink, but still. If he really believes Everett's the one who hit me, I'm surprised Everett isn't in a body bag.

Nibbling on the edge of my thumb, I murmur the only plausible possibility. "He's probably scared I'll ghost him again. I'm not exactly proud of it, but...it's what I've been doing for months now."

As my words hang in the air, Everett pinches the bridge of his nose and sighs. "Did your dad know about Drake?"

Staring down at my hands in my lap, I try to ignore the shame accompanying his question. "Yes and no. It was one of the things I argued with my dad about most. I mentioned I was dating someone, my dad asked to meet him, Drake said he wanted nothing to do with my family, and round and round we went."

"I introduced myself as Everett." He sounds so...detached. Unable to hide my curiosity, I peek up at him only to find him looking as defeated as before. "Not sure if it's gonna mess with your lie," he adds, "but..."

Shit.

"It's fine," I whisper. "I'll figure it out."

"Whatever you say, Raine." Running his tongue between his upper teeth and top lip, he finally reaches for the door handle and heads inside without a backward glance. But the relief I was expecting? Yeah, it's absent. Instead, all I'm left with is silence, which kills me. The way it burrows under my skin and leaves me itchy and uncomfortable. He's hurt or frustrated or…something, and I don't like it.

Without giving myself time to overthink things, I rush after him, desperate to fix this. Whatever's bothering him. Whatever I did to reinforce his need to shut me out and keep his distance from me.

"I'm sorry," I call out.

He slips his shoes off in the mudroom but doesn't answer me. The door to the house closes behind him, leaving me alone in the dark garage.

With a twist of my wrist, I push the door open again and continue. "I really am. I'm sorry."

"And what are you sorry for, Raine?" he demands.

Wiping my sweaty palms against my jeans, I try not to cower from his penetrating gaze and the accusation in it. "I didn't defend you. I was so blindsided by you being in the shop I kind of…froze. And I know it's no excuse, but I promise I'll talk with my dad at my next shift. Make sure he knows you had nothing to do with"—I wave my hand around my face, motioning to my swollen lip—"this."

A dry, gruff laugh escapes him. "Yeah, I'm sure he'll believe you, too."

"Seriously, Ev," I grab his shirt sleeve to keep him from escaping down the hall despite it being my own game plan until he brought up his conversation with my dad. "I'm sorry. I really am. I know how shitty it must feel to be looked at like you'd hit me when I know you'd never cross that line, but—"

"Do you know I'd never hit you?" he challenges. His attention falls to where I'm touching him.

Shit. I would've never touched Drake like this. Not when we're in the thick of an argument. Not that I'm arguing with Everett or anything, but still.

"Answer the question, Storm," he pushes.

I hesitate and let him go. "What?"

"I want to know." He turns those icy blue eyes on me. "You said you know I'd never cross that line. Do you?"

Looking down at his sock-clad feet, I whisper, "Honestly?"

He moves closer and nudges my chin up with his knuckle, silently calling me out for being too much of a coward to look him in the eye as I consider his question and all it entails.

When I meet his gaze again, my abdomen tightens with anticipation.

"Yeah, *honestly*," he repeats, throwing my own word back at me. "I think I'm over the lies for today. Aren't you?"

"Yes." My voice is hushed as I try to combat the swell of butterflies in my stomach. I always knew Everett was attractive, but when he looks like this? All stubborn and direct and prickly, it kind of makes me want to push him more. The realization is startling and only confirms my slip of the tongue from thirty seconds ago. My chin lifts an inch higher, and I whisper, "I know you would never hit me."

A long pause follows. His eyes bounce around my face as if he's a genuine lie detector or something. And even though it makes me want to run in the opposite direction, I keep my feet planted where they are and look up at him. Noting how his eyes are more navy around the outside of his iris and melt into a lighter, sky blue near his pupil. The way his lips are full and soft. My fingers itch to reach up and touch his scruff to see if it's as prickly as it looks. If his jaw is as hard as it appears. I don't know how he does it. How he can seem so genuine yet guarded at the same time. It's confusing, and so is my body's response. But fear? Fear is the last thing I feel. It's so nonexistent I should seriously second-guess my sanity at this point, especially if he keeps looking at me like this. Like he might—

"Then it's enough." His gaze falls to my mouth for the briefest of seconds before he drops his hand from my chin but doesn't pull away. "You don't need to make your life messier by defending me. We're good."

When his minty breath hits my cheeks, I realize how close we're standing. And even without his shoes on and mine firmly on my feet, he still towers over me. It's a reminder of how little power I actually have at this moment. The old me would've been afraid. I embarrassed him. Painted him in a bad light. He has every right to be frustrated with me, and if he was Drake, I'd be terrified of standing in front of him. Admitting my mistake. Yet here he is, calling me out for my shit without yelling or throwing things. Without making me want to run and hide and tuck my tail between my legs. The contrast with Drake is staggering. Even when Drake wasn't physical, he always knew how to throw a verbal punch. Sometimes, those were even worse.

But Everett? Everett makes me feel...safe. And I honestly didn't know if I'd ever be able to feel this way again. But what's even crazier is how he doesn't need my dad's approval. Everett only needed me to confirm *I* know him better than to put him in the same category as Drake.

He has no idea.

I slowly step back, convinced that maybe if I have enough breathing room, my lungs will finally start working, and I won't feel so lightheaded. "You're a good guy, Ev," I confide. "I guess I assumed you must be so used to hearing it you wouldn't need any validation from me or my dad. Even if this is fake," I clarify, though I'm not entirely sure who I'm trying to remind. "But just so we're clear, you are. You're a good guy. I mean it."

It's still dark inside. Nothing but the moon shining through the windows. I wish the lights were on now, though. Wish they could shine a light on how stupid it is for me to say something like this. Everything I've said is the truth, but we have our rules in place to keep any of this from becoming too real. And I'm afraid my little…rambling session hits too close to home. The last thing he needs is for his project—aka me—to catch feelings.

"Can you…get the lights?" I breathe out.

He nods slowly and leaves me near the door next to the garage to flick the kitchen light on. I slip my sneakers off, unsure where to go from here after I kind of, sort of peeled away some of the protective barriers I had in place until now. Until I stupidly started to wonder what it would be like to kiss Everett Taylor. To let him kiss me.

"Anything from Drake?" Everett asks as he tosses his keys onto the corner of the kitchen counter.

It's the same question he's asked at least twice a day since we moved in together. Since the first night we made lasagna, my answer has always been the same.

With a slow shake of my head, I reply, "Not a peep."

He nods and opens the fridge, searching for a late-night dinner, but his absent gaze makes me feel like he's some-where else. It's strange. How easily he can control his emotions. Locking each and every one of them into a small little container deep inside of him until only a stranger stands in front of me. As if he can feel my assessment, he clears his throat and turns to me. "I forgot to tell you I talked with Reeves the other day."

Reeves. Right.

"Oh?" I offer weakly.

"Yeah. He asked if we want to keep laying low like we have been or if we want to lure Drake out."

The name alone causes a ripple of wariness to crawl down my spine. Locking up my own freak-out over his name, I pull one of the leather barstools at the kitchen island out and sit down across from Everett. "And how would we do that?"

"Throw another party. See if Drake comes."

"And if he does?" I ask. "What then?"

"Then we get the ball rolling and push him off a cliff."

I snort. "Sounds like a solid plan."

"Thought you'd like it." A smile toys at the edge of his full lips before he sobers slightly. "What do you say? Keep laying low or throw a party?"

I play out all the potential outcomes as well as the consequences of either option. Not going to lie. It's been nice. Really nice. Lying low and pretending like my past with Drake is where it should be...in the past. I haven't been lying when I told Everett Drake hasn't called since his conversation with Everett the first night. While it should make me feel better, it's only left me with more anxiety. I feel like I could walk into a trap any moment, and I'd never see it coming. I doubt it's been easy for Everett, either. Being my chauffeur. My chef. My freaking butler half the time. And it's all because he made his friend a promise. To protect someone in need. Someone like me.

With a deep breath, I decide, "Let's lure the bastard out."

"All right," he answers. "I'll get the ball rolling."

CHAPTER TWENTY

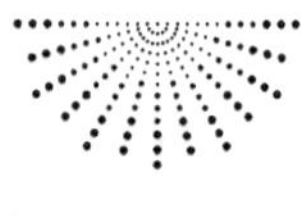

EVERETT

My nostrils flare as I read his message. Another one pops up right after.

I glance up at the house we're parked in front of as my thumbs move across my cell.

Resisting the urge to scrub my hand over my face, I type my response instead.

ME

> Not yet. We never should've let him win last time.

REEVES

> Wait until you hear what he picked. You need to cut us some slack. We were a little distracted by your girl's boyfriend's appearance during the last game night, remember? Get your ass inside.

ME

> Be right there.

I hit send, then tuck my phone into my back pocket as the car idles in front of the house. Turning the ignition off, I wipe my palms against my jeans and glance at Raine beside me.

It's been interesting these last few weeks. I don't think either of us can deny the distance we've kept from each other, but even then, I can't help but have picked up a few things. Like the way she plays with her black nails when she's anxious or distracted.

She's doing it again while staring up at the house. Lost in her own thoughts. In the what-ifs of tonight. The quiet click-click of her nails tapping against each other echoes through the otherwise silent cab, and she wets her lips.

She's nervous.

Beautiful, of course, but nervous.

Her hair's curled and pulled into a high pony. The thick waves hang down her back, and her makeup is kept to a minimum. Yet there's a glow to her skin making her look like a fucking goddess.

A *nervous* goddess.

A nervous goddess who couldn't decide if she wanted to blend in or stand out tonight, if I had to guess by her tight black top and ripped jeans.

Fuck, she looks incredible.

I tear my attention from the slip of skin peeking through the rip in her jeans on her upper thigh and ask, "You good?"

She gulps and looks at me. "You really think he'll show?"

He.

The girl can't even say Drake's name, or she refuses to give him the respect of one. Like he's a mindless drone she'd rather forget. It's not like she even needs to say his name. I know exactly who she's talking about. He might not have reached out since our phone conversation, but I'm not stupid enough to believe he's let her go. Why would he? She's the best thing he'll ever have.

Poor bastard.

I shake the thought off, remembering Raine's question. Do I think Drake will show up tonight? It's a good question. Part of me wants to ask why we're hurrying to poke the bear, but this isn't my game. My plan. Nah, I'm only a pawn. In a way, so is she.

Rolling my shoulders, I answer, "We're on our grounds, so I'm not sure if he'll show, but Reeves promised he told everyone he could think of about tonight, so Drake definitely knows about it. Whether or not he makes an appearance is a toss-up."

Sucking her plump red lips between her teeth, she nods quickly as if mentally psyching herself up for whatever tonight will bring.

I've been trying to do the same thing since she told me she wanted to lure him out of hiding instead of lying low like I'd hoped. Nah, that's a lie. Lying low with Raine as a room-mate is the last thing I need. Not when she's too jaded to want anything real, and I'm too stubborn to cross into relationship territory when I already have enough on my plate. She's making it difficult, though. Besides, as far as I'm concerned, she isn't even available. Not really. Not after the shitstorm her ex put her through. Is *still* putting her through. Or at least, I thought so until I picked her up from Etch 'N' Ink the other night. I could've sworn she was begging me to kiss her. If she was anyone else, I would have. Or if things weren't so complicated.

Yeah. I gotta get this over with.

"It'll be fine," I promise, though I'm not sure who I'm trying to reassure. "We have freshmen posted at all the entrances. They'll text if he arrives, so we'll have a heads-up. Also, Fin volunteered as the whistleblower if it comes to it."

Her eyes widen, and she opens her mouth, but I cut her off. "I know. No cops. Don't worry. It's only a precaution for a worst-case scenario. What I'm trying to say is we have a game plan. You'll be safe. Promise."

"Whatever you say." She pastes on a fake smile and reaches for the door, but I stop her.

"Listen," I start.

The sight of her forest-green eyes nearly knocks me on my ass as she peeks over her shoulder. "Yes?"

"You've never been to one of these parties," I remind her.

"I went to the last—"

"You haven't participated in any of the games," I clarify.

She frowns. "So?"

"So, I don't know what game Cameron chose tonight, but I do know they can be…physical."

Her brows crease. "Okay?"

"Do you have any boundaries?"

"What?"

"Boundaries," I repeat. "Do you have any?"

"Boundaries for what?"

The girl's seriously going to make me say it? I nearly grind my molars but find an ounce of control and explain. "I know this isn't real, but we're supposed to *pretend* it's real. I need to know your boundaries before we walk in there."

Her lips lift when she lets go of the door handle and turns in the passenger seat to give me her full attention. "Are you asking if it's okay to touch me?"

"Yeah."

"Okay?" Her smile widens. "Yes, it's all right if you touch me."

"With my hands?"

"What else would you touch me with?" she counters.

I bite back my own smirk. Oh, the things I could say if the circumstances were different. Instead, I push, "Can I kiss you?"

She hesitates, her gaze narrowing. "For show?"

My eyes drop to her lips, and I force myself to nod.

"Yes, you can kiss me," she whispers.

"What about dancing?"

"What's wrong with dancing?"

"Can I grind against you?" I clarify.

Her jaw drops. "Did you seriously just ask me this?"

"I'm only trying to figure out your boundaries."

"And what are *your* boundaries, Everett Taylor?" she challenges.

With her? I'm not sure there are many. Not if she keeps looking at me like this. You'd think I'd hold a grudge after she threw me under the bus with her dad. But after confessing how she felt safe around me, I couldn't help but let it go, realizing it was all I needed to hear. All that really mattered. Not gonna lie. This entire situation has messed with my head from the beginning. Seeing my similarities to Drake. Our differences. Our attraction to similar girls, no matter how much I don't want to admit it. The whole thing is screwing with me, and I'm not sure how to handle it.

Rolling my shoulders, I shove the thought aside. "I'm up for whatever sells this."

"Good, then so am I."

"Good," I mimic.

"Good," she finishes and reaches for the door handle again. This time, I don't stop her, letting her step outside.

The place is already buzzing. I didn't think Raine's nerves could handle us showing up early, so I figured arriving a little later than usual might not be a bad idea. However, when a drunk-off-his ass-freshman stumbles into her, I immediately regret my decision. Holding her waist to keep her steady, I see Jaxon cutting through the crowd, heading straight for us.

"Hey, have you seen Rory?" he calls.

Jaxon is Dylan and Griffin's older brother. He's also LAU's hockey coach for the girls' team and my former roommate. He graduated and moved out earlier this year. Even then, he was never a fan of our game nights, so why the hell is he standing in the family room tonight while a party rages around us?

"What are you doing here?" I ask.

The guy looks nothing short of panicked as he rises onto his tiptoes and searches for something over the top of my head, barely giving me an ounce of his attention. "I'm looking for Squeaks."

Squeaks is Rory's nickname. She's Maverick's and Archer's little sister and is also in middle school.

"Why would Rory be here?" I ask.

His nostrils flare as he turns back to me. "She asked if she could stay at my place because her parents were going out and she didn't want to be alone. We were hanging out, watching a movie, and she, uh,"—Jax looks down at his feet—"she got embarrassed and ran off. She didn't take Kovu with her, either," he adds, mentioning the family's German Shepherd who hasn't left her side since Archer died. "I gotta find her."

"Why was she embarrassed?" I challenge.

Squeezing the back of his neck, he mutters, "She, uh, she tried to… You know what? It doesn't matter. What matters is finding her. *Now.*"

He's right. This is the last place a girl Rory's age should be, and the faster we find her, the faster we can sneak her out before she sees something she shouldn't.

I stand a little taller and scan the crowded house in search of a small girl who doesn't belong.

"Wait, I'm sorry…who are we looking for?" Raine asks beside me.

"Rory," Jaxon answers for me. "She's Maverick's little sister and way too young to be here."

"I know who Rory is," Raine comments.

I interject, "Are you sure she's even here?"

Jax shakes his head. "No idea, but since this is the only real place she knows within walking distance of the penthouse, I figured it was my best bet. If I don't find her in the next ten minutes, I'm calling her parents. I have a feeling no one wants that."

He's right—again. We don't. Especially when Reeves set this party up as a trap for Drake.

"I'll help you," I offer.

"Me, too," Raine adds. "What's she wearing?"

"Green top, jean shorts, hair in a ponytail. Now spread out."

"I'll check upstairs," Raine offers, taking the steps two at a time.

As she disappears around the corner, I continue my interrogation of Jax. "Does Mav know?"

He shakes his head.

"Why not?"

"I don't want him to ask what happened."

"And what happened, exactly?" I push.

The guy looks like he might puke as he shifts from one foot to the other, avoiding me like the fucking plague. "She, uh… Look, I doubt she wants me talking to anyone about this, so will you help me find her or not?"

"What'd she do, Jax?"

Looking awkward as fuck, he moves closer and drops his voice low. "She tried to kiss me, okay?"

"*What?*"

"Yeah." He scrubs his hand over his face. "Obviously, I turned her down. She's a fuckin' kid. I don't see her like that, but it…it crushed her, Ev." Jax sighs and shakes his head as if it'll erase the situation entirely. If only the bastard was so lucky. "You should've seen her face." He pales. "She'll never forgive me for this."

I don't know what I'm supposed to say. Squeaks has always worshipped the ground Jax walks on. I'm not sure he realizes it, but it's pretty clear to everyone else. We all assumed it was nothing more than a childish crush, though. It's not like it could ever go anywhere. And even now, it hasn't. But what the hell was she thinking? Why would she do it? She had to have known Jax wouldn't reciprocate. She's in fuckin' middle school. None of it matters now, though. It's done, and Jax did the right thing even if it made Rory wish the ground would open up and swallow her whole. Yet here she is, reminding us all how childish she really is by running away. By scaring Jax and me and anyone else who might know about her disappearance.

Unsure what else to say, I offer, "You did the right thing, man."

"I know I did," he mumbles. "Still doesn't erase the hurt in her eyes."

I slap him on the shoulder, hoping it'll pull him out of the memory, and promise, "We'll find her." Then I continue scanning the crowd, barely searching for ten seconds when Griffin appears with a handful of pretzels, looking confused. "Hey, what's Rory doing here?"

Jax shoves me aside and stalks closer to Griffin. "Where is she?"

Grimacing, Griffin hooks his thumb over his shoulder. "She's out back with Ophelia, crying. What happened to her?"

"Fuck," Jax breathes out. "I should…" He turns to me. "What should I do?"

I have no clue, but it's the last thing he needs to hear. Weighing his options, I suggest, "Go out there but keep your distance. Ophelia's probably the best person she can talk to right now."

He nods, disappearing down the crowded hall and heading out to the backyard.

Popping a pretzel stick into his mouth, Griffin watches him leave and asks me, "What was that about?"

"I'll tell you later," I deflect. "I need to find Raine and let her know we found Rory."

"Speaking of the devil." Griffin lifts his chin toward the staircase.

Raine's long legs are the first thing I notice before my eyes trail up her thighs, hips, and stomach, then pause at the way her shirt stretches across her chest until I force myself to look her in the eye.

Shoulders lifting, she grimaces and mouths, "No luck."

I crook my finger at her, silently ordering her to come closer. Once she reaches me, I bend forward and tell her, "Griffin spotted her. Jax and Ophelia are taking care of it."

"Perfect timing," Griff adds, lifting his chin toward the crowded family room. "The game's about to start."

"Do you know which one Cameron picked?" I ask.

Griffin's lip twitches, but instead of answering me, he gives our teammate his full attention, so I force myself to do the same.

This is going to be a long night.

CHAPTER TWENTY-ONE

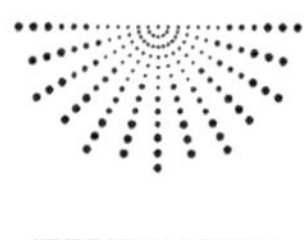

EVERETT

"All right, all right!" Cameron yells from the center of the family room. "By some miracle, I won the last game night, which means, I won this bad boy, too." He lifts the ugly ass gold medallion from his neck, kisses the medal, and rests it on his puffed-up chest like it's his most prized possession.

Dumbass.

"And tonight's game is…*Spin the Bottle!*" he continues. Cheering erupts. It bounces off the walls as my attention drifts to Raine. If she's pissed, she doesn't show it. She almost looks…nervous. Pouty—and now healed—lips parted. Breath stilted. Deer in the headlights glazed eyes while she clicks her black nails together in front of her.

Tried to warn you, sweetheart.

As if she can read my thoughts, she peeks over at me, catches me staring, then turns back to Cameron and lifts her chin an inch higher in the air.

"Rules are simple," Cameron continues. "Everyone splits into groups of ten. Freshmen will pass out bottles for spinning and shots for those looking for a little liquid courage. When it's your turn, *Spin the Bottle*. Whoever it lands on, you kiss."

Reeves steps up beside him, adding, "As always, leave your jealousy at the door. If you don't trust your partner enough to see them kiss a stranger, are you even in a healthy relationship?" Dylan snorts beside him, and he tosses her a wink, adding, "And, as always, consent is necessary. You both must agree on where the kiss should be placed, or you can pass by taking a shot. Like Cameron said, freshmen will walk around with them in case you need one, so just flag them down. And, if anyone has a problem, come talk to me, Griff, or Ev. Any questions?" He barely waits a second before nodding at Cameron, urging him to continue.

"Let's go!" Cameron booms.

Like ants, everyone scatters, splitting up into groups of ten and claiming different territories of the house in preparation for tonight's game. When I catch a flash of Finley disappearing around the corner, I call, "Griff."

"Yeah?"

"Keep an eye on Fin for me."

"You think I can control anything the girl does?" he counters.

"You're the only one I trust. Just do it."

I don't wait for his response as I grab Raine's hand and tug her toward one of the back rooms in search of…fuck, I don't even know at this point. Sanity? Clarity? A moment to fucking breathe and wrap my head around the idea of someone kissing Raine before I even have a chance to?

And since when have I wanted a chance to kiss her?

What the hell is my problem tonight?

Trailing behind me, Raine asks, "We're seriously playing *Spin the Bottle*? What is everyone? Twelve?"

"It's the lazy man's choice," I agree as I push us both into a nook in the hallway. "Fitting, since Cameron's the one who chose."

"You don't like Cameron?"

"No one likes Cameron," I reply dryly. "But yeah, if we're keeping up pretenses, I think we should play."

"Seriously?"

With a shrug, I offer, "At least we have a loophole in case you don't want to kiss anyone."

"Taking a shot?" She rolls her eyes. "Which means the longer you play, the fewer shots are taken, am I right?"

The girl isn't wrong.

Still, she wanted to lure her asshole ex out, and a game of *Spin the Bottle* is the perfect way to prove she isn't his anymore. *If* he shows up.

I lean back, glancing around the corner toward the entrance, searching for Drake, but I come up empty.

"You don't have to play," I remind her.

"Yes, I do."

"No." I give her my full attention again. "You really don't."

"Ev…"

"You can take shots all night."

"I don't like shots," she argues.

"Fine, you can pass them to me, and I'll take them for you."

"And if Drake shows up when you're already shitfaced?"

"I think I can hold my alcohol a little better than you're assuming," I tell her.

"I'll be sure to keep that in mind." She presses her hand to my chest, and I swear I can feel my fucking heartbeat in my throat, so I shut my mouth and wait. For what, I'm not even sure. A reason why she's touching me might be nice, though.

Sometimes, I forget how small she is. How breakable she is. Until she's like this. Within reach. The girl barely comes up to my collarbone, yet she's far from a kid. Far from anyone I've ever met.

I look down at her hand sprawled across the LAU logo on my T-shirt. The black-tipped nails contrast with the red fabric and seriously make me wonder if I've been sent to Hell because this? This is starting to feel like a different kind of torture. If she were any other girl, I'd wonder what it would feel like if my T-shirt didn't separate us. If she's as soft as she looks. As supple.

Her eyes find mine. Those dark lashes tease me as she blinks slowly, letting them brush against her skin until her forest-green eyes meet mine again. "I appreciate your willingness to protect me from kissing a few random guys tonight."

"Yeah?"

"Mm-hmm, but—"

"Hey, Ev!" someone calls.

I clear my throat and step back when I realize exactly how close I'm standing to Raine while searching the room for the culprit.

Reeves strides closer, his curious gaze scanning the place with every passing second. "How's it goin'?"

"About as good as can be expected," I mutter. "Any sign of Drake?"

He shakes his head. "Not yet, but I just got an interesting text."

My brows dip. "What kind of interesting text?"

"It's, uh," Reeves looks at Raine, then turns back to me. "Just to confirm, you two are still faking it, right? Because it kind of looked—"

"Everett's only helping me with Drake," Raine interrupts.

"Yeah." I clear my throat. "Why?"

"The text," Reeves explains. "It's for a job."

My attention shoots to Raine, and fuck me, what I

wouldn't give to know what she's thinking. A job? Reeves wants to talk about a job when my current one stands a foot away from us? Does it bother her? Should it?

"Ev." Reeves snaps his fingers an inch from my nose, and I jerk back.

"Not taking any more jobs until I finish this one," I answer.

"The problem is…" Reeves sighs. "I already agreed to help her, and—"

"What?"

"It was before I started dating Dylan," he rushes out. "But it isn't like the"—Reeves glances at Raine and grimaces—"*current* situation. This one is pretty straightforward. A simple, one-time favor."

I groan. "Not interested."

"Come on, man. Please," he begs. "Remember the puppy? The one from the photoshoot with Dylan a while back?"

I search my memory for a puppy when it hits me. A little while ago, Dylan and Reeves were partners for a photography project. He brought a puppy to the photoshoot. Not sure what it has to do with our current conversation, but I lift a shoulder. "Yeah? What about it?"

"Well, I borrowed it from a friend in exchange for being her plus-one to a wedding."

"So?"

"So, I kind of forgot about it, and the wedding is next week."

I shake my head. "Not my problem."

"Come on, man. What about Dyl?" He grabs my jacket, tugging me closer as a pair of drunk girls stumble down the hall toward the bathroom. Once we're alone again, he lets me go, adding, "I'm not going out with someone else even if it's purely platonic."

"Yeah, well neither am I," I argue. "If Drake sees me with someone other than Raine—"

"He won't," Reeves promises. "The wedding isn't even anywhere close to Cedar Springs, I swear, and there aren't any jealous exes and shit, either. It'll be easy. She only needs a date to get her parents off her back."

"Like I said, not my problem."

"Come on. This is the last one. I swear."

The last one. As in, the last favor I'll owe him. And even though I want to tell him to go to Hell, I know it'll only hurt Dylan in the long run.

"Come on, man," Reeves repeats. "Please?"

My nostrils flare, but I concede anyway. "After this, I'm done. We clear?"

"Ollie!" Dylan calls. "You coming or what?"

"Coming, Pickles!" Turning back to me, Reeves slaps my shoulder. "We should find a circle."

"I'll catch up," I tell him. As he disappears down the hall, I look at Raine, wishing I could read her mind. "You sure you're still good with this?"

"Good with what?" she challenges. "You going on a date with a random girl? Yup. We're here to play, remember? And worst-case scenario, we fake it, right?"

With a soft pat to my chest, she slips past me, grabs a shot of something from one of the freshmen, tosses it back, and lets the burn out with a slow breath through pursed lips. Part of me wants to ask if she needed the liquid courage to get through tonight's game or if it's because she might see Drake. *Or* if it's because she doesn't like the idea of me going out with someone else. Does it bother her? Should I even ask? Is it my place? I don't fuckin' know. Not when our entire relationship is based on a lie. Based on a ruse. One meant to get her ex off her back.

Feeling my stare, Raine gives me a fake smile and steals another shot from a freshman.

Unable to bite my tongue, I point out, "I thought you didn't like shots."

"I don't." She tosses it back, then gives me a sickly sweet smile. "Let's get this over with."

I grab her arm and push her back against the wall behind her, pressing my hands to either side of her head.

"Is there a problem?" she challenges.

I lean closer, consuming her space the same way she's consumed my thoughts since the moment we met. "You mad at me, Stormie?"

She wets her lips, her brows bunching. "Stormie?"

Fuck.

I clear my throat. "Answer the question."

"About what?"

"Are you mad at me?" I repeat.

"Why'd you call me Stormie?"

"Doesn't matter."

Her eyes fall to my mouth. "Of course, it doesn't." She shakes her head, looking up at me again. "And, no, I'm not mad."

"You sure?" I push.

With a quick nod, she answers, "Positive," then dips beneath my arm and sways toward an already full circle of people sitting on the floor.

Well, I guess that's it, then.

"You guys ready?" she asks once she reaches the group.

This should be interesting.

Squeezing between one of my teammates and a guy from one of my classes sophomore year, Raine sits cross-legged on the ground. When one of them grins at her, I clear my throat. His head swivels toward me. Without a word, he stands and moves to a different circle, leaving me space beside the girl who's even more confusing than Finley, and that's saying something.

Speaking of which, where the hell is my sister? I search the crowded room but come up empty. Nic, one of my teammates, reaches for the bottle in the center of the circle. After a flick of his wrist, it spins round and round, landing on a girl named Courtney. She crawls toward him, gives him a quick peck, then moves back to her spot as the guy to Nic's left reaches for the bottle and takes a turn. When it lands on another of my teammates, they both laugh, taking shots from one of the lowerclassmen walking around with trays of different liquors. Each has a designated area to keep an eye on. Their jobs are to pass out drinks and to be available in case anyone needs anything. You know, like a shot of alcohol to keep from kissing someone they aren't interested in. It's a necessity during a game like *Spin the Bottle* where anyone's invited.

Ellie, one of the sorority girls, spins the bottle next. When it lands on Nic, he grins and moves to the middle of the circle, meeting her halfway. Smirking, she reaches up and taps her finger against her cheek. With a laugh, he kisses it and glances at the guy to Ellie's right.

"Your turn, man."

The guy spins, and when it lands on Ellie again, a blush hits her cheeks, and her smile widens.

"Hey, baby," he says as his mouth descends on hers. This time, the kiss isn't a quick peck. With her hands in his hair and his arms wrapped around her waist, they kneel in the center of the circle, going at it like it's their last day on Earth. My phone buzzes, distracting me, and I pull it out of my front pocket.

REEVES

Drake just showed up with two guys and three girls. Keep an eye out, but don't make anything obvious. Remember, you don't care about him. You care about having a good time with your new girl.

"I take it they like each other?" Raine interrupts.

I slip my phone back into my pocket and shift closer to her on the ground. "They've been going out for a few months." Letting my mouth skate across the shell of her ear, I add, "Dickless just showed up." Her muscles tense, but she doesn't pull away from me. "I won't let him touch you. But I need you to play along with whatever happens, all right?"

With a slow nod, she turns to watch the show again and leans back on her hands.

"All right, wrap it up. Let someone else have a turn," Nic orders as Griffin slips into the space beside Ellie's boyfriend, rubbing his hands against his jeans. Part of me wishes he was still keeping an eye on Finley like I asked, but I bite my tongue. If I had to guess, Reeves gave him a heads-up about Drake's appearance, and he's here as backup. Smart. Even if it does leave my little sister vulnerable. Fuck, sometimes I really wish there were multiples of me. It'd make my life a hell of a lot easier.

"Looks like I found where the party is," Griff jokes.

Ellie's lips break apart from her boyfriend's, and they make their way back to their spots on the ground.

"Your turn, Griff," I announce.

My best friend shifts forward and spins the bottle. Around and around it goes until it stops on the girl beside me. I swear the air in the room charges, and a stone falls in my gut as I wait. For what, I'm not sure. The punch of rage beneath my sternum is unexpected, so I dig my fingers into my thighs.

What the hell do I do now?

Head cocked, Griffin looks between me and Raine, a silent question in his eyes. I open my mouth to call one of the freshmen forward but bite my tongue at the last second as Raine scoots toward him without even casting me a glance.

What. The. *Fuck?*

My best friend gives me one more look over the top of her head, appearing as confused as I feel. "You good with this?" he asks.

"Pretty sure it isn't his decision," Raine chirps, drawing his attention back to her.

As she crawls toward him, he sits up a little straighter, giving her a grin. "All right, Raine. Where do you want it?"

She cups his cheek with her dainty little hand, and I swear the image of her black nails against his stubbled fucking cheek is ingrained into my mind for the rest of my life.

As if in slow motion, she tilts her head and leans into him, preparing to kiss my best friend under the guise of a stupid game. I swear it's like watching a fucking train wreck. Time slows. My pulse skips. Sweat breaks out along my hairline when she presses her mouth to his. And even though it only lasts a second, it's the longest one I've endured in my entire life.

My hands fist in my lap, and my attention catches on someone behind her. It's Drake. I don't give a damn right now, though. I'm too distracted by the shitshow in front of me. When Raine pulls away, Griffin's eyes stay closed as a quick laugh falls out of him, and he shakes his head.

"Fuck, man," he says, turning to me. "You're a lucky guy."

"Am I?" I challenge dryly. It's hard to keep my expression in check when all I see is red, but I force it back and quirk my brow, looking bored.

Batting her lashes at me, Raine stays quiet but motions to

the bottle in the middle of the circle, silently urging me to take my turn.

Is this a dare, Stormie?

The question burns in my eyes, but I don't voice it aloud, too amped up from her last kiss to say a single word as I hold her gaze. With a blind flick of my wrist, I spin the bottle, not bothering to wait and see who it lands on for my hands to find Raine's waist and drag her into me as if she weighs nothing at all. A tiny gasp escapes her before I swallow it with a kiss.

Her skin is softer than I imagined it would be. I grab her face, tilt her head, and move her exactly where I need her.

Me. Not Griffin. Not Drake. *Me.*

The kiss is hard and needy, and I tell myself it's because I know her ex might be watching, but the truth is? I have a feeling I'd be kissing her regardless. Seeing her lips on my best friend? It fucked with my head, making me feel like I might be losing my damn mind. But when she kisses me back? When I feel her lips move against mine, when I swallow the tiny whimper in the back of her throat and taste the sweetness of her mouth, I fucking lose it.

I pry her lips open with my tongue, and she sucks on me, letting me pump in and out of her waiting mouth as my dick jumps to attention in my jeans. Wishing—begging—to let him have a turn. To let him mark her.

This isn't me.

This isn't. Fucking. Me.

I don't lose control. I don't get jealous. I don't cross lines. And I sure as shit don't unravel from a single fucking kiss. But this? This feels different. She feels different. And I'm not sure what to make of it. I'm not sure what I *want* to make of it.

Nothing. This means nothing. It's only a kiss. Just a fucking—

Throats clear around us, and Raine pulls away, her eyes wide. Tiny wisps of her dark hair frame one side of her face from where I held her. As she lets out a slow breath between her parted lips, she looks at me, confusion and desire swirling in her forest-green gaze. When her eyes snap to someone behind me, whatever lust was present is replaced with...fear?

Looks like our little show didn't go unnoticed.

I slowly turn my head and stare at the one and only Drake Haitt.

Good to see you again, asshole. Here we go.

CHAPTER TWENTY-TWO

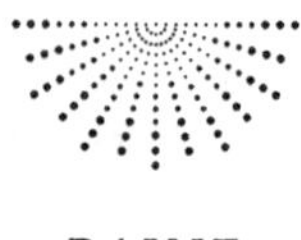

RAINE

He's here. I shouldn't be surprised, and I guess I'm not, but knowing the possibility versus seeing it firsthand are two very different things.

"*Spin the Bottle*, huh?" Drake says. "Mind if we join?"

Three girls are with him, along with two of his guy friends, Johnny St. James and Mikey Knolls. Great. They already have bad blood with this house, so why not make it worse, right?

Blood whooshes in my ears, and my mouth feels like it's full of cotton as I watch him stride closer. Part of me wants to tell him to leave. Part of me wants to get off my ass and run in the opposite direction. But this is the point, isn't it? To prove I'm not scared anymore. I'm not…anything anymore. *We* aren't anything anymore.

"Pretty sure you could have your own circle," Griffin says to Drake before calling for another of his teammates. "Hey, Dreggs, get this guy a bottle—"

"Nah. Nothin' wrong with a little variety, right?" Drake sits across from me without waiting for an invitation while gifting me with a pointed gaze I swear I can feel deep in my chest. But it doesn't leave butterflies. It leaves a sharp burn I want to wipe away, though I'm not stupid enough to believe it would do anything.

As if he can see his affect on me, he smiles. "I think we can all play this game, don't you?"

I feel Griffin's questioning eyes on me, and I have no doubt they mirror Everett's on my opposite side. I don't know what they expect me to say. I don't know how this goes. I have no freaking idea. Like a rubber band stretched too thin, I force my focus to snap from Drake to Everett.

My eyes plead with his as I wait. For what, I'm not sure. Maybe for him to take the reins? To make a decision? To tell me what to do now with my abusive ex sitting eight feet in front of me?

Why hasn't he lashed out yet? Drake, not Ev. He saw me kiss someone who isn't him, and he didn't lose his shit. Why? What's going on? And why do I feel like it only pushed us another step in the wrong direction?

A warm hand hits my thigh. I look down, finding Everett's large, calloused hand on me. His thumb slips beneath the ripped material of my jeans and he runs it back and forth against my bare skin. Back and forth. Back and forth. Slowly. Methodically. As if it has a direct connection to my sanity, I let out a slow breath, forcing myself to calm the hell down.

Satisfied, Everett shifts slightly and bends one of his knees up, resting his forearm against it while keeping his opposite hand on my leg.

Back and forth. Back and forth.

He looks good. I'll give him that much. Like he's in his element. Like he's looking into the face of a lion, and all he sees is a baby kitten he could squash with his bare hands if he wanted to. Everett Taylor. Kitten squasher. It'd be gross if Drake wasn't the kitten in this scenario.

"Rules are simple," Everett explains. "When the bottle lands on someone, both parties have to agree to the kiss and the location. If one or more participants don't want the kiss, you both take a shot, then it's the next person's turn. If there are any issues, you're kicked out of the party. Any questions?"

Drake shakes his head. "None at all, man. I'll go first."

With a flick of his wrist, Drake sends the bottle whirling on the ground. It finally stops on one of the girls he came with. Taliah, I think? Gorgeous brown hair. Olive skin. Sweet smile. I remember her from some of Drake's games. She's one of the girls Drake told me not to worry about. To be honest, I never really did. Why would I? Drake knew I'd leave if he cheated. It was one of the only lines I drew in the sand, and it's one of the rules I think he actually respected. Now, here he is, trying to shove my nose in…whatever this is.

When Taliah realizes she's been picked, she turns to Drake and lifts her head to pay up. He swoops down, shoving his tongue into her mouth like an overzealous porn star. It's over the top and kind of gross, but I'm well aware this show isn't for anyone but me. Too bad Drake missed the mark.

Without even blinking, I watch—hell, I stare—at the makeout session in front of me, being sure Drake knows exactly how little this affects me. How little he means to me, and how far he dropped off my radar as soon as his fist connected with my face.

Or at least it's what I try to show.

The voice is still there, though. It's quieter than ever, but I can still hear it. Telling me I'm making things worse. That I screwed up. That this is my fault. Because even though Drake was an ass. Even though he hurt me. He was still my everything at one point, and here he is, rubbing my nose in the fact I'm the one who chose to leave.

After all we've been through. All we weathered together. I'm the one who walked away. And I don't regret it. I can't.

But it doesn't take the sting away from having a front-row seat to Drake kissing someone who isn't me when he swore I'd be the last girl to touch his lips. That we'd make it through anything. Through everything. Together.

As his lips move over hers, I realize how difficult it is to come to terms with the fact that the man I loved never really existed and the man in front of me wants to cut me deep. Whether it's physically or emotionally, his goal is still the same. To hurt me. And if he can't do it with his hands, he'll do it with his actions.

I deserve more, though, don't I?

Then again, aren't I doing the same thing?

I'm with Everett to prove I moved on. To prove I don't want anything to do with Drake anymore. To prove I'm nothing but a girl from his past, the same way he's nothing but a guy from mine. And I do want it. To leave Drake in the past. So, why isn't he letting me go?

The warm hand on my knee squeezes, snapping me out of my spiraling thoughts. Looking down, I take in the scarred knuckles. The light dusting of hair on his wrist disappearing underneath his shirt. The veins beneath his skin. The strength in his hands. How big they are. How easily they could hurt me. How easily *he* could hurt me.

I peek at Everett, surprised by the understanding in his cool blue eyes. As if he knows exactly what's going through my mind, and he doesn't think I'm crazy or insane or... wrong. It's so different from the look he gave me when we first met. When it was as clear as day how he labeled me as weak and stupid for dating someone like Drake in the first place, let alone running back to him after he hurt me. It's like he finally gets it. Maybe not all of it, and definitely not the little details that will haunt me for the rest of my life. But part of it. The big part. The part saying it's okay. *I'm* okay.

"All right, you two," Griffin jokes. "Either find a room or let someone else play."

Ripping his mouth from Taliah's, Drake turns to me and smirks. "My bad. Seems it's been a while since I kissed someone who actually knew what they were doing."

Asshole.

"Pretty sure we've been kissing different girls, then," Everett counters dryly. "Because Raine has the sweetest lips I've ever tasted."

"Well, since you're used to my sloppy seconds, why don't you give Taliah a go," Drake offers. "You can compare the two." He smirks at me again. "I know I have."

My lungs deflate, my abdomen plummets, and my cheeks flush. Coming from a stranger, it would be a ruthless comment. Coming from a guy I actually trusted and opened up to? It hits on a whole other level.

"Nah. Don't get me wrong. You're beautiful, Taliah," Everett points out as his thumb continues dragging along the slit in my jeans. Slowly. Methodically. "But I'll have to pass. Over the years, I've learned not to fuck up the good things in my life, and I think we can all agree Raine's pretty close to perfect."

"Sure, she is." Drake's eyes darken, and I have no doubt he's close to tumbling over the edge. To losing his shit in front of everyone. "Yeah, she's the real deal until she grabs her shit when she knows you're out of the house, then moves in with a prick and acts like a slut."

"Careful," Everett warns. His tone is sharp. Lethal. Until whatever minuscule speck of hospitality that had been present since Drake arrived shrivels up like an old raisin as Everett stares at my ex across from us. "You can say whatever you want about me, but you might want to remember where you are."

With a scoff, Drake looks around the crowded room. "And where am I?"

"You're in LAU territory. And yeah, you brought a few buddies as backup, but they can't help you here. Not if you run your mouth about my girl."

My pulse lurches as I register his words, no matter how fake they are. I'm not his girl. I'm not his anything.

Drake's friends shift forward, their muscles tense, bodies rigid. Like they can feel the same shift I can. The power dynamic. The commanding aura they're used to their friend sporting is being stripped right in front of them, only to be wielded by the one and only Everett Taylor.

"Is that a threat?" Drake challenges. I can't tell if he's surprised or intrigued, or freaking pissed, though none of the options make me feel better.

Scratching his jaw with his opposite hand since his other one is most definitely still branding me, Everett replies, "That's exactly what this is."

"Yeah, I heard it, too," Griffin chimes in beside him. He turns to the circle next to us and calls, "Mav, did you hear a threat?"

Mav glances over his shoulder at us and grins, proving he's been a hell of a lot more invested in what's going on in our circle than he let on. "It's exactly what I heard. How 'bout you, Reeves?"

Reeves appears out of nowhere and nods. "Yeah, Ev isn't usually known for subtlety, but if you need any of us to spell it out for you, let us know." His muscles bulge as he folds his arms and leans against the wall. "We'll be happy to oblige."

Slowly, Drake shifts his gaze from one LAU player to the next, realizing how surrounded he and his friends really are. When his attention lands on me, the acid in my stomach curdles. He rests his elbow on his bent knee the same way

Everett had earlier, though I doubt he even notices the similarity. Or maybe he does. Maybe he's all too aware of his surroundings and attempting to use them for his own gain. And what does he want? Well, I think we both know who the weak link is here and right now? He's daring me to crumble. To try to smooth things over and let him fly under the radar the same way he has for months.

Swallowing back my trepidation, I murmur, "I think it's time for you to leave, Drake."

If he's surprised, he doesn't show it. Instead, his eyes thin. "Careful, Raine."

It's a warning. One I once would've listened to. When I had to go home with him. When I had to deal with him. When I had to put up with his tantrums and his yelling sprees and his asshole comments and his hands. Whether they were punching a wall or grabbing me, or in the end, hitting me from out of nowhere, his hands were something I definitely had to put up with. I never realized how much I feared them. How rough he could be, even with little things. Like when he would touch me. Both in and out of the bedroom.

It's such a stark contrast to Everett's touch. Even now, with his thumb against my bare skin and the rest of his palm pressed against my upper thigh, there's a weight to it. A strength. But without the underlying possession I grew used to. Like he isn't touching me for him. He's touching me for *me.* And it's strange. Recognizing the difference in real time and with so many people witnessing it. And it doesn't matter if it isn't real. If this thing between Everett and me is all based on a lie. His touch? It *is* real. In this moment, I can feel it. The strength he's giving me. The unspoken reminder I'm not alone, but I am capable.

I. Am. Capable.

"I think I've walked on eggshells long enough, thanks." I grab Everett's hand and lace our fingers together, placing our entwined hands in my lap. "And in case it isn't clear, we're through. *Forever*. And there isn't anything in this world that will change my mind."

It's quiet now. The room. The entire house. Like everyone forgot about the game we're supposed to be playing. They're too invested in the drama unfolding right in front of them.

I have no idea if this is how it usually goes when Reeves helps girls. If they all feel the way I feel. Ashamed. Confused. Close to crumbling. Or maybe it's me. Maybe I'm the problem. The one with the messed up perception of everything including the man beside me and his words from seconds ago.

My girl.

Am I his girl? Obviously not, but after our kiss, I can't help but wonder if…maybe it could be real. This thing. Or maybe I'm just growing addicted to what comfort feels like since it's been so long since I felt it.

And maybe now isn't the time to let my thoughts spiral into what-ifs and what could be. Maybe now is the time to watch Drake walk away for the last time.

Please walk away.

Drake's movements are slow—calculated—as he pushes to his feet. His friends follow, but I don't miss the same rigidness in their muscles. It's like they're poised and ready to fight if their leader gives them an inkling to pounce.

Please don't turn this into a fight.

Please *don't turn this into a fight.*

Tension swirls in the air, leaving me breathless as I glance at Everett. I can tell he wants to jump to his feet. Can see how much he doesn't like being at a disadvantage, and Drake moving toward us while we sit our asses on the ground definitely puts us at a disadvantage. But even though Everett doesn't move, I don't miss the way Reeves watches Drake from right outside the circle. Waiting. Ready. I have no doubt he's the reason Everett's staying put, even if I can feel his restraint radiating off him.

Yeah. Everett wants to hit Drake as much as I know Drake wants to punch him, which is the last thing I need. I know Reeves mentioned this could be part of the process, but now that it's potentially here, I don't want it. I don't want any of this. I'm here with Everett. Everyone just stood up for me. It has to count for something, doesn't it? It has to be enough.

I squeeze Everett's hand gently, silently begging him to let it go. To let Drake go. He doesn't look at me, only continues staring at Drake, but I don't miss the lock of his jaw. The way his muscles are taut and hard. For a fight. For a full-on brawl.

Please, I silently beg.

Teeth grinding, Drake moves toward me through the circle. When his boot hits the edge of the bottle, it rolls to the side. Griffin grabs the long neck, testing its weight while staring up at Drake. Just as on edge. Just as ready.

I lift my head, waiting, refusing to cower as Drake stands over me.

"You're done, Raine?" he asks.

I nod.

"We'll see." Then he turns and leaves, taking his friends and what's left of my oxygen with him until they disappear through the front door. My shoulders slump forward.

Ho-ly. Shit.

The party is silent. It's like in the movies when you swear you're in a vacuum, and everyone's looking at you. Watching you. Studying you. Like you belong in a zoo or beneath a microscope. It's not long until a loud clap reverberates through the air.

Reeves slaps his hands together, demanding everyone's attention. He cups his hands over his mouth and booms, "All right, I'm over this game. Let's meet in the family room for musical chairs!"

Chaos follows as everyone but me stands. Some head to the family room as instructed, while others head to the basement, carrying up folding chairs and placing them along the edge of the family room. Like a well-oiled machine, everyone moves around the space, preparing for the game change as I watch from the side of the room in awe when a hand appears in front of me.

I look up, taking Everett's offered hand.

As he pulls me to my feet, he asks, "Do you want to play, or do you want to call it a night?"

If I call it a night, Drake wins. He'll have ruined my night. If I stay, will I even be able to focus on the game? At this point, I have no idea.

"Raine?" Everett prods. He moves in front of me, blocking out the entire world around us as I look up at him. "I'm proud of you."

I pull back, surprised. "What did you say?"

"I said, I'm proud of you."

"Why?"

"For standing up to him." He lets my hand go and squeezes the back of his neck. "And, uh, you're not a...you're not a slut," he forces out. "It was a dick thing for him to say."

I laugh dryly and fold my arms. "Thanks."

"Don't let him get to you."

"Who said I let him get to me?" I challenge.

His gaze bounces around my face, making me feel vulnerable and more seen than I'd like to admit.

"I can see it," he explains.

"Yeah, well." I lift a shoulder. "Cutting me down is kind of his M.O. when he's frustrated, so..."

"Doesn't make it okay."

"You're right. It doesn't," I reply. "But, it's kind of par for the course with him, so don't worry about it."

"I'm sorry I was such a dick when we first met," he adds.

My brows bunch. "What?"

"I was a dick. I called you stupid for dating him, and"—he looks at the ground as his tongue runs along his upper teeth—"it was a fucked-up thing to say." Meeting my gaze again, he adds, "You aren't stupid, all right? Honestly, you're one of the strongest people I've met, which considering my friends and family, is saying something."

My breath hitches as his words wash over me, but I force my lungs to exhale and peek up at him again. "Well, since we're complimenting each other, I want to thank you, too."

"For what?"

"For not letting him get under your skin, either. For standing up for me without taking the bait and hitting him. I know, in a weird way, it was kind of a big possibility you'd fight with him, but the fact that you didn't means a lot to me." I tuck my hair behind my ear. "Thank you for being more levelheaded than Drake ever was."

His nod is slow as if he can't decide whether or not he agrees with me, and I hate it. The question in his eyes. The slight dip of his brows. The hesitation. I get it. He can be controlling. He can be bossy sometimes and a little over the top. But for him to wonder if he's anything like Drake Haitt? For him to even think he's in the same league?

I open my mouth to say something. Anything. But before I can, he presses his hand to my back and guides me to the family room. "Come on."

"Ev—"

"Want to watch a movie or something?"

"A movie?"

"Yeah. I think we've had enough fun for one night, don't you?"

I nod and let him lead me to the room he shares with Griffin.

Yeah. Whatever just happened in there? I think I've had enough of it, too.

CHAPTER TWENTY-THREE

It's been a weird week. After the last game night, things between Raine and me are different, but…not. And it sucks because I can't figure out if I'm literally hallucinating or if the only thing that's changed is my perception of Raine Anders.

I wasn't kidding when I apologized for being a dick to her when we first met. I assumed so many things, made her feel like shit, and for what? For assumptions so far off base, they're now laughable? It still doesn't change anything. Doesn't change my obligation to her or her obligation to follow through with this bullshit lie on the off-chance Drake is only lying low after our run-in.

Fuck, I don't even know anymore.

My playing is shit, too. I've been so caught up in my own head I haven't really shown up on the ice. I tried keeping it in check, but anytime I'm away from Raine, the possibilities of Drake finding her and hurting her rise to the surface, making me a fucking wreck. Add in tonight's date with whatever-her-name-is, and I'm ready to tap out and surrender.

The fact Raine and I have barely said two words to each

other today doesn't help, either. She knows I'm going out with someone else tonight, even though we haven't talked about it. I don't know why I feel guilty. Why I feel like I'm betraying her when it couldn't be further from the truth.

So why do I feel like shit?

I'm even missing a game for this. Reeves seriously owes me.

As I roughly tug at the tie around my neck, a shadow catches my attention from the bathroom doorway. I look over my shoulder, but she's gone.

"Raine," I call out to her.

Raine reappears at the entrance, giving me a shy smile. "Yes?"

"I have a…thing tonight."

"The wedding, right?"

Fuck, what I wouldn't give to be able to read her mind. To hear her thoughts. To have a glimpse of what's going on behind those forest-green eyes. Instead, all I see is restraint. Indifference. Unease.

I nod. "Yeah, the wedding."

"Yup, I remember."

She walks away again, but I repeat, "Raine."

Stepping back into view, she folds her arms and leans against the doorjamb, giving me her full attention. "Yes?"

"You're staying in, right?" I ask as I start to redo the knot around my neck, which feels a hell of a lot like a noose.

Her gaze stays locked on the silk in my hands. "Not sure where else I would go."

"I'll probably be late," I add, tugging at the fabric again so I can start over.

Stepping toward me, she removes the tie from my hands. "Here." Her movements are slow but methodical as she wraps one end around the other, then slips the end into the gap, creating the perfect knot. Her hands find my chest, smoothing the tie down. "There."

When she starts to move away, I grab her wrist to hold her in place. "Where'd you learn to tie a tie?"

She swallows and tears her attention from my face, staring at my hand wrapped around her wrist instead. "Drake's dad wasn't around much. He would get frustrated anytime he had to wear a suit or whatever, so I learned how to tie one for him."

I nod slowly and let her go. "Well. Thanks."

"No problem." Her tongue darts between her lips, and she clears her throat as she steps back. "Are you...excited for tonight?"

I scoff. "Not the word I would use to describe how I feel about this."

"And what word would you use?"

"Obligated." It slips out of me before I can stop it, and her eyes widen. She recovers quickly, though. Part of me wonders if it's a defense mechanism. If it's something she's had since childhood or only a learned behavior after spending time with Drake.

"I'd say you should take it as a compliment," she replies. "Being so reliable, Reeves doesn't even have to question whether or not you'll bail him out when he asks."

She's right. Reeves and I might not always see eye to eye on shit, but I'd do anything for him. For any of my family. My friends.

"I have a feeling you do it a lot," she notes. "Bail people out."

"I don't mind," I murmur.

"That's because you're a good guy, Everett. I'm sure your date for the evening will think the same thing."

When she starts to turn away, I stop her. Again. It's like I can't help it. "Raine..."

"Have a good night, and don't worry," she adds. "I'll be here."

Then she walks away, and I stand here doing nothing but watching her leave.

A few minutes later, I enter the family room. She isn't there. Not that I thought she would be. Still. I feel like shit. And even though I try convincing myself it's because I'm missing a game for this, I'm not an idiot. I know the real reason, and she's hiding in her room, unwilling to watch me leave the house under the pretense of going on a date with someone who isn't her.

But if this isn't real, why does she care?

And why do I?

CHAPTER TWENTY-FOUR

RAINE

Everett left an hour ago for his date. I keep telling myself the only reason I'm bothered is because if Drake finds out, it'll ruin everything. If only I believed it.

Ev likely won't be home until after midnight, and neither will the rest of the guys since there's an away game today, leaving me with nothing to do but twiddle my thumbs.

With popcorn popped, I prop my bare feet on the coffee table when my phone buzzes. Again. Finley created a group chat with me and the rest of her friends. I didn't think it would have much traction, but ever since we hung out at the cabin, it's basically been buzzing nonstop. Especially today.

FINLEY

Aaaalright, ladies. Drew pissed me off again,
so I want a girls' night out with zero men.
What do you think?

OPHELIA

I think there isn't a chance in hell Everett lets
Raine out of his sight.

DYLAN

Yeah, I've been meaning to thank you for getting Everett off my back, Raine. I used to be his pet project until Reeves came around, but it seems he's right back to his bossy ways. How are things with you two, anyway? I heard your kiss at the party last week was STEAMY.

Usually, I'm a lurker in these kinds of group chats, but when I'm called out like this, I'm left with no choice. Wiping my fingers on a napkin, I pick my phone up but hesitate, unsure what to say because honestly? Well, for starters, the kiss has been haunting me ever since it happened, and so has his absence ever since. Maybe not literally. We do still live in the same house, after all. But in every other way, he's been... distant. We've barely even crossed paths.

I'm not sure if it's because I offended him, or if he thinks our arrangement will end soon, and getting to know me isn't worth the effort anymore, or...I don't even know.

He's probably right about our arrangement coming to an end, though. I haven't heard a thing from Drake, and whatever spies Reeves has informed him of the same thing. Drake's lying low. He might've even thrown in the towel despite his last words to me at game night.

My phone buzzes with another message.

DYLAN

Fine, fine, you can tell me about the steamy kiss later. I also heard about the wedding tonight. How are you holding up?

OPHELIA

Wait, what wedding?

DYLAN

Everett's covering another job for Ollie.

OPHELIA

Ouch.

Yeah.

DYLAN

If it helps, Ev called Ollie last night and tried
to get out of it. Again. So, don't stress,
Raine. You're still definitely the only girl for
Everett.

My heart stalls in my chest before I type my response.

ME

I'm not Everett's girl, remember? I'm his
FAKE girl. There's a difference.

FINLEY

For now ;) But back to the question at hand.
SeaBird? Yay or nay? Please, please, please.
I need a girls' night.

OPHELIA

As long as I have time to go home and
shower after my game, I'm in.

Ophelia is the goalie for LAU's Lady Hawks. I check the
time on my phone, confirming their game is supposed to
start in less than an hour as my phone chimes with another
notification.

DYLAN

I'm in too.

ME

I think I have to pass.

FINLEY

Why?!

ME

Everett's at the wedding, so…

FINLEY

So? You'll be with us. He'll be fine.

DYLAN

I think you're severely underestimating your brother.

OPHELIA

I agree with Dylan. Maybe if Maverick comes?

FINLEY

No deal. Don't get me wrong. I adore Maverick, but I also kind of want to stab anyone with a penis at the moment, so if you have any desire to bear children with the man, it's probably a good idea for him to stay out of this one.

Despite not having a penis, I cross my legs and grimace because I really wouldn't put it past Finley, especially if Drew has already fanned the flame of masculine hate. And honestly, it's kind of sad. The image I have of Finley's boyfriend despite never meeting him.

ME

What'd Drew do this time?

OPHELIA

Ha! Raine's only been around for a little while, and even SHE's starting to see a pattern here. What does it say about Drew, Fin?

FINLEY

It says you guys are all buttheads.

PS- I changed my mind. I'm going to the
source and am talking to my brother. Raine,
be ready by 9 pm. I'll come grab you.

My eyes pop as I read her message, and I sit up a little straighter, wiping the popcorn crumbs from my tank top.

ME

You don't have to. It's like an hour out of
the way.

FINLEY

More time for me to plot my boyfriend's
death.

OPHELIA

Okay, I gotta go. Jaxon's gonna kill me if he
sees me texting before the game. See you
later!

ME

Who's Jaxon?

DYLAN

Jaxon is my oldest brother. He's also the
coach for the Lady Hawks.

ME

Oh yeah! The guy looking for Rory. I
remember now. It's way fun that he coaches
the Lady Hawks.

DYLAN

Yeah, he likes it, even though it kills my dad
sometimes since Jax was basically a hockey
god but "retired" so he could coach the girls'
team. Anywho, I should probably go too.
Finley, want to carpool?

OPHELIA

We live together, so I'm gonna go with...duh
;) See you guys!

ME

See ya.

~

I DIDN'T KNOW WHAT TO WEAR, BUT I SETTLED ON RIPPED jeans and a cropped sweater that exposes one shoulder. It must work because Finley whistles when I open the front door, locking it behind me. The weather is cooler tonight, and I can't help but wonder if it will snow. Then again, maybe it's wishful thinking. I love the snow. The way it muffles the noise around you. The way you can taste it. The way it burns your lungs if you breathe in too deep. It's beautiful. Peaceful. And makes you want to snuggle under a blanket. Seriously, what's not to love?

Putting aside my wistfulness, I head toward Finley's car when my phone rings. I pull it out to see Everett's calling.

"Hello?" I answer.

"Hey."

Silence follows, and my brows tug. A million questions race through my mind. How's the wedding? Is his date pretty? Is her family nice? Does he regret going? Did he kiss her the same way he kissed me? The last thought brings a sharp pain to my chest, but I breathe through the strange ache.

"Are you…already finished with the wedding?" I ask.

"Nah. Needed to step away for a minute."

"Oh." I stop moving, unsure what else to say. A minute? Why does he need a minute? And why is he calling me during said minute?

"What are you doing?" he prods.

"Nothing really." Forcing my feet to move, I close the last bit of distance between me and the car, open the back door, and climb inside. "Finley just picked me up, and—"

"Where are you going?"

"Shit, are you talking to my brother?" Finley interrupts from the front seat.

I glance at her, then close my eyes, hoping to block her out. "Uh, we're going—"

"You shouldn't be going anywhere," he reminds me. It isn't bossy or rude. It's...confused.

Why is he confused?

My eyes pop open, and I stare at Finley. "Did you not call Ev?"

She grimaces. "I knew he'd say no."

"Knew I'd say no to what?" Everett asks through the speaker. "Finley—"

"Nothing!" she calls sweetly, then mouths, "Hang up the phone."

"Raine," Everett warns.

Plugging my opposite ear, I explain, "Finley invited me out for a girls' night."

"You can't go out."

"Why not?"

"What about Drake?"

"What about him?" I ask. "He hasn't even reached out since the game night."

"It's a bad idea," he pushes.

"Seriously?" I laugh. "Don't get me wrong. Drake's an abusive ass, but it's not like he'll toss me over his shoulder and drag me away if I run into him."

"Stay. Home."

"Everett, I mean this in the nicest way possible, but I didn't ask for your help only for you to keep me prisoner," I point out. "You asked if I had plans tonight, and...now I do. Not a big deal."

Something muffled echoes through the speaker, and Everett calls out, "Be right there, babe!"

Babe.

He's talking to her.

Why do I care that he's talking to her? Especially when I'm well aware his relationship with her is fake. Then again, his relationship with *me* is fake, too, which I think we can both agree is for the best. So, what the hell is my problem?

"Raine? You still there?" Everett adds into his cell. He sounds…tense. Like a small part of him already knows what I'm thinking even if neither of us would ever admit it.

"I gotta go."

"Raine—"

"Finley's already offered to drive me home after, so I'll see you at the cabin. Have a great night." I hang the phone up and open my eyes, finding Dylan and Finley staring at me, their jaws practically unhinged.

"Did you just hang up on Everett?" Dylan asks from the passenger seat.

Did I just hang up on Everett?

Yup. Yup, I most definitely did. He's going to be furious.

"I, uh…"

They both laugh, turning back in their seats.

As Finley reverses out of the driveway, she points out, "Well this just got even more interesting."

Ophelia's already waiting at the bar when we head inside SeaBird. She has a fruity drink in front of her, along with two more matching beverages and what looks like a Diet Coke beside them.

When she sees us, she stands from her barstool and waves. "Hey!" Ophelia passes hugs around like they're confetti, then offers each of us a drink. "PS—Maverick says he should get a free shot to Drew's balls since we're ditching him tonight."

Finley laughs. "Nope. Drew's balls are mine to squeeze or caress, thank you very much."

"Caress?" Dylan snorts. "Ew."

"Hey, no kink-shaming," Ophelia quips. "Whatever floats your boat. Right, Fin?"

"Mm-hmm," Finley hums as she takes a long sip of her Diet Coke. "Though there will be no caressing anytime soon, I'll tell you that much."

"Are you gonna tell us what happened?" I prod.

Rolling her eyes, Finley decides, "Not until everyone's had at least three drinks so they don't judge me too harshly."

"You sure you'll even remember the story at that point?" I tease.

She smiles around her straw. "I don't drink, so I think I'll be fine."

My brows jump. "You don't drink?"

"Nope."

"Good for you."

"Meh. Don't be too impressed," she teases, heading toward one of the open booths as we trail behind. Once we're all settled, she adds, "I have epilepsy, and alcohol can be a trigger, so...yay me."

Tilting my head, I look at her again with newfound curiosity. The way she threw it out there so casually. Like we're talking about the weather instead of a pretty serious neurological disease. I've never known anyone with epilepsy. To be honest, I don't know much about it, in general. Seizures and...sensitivity to light? Yeah. That's about as deep as my knowledge goes.

"You have epilepsy?" I ask.

With a syrupy sweet smile, she says, "Yup."

"I had no idea."

"Most people don't." She shrugs and takes another sip of her Diet Coke. "Usually, it's not a big deal, but if I decide to drop to the ground and start convulsing, maybe call my brother."

A surprised laugh slips out of me, and I shake my head, blown away by the girl's nonchalance over the whole thing. "I'll keep it in mind."

She grins back at me. "You're a peach."

Looking at Ophelia, I hook my thumb toward her best friend and ask, "Does she always talk this candidly?"

Ophelia leans closer and drops her voice as if we're discussing conspiracy theories. "You have no idea. Speaking of which,"—she clears her throat and palms her glass, giving Finley a pointed look—"I'm ready for all the reasons why we hate Drew."

"Only I'm allowed to hate Drew," Finley defends. "Because on the off-chance I don't rip his balls off and, instead, decide to marry him, I still need you ladies to be my bridesmaids one day."

"We'll be your bridesmaids regardless of who the groom is," Dylan chimes in. "Now, what happened?"

Digging through her purse, she pulls out her phone, unlocks the screen, then slaps it on the table. "A girl tagged him on Instagram."

I lean closer to look at the photo. They're at a bar. Her arms are looped around his neck, and his hand is on her waist as they smile at the camera. It isn't completely incriminating, but it's enough to make a person pause, especially a girlfriend who's across the country from her boyfriend starring in said picture. And if I had to guess? That's the problem.

Ophelia and Dylan share a grimace and push the phone back to Finley.

"Did you ask him about it?" Dylan questions.

"Yes," Finley huffs. "He swears they're only friends, and maybe they are, but…"

"But something feels wrong," I finish for her.

Swirling the straw in her drink, she nods slowly. "Yeah. And I don't know if it's in my head or if it's real, but when I asked if he wants to take a break, he got pissed at me for even mentioning it, promising he loves me and only me, and he's been nothing but loyal the entire time we've been together, and it would be nice if I could show some trust instead of freaking out over nothing."

Ophelia gasps. "He said all that?"

"Yup." She pops the 'p' at the end and leans in for another long drink of Diet Coke.

Lia's lips bunch as she watches her best friend from across the table while I ask, "Do you believe him?"

"I *want* to believe him. I mean, he's been busy, but I've been busy, too, you know? I'm not stupid. I know a relationship goes both ways." She hesitates as if she's replaying her conversation with Drew for the hundredth time. After a minute, her face scrunches. "God, and then he accused me of having feelings for Griffin. Can you believe it? He said if I can post pictures of me and Griff, he should be able to post pictures of him and his"—she lifts her hands and does air quotes—"*friend* without feeling like I'll jump down his throat." Her eyes go hazy, and she sucks her lips between her teeth. "And then, I'm like…yeah. He's got a point, you know? I hate when he gets all weird and jealous whenever I talk about me and Griff, but we've been friends for forever, so it's not like I can just…cut him out."

"Is Drew asking you to cut my brother out of your life?" Dylan demands.

Finley's expression falls, and she twirls the straw in her glass again, unable to meet Dylan's gaze, and I swear I can feel the shift in the air. The heaviness of it. The resignation. "Maybe."

"You can't do that," Dylan pushes. "You guys live together, he's like family—"

"I know." Finley sighs, picks her phone up again, and checks the screen. "And I also know I'm done thinking about all of this. Someone take my phone. Actually, someone take all the phones."

She pushes her cell into the center of the table, and I follow suit, gladly adding it to the pile in hopes of keeping myself from checking to see if he messaged me. Everett. I shouldn't care. But the radio silence? It's messing with my head.

With a smile, Ophelia opens her clutch, confirms each phone is on silent, slips them inside, and closes it up. "There."

"Thank you." Finley smiles at her friend. "Now…what do you say we dance?"

CHAPTER TWENTY-FIVE

EVERETT

The girl deserves a damn spanking.

As soon as the thought rises, I tamp it down, ignoring the guilt in my chest. It doesn't make me like him. I know I'd never hurt her, and thanks to our conversation after the first time I met her dad, I know Raine knows it, too. Even so, it doesn't erase the similarities between me and Drake. The way we can be controlling. Stubborn. Unwilling to bend.

Could I be like him? Fuck, no. But am I too controlling sometimes? Am I fucked up for wanting to smack Raine's ass for hanging up on me? Will she think I'm like him if I call her?

I set my phone back in the cupholder and scrub my hand over my face. After Raine hung up on me, I went back inside the reception hall and faked a stomach bug. Shae and the rest of her family bought it with ease. Shae walked me to my car and thanked me for coming. For saving her from a night of asshole comments.

After confirming I'd paid Reeves' debt for borrowing

Shae's puppy, I gave her a hug in case anyone was watching from the windows, then got the hell out of there.

Anxious, I pick my phone up again and dial Griffin.

"Hello?" he answers.

"You back at the rink yet?" I grunt. The team rode the bus to an away game, but it ended an hour ago, so they should be close.

"The game was good," he replies. "We won. Thanks for asking."

"Answer the question," I bark.

"We're about to pull in. Why?"

"Have you seen the girls?" I ask. "Heard from them or anything?"

"All right, now you're freaking me out. What's going on?"

"Finley picked Raine up so they could hang out."

"So?"

"So, you really think it's a good idea for Raine to be away from the cabin without protection?"

"You worried about Drake?" he prods.

I'm worried about a lot of things. Like Drake having some magic crystal ball telling him I'm not around tonight and Raine's free game to fuck with. Like I hurt her feelings by being Shae's plus-one tonight. Like other guys looking at her when I'm not sure where we stand. Ever since our kiss during game night, things have been…different. And I don't know if it's only me or if she's feeling the same thing. I don't know if I'm imagining her lingering looks or if they're real. But I do know the idea of Raine being out of the house without me by her side when I don't know where we stand leaves me feeling like razor blades are skating across my skin, and I don't like it.

"Where are they?" Griff prods.

"They didn't tell me." I frown, opening the tracking app

from when I picked Raine up on the side of the road. My mouth lifts. "They're at SeaBird."

"Well. How far are you?"

"Ten minutes," I answer.

"We're pulling into the rink right now. I'll meet you there."

Perfect.

～

THE TEN-MINUTE DRIVE FEELS LIKE TWICE AS LONG WHEN I finally arrive at SeaBird. It's crowded, so I drive around back, looking for a spot and Griffin's car since I have no doubt he let Finley borrow it. Okay, let her borrow it is probably a stretch. My sister has had my best friend wrapped around her finger since they were kids. She probably stole it. *Brat.*

Pulling into an empty spot, I leave my jacket in the back, too amped up on adrenaline to feel the drop in temperature. There's a storm coming. I can feel it.

The quiet creak of metal sounds from my left, where I find Griffin and Reeves climbing out of Reeves' car.

"Mav's already inside," Griffin calls. "He's been keeping an eye on them since they told him they were having a girls' night."

Sneaky bastard.

Relief swells through me, and I nod. "Glad someone could be here."

"Yeah, guess there are pros and cons to the guy having a heart transplant and retiring from the team," Reeves jokes.

With the guys flanking my sides, we nod at the bouncer, then scan the open bar for the girls and, even though I don't want to admit it, Drake. When I don't see him, my muscles relax, and I continue searching for my little sister, Lia, Dylan, and Raine.

My phone buzzes in my pocket.

MAVERICK

They're on the dance floor. Come to the
south side. I have a booth where we can
watch the girls without them noticing.

I look up from my cell and survey the dance floor. Sure enough, there they are. Dylan. Finley. Ophelia. And Raine. They're dancing to the song blasting from the speakers. Raine's shouting the lyrics along with the rest of the girls, each of them belting out the words about a scorned woman or some shit. She looks happy, though. Carefree. The constant divot between her brows is softer than usual, and when she holds her stomach and bends over laughing at whatever Finley said, I can't help but feel…lighter, maybe. My mouth lifts, and my chest swells. The girl's fuckin' beautiful. I've always known it, but this? This is something else. I like this side of her. And honestly, I'm almost jealous I'm not the one who made her this way. Who helped her let go and let loose. It would probably help if I talked to her more. If I opened up. If I let her open up.

"Dylan's wasted," Reeves notes, but there's amusement in his voice as he takes a step toward the dance floor. "Come on."

I lift my arm to stop him. "Wait."

Hesitating, Reeves looks over his shoulder at me. "What?"

"They don't know we're here yet."

He quirks a brow. "Okay?"

"They wanted a girls' night," I remind him. "Let's give them one. For now."

"All right," Griffin agrees. "But I need a drink if I'm gonna survive their shitty singing." He slaps me on the shoulder, steps around me, and heads for the bar as I fill Reeves in on Maverick's text. Afterward, he follows me to the booth.

Mav's right. From here, I can still keep the girls in our line of sight without raining on their parade.

A few minutes later, Griffin brings three beers to the table, setting one in front of each of us. They spend the next thirty minutes filling Mav and me in on the game. It kind of sucks. Growing up with him and his brother on the ice, only to have both of them ripped away in different ways. I guess it's how life is, though. Unpredictable. Unexpected. We're all just making shit up as we go. If you don't learn how to pivot, you're fucked.

When Dylan stumbles a bit on the dance floor a little while later, I glance at Reeves, curious as to what he's gonna do. The girl's clumsy when she's sober. Add some alcohol, and she's pretty much a walking disaster.

When we were little, we were playing hockey together, and I got pissed, so I hit the puck as hard as I could. It kicked up into the air and knocked Dylan in the head. She crumpled like a piece of paper. I still remember it. Seeing her fall. How the life left her eyes before they rolled back in her head. The beeping machines. The heavy silence in the hospital room.

Fuck, if I close my eyes, I can still see it. Still *feel* it. The weight of that moment and the way I irrevocably changed a little girl's life all because I couldn't control my temper.

For years, I carried the burden. The knowledge she'll never be the same person. The guilt over the fact it was me who took it from her. Her future. It threatened to swallow me whole until I was convinced Dylan was nothing but a porcelain doll who could break at any second. And if she did, it would only confirm it was all my fault. My problem. My fuck up.

Then Dylan met Reeves. And even though I wanted him to stay as far away from her as possible, convinced he'd only shatter her further, he refused to play by my rules, giving me two middle fingers as he pursued my little sister's best friend without a single apology for overstepping his bounds.

But here's the strange part. The part I still don't fully understand. As I watch Dylan teeter on the dance floor like an uncoordinated giraffe, the urge to catch her is gone. Because it isn't my job anymore. It's Reeves'. My eyes fall to the brunette bombshell beside her. Red lips. Smokey eyes. Long-sleeved crop top falling off one shoulder, giving me a glimpse of her creamy skin and low-slung jeans. The girl's nothing short of perfect.

And apparently, I'm not the only one who notices.

Like a swarm, guys start approaching, but none of them have a chance to get close because Finley bites their heads off and drags her friends to a different spot on the dance floor. Griffin chuckles as he watches her go head-to-head with a particularly massive dude I've never seen until now. When he reaches for Finley's hips, Griffin is on his feet, and so am I. The guys join us as we stride toward them, our drinks forgotten.

Once we're within earshot, Reeves calls, "Hey, Pickles."

If Dylan's surprised to see her boyfriend here, she doesn't show it. With a smile, she returns, "Hey, Ollie. Perfect timing." Dylan turns to the guys bugging them. "Have you met my boyfriend, Ollie?"

"Nah, I don't think we've had the pleasure yet," Reeves states casually as he moves in even closer.

"Lucky man," one of the strangers offers to Reeves while perusing the rest of the girls as if he can have his pick.

When his gaze lands on Ophelia, Mav steps around Reeves, and Lia darts toward him like a bunny on crack, wrapping her legs around his waist and kissing him. "You've been here the whole time, haven't you?"

"Looks like I've been caught red-handed," he confirms.

"I *knew* it was your bike in the parking lot!"

Mav chuckles dryly. "You really thought I'd let you come here without me?"

"Mm-hmm."

She kisses him again as the stranger turns back to Raine. "Now, where were we?"

"You were just leaving," she reminds him sweetly.

"You sure?" he challenges.

Her eyes lock with mine over her shoulder. "Pretty positive, actually. Right, *babe*?"

I step closer, hook my fingers through the belt loop on her pants, and tug her into me, bringing her back to my chest. "I think it's exactly what he was doing."

His eyes drift over me as if he's sizing me up. Lifting his hands in surrender, he steps back.

"Another one bites the dust," the last dumbass taunts. He's a behemoth but doesn't give Finley an inch. "And then there was one."

"Wrong again, buddy," Griffin says. "This one's taken, too."

Finley stares at Griff, but instead of playing into it like I expect, she shifts back a few inches, leaving space between both the stranger and Griffin. "Griffin's right. My boyfriend might not be at LAU, but he *would* care if he knew anyone here was trying to dance with me."

"It's only a dance," the stranger argues.

"Then I'm sure you can find a different partner." She tucks her hair behind her ear. "Now, if you'll excuse me." Her footsteps are quick as she rushes off toward what I assume is her table. Griffin frowns but follows her, leaving the stunned stranger in silence.

Raine twists in my arms and faces me. "Is this a habit of yours, *babe*?"

"What?"

"Saving the day, even when I don't ask for it?"

"Depends. Are you pissed I used your location to track you down?"

Her forest-green eyes flash with understanding. "Ah, so that's how you did it."

"*Babe*," I finish for her, mimicking her syrupy sweet tone.

Her lips purse, but she stays quiet. I guide her hands around my neck, then hold her hips and sway us to the music. "I'm sorry."

She pulls back, her brows bunching, but she forces her tense body to soften as she peeks up at me. "For what?"

"For helping Reeves out tonight," I admit. "And for using your location to track you down."

"I'm not mad about it."

"Which one?" I ask. "The first or second apology?"

"Does it matter?"

"To me, it does." I bring her a little closer. "I'm also sorry I called her babe, and you had to hear it."

She drops her chin lower, choosing to stare at the top button of my dress shirt instead of my eyes. "It's not a big deal, but...you've never called me *babe*, and we've been fake dating longer," she admits dryly. "I guess it took me by surprise. How easily you fell into the role with her."

"Stormie." I bend closer and brush my lips against the sensitive patch of skin beneath her ear, causing her breath to hitch. But she doesn't push me away. Doesn't let me go. "You deserve more than a generic nickname. You're more than *babe*. You're Stormie. A pain in my ass, but the good kind."

"There's a good kind of pain in the ass?" she challenges.

I tug her even closer, keeping us pressed together as I run my lips against her skin for one more taste when her cool breath hits the side of my face.

She turns toward me, lining our lips up, though I doubt she realizes it. "What are you—"

"I'm your boyfriend, remember? Gotta play the part."

"Is that what you're doing?" Her tongue darts out between her lips. "Playing a part?"

My brows dip as my attention bounces from one forest iris to the next, though I have no fucking clue what I'm searching for. "You tell me."

"Honestly, I'm not sure," she admits, though the words are so hushed, I don't know if they're for her or for me.

"Let's say we're both still playing the part," I offer. "What happens next?"

"If I was playing a part, I'd tell you to kiss me."

"Oh?"

"Mm-hmm." She tugs me closer, making me bend until her lips brush the shell of my ear. "I'm not the only one who can see them watching."

Them. The guys who bothered her a few minutes ago. Fuck, I almost forgot they were even here. I glance to my left, finding them hanging out at the bar. They aren't even looking this way, too caught up in flirting with the bartender, though I'm not sure it even matters.

Bringing my attention back to the girl in my arms, I push, "And what if you weren't playing a part?"

"Depends."

"On what?"

"On you." She leans back, putting more space between us as we continue dancing. "I'm glad the date went well, at least."

"It wasn't a date."

"And this isn't real, right?" she counters, lowering her hands from around my neck. "You looked nice tonight. I didn't tell you that when you left."

"Thanks," I rasp. "You look nice tonight, too."

She laughs quietly and looks down at her outfit. "Thanks." Peeking up at me again, she adds, "I, uh, I think we should call it a night, don't you?"

"Depends," I reply. "Why?"

"Maybe we could both use a breather." She reaches for my fingers and tangles them with hers. "For the crowd. Come on."

We say our goodbyes and head outside. It's snowing now. The flakes float down from the dark sky in small flurries, and Raine folds her arms. When we reach the car, I open the door, help her inside, and grab my tux jacket from the back seat, offering it to her.

Her brows dip, but she takes it and slides her arms through the holes, letting the back of my jacket cover her front.

"Seat belt," I remind her.

"Oh." She reaches for the strap, but I beat her to it, sliding it across her chest and leaning closer as I buckle it in place. When I realize I'm leaning over her, my body freezes, and my eyes fall to her lips.

"They could still be watching," she whispers.

My mouth lifts. "You think?"

"Mm-hmm." A puff of misty air leaves her lips and swirls between us. "You should kiss me. Just in case."

"You still worried about keeping up appearances?"

"I mean, we wouldn't want anyone to catch us in a lie, right?" she argues.

I lift her chin, moving in slowly until I press my lips to hers. The kiss is soft and unhurried. If I don't overthink it, I can say it's because I had half a beer when we both know it has nothing to do with the alcohol and everything to do with the tension that's been building around us for too long with nowhere to go.

But now I've tasted her without people watching. Without an act or a reason to perform for anyone but us. I'm afraid I won't be able to pull away, won't be able to stop this. Her tongue dips into my mouth, and she tilts her head more, letting me in in more ways than one until my head spins.

Forcing myself to end the kiss, I shove my hair away from my face. "We should get going. This'll be a blizzard by the time we reach the mountains."

With a slow nod, she sucks her bottom lip into her mouth. "Sure thing."

CHAPTER TWENTY-SIX

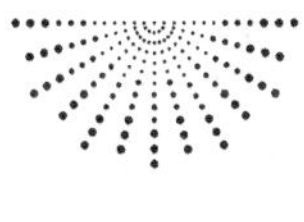

RAINE

Everett wasn't kidding. The snow is like a thick blanket falling down on us as we head inside the cabin. My body feels like it's frozen. From the top of my head to the tips of my toes in my boots. Pushing the front door open, Everett lets me inside. Snow clings to my hair as I drag it over my shoulder and shrug out of his coat, leaving a chill along my limbs I'm afraid will never go away.

"I'm gonna shower," I announce, hoping the hot water will defrost my already chilled bones.

"I'll start a fire," he replies.

"Perfect."

I undress quickly and step into the shower. As I lather my hair with shampoo, I let the heat from the water warm me when, all of a sudden, I'm blanketed in darkness. My lungs stall, and I look through the glass toward the closed bathroom door, but all I'm greeted with is pitch black. I blink a few times, willing my eyes to adjust to the lack of light quickly as I call out, "Everett?"

Silence.

My heart stutters in my chest, and I wipe the fog clinging to the glass with my hand. "Ev?"

A loud knock against the closed door causes me to jump.

"Raine?" Everett's muffled voice echoes through the wooden barrier. "Raine, the storm must have knocked the power out. You okay?"

I nod on reflex, despite knowing Everett can't see me. I clear my throat, answering, "Uh, yeah. Yeah. I'm okay." I let out a soft laugh. "I can't see a thing."

"Yeah it's pitch black out here, too. Do you have your phone?"

"It's on the charger in my room."

"Shit." He hesitates. "I promise I'm not looking, all right?" The hinges squeak quietly as he opens the door. Barely any light spills in from the fire in the main room, but Everett's eyes are squeezed shut nonetheless as his phone practically blinds me with its flashlight.

Partially covering my eyes, I peek through my fingers, and ask, "Don't you need the light?"

"I'll be fine."

He starts to set his cell on the counter, but I call out, "Stay where you are, but give me two seconds, okay?"

His movement stops. He drops his head back, looking toward the ceiling while keeping his eyes closed as I hurry to rinse the rest of the conditioner from my hair. Once I finish, I turn the water off and reach for the towel on the hook outside the shower. As I wrap it around my body, I realize how strained the muscles in Everett's jaw are. My eyes slowly lower, and I take him in. If I didn't know any better, I'd expect him to steal a peek at my naked body.

He won't, though. The man doesn't have a slimy bone in his body.

My attention catches on the bulge in his slacks, and I hesitate. Okay, he might have one bone in his body that's curious. Or maybe it's how the little light bit of light in the room hits his pants. Yeah. It could easily be nothing.

Okay, nothing is a bit of a stretch, since there is most definitely something in the front of his pants.

But why are you still looking?!

I gaze down at my feet, tuck the edge of the towel into itself by my breasts, and step closer to Everett. It's quiet. I can hear his steady breaths. The soft brush of my bare feet against the tile. My unsteady heartbeat as I inch closer to him, daring him to open his eyes. To prove he's like every other guy I've ever been around.

When I reach him, I glance at the door and look back at the man in front of me. My touch is gentle as I drag my fingers against his phone-wielding hand. If he's surprised, he doesn't show it.

"You can open," I whisper.

Those baby blues hit like a wrecking ball as he lifts his lids and looks down at me. They slide down my body for the briefest of seconds then lock with mine.

"You good?" he rasps.

I nod, attempting to ignore the magnetic pull I feel whenever he's around. Like a string, it weaves through me, binding me to him and making it impossible for either of us to walk away. To leave the room or acknowledge exactly how little space is left between my towel-covered body and his.

"Why didn't you peek?" I whisper.

"What?"

"Why didn't you peek?" I repeat. "Every other guy would've peeked."

His Adam's apple bobs. "Didn't want you to feel like a piece of meat." He grabs my wrist, placing his phone in my palm. "Dress in something warm. I don't know how long the heat will be off, but I have the fire going. I'll meet you in the family room."

I nod and watch as he walks away, leaving me alone and even more confused than ever. Considering the whirlwind mess of my brain right now, that's saying something.

I think I like him. Scratch that. I know I like him. I like him a lot, actually. And earlier tonight? When I heard him call someone babe, it felt like a knife to my chest, only for him to pull it out a few inches when we were dancing at SeaBird, and he called me Stormie.

It doesn't really matter, though. I'm still lost. Still a project. Still an obligation.

My cheeks puff out as I force the oxygen from my lungs and make my way into my bedroom. Once I'm dressed in a hoodie and sweats, I head back to the family room. The fire is blazing, the orange and yellow flames licking at each other and highlighting Everett's unreadable expression as he stares into it. He changed, too. Now, he's sporting a pair of sweats and a dark T-shirt stretched across his chest.

What are you thinking, Everett Taylor?

Feeling like I'm intruding on something, I rock back on my heels and whisper, "Hey."

He glances over his shoulder, and his eyes roll down my body like they did before. "Hey."

Stepping closer, I hand him his phone and force a smile. "Thanks."

"No problem."

"The power's still out," I note.

"Yeah, it does this sometimes. I was thinking…"

"Yes?"

"You should sleep by the fire."

I glance at the roaring blaze, then back at Ev. "And where will you sleep?"

"I'll grab a couple extra blankets—"

"Ev." I reach for his hand. "I think the family room's big enough for both of us, don't you?"

A wrinkle forms in his brows as he studies me carefully. "You sure?"

"Pretty positive." I smile, and this time, it's more real—more genuine—as I fold my arms. "Although, I think we might still need those extra blankets. It's freezing."

He chuckles while dragging me into him and hugging me, letting me steal his warmth as he rubs his hands up and down my arms and back. "Want to build a fort?"

"A fort?"

When he nods, his chin hits the top of my head. "Yeah. Fin and I used to build them all the time when we were kids. What do you say?"

"I've never built a fort."

"You've never built a fort?"

I shake my head, but before I can feel embarrassed, a grin practically splits his face in two. "Stay here."

Like a whirlwind, he disappears down the hall, reappearing with his arms full of blankets and pillows. Dropping them at my feet, he jogs into the kitchen and returns with a container full of chip clips.

"Here." He offers them to me, dashes back to the kitchen, and drags each of the chairs into the family room, creating a large half circle in front of the fire. When I finally catch on to what he's doing, I grab the blankets from the floor, help spread them out, and use the chip clips to secure the edges to the chairs, creating our own homemade cave. The entrance opens to the fire, and despite the lack of a furnace, once we're tucked inside, all I feel is warmth.

It's...peaceful.

The crackling fire acts like our own personal DJ and flashlight all at once, making me want to curl up and read a book. I would, too, if it wasn't so late. It's been a long day—a really long day—and I'm not the only one feeling it.

I peek at Everett as he shifts the blankets around us,

mentally checking every box on his list to make sure we're comfortable for the night.

"Do you always take care of everyone around you?" I ask.

He hesitates. "What?"

"I said, do you always take care of everyone around you? Me. Reeves. Dylan. Finley."

His mouth twitches. "Reeves would kill you if he knew you added him to the list."

"No, he wouldn't," I argue, not even bothering to hide my amusement. "He'd probably call you his man-wife for all the heavy lifting you've done in his life lately."

He snorts. "At least it makes me the husband in the relationship."

"What about Griff? Are you his man-wife, too?"

"Nah." He shakes his head. "Griffin's the real rock. Keeps his head down. Focuses on hockey. Tries to make his dad proud."

"I bet," I murmur. "Not sure what's up with him and Fin, though."

Everett frowns. "What do you mean?"

"Nothing," I hedge. "It's just...Finley told us Drew made her promise to kind of...cut ties with him."

Everett's eyes widen. "Who, Griffin?"

I nod.

"Why?"

My shoulder lifts. "I don't know? I think Drew is jealous."

Everett chuckles dryly. "Drew has nothing to worry about."

"You sure?"

"Griff doesn't look at her in that way."

I bite my lip to keep from arguing with him, well aware he's more in tune with his family's dynamics than I'll ever be.

Lifting the edge of the blanket for me, he adds, "Come on. Let's get some rest."

With the glow of the fire, I bring the blanket up to my chest and close my eyes, trying to find sleep.

But I can't convince my brain to shut off. To let me relax. Not when Everett's beside me. Not when I can feel him so close.

I face his back, watching his body move up and down with every breath until my own breathing matches it. Not on purpose. It's like any time I'm around him, we sync. We find our cadence. Our rhythm. And I'm tired of fighting it.

Licking my lips, I whisper, "Hey, Ev?"

The blanket rustles, but he doesn't face me. "Yeah, Raine?"

"W-why didn't you peek in the bathroom?"

He rolls onto his side and faces me. "Are you serious?"

"I want to know."

"I already told you."

"I'm not a piece of meat," I repeat his words from earlier.

"Did you want me to look?"

The weight of his words sits on my chest, making it hard for me to breathe. Did I want him to look? I should say no. Obviously. But the truth is…I don't know. Maybe? Is it so wrong if I kind of did? And what does it mean? What would the fallout be?

I'm so used to walking on eggshells, careful of every single word I say, always keeping my thoughts and feelings close to my chest in hopes of not rocking the boat. Of not causing ripples. But the truth is the idea of saying no. The idea of denying the pull I feel with the man I'm sharing a homemade fort with feels wrong. So damn wrong if I even think of saying that stupid two-letter word in response to his question about whether or not I wanted him to look at me naked makes me sick to my stomach, full of regret. Makes me question my sanity entirely. How could I not want him to look? I've already shared one of my most vulnerable parts with the guy, and instead of letting me down, he let me in. He had my back, albeit grudgingly.

"Stormie?" he prods. "Did you want me to look?"

I nod slowly. "Yeah. Yeah, Ev. I think I did."

A solid ten seconds pass, but I swear it's more like thirty as the light reflects off his light blue eyes, his expression unreadable. A mask of restraint.

Until…

His movements are slow—controlled—as he rolls on top of me and cages me in, resting his weight on his forearms on either side of my head. He pins me to the ground, and even though I can't move beneath him, I'm not scared. In fact, I'm pretty sure I've never felt safer.

Bending closer, his breath kisses my lips before his lips follow with a soft caress. My heart soars, and I open my mouth, letting him in as his tongue sweeps against mine. He tastes like mouthwash, and I smile against him. He dives deeper, adding more pressure, turning me into a puddle beneath him.

Clutching at his T-shirt, I tug him closer, loving the feel of him pressed against me as the fire crackles near our feet. It's sexy and romantic and feels like coming home. Time slows as my pulse races with every touch. Every dip of his tongue. Every caress of his lips.

If this is what a real kiss feels like, I can only imagine what it would feel like to give him everything. Every broken piece, knowing he's the only one patient enough to put me back together.

An ache builds between my legs, so I shift beneath him, spreading my thighs a few inches. As if he can read my thoughts, he groans against my mouth, tearing his lips away and resting his forehead against mine.

"Storm."

"Ev."

"Tell me you want to go to sleep. Tell me this isn't real. Tell me—"

"Kiss me again."

His mouth is on mine in an instant, and I loop my arms around his neck, arching my back off the cushioned ground, spreading my legs fully and hooking them around his waist. It feels good. Having him there. Feeling him there. Feeling him all around. His scent. His heat. His quiet groans and the slight shift of his hips.

A small voice in my head whispers how this is a bad idea. He'll hurt me the same way Drake did. The same way Drake's still trying to.

But then I remember how Everett didn't peek. It's such a simple thing. A silly thing, really. Proving he isn't an asshole in the smallest, most insignificant way, yet it holds more weight than he'll ever understand.

I kiss him harder, praying he can feel it. My need. To connect. To feel. To be with someone. Someone who looks at me like a person instead of…dammit, I don't even know—

Everett pulls away from me again, shifting and grabbing onto my waist right above my hip bone with his strong hand as he stops me from grinding against him.

"What's wrong?" I whisper.

"Who are you here with, Raine?"

I blink slowly, refusing to acknowledge the burn behind my eyes.

"I'm not him," he grits out.

And I can't tell if he's angry at me or himself or—

"I'm. Not. Him," he repeats.

His words wash over me like water. Hot. Almost scalding. Leaving me raw and vulnerable. But it's a good burn. An addictive burn. One I want to lose myself in. To wrap myself up in.

"I know," I whisper. "I know you're not him."

"Do you?"

Opening my eyes, I meet his icy blue ones and nod. "I do. Trust me, I do."

"Then why do you look like you're about to cry?"

"Because I'm terrified of this ending before it even has a chance to begin."

His eyes fall to my lips, his hand moves away from my hip, and he cradles my face. It only makes me fall faster.

This man. Who is this man? He's kind and patient and bossy and talented. He's nothing like Drake and everything I want, which is both terrifying and exhilarating, all wrapped up into one complicated contradiction. And even though I feel like I'm being torn apart, I also feel like I'm being put back together again.

Please put me back together again, Everett.

I lift my chin, silently begging him to put me out of my misery, and by some miracle, he obliges. Shadows dance around us on the flimsy cotton walls as he bends down and kisses me once more. It's the same slow, soft kiss from moments ago. And I melt even more.

With a soft whimper, I cup his cheeks, letting my legs fall open even wider. Nibbling my bottom lip, he moves his hands lower, pushes my hoodie up, peppering kisses along my jaw and neck, and moves to my bare stomach. I squirm beneath him as the heat of his mouth tattoos every inch when his thumbs hook along the hem of my sweats, and he pushes them down, exposing my most intimate places to him.

"Look around, Raine," he rasps. "This isn't a show. This isn't for anyone but you."

Me. This is for me.

"Ev..."

My words die in my throat as he kisses my center with the same soft, slow, deliberate movements. Gently, he sweeps his tongue along my slit, moving up to my clit. I jolt on contact, my jaw dropping as I savor the wet heat of his mouth against me.

With a swirl against the bud, he moves his fingers to my entrance and pushes into me. The sweet stretch makes my muscles tremble as I fist the blankets engulfing us.

I haven't had oral in forever, and holy shit, I almost forgot what I was missing and how good it feels. My breathing turns shallow as he laps at my clit over and over again, pumping his fingers in and out of me at the perfect angle until I swear I see stars.

"So good. So, so good," I chant under my breath.

The world starts to spin as the pressure builds in my core, leaving me desperate and aching. It's so strange, wanting to push him away yet pull him closer at the exact same moment. Squeezing my eyes shut, I fall apart against his mouth and fingers as they play me like a fiddle, the tickle of his scruff against my inner thighs acting like the final strike of a match, leaving me blazing.

My jaw drops as tremors of pleasure pulse through me. Over and over again. My eyes roll back in my head. I shift my hips against his mouth, letting him draw out every wave of euphoria until I swear I can't breathe.

When the sensation is too much, I push his face away from me and try to catch my breath, pulling a low chuckle from his chest as he climbs back up my body.

"Fuck, Stormie. You wanna know what you taste like?" He smirks, caging me in again. "You taste like the fucking rain." Nudging his nose against mine, he lets me smell myself on his lips, adding, "I've always been a sucker for the rain."

I tilt my head up and kiss him greedily, sucking his tongue into my mouth as I fumble with his joggers. He's hard and ready in my palm, and it only confirms every single decision I've made tonight. To do this. To let my walls down. To break his. To ignore the tiny voice inside my head wondering if he'll hurt me like Drake did.

The velvet enclosed steel spurs me on when it jerks against my palm. Running my hands up and down his length, I spread my legs even more and drag him against my wet slit.

With a groan, he rips his mouth from mine and growls, "Tell me you're on birth control."

"I'm on birth—"

He shifts his hips forward, thrusting into me, and I gasp. Holy mother of tortilla chips. He's big. Really big. I squeeze my eyes shut, forcing my body to relax and let him in as he presses his lips to my forehead in a long, slow kiss.

"Fuck," he rasps. "Sorry."

With a quiet laugh, I shake my head back and forth. "Don't apologize."

"You feel incredible."

"I'd say the same, but I kind of feel like I'm being split in two, so—"

"Fuck."

He starts to pull out of me, but I lock my legs around him, preventing his escape. "Don't you dare."

As he stares down at me, he whispers, "I don't want to hurt you, Raine."

Oh, the power of words and the many meanings behind them.

I don't want to hurt you, Raine.

A familiar burn hits the back of my eyes. And it's strange. Because even though I should be scared. Even though I should be terrified. I'm not. Not with him.

Shifting beneath Everett, I slowly lift my hips to his as I keep our eyes locked, praying he can see and feel and hear my sincerity. "You won't."

It takes a second for him to give in. For him to move inside me without being scared of hurting me.

Not going to lie. I kind of like it. The way he wants to put me first. The way he wants to keep me safe. It only confirms my decision to trust him. To let him in. Everett's used to pushing people away. Not because he doesn't care. But because he does. I know he does.

"You're not gonna break me." I drag my fingers beneath his T-shirt and tickle his lower back.

"Raine," he rasps.

I cup his cheek with my opposite hand, encouraging him to look at me. "This isn't my first rodeo, remember? I trust you."

Giving in, he thrusts into me with more force, and I take every inch, craving the slight burn and the way his face twists with pleasure.

Seriously. Even if this felt bad—which it definitely doesn't—it would still be worth it. This. All of this. Keeping himself buried deep inside me, he grabs my waist and rolls onto his back, letting me take the lead. I press my hand to his stomach and churn my hips, rubbing myself against him as I rise onto my knees and slide back down his long, hard length. With one hand on my hip and the other slipping between us to where we're connected, he draws small circles against my clit, and I quicken my pace.

"Seriously, you're too good at this," I pant.

He grins up at me. "Helps when you have a good partner."

I roll my eyes. "Of course it does."

The scent of sweat and sex clings to the air as I chase my second orgasm. When he adds a little more pressure, I snap, falling into oblivion. His groan follows right after, his cock jerking inside of me. I love it. The lack of barrier. The feel of his heat. His cum. To others, it would look reckless. But I know Everett well enough to know he doesn't do anything without thinking things through, and he sure as hell doesn't act impulsively. Which means he's thought about this.

Thought about me. The same way I've thought about him since the moment we met.

Reaching up, he grabs the side of my face and drags me down, kissing me all over again as we both come back to earth. Come back to reality and what we've done.

We had sex.

I just had sex with Everett Taylor.

And I know I should feel regret. I know I should be second-guessing myself. Instead, all I can think about is how good it feels to be held. To feel him inside of me. To feel his lips against mine as his kisses soften, along with his grasp on my hip.

"Fucking perfect," he breathes out. "You're fucking perfect."

My attention bounces around his face as I search for sincerity. I find it in spades. Snaking his arm around my waist, he rolls me back to our original position, then drops another kiss to the tip of my nose.

"Stay here. I'm gonna grab a towel."

I nod as he slips out of me and disappears from sight, only to return ten seconds later with the towel he promised.

After he helps me clean up in the fort, I head to the bathroom and finish the job in the still pitch black bathroom before climbing back into the blanket cave we created in the middle of the family room. The floors are cold, and so are my toes as I climb under the covers. When they brush against his ankle, Everett grabs my foot and tucks it between his thighs, letting me steal his warmth.

"Get some rest," he whispers.

"Okay."

CHAPTER TWENTY-SEVEN

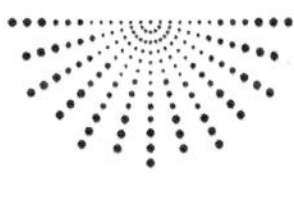

EVERETT

The power turned on sometime in the middle of the night, but I didn't bother slipping out of bed or turning the light off. I should've. I probably would've slept better if I had, but I didn't want to wake Raine up. She's still passed out on my chest. Her soft snore is almost familiar now. I never thought I'd be attracted to a snorer, but I kind of like it.

The fire died down a little while ago, and Raine's been clinging to my chest like I'm her teddy bear ever since. I like it, though. Feeling her against me. I drag my fingers through her hair and study her closed eyes, searching for any lingering bruises, though I know I won't find them. Not anymore. It's been weeks, but I'm not sure time matters when it comes to shit like this. Memory of the first time I saw her and how her face was mottled with bruises haunts me. She's better now. Everything's healed. Her bottom lip. Her black eye. Everything on the outside is exactly how it should be, and after last night, I'm hoping I was able to fix a few of the wounds Drake cut into her that I can't see. The damage beneath the surface. Buried deeper than I ever anticipated.

Her dark lashes flutter in the morning light as she opens her eyes and peeks up at me.

"Hi." Her voice is soft. Raspy. Sexy as hell.

With a smile, I move her hair away from her face. "Hey."

She pushes herself up and leans her back against one of the chairs in our makeshift fort. The distance messes with my head, and I follow suit, sitting up.

"You good?" I ask.

She nods. "Yeah. I'm good."

"Any plans today?" I prod.

She pauses, then shakes her head. "Nope."

"You hesitated," I point out.

Rolling her eyes, she explains, "Lucian texted the other day and asked when I was going to pick my things up from my locker. I was debating whether or not that day was today. I think I'll procrastinate for another week or so."

"You don't want to go?"

"Not in the slightest," she admits. "If I could snap my fingers and have all my things from my locker reappear here, I'd be ecstatic. Unfortunately, it's not the way things work." Her gaze falls to her black nails as she clicks them together.

I make a mental note to swing by and grab her things later today then tilt my head and change the subject. "Any reason why you're sitting all the way over there?"

Her head shifts left and right again. "No?"

"Is that a question?"

She narrows her eyes. "Where should I be?"

I pat my thigh, and she smirks.

"I'm sorry, are you Santa?" she challenges.

I cock my brow. "Are you saying you have a thing for older men?"

"Are you assuming I have a thing for you?"

"I had my cock buried inside you last night," I remind her.

Her mouth lifts. "You did, didn't you."

With a crook of my finger, I order, "Yeah, I did. Now get your ass over here."

"Why? So you can bury your cock inside me again?"

"I mean, if it's on the menu."

Her grumbling stomach echoes in the fort. We both laugh as she crawls toward me and, fuck, it's the prettiest thing I've ever seen. Or at least was, until she crawls right past me, her ass in the air, and disappears through the fort's makeshift exit.

"Where are you going?" I call out.

"I need to brush my teeth!"

Good point. I should probably brush mine, too.

Following her path, I climb out of the fort and head to the bathroom. She's wearing my T-shirt, her bare thighs on full display while she brushes her teeth in front of the mirror. Grabbing my toothbrush, I squeeze some paste onto the bristles, then stick it in my mouth as she peeks at me. Curious. Amused. Entertained. It's strangely…normal. Brushing my teeth with her. Being in each other's space. Doing everyday things. I felt it when we cooked lasagna together our first night here. Feel it when I take her to work and pick her up. Feel it when we go grocery shopping. Feel it when I'm studying at the kitchen table and she's lounging on the couch, watching a show with her bare feet resting on the coffee table or doodling in her notebook.

Even though I've tried to keep my distance. Even though she's been hesitant to open up. It's like we've fallen into a pattern without even realizing it. Like our walls were coming down without either of us even recognizing it.

Bending forward, she spits into the sink, swishes her

mouth with water, and dries her mouth on the towel, giving me a glimpse of her pearly whites. I grab her hand and keep her in place as I finish brushing, spit, and wipe my mouth. Once I'm done, I tug her into me and bring us chest to chest.

As she cranes her neck to look up at me, she asks, "Can I help you?"

"How many boyfriends have you had?"

Her brows bunch. "What?"

"Answer the question."

"One. Well, two if you count Zach Heavensby in third grade, but it only lasted three recesses, so…" She shrugs. "How 'bout you?"

"No boyfriends," I joke.

She shoves my shoulder. "Ev—"

"I've had a few casual relationships. Nothing long-term, though."

Her head bobs in a slow nod as her eyes trail down my body while she toys with the hem of my joggers. "So…why do you ask?"

"Just curious how slow I should take this."

She lifts her eyes to mine. "And what is this?"

"It's me and you."

"Ev…"

Nudging her chin with my knuckle and thumb, I grab the edge of her jaw and bend closer, kissing her. Mint and Raine mingle together on my tongue as I slip it between her lips. When I pull away, her eyes remain closed, and her lips part on a sigh. She swallows and looks up at me again.

"Here's what I know," I murmur. "I know you just got out of a shitty relationship. I know we've been faking like we're together. And I know that, after last night, I don't want to go back to it being fake."

Her mouth quirks, but her gaze narrows. "Are you serious?"

"Yeah, Stormie. I don't want to go back to being fake."

"You're sure?"

"I'm sure."

The same smile teases the edge of her mouth until it splits into a full-blown grin. "Neither do I."

"Yeah?"

She nods. "Yeah."

Her stomach grumbles again. I gather her into a hug, spin her around in the bathroom, and grab the backs of her thighs, encouraging her to wrap them around my waist. I carry her into the kitchen, then set her ass on the edge of the granite island. Once she's steady, I get to work making breakfast because my girl's hungry.

"Omelet?" I ask.

"If I can help, then yes."

"Not gonna let you help."

"Why, because I screwed up the lasagna?" she asks.

"You didn't—"

"I did," she argues.

She's right. She did. But I bite the inside of my cheek to avoid hurting her feelings with my amusement. "You hungry or not?"

She nods. "Fine. Yes. I'm hungry."

"Then let me feed you."

Her lips purse, but she leans back on her hands. "So stubborn."

The girl has no idea.

Satisfied, I open the fridge and dig for vegetables. "Onions?"

"Yes, please."

"Bell peppers?"

"Mm-hmm."

"Jalapenos?"

"Yup."

"Bacon?"

"Oo, yes, please."

"Sausage?"

She hesitates, and I jerk my head back from the fridge, eyeing her. "Sausage?" I repeat.

"Uh, sure?"

I grab her thigh and squeeze.

"Don't you dare tickle me," she warns.

"Then don't you dare lie to me," I volley back.

"Okay, okay." She grabs my fingers, trying to pry me off her. "I can take or leave sausage."

"Not what you said last night," I quip.

Her eyes widen, and she shoves at my shoulder. "Everett!"

"I'm kidding...kind of." With a smirk, I let her go, then turn back to the fridge, searching for anything else I might need. There's a carton of mushrooms on the lower shelf, and I reach for it, set it on the counter next to the other vegetables, and close the fridge door before opening one of the cabinets behind her head.

As she stares at the mushrooms like they're a nuclear bomb, I bite back my grin. Does she really think I don't remember?

"Don't worry, Stormie. I know—"

"It's no big—"

"No mushrooms," I push, giving her my full attention.

"No mushrooms," she confirms.

"But you like the taste." My gaze narrows as I cage her in on the counter. "Unless you were lying."

"I wasn't lying, I swear."

"Then I won't cut the mushrooms and will put them on top so I can pick them off and put them on my plate."

"You don't have to—"

"Let me take care of you, yeah?"

She bites her bottom lip but gives me a small nod, making me feel like a fucking king.

"That's my girl." I give her a quick kiss on the forehead, then grab a pan and set it on the stove.

My girl.

Fuck, it sounds good.

CHAPTER TWENTY-EIGHT

EVERETT

I called before swinging by Eternal. Lucian seems like a nice guy. After a quick conversation, he promised to have the receptionist put Raine's things in a box by the front. Sure enough, it's sitting right next to the same blonde from the first time I stopped by. Fuck, it feels like a lifetime ago. When obligation was the only thing spurring me on instead of the Raine I've gotten to know over the past few weeks.

I introduce myself to the receptionist, explaining the situation. She tells me her name and offers me the box. Tucking it under my arm, I place it inside my car, jump in the driver's seat, and pull away from the curb. My headlights cut through the dark streets while the gas light on my dashboard taunts me, so I pull into the closest gas station a couple blocks down the road.

Turning the ignition off, I climb out of the car, swipe my credit card, and place the pump in my tank. I lean against the passenger door while it fills. A black truck appears at the pump behind me, and a cherry-red Jeep parks up front, blocking me in.

What the hell?

My hair prickles along the back of my neck, but I don't move, keeping both vehicles in my periphery as I unlock my phone and drop a pin of my location to Griffin along with a quick text.

ME

About to get my ass kicked and need you to pick me up. Bring Reeves. Thx.

After hitting send, I slide my phone back into my pocket when a familiar face climbs out of the truck's driver's side. His name is Johnny, and he's Drake's friend.

Apparently, Raine wasn't kidding. Cedar Springs is a small fucking town. All it took was ten minutes for word to get around I was here.

My muscles tense as the Jeep's four doors open, revealing four more Grizzlies players before Drake climbs out last. I scan the station. It's empty. Not a soul around but me and my new buddies. At least Raine isn't here. That's gotta count for something. Probably should've asked Griff to come with me. Not like I expected an ambush, though I don't know why I didn't consider the possibility.

Guess that's on me.

Fuck.

Molars grinding, I rock back on my heels, checking out how close both cars are parked to me. Yup. I'm pinned in. There's no way I'll get out of here. There's also no way I'll win this fight. Six against one.

Six. Against. One.

I slide the handle out of my car, hook it back on the pump station, and face Drake. No need to beat around the bush when I know why he's here. His steps are slow—unhurried— as he strides toward me like the asshole doesn't have a care in the world.

"What are you doin' here, Taylor?" he challenges.

Don't pick a fight, I remind myself. "Just filling up my tank, then I'll be on my way."

Drake rounds the passenger side of my car and glances inside. "Came alone, huh?"

"Not my brightest moment," I mutter.

"Apparently not." He laughs. "It's a shame you didn't bring my girl back."

My mouth lifts. "She was a little tired, so she decided to stay home." I push myself away from my car, unable to help myself. I shouldn't. Fuck me, I know I shouldn't. But as soon as Drake called Raine his girl, I knew I was done for. "In my bed," I add. "A good fuck can take a lot out of a girl, you know?"

His amusement falls, and I cock my arm back, preparing to at least get a few good hits in until I'm surrounded. Instead, a reverberating thud hits the back of my head, and my knees hit the ground, the jarring running up my thighs.

Then, the world goes black.

CHAPTER TWENTY-NINE

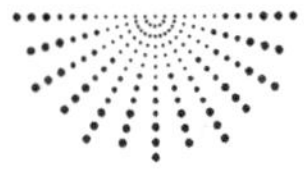

RAINE

"Shit," I seethe. "Are you okay?"

Griffin and Reeves carry a semi-conscious Everett through the cabin's front door and set him on the couch. Reeves had the decency to call me a few minutes ago, warning me they were coming and to not freak out. However, considering the circumstances, it's a hell of a lot easier said than done.

"Got any ice?" Griffin asks.

I rush toward the freezer and snatch a bag of peas out, handing it to him. Griffin passes it off to Everett, and he presses the frozen ice pack to the back of his head, which is saying something, considering the damage to his face.

"What happened?" I ask.

"You can thank your ex for this," Everett divulges, confirming my suspicion.

My lips thin as I take in the bloody mess in front of me. This wasn't a simple sucker punch. He looks like he was hit by a truck. Like he had the absolute shit kicked out of him. What if this ruins his NHL career? What if they did permanent damage, and he'll never skate again? The thought alone makes my knees almost give out, and I grasp the edge of the kitchen island to keep from crumbling to the floor. I'd never forgive myself. I still might never forgive myself. Not for this.

Holding his side, Everett lets out a slow breath, his expression pinched, and eases a little more into the cushions as if there's any possibility of him being able to get comfortable after the hellish ordeal he's been through.

"Ev didn't want me to call his parents," Griffin tells me. "So I made up a bullshit lie about concussions on the ice and asked his dad what to look for." He stares at his best friend, then adds, "Don't let him sleep longer than an hour."

An hour? I look at Everett's best friends standing in the kitchen and shake my head. "What?"

"Ev went to Cedar Springs to pick some stuff up," Reeves explains, setting a brown box on the kitchen table. And just like that, the pieces click into place. Everett went to Cedar Springs, and Drake saw him. I knew he'd watch Eternal's entrance in case I came back, but I had no idea he'd do something like this.

Touching my fingers to my barely parted lips, I whisper, "I'm so sorry. Seriously, I...I don't know what else to say."

"It's fine," Everett grumbles.

"Yeah, but it isn't."

"You're right." His forehead scrunches, and he lets out a slow breath. "It isn't, but it's not on you."

My bottom lip quivers before I suck it into my mouth and bite down. Hard. Praying the sting of pain will keep my guilt and tears at bay. At least until Everett's friends leave. Because he can say what he wants, but the truth is, this *is* on me. If he didn't know me, if Drake didn't know him, this never would've happened. It's all my fault. I squeeze my hands into fists, letting my nails bite into my palms as I stare at the mottled purple along Everett's cheekbone. How can he still look handsome like this? All bruised and broken. I can only imagine what's hidden beneath his blood-soaked T-shirt. I can tell the guys tried cleaning him up before they brought him in. There isn't any dried blood beneath his nose, but his shirt? There was only so much they could do. It doesn't take a genius to see the aftermath and piece together what happened and all he went through.

And it's all. My. Fault.

"You guys can go," Everett says without taking his eyes off me. "Thanks again for your help."

"Sure thing, man," Griffin says. "If you need anything else, give me a call." He heads back to the front door, and Reeves follows behind, not saying a word.

The sound of the latch clicking into place reverberates throughout the otherwise silent house as I turn back to a bruised and broken Everett.

"Talk to me, Storm," he rasps.

"W-what happened?"

"Drake and a few of his buddies jumped me outside the gas station."

My expression falls even more. "Ev…"

"Said I was in their territory." He scoffs, then winces. "What kind of fuckin' life is this? I feel like I entered some alternate universe or some shit. Like I'm in a gang or…" He scrubs the hand not holding the bag of peas to the back of his head from his forehead to chin, wincing even more as he drops his hand to his lap. "What the fuck, Raine? I didn't sign up for this. This isn't… This isn't my life."

The words hang in the air. Heavy. Loaded. Because he's right. This isn't his life. But it *is* mine.

Regret and shame battle inside me as I take a small step backward, ignoring the swell of tears in my eyes and letting out a soft exhale. "I'm so sorry, Ev."

"Shit." His head hangs. "That's not what I meant."

"Doesn't make it less true," I reply. "I'm so sorry."

"Don't apologize."

"How can I not apologize?" I argue. "This is my fault. If you hadn't gone to pick up my things, this would never have happened. You wouldn't have had the shit kicked out of you." I wipe my hand beneath my nose and sit on the cushion beside him. "You're right, you know? This isn't your life. But, apparently, it's mine, and—"

"Raine." He reaches for me, but I shake my head and lean away from him. Desperate for the distance. For the fucking clarity to know what to do in this situation when I feel so damn helpless, it's not even funny.

"Whether we want to admit it or not, whatever's going on with Drake, he isn't going to just let me go, and it isn't fair this happened to you. That he hurt you." I cover my mouth, nearly choking on a sob. "I'm so sorry, Ev."

"Raine—"

"I am," I push, dropping my hand back to my lap. "I'm sorry, and I wish I could take it away, but I can't." My voice cracks. "I can't take it away, and I can't make Drake go away, no matter what I do, no matter how much I try to avoid him, but it isn't your job to put up with this. To deal with shit like this." I motion to his broken face. "I'm so sorry."

I feel like a broken record. Like I can't stop spewing the same rambling apology. But I don't know what else to say. How else to fix this. How to make Drake pay for hurting someone I care about while knowing it's my fault in the first place. "I, uh, I'm gonna need you to do something for me, all right? I need you to break my heart so we can go our separate ways because this? You and me? I can't let you live like this. I can't let him hurt you—"

"Raine," he snaps.

My bottom lip trembles, and I squeeze my eyes shut. Self-loathing swamps my every thought. It seeps through the cracks of my defenses, attacking my logic and self-esteem. In a way, it's comical. This isn't about me. Yet I can't help but carry the burden of it. Because if I wasn't in the picture, this wouldn't have happened, and there's nothing I can do to fix it. To take his pain.

Everett's touch is gentle, making me feel precious as he cups the side of my face and tilts my head up, leaving me no choice but to look at him. Moisture clings to my lashes, but I open my eyes. The same hammer of guilt hits me square in the chest when my gaze connects with his baby blues.

"You're a storm, Raine. Messy and chaotic and a shit-ton of work, but I'm in, all right? I'm all in."

He presses his lips to mine, and I meet him halfway, careful not to hurt him or make this worse. The slight tang of blood hits my tongue as he swallows my whimper, his mouth moving with mine in a slow, cautious kiss. And I hate how I'm the one who's a mess right now. How I'm the one being comforted when he's the one who went through Hell and back tonight. Shame clogs my throat at the reminder that if I hadn't told Everett I needed to pick my things up from Eternal, he wouldn't have gone by himself. If I hadn't dated Drake in the first place, he wouldn't have to keep an eye out for any potential run-ins. If I hadn't approached Reeves, I wouldn't have met Everett, and he'd be safe. He'd be okay.

"You're *my* storm," he rasps against my swollen lips as if he can read my thoughts. As if he can feel my warring emotions. He shifts closer, kissing me harder and branding me in every way he can. As if he knows what I'm thinking. What I'm feeling. And he wants to take it away. My pain. When I'm the one who's desperate to make him feel better. To make this right.

"Fuck." His chuckle is low and throaty as he pulls away and rests his forehead against mine. "I just had the shit kicked out of me, and I still want you." He opens his eyes and smiles. "Yeah, I'm not letting you go anywhere, Stormie."

My chest swells as I press my hand to his, letting the steady rhythm of his heart ground me as I slowly move onto my knees in front of him.

"Raine..."

"You've taken care of me since the moment we met, Everett." I peek up at him and reach for the seam of his jeans. "Let me take care of you for once, will you?"

His blue eyes darken, and if I didn't know any better, I'd say he wants to tell me no. My fingers graze him, but I don't unzip his zipper. Instead, I stay still and study him. The worry lines framing his eyes. The hardness in his jaw. The bruises. The dried blood beneath his nose clinging to his five o'clock shadow. The flare of his nostrils.

"Do you not want me to take care of you?" I whisper.

He pauses, his chest expanding with a deep, forced breath. "Not used to being taken care of," he grudgingly admits.

It doesn't surprise me. Everett doesn't seem like someone who allows people to take care of him. It only feeds my determination.

"Well, there's a first time for everything, right?" I smile, reach for his button, and wait.

When he doesn't tell me to stop. Doesn't tell me to take this slow. Doesn't tell me not to touch him, I continue my path. And I think we both need it. Proof I'm all in, too. Proof I'll do anything to take his pain away, even if all I can give him is a distraction.

My fingers move deftly, the sound of the zipper ringing throughout the otherwise silent room when I tug the thick metal lower. I used to like giving blow jobs. That probably sounds weird, but it's true. It made me feel powerful. Wanted. Desirable. Then Drake filmed me, and instead of it being the compliment Drake insisted it was, his actions made me feel used. Dirty. I didn't like them after that.

A small part of me wonders if I still don't like them, but it shrinks with every slow drag of the zipper, one small metal tooth unclicking after another. Anticipation mixes with the trepidation swirling through my veins, and I continue my pursuit, curious to see if it'll stay. The anticipation. Or if it'll be swallowed whole by my own insecurities and the past refusing to stop haunting me no matter how hard I try to bury it.

What do you taste like, Everett?

I let the question guide my movements as the zipper reaches its end, and his black boxers come into view. The ridge of his cock is outlined by them. They remind me of the ones I borrowed on my first night with him.

I rise onto my knees, blow a kiss through the damp fabric near the head of his cock, and pull him out. The mushroom head tempts me as I drag my thumb along the slit, spreading the precum around the tip as I lift my eyes to his again. I want to watch him. I want to see what I do to him. To see if I can drive him crazy like he's done to me. Spreading my lips, I taste him, keeping my movements slow as I wrap my mouth around the head of his erection, using my hand to massage the rest of his length.

A groan rumbles from his chest. As he reaches out to hold the side of my face, I wait for fear to replace my curiosity and anticipation, but it doesn't. No. I only want to make him needier. To steal another groan from him to see if it's louder than the last. To take him deeper. So I do.

What do I do to you, Everett Taylor?

Running his thumb along my stretched lips, he shakes his head, looking down at me. Not in contempt, but disbelief. Like he's in awe. Like he can't believe I'm the one he's with. The one sucking him off. When I'm the lucky one. The one who can't believe I'm here. Safe. Appreciated. Cared for.

Pulling away from his cock, I swirl my tongue along the

head and catch my breath while trying to keep my potential freak out at bay. I dive back in, bobbing my head up and down over his erection. His hands slip into my hair, push it away from my face, and tug softly against my roots. It spreads tingles along my scalp. They race down my spine, and I press my thighs together. Spreading my hands beneath his shirt, I explore every inch of his body I can get my fingers on, savoring the way his muscles bunch and flex as he fights for control.

"Fuck, Raine," he pants. "Fuck, just like that."

I swallow around him, and he drops his head back, staring up at the ceiling.

"You suck me so good, baby. So fucking good."

I can feel his need. His unsteady breaths.

His hands twist in my hair. My core clenches at the sound of his raspy voice and how it mixes with the wet, rhythmic sound coming from my mouth.

Yup. I'm pretty sure this takes the cake as the most turned-on I've ever been while giving a guy a blow job. Honestly, even my aching jaw and sore knees are a turn-on at this point. Because I want it. I want him. To make him unravel. To make him fall apart and come in my mouth. I press my thighs together and cup his balls, rolling them in my hand while hollowing my cheeks.

"Gonna come, baby," he warns, dropping his hands and threading them together behind his head to keep from holding me against him.

Sucking him deeper, I wait for the familiar spurt to hit the back of my throat. I close my eyes and welcome it. Welcome the closeness. The way he's so close to coming apart. The tiny grunts. The whispered curses. His dick jerks against my tongue before he explodes in my mouth, and I swallow every drop. Desperate for more. More of him. More of this. This intimacy. This connection. I squeeze my eyes shut, the realization hitting me harder than I expect. I really like this man. I really like what he does to me, and what I clearly do to him.

As he softens in my mouth, I slowly slip off him, running my tongue along the sensitive head to see if I can tease anything else out of the poor guy until he pushes me away with a low chuckle.

"Tryin' to kill me, Raine?"

I wipe the corner of my mouth with my thumb and hold his gaze. "Maybe."

Reaching for me, he orders, "Come here."

When I crawl up his body, he winces, and I freeze, lifting my hand from his sore ribs. "Shit."

"I'm fine."

"No, you're not."

"Come here, Raine," he repeats. His tone is gentle. Like a caress. And I'd give anything to wrap myself up in it.

Carefully, I tuck myself against his side and start to rest my head on his chest until he grabs my chin and kisses me, shoving his tongue into my mouth and tasting himself. Tasting what I did to him. If only he knew how mutual the feeling really is. And if he wasn't jumped earlier tonight, I'd have no issue proving it.

Instead, I slow the kiss and pull away, pressing one softer, more gentle kiss to his lips. "You need to rest."

"No, I need to get you off."

"No," I repeat with a laugh, pressing my hand against his chest as he tries to sit up. "You really need to rest."

"Not gonna let you swallow my cum without giving you an orgasm, Storm."

"Are you always this transactional with sex?"

He quirks his brow. "Most girls don't complain."

"Not complaining," I clarify. "But I *am* going to pass. You need to rest."

Grudgingly, he settles back and takes a slow breath, looking down at me and pushing my hair away from my face as he studies me carefully. I wish I knew what he was thinking. If he's falling the same way I am.

I think he is. I hope he is.

"I'm not going anywhere, Raine," he promises, and I swear the words are a balm to my soul.

Sucking my lips between my teeth, I bite on the plump flesh and swallow around the lump in my throat. "Good… 'cause neither am I."

RAINE

"You ready yet?" my dad asks.

I peek up from my sketchbook and frown. "If I say no, will I be in the doghouse again?"

My dad's been suggesting I give him or my mom or my brother or even one of his favorite clients a tattoo almost every day this past week. At first, it was only here and there. His offer to walk me through giving my first official tattoo. But lately, he's more persistent. More pushy. I think he's caught on to my fear, no matter how ridiculous it really is. But I'm not him. I'm not my dad. I'm not some…prodigy. I'm just me, and a small part of me is terrified I'm not enough. Terrified I'll make a mistake. One someone will have to wear for the rest of their life unless they're willing to pay for removal, and how would that look? The infamous Milo Anders' youngest daughter. The screw up. The failure. The girl who couldn't hack it.

At first, it was pretty easy to shrug off my dad's offer to be my first guinea pig, saying I wanted to finish a piece in my notebook or do a few more practice runs on the fake skins instead. Apprentices use them to work on their craft and make sure the needle doesn't go too deep or shallow. It's great for newbies like me, even though I'm not stupid enough to believe tattooing on the fake stuff is anything close to the real thing. Human skin. Regardless, when I began working here, my dad bought my excuses, but over the last couple of weeks, he's wisened up to my stalling tactics.

He plops down onto the swivel stool and casts a quick glance at the clock on the wall, giving me his full attention. "I have a few minutes before my next appointment. You can always give me a quick—"

"Not ready yet."

"Rainbow." He scoots his chair into my periphery, grabs the edge of my notepad, and lowers it. "What's going on?"

With a smile, I turn back to my half-finished drawing. "Nothing."

"Is it about your boy?"

I scoff and look up at him again. "One, no, this has nothing to do with my boy. His name is Everett, by the way. And two, I thought we'd moved past this."

"Not until you let me officially meet him," my dad volleys back at me. "I'm still waiting for our introduction."

"You've already had your introduction," I remind him.

"I'd hardly call a two-minute run-in when you're covered in bruises an introduction."

With a sigh, I shift in my seat, running my tongue along the inside of my upper lip and across my teeth. I hate how he hasn't dropped it yet. His determination to find the culprit behind the bruises Drake gifted me with. He doesn't get it, though. Why I need him to let it go. Why I need any reminder of all things Drake to be shoved under the rug, never to see the light of day. But making assumptions and piecing together nonexistent strings, like Everett's connection to said bruises, is a joke. And it's one I don't find very funny, especially if there's any chance of my dad actually accepting Everett as my boyfriend and welcoming him with open arms.

Pinning my dad with a sharp look, I say, "Let's cut to the chase."

His mouth twitches as he shifts on the faux leather stool. "By all means, Bo. The floor's all yours."

"He didn't do it," I announce.

"And who did?"

"Dad," I repeat. "He. Didn't. Do. It."

"And. Who. Did?" my dad returns, mirroring my inflection. He isn't mad. Not really. But it's still infuriating.

Curtly, I offer, "It doesn't matter. I'm fine."

"You know, sometimes our conversations feel like I'm pulling teeth," he points out, stating the obvious. "Who are you trying to protect?"

"I'm not trying to protect anyone."

"Then why can't you tell me the truth, Bo?"

Trepidation swims in my gut, and I push aside the tiny voice inside my head. The one willing me to open up to him. It likes to flare up when my dad looks at me like this. Like he cares and loves me and wants to make sure I'm safe. The funny thing is, since moving in with Everett, I've never felt safer.

"You want the truth, old man?" I ask.

"Before I turn eighty? Yes."

I lean closer to him and wrinkle my nose, giving him a mock glare. "Here it is, but you won't like it."

"Ready whenever you are."

"The truth is…" I pause for effect. "You need to look into cleaning out your ears because I already told you it was a bar fight—"

His groan cuts me off. "And I already told you, I think you're full of shit."

I'm not surprised he doesn't buy it. Thankfully, I also

know he'll drop the interrogation after he says his peace, the same way he has at least once a week since I started working here. Even so, it still makes me want to wrap up this conversation as quickly as possible so we can move on to things like my oldest niece's first word or what kind of chaos Dodger is stirring up while on the last leg of his tour.

I paste on a fake smile and tilt my head. "Maybe you should have a little more faith in your daughter."

"Maybe you should have a little more faith in your old man," he counters. "How are things?"

"Honestly?" I hesitate as I reflect on the last few weeks since Everett's attack. He didn't go to the cops even though I told him to. Why? Well, call it a hunch, but I think it's because of the original promise he made to keep the cops in the dark. In fact, he's been quite stubborn about it, even giving me shit for telling him to press charges.

"*Oh, so I can call the cops about Drake, but you can't?*" he asked.

"*I'm fine.*"

"*Yeah? Well, so am I. What's done is done. Now, come over here and kiss me.*"

I let it go after that. Not because Drake deserved to get away with jumping Everett without repercussions but because Everett deserves to have a say in the matter like I did. It also doesn't help knowing the owner of the gas station is a huge Grizzlies fan and most likely wiped the security footage before Griffin and Reeves even arrived on the scene. It's also probably why Drake brutally pulled the trigger in the first place. Right time, right place, and all that.

Asshole.

Even so, it's been nice. Having Everett all to myself while he's healing. After the incident, he had to sit out of a couple of games, much to his dismay, but it's been kind of fun to go to them together. Okay, *together* is a bit of a stretch. He's still on the bench, and I'm still in the stands with Finley and Dylan, as well as Maverick and Ophelia when she doesn't have a game. Yeah, you better believe Maverick sits front and center during every Lady Hawks game when Ophelia plays. It's pretty adorable. But I've still been able to drive with Everett to the men's games instead of separately, so I think it still counts.

The bruises have finally faded, and he doesn't grunt when he stands from the couch anymore. Still, it hasn't erased the image of Griffin and Reeves carrying him inside, no matter how much I wish it would. We don't talk about it, though. The incident. Drake. Or any of the repercussions. I'm not sure there's anything left to say at this point. Hopefully, Drake made his point, feels like he was vindicated, and it's over. Done.

Hopefully.

The possibility is like a huge weight lifted from my shoulders.

Please let it be over.

Everett still drives me to and from work, and I still live under his parents' roof. It's strange. How comfortable we've gotten. I like it, though. The comfort. The routine. I was almost sad when Everett's coach agreed to let him play at practice today. Apparently, the coach bought the whole "I don't know who jumped me" line Everett fed him.

After their team physician checked Everett out and cleared him for playing, he's been consumed with all things LAU. Well, and me. He's been pretty consumed by me, too. My lips curve up at the memory of last night and the way he ate me out on the kitchen counter.

"Bo?" my dad prods. "How are things?"

I clear my throat and smile back at him. "Things are... really good, actually."

"You sure?"

"Yeah." *Other than Everett having the shit kicked out of him, anyway*, I silently add to myself.

"And you and the guy are doing well?" he prods.

"His name's Everett," I remind him, well aware I've already mentioned it a handful of times during this conversation alone. "And, yes. We're doing really well."

He quirks his brow. "Well enough for an introduction?"

"You really won't quit, will you?" I humph.

He grabs the base of my chair and drags me to face him. "Where do you think you got your stubbornness from?"

I bite the inside of my cheek and stay quiet. Part of me wants to laugh at the man's audacity. The other part wishes I could take it back. Their first meeting. That I could bring Everett to a family dinner without any prejudice. That I could trust my family to give him an actual chance instead of assuming Everett's the one who hurt me and lumping him in with assholes like Drake when it couldn't be further from the truth.

"Your brother's coming into town for a concert at SeaBird," my dad adds. "I want you to bring him."

I open my mouth to find an excuse but close it quickly, knowing he won't buy it. Not in the long run. Not when this is the *other* question he can't help bringing up every time I'm at work. Every time he sees Everett's car parked in the front parking space. Every time he catches me climbing out of Everett's car when I'm dropped off. Every time he asks about my love life or living situation, I have to dodge his questions instead of telling him the truth. My dad wants me to let him in again, and after months of pushing him away while he refuses to go anywhere, I have a feeling it's the least I can do.

Chewing on the end of my pencil, I avoid my dad's stare and mumble, "Not gonna let this go, are you?"

"Just trying to show I care while respecting your boundaries, Rainbow."

My lips bunch on one side as I take in the crinkles around his eyes. He really is a good guy. One of the best.

Giving in, I exhale, "I'll see what I can do."

He nudges my chin up and smiles. "That's my girl. Is he picking you up today?"

I shake my head. "His friend is."

"And who is this friend?" he prods.

"His name is Griffin, and before you ask, no. You can't meet him, either."

Clutching his chest, my dad spins his swivel chair away like he's been dealt a fatal blow. "Breaking my heart, Rainbow. Breaking my heart."

"Sure I am," I toss back at him without bothering to hide my grin or rolling eyes. "Now, if you'll excuse me, I'm going to finish this drawing in private."

"You do know I'm your boss, right?" he challenges as I stand up and press my notepad to my chest.

My gaze flicks to the waiting area. "Your next client's here."

"Perfect. You can prep the stencil." He snaps his fingers and points back to my chair. "Chop, chop."

"Okay, but no actual tattooing yet. Right?"

"And why would we do that?" He snorts.

My butt hits the seat, nonetheless. It looks like I'm off the hook for another day.

Perfect.

CHAPTER THIRTY-ONE

RAINE

It's raining when I step outside. And not a little sprinkle, either. Like, buckets of icy sleet I have no doubt is a full-blown blizzard at the cabin. Tucking my notebook into my jacket, I dash toward Griffin's car and yank the passenger door open.

"Hey," I greet him.

He doesn't bother looking at me. His sole focus is on his phone until he tosses it into the backseat like it personally offended him. Then, after a grumbled, "Hey," he grabs the back of my seat and turns around to face the rear bumper as he pulls out of the parking spot in front of Etch 'N' Ink.

"Is everything okay?" I ask carefully.

We haven't really spoken since our game of *Spin the Bottle*. Even when he dropped Everett off after he was jumped, we barely said two words to each other. To be fair, we've never really talked, and I'm not sure if it's because he respects my situation and doesn't want to overstep his bounds or if it's because I'm kind of sort of dating his best friend, whom I've only brought trouble to from the very beginning. Well trouble and orgasms. Lots and lots of orgasms. Add in the fact Everett asked him to pick me up and drive me to the duplex until Everett finishes helping his mom with something, and I'm basically a bundle of nerves.

"Thanks for picking me up, by the way," I add.

His jaw clenches as he turns back in his seat, facing the windshield and driving toward the main road. "No problem."

A minute passes, and I suck my lips between my teeth. "Listen, about *Spin the Bottle*, I'm sorry if—"

He chuckles darkly. "What happens at game night stays at game night."

The windshield wipers pick up their pace, and I twist my hands in my lap, surprised by how quickly he shut me down. "Right."

"Besides, it's all good. It was only a kiss."

I nod but stay quiet.

"I'm sorry I'm acting like I have a stick up my ass," he continues. "There was no hot water after the game, and..." His eyes fall to the backseat where his phone still rests. His eyes return to the road in an instant. Nostrils flaring, he adds, "Can I ask you something?"

My brows hitch, and my head bobs again, making me feel like a bobblehead. "Sure, what's up?"

"Do you wish your friends would've stepped in?"

Blindsided, I jolt back. "What?"

"When Drake started acting like an ass," he explains. "Do you wish your friends or family would've stepped in?"

I open my mouth to answer, but he barrels right past waiting for my response.

"Or better yet, did you even see them? The signs?" he questions. "Or were you really so disconnected from everything you thought the red flags were normal relationship shit?"

"Are you asking about my experience or...are we talking about someone else? Hypothetically," I rush out.

He gives me the side eye. "Fin wants to cut me out of her life all because her fucker of a boyfriend told her to."

My nose wrinkles as I watch the wipers move back and forth, squeaking with every pass. So this is about Finley. I should've known. But seeing Griffin like this? Distracted and lost in his own head? It's…well, it's a little confusing because, from what I've been told, Griffin and Finley are only friends. Or at least, they were until her boyfriend drew a line in the sand.

Unsure what to say, I admit, "She, uh, she might've mentioned it to me, yes."

"And?" He glances at me again. "It doesn't seem messed up to you?"

"I mean, yes," I offer. "It's a little messed up, but—"

"Do you know if he told her to cut anyone else out? Like Mav or Reeves or…anyone?"

I lift a shoulder, hating the position I find myself in and how distraught Griffin is because of it. I've never gotten this vibe from him. He's always so laid back. So easy-going. Pretty sure Griffin is the definition of Golden Retriever energy, yet here he is, looking closer to a Rottweiler.

"Just you," I admit.

His knuckles turn white around the steering wheel. "That's what I thought."

"I'm sure he'll cool down and let it go," I add. "Just give it some time, you know?"

Griffin scoffs. "Yeah, I thought so, too, but she hasn't answered any of my texts since the bar."

Shit.

Not exactly a good sign. No wonder he was giving his phone the death glare when I climbed in.

"Do you like her?" I whisper. Maybe it's a stupid question, and maybe I shouldn't even ask, but stepping into a friend group as close-knit as this one makes me feel like I'm ten steps behind. Like there are dynamics and relationships right below the surface, making each scenario hard to read. Like this one. Finley and Griffin. Griff has been so busy with hockey and…who knows what…that we haven't really gotten to know each other. Hell, we've barely talked. He's the quiet one of the group. The thinker. The one easily overlooked. And for some reason, it makes me more curious than ever. Honestly, he couldn't be more opposite to Finley if he tried. Even their complexions are different. Light brown hair with gold highlights and tan skin to Finley's dark brown, almost black hair with pale, ivory skin. He's tall. She's short. He's quiet and observant. She's loud and impulsive. He eats, sleeps, and breathes hockey, and she couldn't care less about the sport.

His silence is deafening, though. It makes me squirm in my seat and pick at my nails until I can't help but give into my own impulsiveness and add, "Let me rephrase. Does Drew have a reason to be wary of your relationship with Fin?"

He presses his forefinger to his temple, rubbing in slow, small circles like he's fighting an impending headache, and states the obvious. "She's Everett's little sister."

"Not exactly an answer," I point out.

"I think she deserves better."

"Someone like you?"

He shakes his head. "Nah. We wouldn't be good for each other."

My brows lift. "Why not?"

"For one, she's Everett's little sister."

"You mentioned that." I bite the inside of my cheek. Seriously, how did I not see it before? One, that this guy is absolutely adorable, and two, that he's clearly in love with Finley. Curious, I push, "What does Ev have to do with it?"

His full lips are nothing but a slash of white as Griffin

turns down the road toward the duplex. He's still in his head. Still overthinking. Still going crazy. Scrubbing his hand over his messy hair, he finally says, "He's protective of the people he cares about."

"Yet he's fine with Finley dating Drew," I point out. "Which, as you've already alluded to, is problematic because Drew has a few red flags, right?"

"Finley's stubborn," Griff argues. "And Ev's been distracted lately." His eyes find mine again. "No offense."

"None taken," I reply.

"I don't think Drew's good for her, but I also don't think it's my place to throw a fit about it, especially after the shit she pulled at the bar. If I do say something, I have a feeling they'll look at me like you are."

"And how am I looking at you?" I ask.

"Like I'm a pathetic, lovesick puppy." He pulls into the driveway and shuts his car off. "I'm only thinking of Fin, is all."

"I think Fin can take care of herself," I reply, carefully. "And if—or *when*," I emphasize, "she realizes Drew isn't the one for her, she'll come back around. She has to."

He nods slowly, his eyes glazed. "Yeah, we'll see."

Reaching for the door handle, I add, "Thanks for the ride."

"Thanks for the therapy session," he quips, giving me a full-blown, contagious lopsided grin.

Oh, yeah, Fin. You're in trouble.

CHAPTER THIRTY-TWO

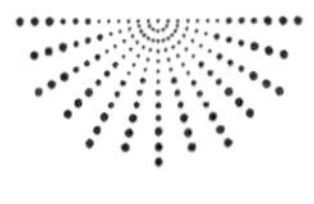

RAINE

If days could be labeled as perfect, this one would have the title. We spent the day outside in the snow before sharing a steamy hot shower. He insisted it was two degrees shy of Hell but stopped complaining after I grabbed his erection and turned the heat up until we were both coming. Afterward, we made chicken noodle soup. Now, he's giving me a foot massage while I draw in my notebook as an NHL game plays on the television.

See? *Perfect.*

As my pencil scratches against the paper in a long, thin stroke, I feel Everett's stare and stop moving. When my eyes flick over to him, I ask, "Is there a problem?"

"You move your lips when you draw."

I frown. "I do?"

He nods gently. "Yeah. It's cute as shit."

I roll my eyes and start drawing again, but he squeezes my foot, demanding my attention.

"Yes?" I ask.

"Can I look?"

"You've looked before," I remind him.

"Can I look again?"

Instead of offering him the notebook, I close the cover and hug it to my chest. "Depends."

"On what?"

"On why you want to look."

"Someone's protective of their work," he notes.

Part of me feels like I should point out I'm only protective when I care about the person's opinion, but I cough up the notebook anyway and offer it to him.

Gently, he takes it from me and carefully flips through the pages while I keep my feet in his lap and study the side of his face. I'm not sure I'll ever get used to it. The sharp edge I sit on whenever someone sees my work. The way I prepare myself for criticism or compliments, unsure which one I'll receive. That's the thing about art. How differently it can be taken. And putting something down on paper to open your-self up to criticism? It's terrifying. But bottling it up isn't any better. So, where does it leave me? On pins and needles, that's where.

"Hmm," Everett hums. The sound is low and throaty and makes me want to scoot closer as his gaze flits across the paper. "I like this one."

"Which one?" I ask.

"The hawk."

Relief shoots through me. "Of course, you like the hawk," I tease. "LAU through and through, right?"

"It's in my blood," he agrees.

"Want to know something about him?"

He shifts the notebook a bit to the left, changing the angle as he continues staring at the hawk. "What?"

"I drew it the night we met."

His gaze snaps to me. "No shit?"

I laugh. "It was during the game. You managed to grab my attention even then, Everett Taylor."

His smile softens, and he reaches for my wrist, tugging me to a seated position while keeping my feet in his lap and my notebook in his opposite hand. Once I'm hauled up, I rest my head on his shoulder, and he lets me go, continuing his perusal of my work.

"How long have you wanted to be a tattoo artist?" he asks.

"A while."

"You don't have any tattoos."

"You noticed, huh?"

"Most tattoo artists I've seen look like your dad."

My lips curve up as I nuzzle a little closer to his side. "Technically, I'm not an official tattoo artist yet, but yeah. My dad's a sucker for tattoos."

"And you aren't?" he challenges.

Resting my chin on his shoulder, I peek up at him and hedge, "I am."

"Yet you don't have any," he repeats.

"I'm, uh, I'm waiting."

"For what?"

My cheeks heat. "I haven't actually tattooed anybody."

With a frown, he tilts his head. "What does that have to do with you getting one?"

It's a good question, one I'm embarrassed to answer. No one knows this. Not my dad or mom. Not Drake. It's a secret I've kept close to my chest for as long as I can remember. But for some reason I genuinely can't explain, I'm tempted to tell him the truth, no matter how juvenile it might sound.

Shielding the side of my face with my hair, I look down at my feet in his lap and warn, "It's weird."

"You should tell me," he pushes. "Please?"

Please.

Oh, what this man can make me say.

"Honestly?" I pause, hating how stupid my answer feels now that I'm about to actually voice it aloud. "I kind of want to, like…commemorate the first tattoo I give by getting a matching one. My first job with my first tattoo. Weird, right?"

He stays quiet, and I roll my eyes.

"I'll take that as a yes."

"It's not a yes, just, uh, *damn*." He turns back to the notebook and drags his fingers along a pair of hands sketched onto the paper.

"Damn?" I repeat. The familiar pang of shame and fear swirl together, leaving me on pins and needles as I study the side of his face.

"It's a lot of trust in a random stranger." He keeps perusing my work, slowly lifting the pages one after another. "What if they want you to tattoo a dick or something?"

I snort. "They're not gonna ask for a dick."

"You don't know that," he argues. "It could be anything. It's their choice. All I'm saying is it's a lot of trust in someone you don't know."

"Guess I'll have to choose my first client wisely," I concede.

It's interesting. Watching him analyze my art. The way his tongue darts out between his lips and his eyes drag across the page. Seriously. It isn't fair how handsome he is. And I don't know if it's because he actually cares about my work or if it's because I've managed to slip past his asshole personality and see the ooey-gooey center he hides from the world, but I like it. I like *him*. Way more than I ever thought possible.

Oblivious to the heart pangs I get any time we're in the same room together, he challenges, "What if it's a girl's name or an anniversary date or a heart tattoo with I love Mom in the middle?"

With a laugh, I lift one shoulder. "Hey, I love my mom as much as the next person, so…I guess it's fine?"

He looks up at me and quirks his brow, like I'm literally the craziest person he's ever met.

"And will you please stop looking at me like I've grown a second head or whatever?" I add.

Hands raised in defeat, he concedes, "All right, all right. When do you get to do your first tattoo? Is there a checklist or something?"

"I mean, yes and no," I hedge. "Technically, I have my own machine, so I could do it whenever, but…"

"But?"

Stalling, I wet my lips. "I don't know. I guess I'm waiting."

"For what?"

My lips bunch, and I lift my shoulder again, knowing I don't have an answer, let alone one he'll accept.

"So, you're a coward," he teases. And honestly, it's surprising. Witnessing this side of Everett. The playful side. The softer side. The non-asshole Everett. Even if he did call me something offensive.

Biting back my amusement, I argue, "I'm not a coward, it's just…"

"Just what?"

"It's a lot of pressure, okay?"

His laugh turns my insides into knots as he flips through my notebook at a quicker pace. "This is awesome. This is awesome." He pauses at a picture of a bull with massive horns and a pierced nose. "Even this is awesome." Slapping it closed, he gives me his full attention again. "You're talented, Stormie. There's no shame in that."

My heart flutters in my chest, but I shake it off and reopen my notebook, attempting to see my hard work the same way he does. Without the mistakes or the erase marks or the tiny details driving me nuts, no matter how minute they are.

"See?" His warm, minty breath hits the side of my face. "Talented."

"Let's say you're right." I peek up at him again, my notebook forgotten. "Being talented on paper doesn't mean I'm talented on skin."

"And I think you need to give yourself a little more credit." He folds his arms and settles back into the cushions. I know this look. I've seen it when he's around his friends. His sister. It's confidence. Confidence in me. My potential. My talent.

Ignoring the way it makes me want to squirm, I murmur, "I'll work on it."

"Good. And while you work on it, I'll pick my tattoo." He reopens the notebook, but I snag it from him and toss it onto the coffee table in front of us.

"You think you're so funny," I quip.

He smirks. "Not usually, but I'll take it."

I snort and loop my hands around his bicep, squeezing tenderly. "Speaking of tattoos, though."

"Yeah?"

"My, uh, my brother's coming into town for a concert, and…" I look down at my hands, unable to finish the sentence while simultaneously preparing for a fight.

"And your dad's calling in that introduction," Everett finishes for me. "Not sure if you remember, but he mentioned it when he almost ripped my head off."

I asked Everett to sit in the car while waiting for me to finish my shifts. It's probably the coward's way out, but I can't help it. My dad hates him. He didn't even have to officially meet the guy, and he still hates him. The prospect of Everett meeting my brother on top of my dad makes me feel about as comfortable as getting a nipple piercing without numbing cream.

No, thank you.

"I've been putting it off," I admit, "but with my brother coming into town, I don't think I can push it off any longer. Not when you take me to and from work, and—"

"Okay."

I jolt back, surprised.

He gives in so easily. Like it isn't a big deal. Meeting my family. I spent months trying to convince Drake to give my family the time of day. To give them one afternoon. One meeting. Yet here Everett is, complying without batting an eye.

I look up at him again and search his expression for any hint of frustration or annoyance, but I don't find anything out of the ordinary. Nope. Just the unapologetic Everett I've grown accustomed to since moving in with him.

"You're still okay meeting my family?" I ask.

"Why wouldn't I be?"

"I don't…I don't know?"

His warm hand envelops my calf once more, and he squeezes softly. "Before the fort, I'd say we might need to figure out a game plan or something, but now this is real, so I don't see a problem with meeting your family. Do you?"

Damn, those baby blues. The way I swear they pierce every single protective layer I've woven around my heart with a single look. It leaves me vulnerable and…curious. What it would be like. To trust myself enough to let him in completely.

Don't get me wrong. I have been letting him in. One day at a time. One positive interaction at a time. One homemade cookie or from scratch meal at a time. He's a guy I'm proud of. A guy I want beside me. But Drake used to be that guy. What if I'm wrong again? What if my gut is…a bad judge of character?

I bite my bottom lip, unsure what to say because honestly? I don't have a problem with Everett meeting my family for real, but I also don't know how to handle Everett being so...easy about meeting my family for real when all Drake ever did was bitch and moan about the prospect alone.

"Is there a problem, Stormie?" Everett prods.

"They're going to interrogate you," I point out.

"Okay."

"And they're going to threaten you."

He smirks. "I wouldn't expect anything less."

"And they'll follow through on it, too."

"If Drew hurt Fin, I'd be the same way," he volleys back.

I frown. "You're really okay with this?"

"I said I was," he reminds me. Crinkles of amusement line his eyes, but even then, I'm not sure what to say or do or... anything really. "Is this about Drake?" he prods.

His name hits like a baseball bat, but I try to hide the air as it whooshes from my lungs.

"No?" I offer.

The same soft smile toys at the edge of his lips. "You sure?"

"No?" I repeat hesitantly.

"I'm gonna go with yes, this is about Drake." He squeezes my calf again. "With all the shit he put you through, I want you to know I get it. And I know you know this, but I'll reiterate it anyway, all right? I'm not him."

"I know you're not."

"Raine." His touch is gentle as he grabs my chin and turns me toward him. "I'm. Not. Him."

Nibbling the inside of my cheek, I nod, willing myself to believe him. "I know you're not."

He searches my eyes as if debating whether or not he believes me either. Dropping his hand, he leans forward and brushes his lips against mine. The kiss is warm and sweet and innocent and only makes me fall for him more.

When he pulls away seconds later, Everett asks, "So, when do I meet the infamous Dodger Anders?"

I square my shoulders and prepare myself for the inevitable. Everett's going to meet Dodge. And my dad.

Shit.

"In two weeks," I force out.

"Two weeks." He nods. "Got it. Which brings us to our next order of business."

"What's that?"

He pauses, and I swear I can feel the shift in the air, like he's preparing himself for a kick to the crotch. "We, uh, we play the Grizzlies next weekend."

My abs tighten on reflex, and I exhale slowly in an attempt to cover the flight or fight response flooding my system from the mere mention of Drake's team, let alone the devil himself. Surprisingly, Drake isn't a usual topic of conversation between me and Everett. Bringing him up twice in a two-minute span is more than I can handle.

My mouth feels like it's been coated in cotton, but I force out, "Oh?"

"On their ice," he adds.

My stomach bottoms out, and I stare at my hands, clicking my nails back and forth as I fight back the urge to yell at Everett when we both know he doesn't deserve it. Still. The timeline makes sense. Why Everett's been begging his coach to get back on the ice. He wants to play against Drake. To prove whatever shitshow Drake put him through a few weeks ago means nothing and he's still the better player. The better man.

It shouldn't terrify me, but it does. The idea of them facing off. The idea of anything to do with Drake, in general. I wish I could take it back. Every moment with him. Wish I could erase it from everyone's memory, including my own.

Wish I could've been stronger. Could've seen who he really was.

"Stormie," Everett murmurs.

The warmth in his voice cuts through the ice in my veins, and I peek up at him. "You're going, I assume?"

"Yeah. Yeah, of course I am." He squeezes my calf again. "You think I'd stay away when I finally have a chance to legally beat the shit out of the guy?"

My expression falls. "Ev—"

"Sorry, Stormie, but I wouldn't miss this game for the world." He leans forward and kisses me again, though I'm too frozen to reciprocate. "Have you heard from him lately?"

I shake my head. "Not since *Spin the Bottle.*"

"Do you want to come?" he prods.

My lips part on a staggered breath as I carefully consider showing up. Of facing him again. It's stupid. He's merely a person. A shitty person. A shitty person I want nothing to do with yet can't seem to escape, no matter how much I try.

Do I want to see him again? No. No, I really don't. But do I want to give him the power to keep me from attending a game my boyfriend's playing? Not really. He's already stolen enough moments from me. Adding this to the list feels… wrong. In a way, all of it does.

"Raine?" Everett prods. "Do you want to come?"

"I don't…I don't know," I whisper.

It's so weird. Talking about this. How easily Drake can completely taint a conversation, let alone a pretty awesome evening together.

"My parents are coming, too," Everett adds.

"To the away game?"

He nods. "Yeah. You could sit with them. If you want."

Sitting with his family? Why does it feel even more intimate than actually holding hands and snuggling on the couch with the guy?

Because it's the next step. The next phase. Making this even more real. More...*more.*

I never got this far with Drake. In a way, I'm not sure I ever wanted to, even though it was so easy to blame him for not being interested in crossing that particular bridge. The truth is, I'm not sure either of us wanted to cross it. To move our relationship to the next level. But with Ev? Am I crazy for considering it? Maybe.

"Is it a bad idea?" he asks. "You sitting with my family?"

"Do you want me to sit with your family?"

"Yeah, of course I do. If I didn't, I wouldn't have invited you."

"You sure?" I ask.

"You're important to me, Storm. They'll love you."

"Then, no," I answer. "I don't think it's a bad idea."

"You sure?" he asks, throwing my own words back at me.

Am I sure?

My brows crease before I smile back at Ev. It's small and weak, but I cling to it nonetheless. "Yeah. It's actually...really sweet of you," I decide. "Wanting me to meet your family."

"I can be sweet." He kisses my cheek, and I close my eyes, savoring the feel of his lips against my skin.

"You can be very sweet," I agree.

He kisses my cheek again, this time closer to my lips. "I want you there."

With a slow nod, I give in. "I wouldn't miss it."

"That's my girl."

CHAPTER THIRTY-THREE

RAINE

I'm nervous. It feels like a thousand bees are buzzing around in my stomach, and I can't figure out if or when they'll sting. Finley's gone. Apparently, she bought a plane ticket and flew out to see Drew last night and, therefore, wound up ditching me with her parents in the process.

It's fine. I understand she needs to put out a few fires in the relationship department, but I could've definitely used her as a buffer right about now.

I also probably should've rethought my first time meeting Everett's parents with the added distraction of being in the same vicinity as Drake, but it's too late now.

Shoulda, woulda, coulda, Raine.

Everett offered to talk with his coach and explain the situation so he could drive me to the rink. I declined, not wanting to rock the boat after already being the reason behind why he missed the last few games. Grudgingly, Everett agreed, then suggested I catch a ride with his parents to the game. The idea of being stuck in a car with them for an hour or so felt pretty miserable, so we compromised. I drove his car, promising I wouldn't get out of it until his parents could walk me in.

Did it make me feel a little bit like a child? Yes. Did I appreciate Everett's thoughtfulness, especially after being jumped the last time he was in Cedar Springs? Also, yes.

Although now that I'm here, I'm seriously second-guessing my decision to drive alone instead of taking Everett up on his offer to call in a favor with his coach. I don't want to be here. This place holds too many memories. Too many experiences I wish I could erase. Facing them with Everett is one thing. Facing them alone, or better yet, with Everett's parents as witnesses? Yeah. It feels even more unbearable.

But so does hiding away in Everett's cabin instead of moving forward. Moving on. Even if this feels like trudging up a snow-covered hill barefoot. Sometimes numb. Sometimes painful. It's better than being paralyzed with fear.

Breathe, I remind myself. *You're here for Everett, not Drake.*

When my phone buzzes in the cupholder, I flinch, then pick it up to read the message.

555.236.0595

> Hey, Raine! Everett gave me your number. This is his mom, Kate. We're so excited to meet you! We just turned into the parking lot. Where are you?

ME

> East side. Fourth row back. Do you want to meet at the entrance?

MRS. TAYLOR

> No worries. We'll come to you.

My shoulders fall as I read her message. Not because she isn't being super thoughtful, but I can't help wondering if she knows about my situation with Drake and if it's the reason why she insists I wait for her and her husband in my locked car. I should've asked Everett if he told them, but I didn't think about it. I guess I assumed he'd keep it between us. He promised to not tell my family, but he never promised to keep his own in the dark. And let's not forget about his blabbermouth little sister. Yeah. There's no way they don't know.

Great.

I reread Mrs. Taylor's text. It doesn't exactly ease the buzzing in my gut. She knows. She has to. And here, I wanted to make a good impression.

Puffing my cheeks out, I type my response.

ME

Sounds good. See you in a minute.

MRS. TAYLOR

Perfect! We're in a white Jeep.

I look up and scan the parking lot when a pearly white Jeep pulls into one of the closest spots. Seconds later, a man and a woman climb out of the SUV. The man is broad-shouldered with short brown hair and a five o'clock shadow. The woman beside him is short, curvy, and has long, straight black hair reaching her mid-back. Both wear LAU hoodies, jeans, and white Nikes. It makes them look like the perfect match. And even if I hadn't seen their pictures at the cabin, I feel like I would still recognize them. It's like Everett's the perfect mix of the two. He has his dad's eyes and height. His mom's hair and nose.

As Everett's dad's hand finds Mrs. Taylor's waist, she smiles up at him. All it takes is one smile to know they're good people. Loving people. And I swear I recognize it. The smile. It's the same one Everett's given me. The same one he uses to settle my nerves more times than I can count, and even though Mrs. Taylor's isn't directed at me, I still manage to let out a slow breath.

It's going to be fine.

Turning Everett's car off, I grab my purse from the passenger seat and open the door.

As soon as my feet hit the ground, I offer, "Uh, hi."

"Hey, I'm Kate," the woman replies. "And yes, please call me Kate. Mrs. Taylor is Macklin's mom."

I smile back at her. "Hi, Kate. I'm Raine."

"And I'm Macklin," her husband adds, stretching his hand out. "You can call me Mack. Nice to meet you."

Shaking his hand, I say, "Nice to meet you, too, Mack."

"Shall we?" he suggests.

The building is bustling. The majority of the fans are decked out in yellow and brown, the Grizzlies' colors. It makes me and Everett's parents stick out like a sore thumb in our red, black, and white jerseys. When we find our way to the visitor's section a few minutes later, I can't help but curl in on myself despite Everett's parents being nothing but friendly.

I've been here a hundred times. But I've never sat in these seats, and I sure as hell have never worn these colors. Not here. My knee bounces, and I slouch in the plastic chair while trying not to have a full-blown meltdown in the visitor's section as the fans stand up, preparing for the home team to take to the ice while I keep my butt planted where it is.

"So, Raine," Macklin leans forward in his seat, resting his elbows on his knees. "How do you like the cabin?"

"Cabin?" I turn to him and frown. Not because I don't know what he's talking about, but because, well, he knows I'm living in his cabin?

"Everett said you're sleeping in the guest bedroom?" he prods.

"Oh. Yes." I force a smile.

So, Everett's a blabbermouth. *Noted.*

"It's really nice," I add. "Thank you for letting me stay there."

"It's a good place to escape to when you need it," he replies.

Sandwiched between us, Kate explains, "Macklin went through a nasty divorce and wound up moving to the mountains and building the place before we met. We're glad it's getting some more use."

Macklin was divorced when he met Everett's mom? Wait…I think I knew that. He also has two older daughters. Miley and…Hazel, I think?

I shake myself out of replaying one of my earlier conversations with Everett and reply, "Thank you. It's really beautiful."

"He worked hard on it," Kate gives her husband a look and smirks. "I'm sorry Finley couldn't be here, by the way."

"It's fine. She told me about her little trip to see Drew."

"Yeah, she really loves the boy. Speaking of my youngest child, Finley's told us a lot about you," Kate adds.

Called it.

Finley's *also* a blabbermouth.

I look down at my hands. "Sounds…promising?"

"Only good things, I swear," Kate teases but sobers quickly. "Well, mostly good things. I heard about your ex."

My smile falls. "Did you, now?"

"Yeah." She grimaces. "I hear it's how you met Everett?"

I force myself to nod. "Uh, yeah. He stepped in and made sure my ex couldn't…couldn't bother me anymore."

"Ever the protector," she quips. "I'm sorry about your situation, though."

"It's fine."

"It isn't, but I understand why you don't want to talk about it," Kate interjects. "Just so you know, my daughter's a vault most of the time, I promise. But when it comes to her big brother, she isn't afraid to break the rules and fill us in."

Nodding, I pick at my cuticles.

"He's so used to taking care of everyone else," Macklin adds. "Dylan. Ophelia. Tatum. Finley. His mom."

Kate smiles and grabs her husband's knee like they're both privy to some big secret. I bite my bottom lip to keep myself from asking what it is.

"I have epilepsy," Kate explains. "And unfortunately, it's genetic, so I passed it along to Finley."

"Finley mentioned it," I reply, remembering the way she blurted out her diagnosis at SeaBird not so long ago. "It must be…scary."

"It can be," Macklin says, "but I'm a paramedic, so I know how to handle it."

"You also signed up for it," Kate muses. "Everett, on the other hand…"

"You're an amazing mom," Macklin reminds her.

"I know I am." Kate grins back at him, then turns to me again. "But what I'm trying to say is Everett didn't sign up to be his mom's and sister's pseudo-protector when his dad isn't around."

"Pretty sure he's the pseudo-protector no matter who he's around," I point out with a laugh.

Kate joins in. "You're totally right. What we see and experience in this life molds us into who we are. And sometimes, it sucks. Then, add in what happened with Dylan and how terrible he felt, and…well, no wonder the poor boy has a bit of a hero complex, you know?"

"Yeah, I've noticed that, too," I admit. "The way he's always so quick to swoop in and protect the people he cares about. Like me," I add.

"It isn't a bad thing," Kate rushes out. "I think we all need someone to swoop in and save us every once in a while." She tosses another smile at Macklin, and my chest squeezes.

"I'm sorry if you feel like Finley betrayed your trust by telling us about your situation," Macklin interjects. "She likes you. Actually, they both do."

"I like both of them, too," I reply.

"They're easy to like," Kate agrees. "It's just…," she pauses. "I want to make sure someone's taking care of him, too."

I swallow thickly, unsure what else to say, as my pulse quickens. "Yeah, I…I completely understand."

"Good because I want to make it clear that I've never seen my son happier," Kate points out.

"He's also never brought a girl around until now," Macklin adds. "You're special to him."

"He's special to me, too," I whisper. "And I'll, uh, I'll do my best to take care of him. I promise."

The same familiar smile stretches across Kate's face. "I know you will. Honestly, you already are. We heard about his concussion and how you rose to the occasion to take care of him." She pats my knee, the same way she did to her husband. "You're good for him."

"Everett…Taylor!" the announcer booms.

The words snap us from our conversation, and I notice most fans have sat down again, giving me a perfect view of the rink. The teams are lined up on the ice. I was so distracted by our conversation, I didn't even realize they'd filed out of the locker room and down the tunnels.

Sitting up a little straighter in my seat, I wait for both centers to meet at the blue line and the whistle to blow. But I can't shake Kate's comments. For the first time since meeting Everett, I finally grasp why he is the way he is. So vigilant. So on point. So laser-focused on everyone around him. Because if he has a mom and sister who deal with epilepsy, and a friend who hid a fatal disease, and another friend who died in a car accident, and another friend who struggles from head trauma, what other choice does he have but to always watch and wait, to anticipate if and when something will go wrong while also juggling his own life. His own struggles. His own goals and hopes and dreams.

I can't even imagine.

No wonder he was so hesitant to add me to his plate in the beginning. To make sure I'm taken care of and staying safe. It isn't only who he is. It's who he's had to be, and my heart aches in understanding. For the little boy and the pressure he must've felt on a daily basis. Scratch that. The pressure he still feels on a daily basis despite never having signed up for it.

Am I adding to it?

The question is like a barbed caress as it rises to the surface. He moved out of his place because of me. He was jumped because of me. He had to worry about how I was going to get here and whether or not I was safe. He had to give his parents my number and arrange for them to walk me inside a stupid building all because of a potential interaction between me and my ex. It has to be exhausting, doesn't it?

"I want to make sure he's being taken care of, too." Kate's words filter through my mind, bringing with them a heaviness I feel down to my bones.

I'm trying to protect him. To make sure he's happy and fulfilled. But obligated? I don't want him to feel obligated to be with me. I don't want him to feel obligated to keep me safe, or to put me in a box with the rest of the people he cares about.

Is that so wrong? At this point, I don't even know.

Shoving the thought aside, I wipe my sweaty palms on my jeans and try to focus on the man I've most definitely fallen for, who's going head-to-head with my ex.

Look at the bright side. If I wanted a distraction from being in the same area as Drake, I got it, right?

CHAPTER THIRTY-FOUR

EVERETT

Not gonna lie. I've been waiting for this. For this moment. When I can beat the shit out of Drake under the guise of a hockey game. Without pissing off the police or messing with Dylan's investigation.

Just me and him on the ice.

No bullshit.

Only retribution.

It's funny. Hearing my Aunt Mia and Uncle Henry's account of the guy who used to beat the shit out of her when she attended LAU. His name was Shorty. Fitting since only a guy who's small would choose to beat the shit out of a woman. Drake's small, too. Maybe not literally—Shorty wasn't, either—but small all the same.

Rolling my shoulders, I head to the blue line as the crowd chants around us. It'll be even sweeter this way. Beating the shit out of Drake on his own ice. Proving he's the lesser man in front of his biggest fans.

I can't. Fucking. Wait.

Looking up at the stands, I search the crowd for Raine and my parents. When I find them, my brows dip. Raine looks nervous. Did one of the fans do something to her? My mom's beside her. She looks okay for now. I was worried when I came through the tunnel, and strobe lights were flashing. I've seen it a hundred times. Hell, maybe a thousand if you include Finley. I still remember when we were kids and how many times she seized until the doctors figured out the right dosage of her medication. Doesn't erase the memories, though. My mom's is worse. Or maybe it isn't. Feels like it, though. Sometimes, I wonder if it's because she's my mom. She's supposed to be strong and unbreakable. And yeah, to be fair, she's definitely the most resilient person I've ever known. But watching her battle her seizures will never get easier. She looks all right, but if she has one here? On the fucking concrete or in the plastic seats? My hands shake, and my gut churns.

"Your dad's got her," Griffin calls out as if the bastard knows exactly what I'm thinking.

He's right.

My dad's beside her. He knows her better than anyone. Has been able to read the signs, whenever he's given any, better than her own doctors. Hell, better than my mom herself. And she looks…fine for now.

She'll be fine.

She'll be fine.

She'll be fine.

The sound of skates gliding against ice cuts through my spiraling thoughts as the referee approaches us.

Preparing for the game to start, I shake my head and squeeze the stick in my palms a little tighter.

Focus.

Reeves is on my right. Griffin on my left. Drake and the rest of his team skate into position. It's a shame we can't meet at the center line or face off since Drake's a defender. I'm not too worried, though. We'll have our time. His movements are slow as he skates into position, though I can feel his stare. Motherfucker probably feels like he's on top of the world right now after the last time we saw each other. Joke's on him. He didn't play fair, and now it's my turn to knock him down a peg or two. Leaning forward, I block him out and palm my stick, preparing for the ref to drop the puck and blow the whistle.

Three. Two. The puck slips from the ref's fingers and falls to the ice. I slap it to my left toward a waiting Griffin and dodge the Grizzlies' center. Charging around one of the defenders, I move into the pocket, stopping short. Ice sprays as I screech to a halt, turn, and prepare for the pass I know is coming. Like clockwork, Griffin chips it off the board, and I dribble it around the back of the net. From my periphery, I catch a flash of yellow.

Yeah, I see you.

Drake sprints toward me, thinking he's caught me off guard, but I slap the puck through his spread skates where Griffin stands. With his stick wrenched back, he waits for the perfect moment, then slaps the puck into the corner of the net. The flight flashes red, and the siren wails.

One to nothing.

Fuck. Yes.

The Hawks whoop on the ice and at the bench, celebrating our first point, and, not gonna lie, it feels good. A huge part of me wanted to come out here and beat the shit out of Drake before the whistle even had a chance to blow. But winning like this? Embarrassing Drake on his own ice? It might even be sweeter than ending the night with split knuckles and Drake's blood on my fists.

Then again, it's still early. Anything can happen.

We go again, setting up for the next play. This time, the Grizzlies' center steals the puck, but one of our defensemen manages to bat it away from him, recovering it and shooting it across the blue line. Reeves receives the pass, handling the puck like a seasoned pro as he spins around a Grizzlies' defenseman, then slaps it my way. Drake's close, but I manage to dodge him at the last second. He slams into the glass, causing an "Ooooh!" to echo throughout the arena as I pass the puck to Griffin, then turn around and wiggle my fingers in a toodle-oo motion. Yeah, I'm acting like a dick, but at this point, I don't really give a fuck.

Drake's face is red beneath his mask, and my grin widens before I get my head back in the game and try to help my teammates out. Then, like a fucking bull, Drake charges straight toward me. Clearly, he doesn't give a shit about the penalty we both know he'll face if he does what I think he's going to, but if he's game, so am I. With a heavy thump, the air whooshes out of my lungs as I'm pushed back, sliding on the ice and trying to keep my balance while fighting off the uppercut to my gut.

Apparently, Dickless didn't like me toying with him.

"Don't worry, asshole," I say between grunts as he pins me to the boards and hits me over and over again. "I can embarrass you this way, too."

Whistles blow around us as Drake throws off his gloves, and I do the same, ready to finally blow off the pent-up frustration that's been building since the moment I saw Raine's bruising. I dodge his right hook, land a jab to his nose, and wind up for a cross-hook combo. His head snaps back from the impact of my hits, but he recovers quickly and yanks me into a bear hug.

"You want your ass kicked again, Taylor?" he spits. "You're lucky I didn't break your fucking kneecap."

When he connects another brutal uppercut, my abs scream in protest as I twist his jersey in my fist, hold him in place, and land a right hook to his eye.

"And you're lucky I didn't call the cops." I wind up for

another hit. A searing pain explodes across my knuckles, but his grunt is like music to my fucking ears. "Never been one to fight fair. Right, Haitt?"

I shove him away from me and prepare for another hit, only to be torn apart by the refs and my teammates. Like my head breaking through the water's surface, whistling ensues, and the booing of the crowd finally registers as the referee drags us both to the penalty box.

It's only the beginning.

Ninety-eight seconds later, Griffin scores again. Yeah, I'm counting. The red light glows behind the Grizzlies' net, and the crowd boos again as Griffin skates around the rink with his glove raised in the air. With a grin, he moves past me in the sin bin, and I slam my hands against the glass, cheering him on. Seconds later, the Grizzlies take possession of the puck and dart toward our goalie, looking for blood. Keeping his stance low, Dreggs watches the Grizzlies' left wing dribble the puck down the ice toward him. When the opponent winds up and slaps it into the left side of the net, anger surges through my veins.

Fuck.

So much for having a big lead. After the power play, the ref lets me out of the box, and I'm more than ready. Racing forward, I let the ice spray as I stop short at the blue line, anxious for the face-off again and scoring our team another point.

It takes a little while, but before the whistle blows ending the first period, we manage to do exactly that, putting the score at three to one.

The second period is uneventful, but by the third period, I'm ready to end this thing.

As I head toward the blue line, I catch Drake glaring at me. His mouth is swollen from earlier, and it makes me grin back at him. Yeah, he'll be feeling it tomorrow. I crouch forward, preparing for the next play. When the puck slips from the ref's fingers, I slap my stick against my opponent's, then snap the puck off the boards, passing it to a waiting Reeves. In a flash, he dodges the Grizzlies' defender, and I race toward the red line, trying to put myself in position. The puck flies through the defender's legs, and I catch it just in time, dropping it into the bottom corner of the net.

The red light flashes, and I grin, skating toward the bench where Cameron waits to swap places. It feels good to be here. On the ice. The crowd booing. I hide my amusement as I bask in the sound. Little do they know, it only feeds my adrenaline and the high accompanying every fucking score. As I steal a drink of water, I catch Drake staring up at Raine in the stands with a smirk. It makes my blood boil. Just like that, my high disappears, and I want to kill him.

I want to tell him to stop looking at her. To stop noticing her. To stop proving she's still on his radar despite his absence lately. It doesn't matter that she's sitting next to my family. That they're trying to make her comfortable by talking to her. I can still see it. The way her spine is rigid. The way she's chewing on her long black nails. The way her eyes keep darting around the arena.

"Get your head in the game," Griffin grits out beside me.

Where the hell did he come from?

I tear my attention from the asshole across the ice and look at my best friend. "It *is* in the game."

"Nah, it's in the stands," he argues. "Come on. We got this."

He's right. We do.

Rolling my shoulders, I watch the rest of my team on the ice until Coach puts me in again, and I move toward the blue line. Anxious to prove it. To prove we've got this game. To prove we're better. Not just the Hawks, but me. I'm better. I deserve this. I deserve her.

Focus, I remind myself.

As soon as the puck drops from the ref's fingers, I'm ready to slap it toward Griffin, but the Grizzlies' center gets to it first. He hits it toward the Hawks' side of the ice. One of our defenders intercepts and chips it off the board as I race into position, barely catching the pass. Left, right, left, right, I dribble down the side and find Drake in my periphery.

Yeah, I see you, asshole.

When I stop short, he slams into the glass as, *"Oof,"* echoes throughout the arena.

"That one's gotta hurt," the announcer adds.

He's not wrong.

Frustrated, Drake pushes off the glass, but I'm already around him, moving toward the net as he races to catch up to me.

Not today, Drake.

I pass the puck to Reeves, then move toward the pocket as sweat slides down my temple.

"Come on, come on, come on," I mutter under my breath. My gaze is glued to the black biscuit when I'm hit from behind. With a crack, my helmet hits the glass, and I blink the stars from my eyes, realizing I'm pinned between Drake and the slick barrier. It's a dirty move, but I'm not sure why I'm surprised.

"How'd you like that?" Drake growls.

I spin around and shove him off me. My gloves are on the ground again, and all thought of the game, of being thrown out or what numbers are on the scoreboard, dissipates. I cock my arm back and deck him in the face, causing an explosion of pain to erupt in my knuckles, but I don't stop. I keep hitting him over and over until the refs rip me away, and I flex my hands. Yeah. My knuckles are split, and fresh blood coats his jersey.

"You're out!" the ref yells. "Both of you!"

I look up at the scoreboard and grin. It's four to one. Thirteen seconds left in the third period. We've got this game in the bag.

"Fine by me," I answer. Turning to the bloodied Drake, I add, "Good game, Haitt."

Then I look up at the stands, confirming my dad's still seated next to my mom and Raine, and skate toward the locker room.

CHAPTER THIRTY-FIVE

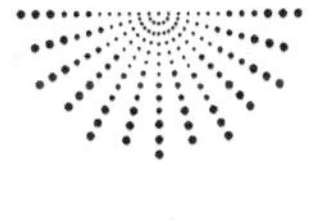

RAINE

LAU won. And I survived being in the same room with my ex without puking my guts out. It should feel like I win on all counts, but I haven't been able to quiet the little voice inside my head ever since I sat down in my seat and put myself in Everett's shoes.

Ripping the paper towel from the dispenser in the women's bathroom, I dry my hands, then toss it in the trash. Everett's parents are waiting by the visitor's locker rooms, but I snuck away to use the restroom.

As I push the door open, I nearly run into a yellow and brown jersey but stop short and crane my neck up. "Excuse me."

"Hey, traitor," the stranger grunts.

My brows pull as I look up at him again. "I'm sorry. Do I know you?"

"Rick, one of Drake's friends," he clarifies.

I squint, trying to see if I recognize the guy, but honestly, I think the term *friend* is probably a stretch. If I had to guess, he's a big Grizzlies fan and worships all the players like the rest of Cedar Springs, meaning he's likely not a fan of me.

Perfect.

"Nice to meet you, Rick," I mumble. "Now, if you'll excuse me." I start to step around him, but he mirrors my movements, blocking my escape.

"What the fuck are you doing here wearing the enemy's colors?"

I look down at the Hawks jersey with Everett's number printed on the front. It's peeking out from underneath my unzipped North Face jacket, and I frown. "W-what?"

Before I even register what's happening, the asshole dumps soda over my head. Ice skitters around my feet, and I gasp, jumping back with my jaw slack as I realize I'm now drenched in sticky brown liquid.

"Are you kidding me?" I screech.

"That's for my boy." Rick's gaze slides down my body, and he grins, taking in his handiwork. "Now, get the hell out of our arena."

I'm so shocked it takes me a second to pick my jaw up from the floor as I stare up at the Grizzlies fan. Like seriously, who does this? How does this even happen?

Rick bends closer, bringing us nose to nose. "Or you can wait until Drake comes out of the locker room. Bet he'd love to see you again and put you in your place. *Bitch.*"

"Raine!" a voice calls.

My heart jumps to my throat, and I turn toward the culprit when a freshly showered Everett appears. His hair is still wet and pushed away from his face like he combed his fingers through it as he balances his massive hockey bag over his shoulder. With long strides, he moves toward me, his parents flanking his sides. It only makes me feel like more of an idiot. An outsider. A weak damsel in distress. My cheeks flame, and I stare at the ground, desperate to disappear.

Rick scoffs but steps back, giving me more space, only for

it to be replaced with Everett's back as he moves between me and Drake's so-called *friend*.

"There a problem?" Everett growls. I shouldn't be surprised he's coming to my defense. It's what he does for everyone, apparently. The reminder kind of makes me want to cry.

Lifting his hands into the air, Rick takes another big step backward. "No problem."

Everett glances over his shoulder at me, taking in my wet, sticky clothes and hair, and turns back to Drake's buddy. "Did you pour soda over my girlfriend's head?"

"Everett," Macklin warns beside him.

Everett's fists squeeze at his sides, and I wait for the spiral. The chaos. The reared back arm, followed by the grunt of pain and the sound of flesh hitting flesh. Instead, Everett steps back, creating more distance between him and the stranger. Desperation and shame nearly split me in two as I grab the back of his shirt and keep my feet planted where they are, grateful for Everett's heat and maturity because I'm pretty sure if I was dating anyone else, there would be a full-on brawl, and thanks to today's location, I'm not sure it would end in our favor.

"Best get going, *Hawk*," the fan grits out. He says the word like it's a curse.

"You're right. We gotta celebrate tonight's win. Good game, though." I can hear Everett's amusement in his voice, and even though none of this is very funny, I can't deny how the sound tugs at my lower belly.

The fan flips Everett off but turns around and disappears through the exit, leaving me with Everett and his family. In an instant, Everett faces me again and shrugs his jacket off, his eyes brimming with concern. "Here."

"I'm fine," I murmur.

"You're not."

"I don't want to ruin it."

"You won't." He offers the coat to me again. "Take it."

"Ev," I beg. The dry jacket hangs between us, and I fold my arms. "Can we please…?" My words trail off, and I press my lips together, unsure what to say. I'm embarrassed. Cold. Sticky. I just want to go home.

"Hey." Everett's mom interrupts our little staredown. "Your dad and I should probably get going, anyway. I know we talked about grabbing dinner, but how about a rain check?" She steps closer to her son, kisses his cheek, and gives me a smile. "It was really nice to meet you, Raine."

"Nice to meet you, too," I whisper.

Macklin pulls his son into a quick hug and slaps his hand against his back, mirroring his wife and giving me the same reassuring smile she did. "Nice to meet you, Raine. We'll see you around, yeah?"

I nod. "Of course."

"See you, son," he adds to Ev.

As I watch them go, I tug my wet jacket tighter around me, trying to curl in on myself, when a couple of puck bunnies move toward me. My spine straightens as they giggle. One of them calls me a slut under her breath as they slip past me and head into the bathroom. It only makes me feel more awkward and uncomfortable.

I know Everett hears it, too, because his glare follows them until the heavy bathroom door cuts off his view. He turns to me, his gaze softening. "Let's go, yeah?"

I nod and let him lead me to his car. Apparently, his coach gave him permission to drive home with me instead of riding with the team, and I don't even give him crap for calling in a favor. I've been too lost in my own head.

It's cold out. Dark, too. The sun set at least an hour ago, and flecks of snow fall from the sky. I push my wet, sticky hair away from my face, and Everett opens the passenger door, guiding me into his car.

After rounding the front of it, he turns the ignition on, sets the heat to full blast, and forces my cold hands to the vents. "You okay?"

I shake my head and avoid his gaze, staring out at the falling snow instead. "I've been better."

"What happened?"

"Apparently, he knew me, or at least knew *of* me," I clarify. "Called me a traitor for wearing a Hawks jersey and said I didn't belong at the Grizzlies' arena." I scoot a little closer to the door and rest my head against the cold passenger window. "To be fair, he isn't entirely off-base."

"I should've kicked his ass," Ev replies.

"Pretty sure you've already kicked enough asses because of me."

"What's that supposed to mean?"

I bite my lip but stay quiet, shaking my head again. "Nothing, I'm just...cold."

I can feel his stare on the side of my face, but I don't look at him to confirm my suspicion. I'm too caught up in everything that happened tonight and the aftermath I need to wade through.

"You seem...off," he decides. When I don't reply, he puts his car in drive and turns onto the main road. "You sure everything's okay?"

Am I sure everything's okay? I want it to be. I hope it is. But is it selfish? Am I the problem?

"How was sitting next to my parents?" he prods, and I know he's trying to change the subject, but it only fuels my muddied thoughts. "Were they okay?"

"Your parents are amazing." I peek at him and force a sad smile. "I really like them."

"They really like you, too."

I don't know if it's true or if Everett's only being nice, but I hope it is.

"They're good people," I reply.

With a soft smile of his own, he nods. "Yeah, they really are."

"It's fitting," I add. "That your dad is a paramedic, what with your mom's and your sister's epilepsy."

"Yeah." He draws in a breath. "I don't know what they'd do without him."

"And you."

He frowns. "What about me?"

"You're their other hero. Their other protector."

Squeezing the back of his neck, he rests his elbow against the driver's side window and mutters, "I don't know about that."

"I do," I argue. "And then with Dylan's head injury—"

"How do you know about it?"

He doesn't sound mad but wary? Yeah. I'd say it's fitting. To be fair, I don't blame him. The way I just...threw out a huge event in his life, which likely altered his own brain chemistry the same way it did Dylan's.

"Finley told me a little while ago," I explain. "Not in a gossipy way or anything. It kind of just...came up. And then, your mom mentioned how you're always looking out for her, too, and...I don't know. I guess everything clicked into place."

"Hmm." He gives me the side-eye as the trees whir past us. "Seems you were pretty chatty during the game."

"Guess you could say so."

"Anything you want to talk about with me?" he prods.

I bite the inside of my cheek, considering his question. The opening he's gifted me. I could drop it. I could sweep it under the rug and pretend like everything's fine—and it is—

or I could open the wound. I could tell him what's bothering me, hoping and praying it doesn't blow up in my face.

The old me would've bottled it up. Would've shoved it aside. Part of me still wants to. The other part? It's screaming at me to let him in. To be open and vulnerable even when it's scary. Even when it feels irrational. Not the being vulnerable part, but the voicing my concerns out loud part. If you can even call my reservations a concern.

"Talk to me, Stormie," he prods.

I force out, "Are you only interested in me because you want to save me?"

His eyes bulge like I've told him the earth is flat. "What?"

"Let me rephrase." I lick my lips. "Have you always felt the need to be everyone's hero?"

Flicking his blinker on, he merges onto the freeway, but I can tell he's considering my question by the tiny flex of his jaw and the way his knuckles squeeze against the steering wheel. They're bruised and red and raw, thanks to his fight with Drake. I still can't believe he was thrown out of the game because of it.

"Where is this coming from?" Ev finally asks.

I tear my attention from his battered hand and peer up at him again. "Your mom mentioned how well you take care of her and Finley and Dylan and...everyone else in your life," I offer weakly.

"Is there a problem with wanting to protect the people I care about?"

"No, it's just...it has to be exhausting, doesn't it?" I whisper.

He pulls off at the next exit, and I swear my stomach flips inside out as he moves onto the side of the road and faces me fully.

"What are you getting at, Raine?"

Raine. Not Storm or Stormie.

Hello again, walls.

"I…I want you to know I don't need your protection. I mean, I do," I rush out, " but…I don't know. I guess, what I'm saying is…" I look down at my hands and fidget with my nails, picking at the cuticles. Clicking my thumbs over each other. It feels strange. Bringing this up. Giving him an out, almost. I'd never want him to take it, but the idea of him feeling backed into a corner or something only to wind up dating me because he doesn't know how to *not* be backed into a corner feels…wrong.

"Tell me," he pushes.

Staring at my hands, I whisper, "I don't want you to be with me because you feel obligated to be. I don't want you to think I'm…like I'm some scared little girl who has a boogeyman chasing after her, and the only way to keep him away is if we're together or something. And I know it's stupid. I know I literally hired you to keep the boogeyman away, but…I don't know, ever since we slept together…" I blink the burn behind my eyes away and look up at him. "I need to make it clear that I don't want to be an obligation." My teeth dig into my bottom lip as I search for the right words, knowing I'll never find them. "This is your official notice that you're…relieved from duty, or…whatever."

"Raine—"

"I'm serious," I push. "If this is as real for you as it is for me, then I need to know you see me as more than a victim."

"Raine."

"Ev—"

"Raine," he snaps. It's sharper this time, and my mouth snaps shut when he grabs my chin and forces me to hold his gaze. "You're not a victim. You were never a victim."

"You said I was a victim," I remind him. "When we first met."

He lets my chin go and hangs his head. "I was wrong. So fucking wrong, Raine."

I can taste his regret. His remorse. It's sharp and pungent and makes me want to cry. Or maybe it's my own guilt I taste. My own shame for being in this situation in the first place. For putting him in this situation when it's the last thing he ever deserved.

"Were you?" I whisper. "Were you wrong?"

He looks up at me again. "Do you really not see how strong you are? Raine, you dated an asshole, decided to leave, and he hit you. You then found someone willing to help, approached them, and got out."

"I should've seen the signs, though," I argue.

"Yeah, and I should've seen how I was overstepping my bounds with Dylan...for *years*," he emphasizes. "And if Dylan won't hold it against me, then you're not allowed to hold your own shit against yourself, either."

"Pretty sure it's different," I point out.

"Pretty sure it isn't. But you're right about one thing. I do have a hero complex. And I do feel the need to protect my mom and my sister and you."

"Ev," I breathe out.

"But it isn't because you're a victim. It's because I care about you, and no matter how much I try, I know it isn't something I can just...shut off, so I hope you can cut me some slack every once in a while. All right? Because I sure as shit am not letting you go. Do you hear me?"

I scowl at him before my expression softens, and I nod. "I hear you."

"Good."

"Can I ask you something else?" I push.

He sighs. "Depends. Is it gonna piss me off?"

"Maybe." My mouth curves up for the smallest of seconds but I quickly sober. "Your mom asked if I take care of you, too, and…I don't know. I guess it got me thinking… Do I?" My brows wrinkle as I consider her question for what feels like the thousandth time tonight. "You're so…strong. And I don't mean only physically." My mouth lifts again, and I meet his gaze. "I mean in every way, Ev. You're like this…this giant protector. And I dunno, I…I started thinking about how or *if* it's even possible for me to take care of you the same way you take care of me, you know?" I suck my bottom lip between my teeth and bite down hard, analyzing every single moment we've shared together since we first met. "Relationships are a two-way street, and I feel like you're always swooping in to take care of me. Even today, you swooped in and threatened to beat the shit out of a random guy. Like who does that?" I shake my head and raise my hand to stop him from interrupting me. "You're always the first to make sure I'm safe and well-fed and happy and warm and…I want to deserve you."

"Fucking hell, Storm," he rasps. Reaching out, he grabs the side of my face and brings me closer, pressing his forehead against mine. "You have no idea how incredible you are. How you make me stronger every single moment of every single day. You're patient and kind and talented and fucking beautiful. You see past my asshole behavior and make me smile, Storm. You make me smile more than anyone else in the world. You give me purpose. Support. Hell, you came to a game I know you wanted nothing to do with. You…" Those icy blue eyes bounce around my face. "You're my girl, Storm. *Mine.*"

I continue leaning over the center console and lift my chin, silently begging for a kiss. He meets me halfway without hesitation. And it's silly. Because we didn't even have a fight, but this still feels like a makeup kiss. Like I could've lost him. Like I almost let him go under the guise of protecting him from himself. From his own obligations. From the way he looks at everything and everyone around him. Like it's his job to step up. To be enough. To become the rock. Is it so wrong for me to want to do the same for him?

I kiss him gently, pinning his bottom lip between mine, and suck on the plump flesh softly. It pulls a groan from Everett's chest and spurs me on. Reaching up, I let his stubbled jaw tickle my fingertips. Then, I grab his shoulder and use it for leverage while I climb over the center console and deepen the kiss.

"What are you doing?" he rasps against my lips.

"Proving I'm yours." My mouth is on his again, and his hands find my ass, cupping my upper thighs and turning me on even more.

It's dark. We're in the middle of nowhere. And I can't help but want to take this to the next level. To see if I can convince him to let go of his control a little more. Not gonna lie, though. It's squishy. Like, super squishy. Rolling my hips against him, I suck on his tongue and tug at the short hair at the nape of his neck. The denim of my jeans rubs against my clit. It's like a spark on a puddle of gasoline, and Everett's strong hands tighten, pushing me against the edge of his cock.

"Fuck, Storm," he groans.

"Get in the back with me."

He smirks. "Is that a request?"

"Either that or you get a blow job while I get off on my fingers—"

His groan cuts me off, and he leans his head against the headrest. "Fuck. Storm."

"You like the imagery?" I nip at his bottom lip, ignoring the way my own pulse ratchets at the thought of it.

Opening his eyes again, he kisses me. Hard. Swallowing my moan as he thrusts his tongue in and out of my mouth like it's his thick cock nestled between my legs.

Dammit. I could seriously get off like this, and we're both

still fully clothed. It's torture. Freaking torture. But I can't make myself stop. I want him. Mind. Body. Soul. I want every piece he's willing to give, well aware of how many of mine he's already collected over the past few weeks. Honestly, it almost isn't fair. How much of me he owns. And even though I should be terrified, the warning bells are growing softer and softer with every kiss. Every touch. Every smile. Every confirmation I'm safe with him. He would never hurt me. Not intentionally.

With a loud thwack, his palm connects with my butt, and I yelp.

"Back," he orders. "Now."

Laughing at the irony of my thoughts and the burn of my ass, I scramble off his lap and climb into the backseat.

"Pants off," he adds, opening the driver's side door. Shimmying the thick denim down my thighs and off my feet, I scoot to the opposite side as he opens the door and climbs inside. His hands are already on his jeans, but he hesitates, his blue eyes practically glowing in the dark cab of his car.

Pressing my thighs together, I whisper, "What?"

"You look incredible like this."

"Naked and horny?" I offer dryly.

"Naked and *mine*." The word is nothing but a growl as he reaches for my ankle, dragging me closer until I'm sprawled out on the seats. Setting my phone on the center console, he skates his calloused palms along my calf, knee, then inner thigh as I wait with bated breath. "Don't. Move."

"Someone's bossy," I note.

"Hungry," he clarifies. Cupping my ass, he lifts me up. My heel digs into the center console while my opposite one digs into a seat belt clip as I struggle to keep my balance. And then, his mouth is on me, and my jaw drops.

This. This selflessness. I'll never get used to it. Never take it for granted. Like it's the most natural thing in the world.

For him to worship me. Crave me. Want to taste me. It's the most surreal feeling, and I bask in it. As if I'm a freaking ice cream cone, he licks my slit, dragging his tongue along my center and dipping inside like I'm the most delicious dessert he's ever tasted.

"Oh my fucking—" my words catch in my throat as he holds me to him and sucks on my clit, gently nipping at the sensitive bud before thrusting his tongue into me all over again. My eyes roll back in my head, and I squeeze my eyes shut. Pressure builds, and my body aches from its position, but I can't help it. I'm more turned on than I've ever been in my entire life.

I could come like this. I could actually come like this. With my body feeling like a freaking pretzel. The cold air caressing my bare thighs. And Everett's wicked mouth kissing my center and clit like it was made for me. Like he was made for me. In a way, maybe he was—is—made for me. Hooking his arm around my lower back, he spreads my folds with his opposite hand and massages tiny circles against my inner walls as his mouth finds my clit again. Stars erupt behind my eyelids, and I lose it. My body spasms against his tongue and fingers. I moan Everett's name, craving him now more than ever. Hell, I'm pretty sure I'm still orgasming as I smack his hand and force him to lower me from his mouth. I climb into his lap, pull his dripping cock out, and line him up with my entrance.

Then down I go, my slick heat swallowing every inch of him until I'm fully seated. He leans back, spreads his thighs beneath my ass, and grabs my waist, silently encouraging me to take the lead. And I like him like this, too. With his gaze glued to where our bodies connect. A slight sheen of sweat along his hairline, and his full lips parted. As I slowly lift up a few inches, his tongue darts out, and he licks his bottom lip.

"Fuck, I can still taste you." His eyes snap to mine. "You gonna fuck me, Storm?"

I nod and shift my hips, forcing him a little deeper. I lift up and do it all over again. He's so deep I have no doubt I'll feel it tomorrow, but the idea only spurs me on. I like the reminder I'm left with every time we're together. The slight ache. The smile I catch myself wearing as I replay it. Our moments together. It's a high. One I've never felt with anyone else. And I can't help but crave it more. Crave *him* more.

"You have no idea how pretty you look like this," he rasps. "Taking me like this."

I grab onto his shoulder and quicken my pace. My thighs burn as I fuck him harder and harder, letting his hands guide me until he slips his thumb between my legs and presses it against my clit. My body trembles from the pressure, and I swear I'm about to come again as I rest my head against his shoulder and move my hips against him over and over again.

"Gonna come, Storm," he warns.

His cock jerks inside of me, and I bite his shoulder, falling apart with him until I swear I'll never be able to walk again. But it's a good burn. A deep burn. A satisfying burn. One I never want to forget or lose. Because it's Everett. And I'm officially a sucker for all things Everett Taylor.

Dragging my hair to one side, he cups my face and lifts my head from where it's tucked against the crook of his neck. Then he kisses me. It's soft. Slow. Gentle. And I swear I can feel it from the top of my head to the tips of my toes.

When I finally pull away, he rubs his thumb along my cheek, and I smile, burrowing closer to him. His fingertips gently run along my spine like he isn't in a hurry for me to climb off, either, and I kind of love it. The steady rise and fall of his chest. The rhythmic pass of his fingertips. It's quiet. So freaking quiet. I can feel him softening inside of me. But I don't want to move. I don't want to leave the back of this car. I don't want to let this moment end. I don't want this to end. Me. Everett. Pretty sure I could stay here forever, and I'd die happy.

Everett Taylor, I think I might love you.

And even though I'm terrified of falling, I can't make myself stop.

CHAPTER THIRTY-SIX

RAINE

"**S**hould I be prepared for anything specific?" Everett asks as he removes the keys from the car's ignition.

"Other than an interrogation?" I quip. "Not that I know of."

"So, I'm going in blind. *Noted.*"

I rub my sweaty palms on my thighs and remind him, "You're the one who decided to walk into Etch 'N' Ink when I specifically told you to wait outside. And after the way I kept my family in the dark when it came to my dating life, I don't think my dad's gonna let you off the hook until he officially gets to know you. The good news is my sister had a baby a few weeks ago, so my mom's at her house, helping with my niece, which means you'll only meet my dad—"

"Whom I already met."

"And my older brother, Dodge," I finish. "He's the one you have to impress." Hesitating, I turn to face Everett fully. "Which, now that I think about it, will be pretty impossible, so don't get your feelings hurt if he's an ass."

Everett's mouth twitches. "Your brother's an ass?"

"My brother's my dad's son," I clarify. "And even though

my dad's mellowed out over the years,"—Everett scoffs, but I ignore it—"Dodger's holding strong to his assholery phase. Actually, I should give my dad more credit. Maybe it's less of his genes and more of Dodge's career choice. Being a rockstar is pretty much the quickest way to inflate a guy's ego, and Dodge is...*Dodge.*"

"I'll keep it in mind." Everett eyes the front of SeaBird warily. "Although, you're not exactly making it easy to walk in there."

"Why? Afraid they won't like you?" I tease.

"It's exactly what I'm afraid of."

My brows raise. To be honest, I didn't think Everett was afraid of anything. Did I find a chink in his armor?

When he catches me staring, he asks, "What?"

"Nothing, it's... I figured you weren't one to care about what others think."

He reaches over the console, grabs my hand, and brings it to his lips. "It's my girlfriend's family. Of course, I want them to like me."

Fireworks erupt in my stomach, and I bite the inside of my cheek to keep from grinning like a lunatic. "Did you just call me your girlfriend?"

Tugging me closer, he drops a kiss to the corner of my mouth and rasps, "Did I stutter?"

"You didn't say *fake* girlfriend," I clarify. "You said girlfriend."

"Pretty sure we already discussed this."

"Pretty sure a girl can't take anything seriously if it comes out of a guy's mouth twenty-four hours after sex," I argue.

The same low chuckle rumbles up his throat. "If we're playing by those rules, my comment tonight doesn't count, either. I did come down your throat on the way here, remember?"

My eyes bulge, and I smack his chest. "Everett!"

"You're the one who brought it up," he reminds me.

I roll my eyes, but the man *does* have a point.

"Whatever." I tuck my hair behind my ear and take a deep breath. "Let's get this over with."

"Okay." He kisses my knuckles one more time, then lets me go. "Girlfriend."

The air is a hell of a lot warmer inside the building than it was outside. As it thaws my already cold cheeks, Everett shrugs out of his coat, and I do the same. Without a word, he grabs my jacket, hooks it over his arm, then offers his ID to the bouncer. Following suit, I pull mine out and hand it to the big, burly man at the front. Once he's satisfied, he tilts his head toward the bar, and Everett adds, "Lead the way, Stormie."

The place is crowded. Even more so than usual, which is saying something. SeaBird has always been the place to be. Or at least, that's the way my dad has always explained it. I never really came here. Not unless his rockstar friends, the leading men in Broken Vows, were playing and they snuck me backstage with the rest of the families. After they had kids and stopped touring, I never really came back. Never really could, and by the time I was over twenty-one, I'd already moved to Cedar Springs. Whenever I came back to visit my family, I hung out at my parents' house.

It's just as crowded as I remember. I'm not really surprised. My brother's band sells out massive venues year-round. Of course, their fans would be lining up to hear them play in their hometown. It's been a while since they've been back. Dodger. Judge. Paxton. And Tuke.

Now, if I could only convince my body to stop feeling like a shaken-up can of soda, that would be great. My relationship with Dodger has always been...strange. Less like we're equals and more like he's the king and I'm the princess he'd prefer to keep locked in a tower somewhere.

Thanks to Mom's miscarriage, there's quite the age gap between us. Penelope's sixteen years older than me, and Dodger's ten. I was the surprise baby. The miracle baby. The rainbow baby. If anything, the gap only made my sister more motherly and my brother more protective and more…big-headed and bossy and overbearing to the point that when he moved away, I felt like I could finally… breathe.

The reminder of how I spent said breathing room by hooking up with an abusive ex-boyfriend is the cherry on top of a craptastic sundae, though.

Way to prove him right, Raine.

If only he knew.

Part of me is grateful Drake never wanted to meet my family. Now, I have a fresh start with Everett, and I'm really hoping I don't screw it up tonight. My dad hasn't stopped asking about him since their first run-in at the shop. Surprisingly, though, he's been kind of aloof overall, and I haven't figured out why yet. I guess I'll find out tonight.

When I spot my dad at the bar nursing a tumbler of whiskey, I square my shoulders and weave between the crowd. Ever the protector, Everett follows my lead, staying right behind me as I move toward my father.

"Hey, Dad." I kiss his cheek, steal his drink, and take a sip, desperate for the liquid courage. My nose wrinkles at the burn, but I breathe the heat out, preparing for the inevitable.

I was anxious over the possibility of him running into Everett before this was real. Now? Now, there's even more weight to it, and the idea of my dad not liking my boyfriend feels pretty freaking miserable.

Narrowing his gaze, my dad watches me down half his beverage, chuckling lowly and motioning to the bartender for another one. Then, he glances at Everett and tilts his head. "You drinkin' tonight?"

"One beer. I'm driving," Everett answers. "Good to see you again, Mr. Anders. Thank you for the invitation."

"Is that what my girl called it?" My dad cocks his head. "An invitation?"

"More like a thinly veiled threat," I interrupt dryly. "Have they played yet?"

My dad shakes his head. "Not yet. They're supposed to start at eight."

I check my phone for the time. "It's 8:10."

"You know Pax," he says into his glass.

Yeah, I know Pax. Everyone knows Pax. Like how everyone knows Dodge. When the original guitarist died from a drug overdose while in town a few years ago, Paxton showed up and convinced my brother and Judge, the band's founder, to let him audition.

Thirty minutes later, he was in, and they never looked back. Even though there's a solid age gap between Pax and the rest of the members, he fits in seamlessly and basically turned into my brother's unpredictable shadow.

The pulse of the bass drum from the stage grabs our attention, so I turn to it. The lights are still dimmed, but we're close enough to see the members' silhouettes. My brother's at the mic. Judge is on the drums. Tuke is on the bass. And Pax is…I search the stage for the baby-faced guitarist. A shadowed figure appears from the side, slipping a guitar strap over his neck before playing the intro to one of IndieCent Vow's popular songs.

I glance at Everett, curious as to how he'll react. If he's intimidated or if he likes my brother's music or…honestly, I don't even know.

His head bobs to the beat as my brother's voice echoes through the speakers, and when Everett's lips mirror the lyrics, I smile.

He knows my brother's music.

My dad must notice, too, because he grunts into his drink, finishes the rest, and sets the glass down with a quiet clink on the bartop. Then, he steals the order he'd made for me as the bartender places it in front of me. "She needs another one."

He gives me a disgruntled look over the rim and steals another sip, making my lips twitch with amusement. Apparently, Everett earned a brownie point despite my father's stubbornness, and he doesn't even know it. Maybe there's hope after all.

Everett doesn't ask me to dance. Okay, that's a lie. He started to, but I interrupted and changed the subject. It's for the best. If Dodge sees us from the stage, no matter how innocently we're dancing, I'm pretty sure he'd jump off mid-verse or call us out over the speakers.

Instead, we watch from the bar as my brother belts out lyrics, and girls swoon up at him like he hung the moon. To be fair, I get it. My entire family was blessed with some pretty good genes, thanks to my mom and dad. And Dodge? He capitalized on each and every one of them. Light brown curly hair cut close on the sides and longer on the top. Freshly shaven face to show off his chiseled jaw. Strong biceps and veined forearms as he cradles the mic. And the voice of a fucking angel, though I have no idea where he got that particular talent. Scratch that. I blame my Aunt Dove. She's my mom's little sister and one of the lead singers in the insanely popular band, Broken Vows, so...yeah. I guess it's her fault.

And even though Dodger and I don't always get along, I am kind of jealous watching my brother kick ass at life. Meanwhile, I feel like I'm barely flailing along. Or maybe it's the alcohol. I'd hoped it would settle my nerves, but when it's combined with my dad's silence? Yeah, I'm kind of on edge.

Why hasn't he said anything to Everett yet? I mean, yeah,

my brother's band is playing, but still. Nothing? It's...weird. I finish the last of my drink and set it down, climbing off my stool and smoothing my sweater out, anxious for a breather. "I'm gonna head to the bathroom."

"Want me to come with you?" Everett asks. It isn't because he doesn't want to be alone with my dad. He's anxious about Drake. About leaving me alone for a minute on the off-chance I'm cornered. It's kind of silly since one, SeaBird isn't exactly Drake's stomping grounds, two, he doesn't know I'm here, and three, I haven't even heard from him in weeks. Pretty sure Everett can let his guard down, but it's nice knowing he cares.

I really wish my dad could see it, too. How Everett wouldn't hurt me. How we literally started dating so he could protect me. From my bad choices. From my demons. From my consequences. Even if I don't deserve them—the consequences—I *chose* to date Drake. I chose to be with him and to open up to him, and now...now, I have to deal with looking over my shoulder until long after he grows bored. And what's worse? Maybe he already is, and I have no idea. Even then, I'm not sure how long it'll take until the feeling goes away. Until I can stop looking over my shoulder or questioning who's on the other end of every random call I receive or if it's okay to voice my opinions without pissing someone off.

Oof. That escalated quickly.

"Bo, you good?" my dad prods.

"Yup." Patting Everett's chest, I add, "I think I can handle going to the bathroom on my own. Thanks, though."

Everett takes in the short line and nods, satisfied he can see it from where we sit. "Be safe."

"It's a bathroom." I laugh. "But, yes. I'll be safe. Be right back."

CHAPTER THIRTY-SEVEN

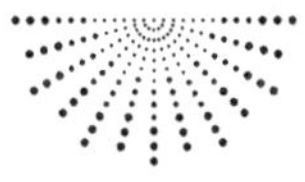

EVERETT

s I watch her go, I realize Raine's dad isn't looking at her. Hell, he isn't even watching his son on the stage. His sole focus is on me, and I don't know what to make of it until the song ends and squeals ensue.

Turning back to the stage, I see why. Dodger has jumped off the edge and is now strolling through the sea of fans, nodding to some, stopping for a quick picture with others, until he waves everyone off, asking for a minute with his dad.

And just like that, his fans listen. Keeping their distance. Giving him space. The guy's arrogance radiates off him like cologne as he strides toward the bar, bringing his dad in for a quick hug and slap on the back. After, both of them turn to me.

I get it now. The timing. The reason why Raine's dad stayed quiet, barely casting me a glance until this moment. This is an interrogation. And a decently orchestrated one, too. My sister would be proud.

I wait for pleasantries. For something. For whatever they

want to say to be said. Instead, they only stare at me, waiting for me to crack.

I've played this game before, though. I'm used to the pressure. The heavy, charged air. The silent game of chicken.

Dodger's eyes thin slightly before he gives in and demands, "How long you been dating Bo?"

"I'm Everett," I reply dryly. "Nice to meet you, too."

"Ah, you're a funny one," Dodger returns. He grabs a pretzel and tosses it into his mouth. "You the reason she's pulled away from the family since last year?"

My jaw tics, and I fight the urge to defend myself, breaking Raine's trust in the process. Reaching for my glass, I take a sip, then set it back on the counter, choosing my words carefully. "Have you asked Raine about any of this?"

"Raine's good at keeping us in the dark. The more we push, the less she comes around," her dad answers. "Honestly, it's a miracle she even agreed to come work with me after moving back to Lockwood Heights. You the reason?"

"For Raine moving back?" I ask.

His chin dips.

"You'll have to ask her," I deflect.

"Why is she working with my dad, anyway?" Dodger demands. "And why do you drive her when she has a perfectly good car?"

"I see you two are close," I note, swallowing the last of my beer and setting the empty glass on the counter. "I'm close with my family, too."

"And my sister," Dodger points out. "You seem awfully close with—"

"Hey, Dodge," Raine interjects. With her hands up and a what the fuck expression on her face, she adds, "Way to wait until I was gone to end the set."

"Hey, Bo." Dodger yanks her into a hug and squeezes her. "Missed you."

"Missed *you*." After patting his back, she wiggles out of his hold and looks up at him. "So? Are we through with the interrogation?"

"His part in it," Dodge shrugs. "*Sure*."

Scoffing, Raine drags out, "Aaaanyway. How was the tour?"

"Long," he admits. "I could use a few months off, but our manager wants us to do a quick world tour before taking a breather and writing our next album."

"A *quick* world tour?" Raine snorts. "Dude, our lives are total opposites. You know that, right?"

Scratching the scuff of his jaw, he lets out a quiet chuckle. "Yeah, it's wild. So, who's this?" He lifts his chin toward me.

"This is Everett," Raine announces. "Everett Taylor. Although I have a feeling you already know."

"Hey." I offer my hand to Raine's brother, but he only stares at it.

"Are you the reason my baby sister's been so absent this last year?" he demands.

Apparently, he didn't like my answer the first time. I keep my expression blank and drop my hand. Raine's right. This guy won't give me an inch. Not willingly.

"Dodge," Raine warns.

"Just asking him a question," her brother returns, pinning me with another look. And it's crazy. To see his easy-going persona from the stage slip, turning him into a fucking Rottweiler who wants to rip me to shreds.

Honestly, I admire it. His desire to protect Raine. To keep her safe, even if it pisses her off. He doesn't know it, but I relate to him more than he'll ever understand. It's how I feel about Finley. About Dylan. And Ophelia and Tatum and everyone else I grew up with. A need to keep them safe. Protected.

"No, he's not the reason I've been absent," Raine argues. "We've only known each other for a few months."

Dodger's eyes thin. "Before or after you showed up at Dad's work with a split lip and a shitty excuse about where it came from?"

Raine glares at her dad, and suddenly, it all makes sense. *Milo didn't need to put me through the wringer. He knew his son would do it for him.*

When Raine and I stay quiet, Dodge asks, "What? Nothing to say?"

My molars grind, but I manage to keep my mouth shut. Because I have a lot to say. Like I would never hit Raine. And she has a crazy ex-stalker who not only hit her but filmed them together without her permission. Then, he stalked her place of work until she had to leave, potentially ruining her future in the tattoo industry if it wasn't for her dad's help. But I can't say a fucking word because if I do, I'll betray Raine's trust, and Drake already obliterated it hand over fist, leaving nothing but pieces for me to put together all by myself. So that's what I'm doing right now. By keeping my mouth shut. By biting my tongue until I swear I can taste blood. Because it isn't my secret. It's Raine's.

"Can we not do this?" she begs. "I'm here to support you and your band, not be interrogated over something you know nothing about."

Cracking his knuckles in front of him, Dodger laces them together and cups the back of his head. "Now, if that isn't incriminating, I don't know what is."

Raine's body tenses, and she turns to her father. "Thanks a lot, Dad. Thank you *so* much for reminding me why I should've never accepted an internship with you."

"Raine," her dad starts, but she stands up and heads outside, not bothering to grab her coat and put it on despite the dropping temperature.

"Did you accomplish what you came for?" I ask Dodge. "Don't get me wrong. I get it. I have a little sister, too, but—"

"Finley Taylor." His mouth stretches into a sneer. "I did my research."

Fuck me. If this guy was anyone else. Anyone. I'd beat the shit out of him for digging into my life as if I have something to hide. The fact he's been sniffing around Fin, though? This asshole's playing with fire. Unfortunately, kicking the shit out of my girlfriend's brother isn't on my to-do list. Not yet, anyway, so I try to rein in my temper.

"If you've done your research, you should already know one of the things I stress about more than anything in my life is whether my little sister is or isn't being treated right by her boyfriend," I tell him. "And no, not only physically, but emotionally, too."

"Yeah, her boyfriend seems like a real piece of work," he counters. "Might wanna stop fucking up on that front. But, hey, you do you."

My molars grind, and I squeeze my empty glass, surprised it hasn't splintered. "I understand the interrogation. The desire to check on Raine and make sure she isn't making bad decisions or winding up with an asshole. But despite your desire to protect her, you're only fucking up your relationship by implying you don't trust her."

"Where'd the split lip come from?" her dad demands.

My gaze slices to him. "I won't break Raine's trust—"

"What if it was your sister?" Dodge interrupts. "What if Finley was the one pulling away? The one hiding things. The one who showed up with a split lip and a new boyfriend no one knew about who doesn't let her out of his sight. What then?"

They're right. If I was in their position, I'd be a mess.

Scrubbing my hand over my face, I try to figure out how I can put their minds at ease about me without breaking

Raine's trust. None of it makes me feel better. I hate how there isn't a simple solution. It'd be one thing if I didn't like Raine the way I do. If I didn't care about her as more than a human, a human I actually like. A human I want a future with, and said future should sure as shit include her family.

Nostrils flaring, I glance at SeaBird's exit. "I'm not the one who hurt her, all right?"

"Who is?" Milo challenges.

"Someone I'm trying to protect her from," I reply carefully. "And the sooner you become a safe space for Raine, the sooner she'll open up to you without feeling like you'll overreact or be disappointed in her. Now, if you'll excuse me."

I stand up, but Dodge blocks my way. We're eye to eye. Nose to nose. And the asshole might be a rockstar, but he's built like a fighter. One who isn't afraid to fight dirty.

I hold his gaze, refusing to back down but not egging him on, either. No use adding fuel to the fire, not when he's already close to losing his shit. Yeah, I've seen this look before, both on and off the ice. This guy's a loose cannon.

"What are you gonna do, Dodge?" I ask. "Your move."

He cocks his head. "If you're lying, I'll kill you," he growls.

"That's what your sister's afraid of," I reply. "You doing something stupid and fucking up your future for her." My mouth twitches. "The irony is, if I was in your position, I'd be the same way. Don't worry, though. I'm not the enemy. I'll keep her safe. Promise."

"Dodge," a grumbly voice echoes from the stage. It's a command. My head snaps in its direction. Sure enough, a guy in his early thirties with tats covering every inch of his skin from the neck down is at the mic. It's the drummer. Judge, I think? The name's fitting. Or maybe not. Executioner is a better choice, and right now, his sight is set on me and Dodge.

"Duty calls." Dodge shifts back on his feet, leaving me

space to move past him. "Talk soon." Then, the same carefree smile takes up his expression when he jogs toward the limelight like he was made for it.

My head spins as I watch his entire demeanor change right before my eyes. When the intro to the next song starts playing, Dodge winks at me from the stage, and Raine's dad stands up, offering his hand.

"I'm letting you pass," he decides. "Don't make me regret it."

With a snort, I take it. "Thanks, I guess?"

"Now, go make my baby girl feel better." He tugs me closer. "And I mean that in the most PG way possible."

My mouth lifts. "I'll see what I can do."

CHAPTER THIRTY-EIGHT

EVERETT

She didn't want to talk. She wanted a hot shower, then a cuddle. Her words, not mine. Honestly, I'm surprised she even asked. The girl's been so skittish about her own wants and needs, having her voice her desires felt like a win in my book, so I gave her exactly what she asked for.

A hot shower and a snuggle.

No questions asked.

The sheets are cold now, though. I lift my eyelids and search my room, only to find it empty. It's four in the morning. With a frown, I shift out of bed, heading to the kitchen. The lights above the island are on, and the fire is crackling, but otherwise, it's dark. Raine sits on the couch, her bare feet resting on the coffee table as she balances an open notebook on her knees. Brows bunched, she tilts her head and glides her pencil across the paper, oblivious to my presence.

Fuck, I could watch her like this all night. Her concentration. The way her lips move. As if she's talking to the drawing. Or maybe herself. Hell, maybe a song is stuck in her head or something, but it only feeds my curiosity.

A loud crackle from the fire snaps her out of her daze, and her attention shoots to it until she finds me leaning against the edge of the mantle.

The surprise in her eyes turns to warmth, and her mouth lifts in a smile as she whispers, "Hi."

"Hey." I push myself away from the fireplace and stride toward her. "Pencil this time, huh?"

"Figured I could use the backspace button today."

"Is that what you call it? A backspace button?"

"I mean, it does the same thing, right? Gives you an opportunity to fix your mistakes."

"Have you ever considered using an iPad or something instead?"

"Sometimes I do but only at work. I'm a sucker for paper." She lifts her notepad and wiggles it back and forth.

I nod and motion to the cushion beside her. "Mind if I join you?"

She scoots a little closer to the armrest, giving me room, and I sit down. On the paper is a tree. It's similar to the one from weeks ago. When I tracked her down at Lucian's shop. The one with messy, twisted branches. But this one is… softer somehow. Less prickles. More leaves. Sunshine slips through the branches, casting light and shadows along the paper. Even the bark feels delicate somehow.

"What do you think?" she asks. I can hear her reservations. Her anxiety. The way she wants to clam up, like all the other times she's shown me her art.

Tearing my attention from the drawing, I look up at Raine. At the little divot between her brows. The way she chews on the soft flesh on the inner edge of her bottom lip. The hesitant sheen in her eyes. Fuck, what I wouldn't give to erase her fears. Her reservations. To rip away the bullshit insecurities surrounding her brilliance in hopes of her seeing what I see. What I've seen since the moment we first met.

"It looks amazing, Stormie," I tell her.

"You think?"

I nod. "You're insanely talented."

"You've mentioned that a time or two."

"Now if only I could convince you to believe it."

She shrugs, then tears her gaze from mine and uses the side of her pencil to add shadows to the right side of the tree. "There's always room for improvement, but thank you."

Unable to help myself, I ask, "Did you do this before Drake?"

"Do what?"

"Shy away from compliments."

Her lips purse. "I don't shy away from compliments."

"You do," I push. "Especially when it comes to your art." When she stays quiet, I add, "I Googled your dad, you know."

A stray line of graphite taints the shadow she was working on, and her brows wrinkle with frustration. She sets the wooden pencil on its side and turns to me. "Oh?"

"He's really good."

"He is really good," she agrees. "And with no formal training or anything. It's kind of insane."

"Says the girl who also has no formal training," I point out.

"I mean, my dad *is* Milo Anders. He taught me everything I know."

"Maybe not everything."

With a laugh, she argues, "No, pretty sure it's everything."

"All right, let's say it is," I concede. "If that's the case, how come your drawings look nothing like his?"

She frowns and looks down at the tree again. "Rude."

I laugh. "That's not what I mean. Humor me for a second, okay?" I reach for my laptop on the coffee table and open it, typing in Milo Anders and tree. Almost instantly, sketches upon sketches appear, and I click on the top result. Vibrant shades of green and yellow appear, along with a thick, sturdy trunk and roots winding beneath the surface in an intricate pattern. I shift the laptop toward her, making sure she has a front-row seat to the screen. Barely casting it a glance, she reaches for the top of the laptop and starts to close it, but I shift the computer away from her.

"Humor. Me," I repeat.

With a huff, she asks, "What's your point, Ev?"

"My point is, your tree looks nothing like your father's, but both are incredible."

"That's kind of you to say, but—"

"No, buts. You're talented, Raine. And it's not because of your dad or the things he taught you. Yes, you might not be where you are today without his help, but he isn't the one holding the pencil. You are." I tuck her hair behind her ear, praying she's listening. "You. Raine Anders. No one else."

I can see it. The way her eyes glaze slightly. Or maybe it's the firelight dancing in her forest-green gaze playing with me, but I don't think it is.

No. This means something.

Leaning into my touch, she closes her eyes and whispers, "Thank you."

"Do you have your machine here?"

Opening her eyes, she tilts her head, confused. "My tattoo machine?"

"Yeah."

"I mean, yes? But—"

"You should go get it."

Her eyes bulge. "Everett—"

"I'm serious," I push.

"So am I," she argues.

"I want you to give me a tattoo."

"Everett, a tattoo is…it's permanent."

"So?"

"So, you don't have any tattoos, which means you know how permanent they really are, and—"

"It's just a tattoo, Stormie." I grab her hand and bring it to my lips.

"Is it, though?" she whispers.

"All right, let's say it's more." I kiss her knuckles again. "I'm still in."

Her eyes flick to mine. "You're sure?"

"Yeah." I nod. "Positive. Besides, the idea of being your first is hot as fuck."

She snorts. "So that's why you want me to give you a tattoo."

"No, I want you to give me a tattoo because you're talented. Really talented. And if you can't see it. If you can't take the plunge without someone giving you a little push, I'll do it. I'll give you the push." I lift my chin toward the hall. "Go get your machine."

Sucking her lips between her teeth, she stands and scurries down the hall like a little mouse, quickly returning with a black box. "You're really sure? I mean—"

"Open the box, Raine," I order.

Her nostrils flare, but she rounds the coffee table separating us and sits on the edge of the couch cushion beside me. Then, I watch in fascination as she spreads a bunch of things I've never seen out on the coffee table.

After straightening a black tube, she fidgets with a small clear bottle and asks, "Do you…do you know what you want?"

"Surprise me."

"Ev," she scolds. "I'm already going out on a limb by giving you a tattoo. Pull your weight, will ya?"

Chuckling, I settle further into the cushions and stretch my legs out. "All right. I know what I want."

"What?"

"A storm cloud."

Her fidgeting ceases, and she peeks over her shoulder at me. "You're joking."

"Not joking."

"You want a storm cloud?"

I nod. "Yeah, Raine. I want a storm cloud."

"Is this because my brother bullied you, and you feel bad, and you're trying to make me feel better? Because if anyone should apologize, clearly it's—"

I kiss her, stealing her unnecessary apology before it even has a chance to slip past her pretty pink lips. She tastes sweet. So fucking sweet. Dragging my tongue against the seam of her lips, I swallow her soft sigh, craving it more than my next breath.

When I pull away, she bites her bottom lip, her eyes shining with the fire's reflection. It's almost enough to distract me from the questioning look accompanying the flames. Almost. But I still see it. Her reservations. Her fear.

"Ask me, Raine," I push.

"H-he didn't scare you away?"

I shake my head. "Not going anywhere. Promise."

She leans in for a second kiss. It's softer. Sweeter. When she pulls away, her quiet breath falls on my lips, and she whispers, "Where do you want your storm cloud?"

My mouth lifts. "I mean, other than on my cock—"

"Everett!" she squeals. Her hands fly to cover her face and her shoulders shake with amusement.

"I mean, you asked me where I want my storm cloud," I remind her.

"I meant the tattoo!"

"All right, all right." I grab her fingers, lower her hands, and lift my right arm, pointing to the inside of my bicep. "How 'bout here?"

Her eyes fall to my arm. She sits up and caresses the skin. It's gentle. Her touch. Like her fingertips are covered in silk. It only makes me want to feel her touch everywhere. Every single fucking inch of me.

"How big?" she asks. "How big do you want it?"

"Whatever you think."

She looks up at me again and tilts her head. "Ev…"

Fuck, I love when she says my name like this. Soft and light and airy, but with a subtle undertone of…something. Annoyance? Nah. Interest? Probably not, but I'll pretend that's what it is.

"I'm your canvas, baby girl," I murmur.

Her eyes soften even more at the nickname, but she doesn't comment on it, choosing to fidget with the tattoo machine again like the damn thing's broken. "Well, sweat can hinder the healing process, so unless you want to wait—"

"No waiting," I push. "I want it now."

Her attention flicks up to me before she stares down at her machine again like it's the most fascinating piece of equipment in the world. "Okay, then it should probably be something small since it's the middle of the season." She nibbles her lower lip. "First, I need to make a stencil—"

I reach out and grab her wrist to stop her from standing. "No stencil."

The girl looks at me like I've lost my damn marbles. "Do you really want to walk around with a permanent, wonky tattoo—"

"Not gonna regret anything with you. Besides." I hook my arm around her waist and kiss her again. Fuck, I can't help myself. The girl's gotten under my skin, and there's nothing I can do to stop it. I force myself not to lean in and steal another taste as I remind her, "If I have to walk around with a wonky tattoo, then you do, too."

Her eyes are a pool of green, and her teeth dig into the inside of her bottom lip again as she stares up at me. "You remembered that part, huh?"

"Yeah, I did." I kiss her nose. "But even if it wasn't part of the arrangement, I'd still want to be your first. Now, come on. Let's see whatcha got."

CHAPTER THIRTY-NINE

EVERETT

There's nothing like the high from a win when your girl is in the stands. After I drop the puck into the top corner of the net, the buzzer sounds, and I look toward the crowd. There she is. Raine's hands are cupped around her mouth as she screams my name, jumping up and down, cheering for the Hawks while sandwiched between Dylan and Finley. Mav and Lia are on Finley's opposite side, and even though I know they're stoked about tonight's win, I can't tear my eyes from Raine. Pointing my gloved hand toward her, I mouth, "That was for you," as a hard body slams into me. Griffin, Reeves, and the rest of the team meet me at the blue line, each of us celebrating the win, when Reeves announces we're having an impromptu game night at our house. Not gonna lie. I'm not always in the mood for a game night, but after our win, the idea of hanging out with some of my favorite people, including the girl in the stands, sounds like the perfect ending to my evening. As long as Raine's on board.

After showering quickly, I dress, meet Raine outside, and ask if she's interested in attending the party. When she agrees, I drive us back to the duplex. The place is already bustling. Cars line the street, and our front yard is overrun with people waiting to be let inside as Reeves approaches. With one hand linked to Dylan's, they weave through the crowd to unlock the front door.

Leaning toward the windshield, Raine watches the people spill through the front door while we stay parked outside. With a quiet laugh, she admits, "I'm not sure I'll ever get over the chaos of game nights. They are fun, though."

"Yeah, they're something." I grab her hand and bring it to my lips. "We could always go back to the cabin if you prefer."

"And miss the celebration?" She tears her attention from the crowd outside and smiles. "Hardly. You're the MVP, Everett Taylor. Soak it up." Bouncing her eyebrows up and down, she reaches for the door handle with her opposite hand, slips out of my grasp, and exits the car. I follow suit, and we head inside. As soon as we step over the threshold, my team starts chanting my name. The rest of the partiers join in when someone hands us red Solo cups and bombards me with requests for a play-by-play of the last forty-two seconds of tonight's game.

I keep my hand on Raine's the entire time, and even though the words coming out of my mouth are all things hockey, I can't stop rubbing my thumb along her soft skin, blown away that she's really mine.

"Yo!" Finley calls. "Let your girlfriend go. We want to hang out with her, too!"

"You had her during the game," I remind her.

"Yeah, well," my little sister loops her arm through Raine's, "now we get her until you're done reliving the glory days."

"It happened like…two hours ago," Raine points out, but she lets go of my hand and tucks her hair behind her ear, giving me a glimpse of the little storm cloud hidden behind it.

Fucking beautiful.

Her dad gave her the tattoo since she couldn't reach the spot to do it herself. Not easily, anyway. He didn't ask any questions, though. He took the stencil she created and got it done. She's been taking on a few of his clients, too, and is kicking ass, but she'll never admit it. The girl's gifted. More than she knows. But it's nice knowing her dad sees it the same way I do. We haven't really spoken since the concert, but Raine assures me things are...good overall. Dodger asked if she could come to another of his shows before he leaves, too. He's picking her up from her shift at Etch 'N' Ink next weekend, which works since we have an away game.

"I'll bring her back in a few," Finley promises.

My attention snaps from Raine's tattoo to my little sister. "Where are you taking her?"

"We're preparing the game."

"What game did you guys pick?" I ask.

"*Close Your Eyes and Open Wide,*" she quips. "The gentlemen's version."

My nose wrinkles. "Of course, you'd pick that one."

"Hey, Reeves is the one who crowned me queen at the last game night."

"Only because there are no winners in *Spin the Bottle.*"

"Not when your boyfriend is a billion miles away, anyway," she grumbles. "Especially when I spent the whole night taking shots—"

"Of cranberry juice," Raine interrupts with a laugh. "Griffin told me."

"Of course he did," Finley mutters. "But, I digress. I need Raine's help, and don't even think about convincing her to give you any hints."

I watch as they move toward the kitchen, nearly groaning at the turn tonight took with a few simple words.

Close Your Eyes and Open Wide is basically Russian Roulette with a food element. It either leaves you puking or snacking on your favorite food. It's a game of balls and luck. The rules are simple. Random food is hidden underneath a tablecloth, and since it's the gentleman's version, the guys are the only ones playing while the girls watch us be miserable. Every guy lines up around the table and picks a covered food item. Once the tablecloth is removed, you have to eat the food in front of you, or you're eliminated from the game. Winner takes all. Sometimes, you might be lucky enough to have a candy bar or some shit. Other times? You might get dog food or month-old Chinese from the back of the fridge. After each round, the guys left standing leave the room, and the girls reset the food placement. Last one to bow out wins.

Knowing Fin? She'll be merciless. Maybe Raine will hint at where to stand so I don't puke during the first round, though I won't be surprised if she keeps me in the dark.

About ten minutes later, Finley reappears and moseys into the family room. The same thick medallion we use to crown the winner of every game night hangs around her neck. It swings side to side as she climbs onto the coffee table in the center of the space. Too bad for her, she's still short as shit and barely grabs anyone's attention until she places her thumb and forefinger between her lips and whistles.

The high-pitched sound makes my ears ring, but it does the job because the party quiets, and she beams with satisfaction.

"Ladies and gentlemen, boys and girls! Welcome to Game Night!" she announces. Cheering ensues, and I clap my hands slowly. Finley's grin widens. "First, I want to congratulate LAU on their phenomenal win tonight! You showed determination! Strength! And grit!"

"Woo-hoo!"

"Fuck yeah, we did!"

"And now, to see if you can continue to show such qualities for tonight's main event," she adds. I swear the girl's eyes twinkle when she pauses for effect. "Tonight, we're playing *Close Your Eyes and Open Wide*, gentlemen's edition!"

Bellows ring throughout the air. It only adds fuel to the fire, and I've never heard such a contrasting collection of sounds. Cackles of amusement from the girls. Low groans from the guys. Yeah. They know what's in store for them, too. Poor bastards

"As always, rules are simple," Finley continues. "Girls, you're spectators and judges tonight. Make sure to keep these boys in line. Gentlemen? You'll be the main event. Let's see how big your cajones are, shall we?" The girl rubs her hands together mischievously. "In the kitchen, we have bowls covered by a tablecloth. Pick a bowl, any bowl, but don't peek. If you do, you're disqualified," she warns. "Once everyone has chosen, I'll announce when you can remove the tablecloth. From there, you either eat the contents or tuck your tail in shame. Any questions?" Finley doesn't even wait a millisecond. "Perfect! Let's go!"

She jumps off the coffee table and ushers us into the kitchen while my stomach swims in response. The smell of fish clings to the air, and I cross my arms as I walk around the room, studying the red and white plaid-covered lumps lining the island, kitchen table, and countertops. Yeah, my sister is rarely up to anything good, and I have a sinking suspicion tonight's no exception. Feeling Raine's gaze, I look up and tilt my head. "Should I be worried?"

Her attention drifts to one of the bowls closest to her for a split second before she links her fingers in front of her and shrugs. "Guess we'll see."

There's my girl.

I follow her lead, moving into position behind the bowl in question. Griffin flanks my left, and Maverick shifts to my right as Finley rounds the room, giving all the guys curious, knowing looks, and fuck me if it isn't intimidating.

Watching her warily, a knot forms in my gut, and Griffin leans closer, dropping his voice low. "Do you think she knows how terrifying she is?"

Mav chuckles. "Trust me. She knows."

With only the island separating us, Raine moves closer—distracting us from shaking in our sneakers—and taps her perfectly painted black nail against her chin. "Remind me, what do you get if you win?"

"Other than bragging rights?" Griffin offers for me as he tears his attention from my little sister prowling the kitchen like a caged tiger. "Nothing."

Raine snorts. "Well then. Good luck."

Finley appears beside Raine seconds later, shoots my girl-friend a warning look, and places her hands on the counter separating us. She's careful not to touch the bowl beneath the cloth as she pins me with an unreadable look. "You sure this is the one you want?"

My gaze meets Raine's again, and I smirk. "Pretty sure."

"Hmm." Finley sneaks a quick peek at Griffin but doesn't say anything as she casts her stare at Mav. "How 'bout you? You sure this is a safe bet?"

"None of this is safe," Mav replies dryly.

The bastard makes a good point.

She smirks, steps back, and calls out, "Lift the tablecloth!"

I pinch the corner and raise the checkered fabric. Dropping it immediately, I look at the ceiling and groan, "You've gotta be kidding me." Turning to Raine, I growl, "I thought you said this was a safe one."

"Finley dared me to do it," she rushes out, barely containing her laughter. "I swear—"

"And you fell for it!" Finley interrupts. The girl's practically giddy as she claps her hands and throws her head back in laughter. "I can't believe you actually fell for it! Wait, wait." Fumbling with her phone, she pulls it out of her back pocket and points it at me. "I gotta get this on camera."

I lift the fabric again, my body already threatening to heave. Tuna fish, peanut butter, and chocolate sauce are swirled in the bowl, creating a diarrhea-brown concoction with chunks of flaky fish. My nose wrinkles, and my throat knots as I look up at my sister again. Her phone is pointed directly at me, and I glare at her through the screen when her brows pinch. Slowly, she lowers the phone, letting her thumbs fly across the screen as she watches...something. Eyes wide, she turns the screen off and shifts her panicked look to Raine.

Confusion lines Raine's forehead as she stammers, "W-what is it?"

My phone buzzes in my pocket, distracting me. I must not be the only one receiving a text because buzzing and ringing start chirping throughout the entire kitchen. I watch as everyone pulls their cell phones out, one after another, while the blood drains from Finley's face.

"Don't," she begs. Rushing toward a few guys, she grabs their phones from their hands and holds them close to her chest, her eyes growing wider and wider with every passing second as she searches the room for...what, exactly? A solution? A safe spot to stash the phones? Don't get me wrong. My sister's known for acting unstable on occasion, but this? This is a new level, and if I had to guess, it has something to do with my girl standing beside her.

"No freaking way," one of the puck bunnies giggles. When her attention snaps to me, she covers her mouth.

"Fuck, man."

"Looks like she knows what she's doing," a freshman says to his friend beside him as he shows him his phone.

I unlock my cell and find a video from an unknown number. Dread coats my stomach, but I open it anyway. It only takes me a second to recognize it. The cabin. I'm on the couch with Raine on her knees in front of me. My cock is out as she bobs her head up and down on it. Her hair is pushed away from her face, and I can see the hollows of her cheeks as I clutch the back of the couch, my eyes rolling back in my head. The sound doesn't entirely match the footage like it's been dubbed over or some shit. But even if the video was silent, it would be just as incriminating. And maybe it's my imagination, but if I close my eyes, I can still hear it. My grunts of pleasure. The slick sounds of me pushing in and out of her lips. The tiny mewls and whimpers of appreciation as she sucks on me. I don't know how anyone would've gotten this footage, but I know exactly when it happened. And the angle? It only feeds my confusion. It looks like it was taken from the balcony. Like someone actually climbed up the trellis and filmed through the back window. At least, I hope it's what it looks like. That the slight blur is due to the window. Because the idea of Raine thinking I'm the one who filmed this is enough to make me sick to my stomach. I shut the screen off and look up. Everyone in the room is staring at their phones. And those who aren't are looking at me or the flash of brown as Raine rushes out of the room.

Fuck.

Forcing my body to move, I charge after her. "Raine!"

The front door slams behind her. I almost crash into it but manage to stop in time. Twisting the handle, I shove it open.

"Raine!"

What if she thinks it was me? We're at my place. She's sucking me off. Who else would she think did this? Drake doesn't know where the cabin is. If he did, he would've pounded down the door to get to her the first night she arrived. So, where the hell did this video come from? Panic surges through me as I realize the easy assumptions she's likely made about the humiliating video footage and how easily it might've broken her trust—did break her trust—if her running out the door is anything to go by. What if she never forgives me? Fuck. What if she thinks I would betray her like this?

"Raine!"

I look left and right, desperate to find her. To fix this. To apologize and see if she's okay. What kind of question is that? Of course, she isn't. No one would be okay after finding out that not only were they filmed without their knowledge, but said film was distributed to dozens, if not hundreds, of people.

It's dark, and even with the streetlights, there are so many cars it would be easy for her to disappear. To hide herself from me and anyone else who might've seen the video. By the look of things, I'd say it's damn near everyone.

How did he get their numbers? It had to have been him. It had to. There's no other explanation. No other culprit who would stoop so low.

I'll fucking kill him.

"Raine!" I yell. "Raine, I swear it wasn't—"

"Open it, please," a quiet voice begs. I search the street again and find a lump leaning against my car's passenger door.

Patting my pockets, I find my keys and unlock the vehicle. Part of me wants to rush toward her and drag her into my arms, but I stay glued to my spot instead. Does she think it was me? Does she think I would do this to her? Her movements are slow but controlled as she climbs inside, rests her head against the headrest, and stares at the ceiling.

Forcing myself to move, I wipe my palm against my jeans, then join her. I've never been good at this. Feeling helpless. Handling emotional shit. Putting out fires, I can do. Feeling like my hands are tied? Not so much. I know she thinks I handle it all the time, and fuck if I don't try my best, but this? Seeing her like this? It wrecks me. My hands itch to reach out and hold her. To pull her to my chest and promise to gut the motherfucker who filmed us together, let alone shared it. But is this what she wants? Or is space what she needs? Do I take her home? To a hotel? What can I fucking do?

She doesn't look at me. Doesn't say a word. It's quiet. Too fucking quiet. Only her shallow breathing is heard as she tugs at the sleeve of her shirt and wipes at her eyes. I swear, I've never felt anything like it. The silence. Heavy. Thick. Charged. It's like a live wire, and I have no idea what happens if I reach out and touch it. If I plead my case. If I ask if she's okay when I already know she's the furthest thing from it. But the silence? The unanswered questions? The what-ifs? I can't fucking take it, and I sure as shit can't spend another second letting her believe I had anything to do with this when I would never, *ever* betray her like this.

"It wasn't me," I rasp. "I swear—"

"I know." Her voice cracks. "I know it wasn't." She sniffles and stares out the passenger window, refusing to look at me. "I'm ready to go to the police station now."

"T-the police?"

Chewing on the edge of her sleeve, she gives me a jerky nod. "It's time, don't you think?"

The car rumbles to life, and I pull away from the curb. "Whatever you need."

CHAPTER FORTY

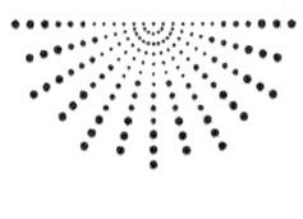

EVERETT

It's funny. With my fear of Raine thinking the video was in any way my fault somewhat resolved, I'm fucking pissed. Who the hell does this asshole think he is? I hate feeling out of control. Feeling like I can't protect what or who's mine, and Raine is mine. Keeping my grasp tight on her, I tug her into the precinct, my nostrils flaring when we approach an empty reception desk. A man appears around the corner before I can barrel into the bullpen but stops short.

"Can I help you?" he asks.

"Is McDonnell here?" I growl.

"Uh," he glances toward the bullpen, and I move around the front desk, heading straight toward the only officer I know firsthand.

McDonnell was Reeves' dad's partner until Reeves' dad planted cocaine in the back of Reeves' car, hoping to arrest him. Yeah, Drake's not the first abusive asshole we've dealt with as a friend group, but I'm determined to make him the last.

"McDonnell," the man from the front calls.

340

Officer McDonnell's head snaps up. His eyes fall on Raine and me as I tug her with me.

Grabbing the closest chair, I set it beside the one tucked on the opposite side of McDonnell's desk, then motion to it for Raine. Once she's seated, I do the same while McDonnell watches us carefully.

"Can I help you?" he asks.

"I'm Everett," I say, forcing myself to keep a straight head when in reality, I feel like I'm fucking spiraling. "Everett Taylor. Oliver Reeves' friend. And Dylan," I add, hoping her name sparks his memory. "I'm Dylan Thorne's friend."

His brows pull. "Okay? Uh, how can I help you, Mr. Taylor?"

"My girlfriend's ex is stalking her."

Raine's breath hitches, and I close my eyes, hating the pain she's being put through while knowing that tiptoeing around the situation won't get us anywhere. Not anymore.

McDonnell's attention shifts to Raine beside me. "You're the girlfriend, I assume?"

Raine nods, gently pulls her hand from mine, and twists her fingers in her lap. Not gonna lie. It stings a little, but this isn't about me. Not right now. This is about Raine, and if she needs to pull away for a minute to cope with this shitshow, I'll be by her side until she's ready to open up again.

"My, uh, my ex won't leave me alone," she whispers.

Concern spreads across his features. He closes a manilla folder in front of him, places it on the edge of his desk, and leans closer. "Okay. How long has this been going on? Do you have evidence?"

"Um…" Tucking her hair behind her ear, Raine stares at her hands. "We were seeing each other for a while. The abuse didn't turn physical until I tried to break up with him. Then he hit me, and…then he hit me again, and…then I moved in with Everett"—she peeks at me and gives me a pathetic smile

—"then he filmed me being…intimate with Everett, and then tonight, he shared it."

"With who?" he asks.

"Everyone," she whispers.

The divot between McDonnell's brows deepens. "And you have proof of this?"

Raine shrugs, turning to me. "He took the video. I know it. And who else would be vindictive enough to share it?"

"Did he send it from his phone?" McDonnell prods.

"I have no idea, but…" I unlock my phone and start to hand it to him, but stop myself. Instead, I look at Raine. "You good if I show him?"

Her cheeks turn red, and it's like gasoline on an already blazing flame.

I'm gonna fucking kill him.

"Raine?" I try keeping my voice steady, but fuck if I'm not fuming.

"Take my phone." She pulls it from her back pocket and gives it to me but doesn't look up. "If he tries to call or… anything, you can use it as evidence, right?"

Hating that this even needs to be done, I hand her phone to McDonnell, shoving mine back into my pocket. "It didn't come from his number, but I know it was him," I add. "No one else would film us, let alone send a video of it to the entire school."

With wide eyes, McDonnell takes the phone but sets it face down in front of him. "The entire school has this? Are you sure?"

I replay the evening for the thousandth time, but even now, I can't find a way to erase it. To make it go away like it never happened. If I could, I would've done it already.

"We were at a party when the message was delivered," I explain. "Everyone's phones started buzzing at the same time. I don't know anyone who didn't receive it, but I guess he could've targeted the hockey team and regular fans. I'm not sure."

"I'll see if I can have one of my guys look into this," McDonnell promises. His focus moves to the Raine again. "Miss, you said he hit you?"

She nods but doesn't look up.

"Do you have any evidence of this? Photographs or... anything?"

Chewing on the inside of her cheek, she pauses before her shoulder lifts a few inches. "Honestly, I don't, uh, I don't think I took any pictures."

He exhales and reaches for his pen, clicking the top. "That's unfortunate."

"I saw them," I interject, cursing myself for not taking pictures when I picked her up on the side of the road. "The bruises. My friends all saw them, too. We'll make a statement as witnesses or...whatever you need. However it works, we'll cooperate, but I promise she's telling the truth."

"I'm sure she is," he replies. "Unfortunately, physical proof has a lot more sway in these situations. Considering the circumstances, we need to be careful exactly how much we push. The video's good," he adds, "as long as we can connect it to the perpetrator. For now, I think the best we can do is file a restraining order and go from there."

I shake my head. "Not good enough. Can't she press charges for assault or something?"

"She can," he confirms, "but without evidence, I'm afraid it'll be hard to prove."

"And the video?" I push. "It isn't enough evidence?"

"Of assault? Not at all."

"He's stalking her," I argue, waving my hand around. "He hurt her in the past—"

"I'm sure he has, all right? I'll do my best to see if we can connect the video to him, and we'll file a restraining order as well, but I have to be honest with you…"

When he hesitates, I know I've already heard enough. I want to stand up. I want to throw everything off his desk. I want to yell and scream and force him to do his fucking job and keep my girl safe. Instead, he only sits there.

"With the other open case against you and your friends, this is a…delicate situation," he adds. "We need to tread lightly. I suggest only pursuing what we have solid evidence for."

"What case?" Raine questions.

McDonnell's jaw clicks, but he doesn't answer her, and I can't decide whether or not I appreciate his silence.

Shifting in my seat, I grab her hand, placing it in my lap. "Reeves' dad was on the force—"

"*Is* on the force," McDonnell corrects me.

My gaze snaps back to his and narrows. "Tell me you're joking."

"He's on a forced leave of absence, but he still has his badge until they conclude the internal investigation," McDonnell explains. "Which is why you being here and seemingly interfering with it is…a little precarious."

"I'm not interfering with shit. This isn't related—"

"But you are," he warns. "And unfortunately, so am I."

Shifting forward in my seat, I rest my elbows against my knees and continue cradling Raine's delicate hand in mine as I pin McDonnell with a stare. "Let me get this straight. Because of your involvement in ratting out one of your own, your hands are tied in general, or at least when it comes to any kind of association with me and my friends."

I can tell I'm right by the glint of pity in his eyes.

"Not absolutely," he offers weakly.

"Then find me another officer to work with," I snap.

"Not sure that's in your best interest at the moment, either."

"So we're fucked." My molars grind. "You can't stop Raine's ex from stalking her or filming her without her consent or sharing it with her friends and family. Am I hearing you, right?"

"Let me explain something to you." McDonnell drops his voice low, scanning the bullpen as he shifts even closer. "I'm a rookie, Mr. Taylor, and I stuck my neck out for your friends, calling out my superior officer for some…"—he hesitates again and grits his teeth—"nefarious decisions. And even though we both know my partner was in the wrong, there's a ripple effect we're dealing with until the internal investigation proves what we already know. Now, it does not mean I'll leave you two high and dry. I'll hand your phone to a member of my team who will run some diagnostics on the video to see if they can pinpoint the person who filmed it, let alone sent it to everyone without Ms. Raine's consent. If we can at least identify the sender, we can charge him with distribution of pornographic material, even if we can't prove your ex filmed you together. I will also grab the paperwork for her to fill out so we can file a restraining order. Other than that, there's nothing more we can do except wait for the results. However, storming in here and causing a scene won't help either one of you, let alone your friends Dylan and Oliver. Do you understand?"

"What if he comes around?" I demand. "What if a single piece of paper doesn't stop Raine's ex from bothering her again?"

He settles back in his chair and folds his arms. "Then we go from there."

"Go from there?" I scoff. "A piece of paper isn't gonna do shit to a guy like Drake!"

"Careful, Mr. Taylor," he repeats. "Things are already

dicey enough with your friend group as it is. Don't do anything rash."

My expression turns to fucking concrete as I read between the lines and all he isn't saying. Yeah, his hands are fucking tied, and there's nothing he can do. Not without concrete evidence.

Meaning if push comes to shove, I might need to take shit into my own hands.

Carefully.

"Don't do anything rash, Mr. Taylor," McDonnell repeats as if he can read my fucking mind.

I lean back in my chair and give him a blank stare. "Wouldn't dream of it."

CHAPTER FORTY-ONE

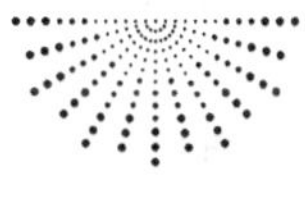

RAINE

Restraining orders are no joke. Everett was pissed when we first walked in, but we gave our statements and filled out a shit-ton of paperwork. The main thing that stuck with me since then is how I should've taken more pictures. Officer McDonnell was…kind, I think. A little robotic, maybe, but a decent listener despite Everett's constant death glare. I'll give him that much.

They're still digging into how Drake sent the videos to everyone at one time. Who knows who else he sent it to outside of LAU. His friends? His teammates? I wouldn't put it past him.

Or maybe not, since it shows his precious ex-girlfriend being intimate with someone who isn't him. My nose wrinkles at the reminder of our connection. Physically. Emotionally. Socially.

I can't believe I dated him. Part of me wants to go home and scrub my skin until it's raw. The other part? It wants to curl into a ball and sleep for a week, but only if Everett holds me while I do.

It didn't help when Officer McDonnell had to watch the

video, either. My stomach twisted, and I played with my fingers in my lap, unable to look up or do...anything at all, really. Not since I saw everyone's faces while they watched the video last night.

Everett's phone has been ringing off the hook. Or at least it was until Everett sent a mass text to all our friends, telling them to give us some space, and turned it off so it wasn't a distraction. Honestly, I'm almost grateful I handed mine over to Officer McDonnell. At least I don't have to deal with it for a little while.

I can feel Everett watching me from the driver's side. He's been staring at me constantly since the video. Part of me wants to tell him I'm okay. Part of me wants to ask why he keeps looking at me like I'm a ticking time bomb. Part of me wants to disappear entirely. Instead, I've stayed silent. Besides, what exactly am I supposed to say? Sorry I dragged you into this? Sorry your dick has now been recorded and passed around to everyone you know? I mean, it's a really nice dick. Thick, long, impressive. He has nothing to be ashamed of on that front, but it still doesn't make it okay or any less violating.

Seriously, what the hell am I thinking? I'm exhausted, and it's clear I'm not the only one. I can't tell if Everett's frustrated with me or just the situation in general, but he's been mostly quiet since we left the precinct last night. When Everett pulls the car into the Bean Scene's parking lot, then disappears inside, only to return with two cups of coffee a few minutes later, I almost cry.

He didn't ask if I wanted to go in with him. I'm grateful but can't help being curious if he's embarrassed by me now. If he doesn't want to be seen with me anymore. Not near LAU's campus. It's stupid. It takes two people to tango, and we were both in the video, but it doesn't make me feel any better, and it doesn't erase the fact that I was the one on my knees. The one who's now been filmed multiple times against my will. He'll be labeled a player. Me? I'll be labeled a slut. A whore.

I can't convince myself to ask what he's thinking. To ask if he's okay or if he's mad at me or if…if he's ashamed.

"Hey." Everett offers me a cup, and I force my body to respond. To move. To do something other than drown in my own pity party.

Taking the cup from him, I bring it to my lips and blow on the small hole until a whimper escapes me.

"Hey," he repeats. This time it's less of a greeting and more of an attempt to comfort me. To put me back together again. Reaching across the console, he tugs me into him, and I burrow into his chest, careful not to spill my coffee on him. I'm so…exhausted. Emotionally. Physically. God, I feel fucking broken.

"I can't even blow on a cup of fucking coffee w-without—"

"Sh…," he coos. "Sh…it's okay."

"It's not okay."

He squeezes me harder. "You're right. It isn't. Nothing he did was okay."

Nothing *he* did was okay. He. Not me. Drake. So why the hell am I carrying his burden? It only messes with my head more. I know Drake's the one with the problem, not me, yet here I am, having a pity party and drowning in shame and misery and disgust.

"I'm so sorry, Ev," I whisper.

"You have nothing to apologize for."

My eyes well with tears, but I don't pull away, too afraid if I do, I'll spiral even further. He's wrong, though. I do have something to apologize for. Something I've been carrying since the moment I saw the video. Honestly? Even before then. When Everett showed up at the cabin after Drake got his hands on him. What kind of sick fuck does these kinds of things?

My eyes burn even more, and I let out a shuddering breath. "I'm sorry because…because I wasn't the only one in the video."

I wait for him to let me go. To push me away. To tell me he wishes he'd never met me because if he hadn't, he wouldn't be in this mess. He wouldn't have some psycho recording him through a window like a fucking stalker.

Not *like* a stalker.

An actual stalker.

Since when did my life turn into a freaking horror movie?

"I don't give a shit about the video," Everett rasps against the crown of my head. "I give a shit about *you*. All right? I'm fucking crumbling right now because of what this bastard has put you through. What he's still managing to put you through, despite our best attempt to make him go away."

I let out a shaky breath and twist the fabric of his shirt in my hands as I breathe him in. Cedar. Pine. Like the trees surrounding the cabin. And rain. Fresh. Clean. Rain. It makes me want to burrow under his skin and never come out again.

"I love you, Raine," he murmurs.

My pulse spikes, and I hold my breath, convinced I heard him wrong. I'm too much of a coward to ask him to repeat himself and confirm I'm right. That he didn't just drop the L-bomb in the middle of Bean Scene's parking lot.

"I know right now probably isn't the best time to tell you this, but I do," he adds quietly. "I love you so fucking much, and I'm so sorry Drake refuses to leave you alone, but I promise you, baby. I promise he'll never hurt you again."

I untuck my head from the crook of his neck and blink slowly, letting the tears fall freely as I hold his icy-blue gaze. I never thought I'd trust someone enough to let them pick up the pieces and put me back together again. Never thought it was even possible. But this man? This man has surprised me more times than I can count, and the idea of him loving me and not knowing I feel the same is worse than anything we've been through since we met all those weeks ago. And it's strange. Because I thought I knew what love was. What it felt like. The truth is? I had no freaking clue. Not until Everett walked into my life, er, not until I walked into his.

Licking the salty tears from my lips, I whisper, "I love you, too, Ev."

His mouth lifts. "Yeah?"

I nod. "Yeah."

"Good. 'Cause, uh, pretty sure your love is the only thing that's going to keep you from wanting to stab me."

"And why would I want to stab you?"

"Because I've been fielding your dad's calls since last night."

My breath hitches. "What?"

"I'm not sure how he got my number, but when you weren't answering your phone, he tracked it down."

"Why?" I whisper.

"Drake, uh," he scrubs his hand over his face, "Drake sent him the video."

The video.

The blasted fucking video.

Can I seriously not catch a break?

Rage and defeat and resentment battle within me, threatening to rip me to shreds. I rest my head against his shoulder and pray for strength. "Perfect."

"I told him we'd stop by."

"What?"

"I know you probably don't want to, but if I was in their shoes, I would want to make sure my daughter's okay, you know?" He drops a kiss to the top of my head. "Don't hate me."

"I don't hate you," I whisper. "I hate Drake."

His chuckle is dry and low as he kisses my hair again. "You're not the only one. Come on," he prods. "Drink your coffee. You're gonna need the caffeine."

"And here I thought we'd head back to the cabin and sleep for a week."

"Not yet." He nudges my head with a gentle pop of his shoulder, and I sit up as he adds, "Soon, though. First, we gotta talk to your parents."

"Sounds...*great*."

A ghost of a smile plays on the edge of his lips, and he shoves his car into drive.

BITING ON THE INSIDE OF MY CHEEK, I LIFT MY HAND AND RAP my knuckles against the front door. I don't know why I didn't think Drake would stoop this low. But the idea he would send the video to my dad never even crossed my mind. I think it's because he knew there would be no going back if he crossed that line. No second chances. Apparently, he's finally gotten the message, and the gloves are officially off. If only I knew how to throw a punch back at him instead of just cowering in the corner and taking it on the chin.

It's freezing out. Everett had an extra hoodie in the back of his car, but I left my coat at the house. I was too distracted to grab it when I rushed out the front door like a bat out of hell last night. It's crazy, though. To think how much has changed in such a short period of time. Life is funny like that, I guess. The way time moves. Sometimes at a snail's pace. Other times it's faster than light speed. Now, here I am. On my parents' front porch. Unable to do anything but knock and wait for their disappointed looks. I should walk in. If it was any other day, I would. This is my family home, so why do I not feel welcome?

"You good?" Everett questions.

"What did you tell him?" I glance at Ev and clarify, "My dad."

"Nothing other than we'd swing by to chat this morning."

"Chat," I repeat.

"Not sure what else you want me to call it."

He's right. This isn't a confession. It's what? An update? On the culmination of shitty decisions I've tried running from to no avail?

Yeah, *chat* fits fine, I guess.

With a nod, I let it go and face the solid piece of oak, preparing myself for the inevitable.

Footsteps echo on the opposite side of the door before it swings open, and my mom tugs me into a hug.

My body stays stiff for all of two seconds. Then, I wrap my arms around her and close my eyes. "Hey, Mom."

"I love you. So. Damn. Much."

I sag into her even more. "I love you, too."

She squeezes me again, then lets me go and turns to Everett. "I believe your introduction is long past due."

"Hello, I'm Everettt," he offers. "Everett Taylor."

"My husband mentioned it." She tilts her head but doesn't move away from the doorframe. Don't get me wrong, my dad and brother are fierce, but my mom? She's something else, entirely. The woman grew up with religious zealots for parents who kicked her out before she was even a legal adult. After that, she was basically a nomad until she met my dad and managed to tame the grumpy tattoo artist. The rest, as they say, is history. And even though it's been relatively smooth sailing ever since, anyone who's met my mom knows she's not someone to trifle with. And right now, I'm seriously squirming from her scrutiny. Not of me, but Everett. I have a feeling she's debating on whether or not he should be on her shit list after my long absence. If only she knew he was the one grounding me in this moment. Giving me the strength and courage to stand here and admit my mistakes to two of the people I look up to most.

Tattoos cover her arms and back, though they aren't on display now. Instead, she's wrapped in a thick, baby blue sweater, and her long blonde hair is tied into a messy bun on the top of her head. She would almost look welcoming if it wasn't for her unwavering—and a bit unnerving—gaze. "You're lucky I've been preoccupied with my newest grand-baby," she adds.

"Congratulations," Everett offers.

"Thank you." She glances at me. "I'm sorry it's taken so long for an introduction."

"We've been…busy," I lie.

"Busy, huh?" Her lips press into a thin line. "Listen, from what your dad said, Everett's already been through the wringer, so I won't push it. I trust your dad's judgment, but I do want to make sure you're okay and if there's anything we can do to help with…whatever the hell's going on. Unfortunately, because you've kept us in the dark, it's kind of difficult to know what that is."

I can see the hurt in her eyes. The undertone of disapproval. Not at whatever I need help with, but at my lack of candor. She has every right to disapprove of me keeping them in the dark, though. I know this. It doesn't make the idea of ripping the Band-Aid off and telling them everything feel any easier, though.

"I know," I murmur. "I know I've screwed up—"

"Rainbow, we all screw up," she interjects. "With my history, no one knows it better than I do. Now, your dad's in the shed out back, working off his pent-up energy thanks to the video we never want to see again. I'm sure he saw the doorbell notification, so I bet he'll be here in a minute. But before we go any further, I need you to tell me whether or not your friend had anything to do with the video being distributed."

I grab Everett's hand and tug him closer to me. "He wasn't the one who filmed us, let alone shared it. I promise."

She hesitates, studying Everett again as if she's a well-seasoned detective. "You trust him, Raine?"

I nod. "With everything."

"Then I'll try to do the same." She turns to Everett again and offers him her hand. "Hello, Everett. Let's try this one more time. I'm Maddie Anders, Raine's mom. You can call me Mrs. Anders."

Everett takes her hand and shakes it once. "Nice to meet you, Mrs. Anders."

"You, too," she replies. "Although I do wish it was under different circumstances."

Everett's mouth twitches. "Same."

"Shall we?"

My mom steps aside, motions for us to come in, and closes the icy chill out with a quiet click of the front door. When my dad rounds the corner from the back of the house, I offer him a pathetic wave, and he picks up his pace.

When he reaches me, he gives me a giant bear hug and grunts, "Who do I need to kill?"

"Dad—"

"You're right, you're right." He lets me go and pins Everett with a stare. "Who do *we* need to kill?"

Pushing myself between them, I break my dad's line of sight and interrupt, "There will be no killing!"

"*Yet*," Everett chimes in from behind me.

My dad smirks. "I knew I liked him."

"No, you didn't," I argue. "You thought he was beating me, remember?"

"Yeah, and then you introduced us," my dad volleys back. "I might not be a saint, but I am good at reading people. And so is your mom." He glances at his wife. "Does he pass your vibe test, Mads?"

"It's still a little early, but yes. I don't think he's the one who did it."

"I already told you he wasn't," I point out.

Ignoring me, my dad scratches his five o'clock shadow and tilts his head. "So the question is, who *did*? Or better yet, let's start at the beginning?" He motions to the soft leather couch in the family room.

The beginning. Right.

I grab Everett's hand, lead both of us around the arm, and sit on the edge of the sofa while my parents each take a seat on the matching couch across from us. Once they're seated, my mom crosses one leg over the other and snuggles into my dad's side as he hangs his arm over the back of the couch, their looks expectant.

Deep breath, I silently remind myself.

I open my mouth and square my shoulders, preparing myself for the inevitable. For the shame and disappointment and—

"Can I say something before you start?" my mom interjects.

Surprised, I dip my chin in agreement, and Everett slowly tugs me into him.

"Why didn't you walk in?" she asks.

My brows crease. "What?"

"When you got here. You didn't walk in like you usually do."

Feeling tongue-tied, I look down at my hands, unsure what to say or do or...anything really. Because it's stupid. My reason for knocking. Honestly, I don't even know if I have a reason. Not one I can put into words, anyway.

"All right, let me say one more thing," my mom continues. "I don't care what you've done, who you've slept with, or what choices you've made in your life. I don't. All I care about is whether or not you're happy and whether or not you're safe. Like I've already pointed out once today, we both know I wasn't a saint when I was your age. And I sure as shit don't blame you for filming yourself while having some spicy time with someone you care about."

My dad balks. "Mads!"

"Oh, shush. We both know we have our own kinks, Milo," she points out. "What I care about is whether or not you're comfortable in your own skin, let alone comfortable with me and your dad and your siblings. What I care about is why you haven't come around lately and why you felt like you couldn't walk into your childhood home without an invitation." Tears gather in her eyes, and she moves from her couch to mine. "Baby, you are my world. And I'm so sorry if you've ever felt like you could do anything to make me ashamed of you or make you feel like you aren't our pride and joy."

Her words are like a balm on an open wound, and I dig my nails into my palms to keep from bawling like a baby. I'm not sure it ever goes away. The desire to please your parents. To make them proud.

"Don't get me wrong. I know you're not perfect," she continues, "just like how I'm not perfect, and your dad isn't perfect, and your sister isn't perfect, and your brother isn't perfect, and"—she glances at Everett—"I'm sure you're a great guy, but I know you're not perfect, either."

"Far from it," he quips.

Her smile widens, and she bumps her shoulder with mine. "That's the beauty of family, though. Especially ours. We like messy. We like mistakes. We like flaws and life lessons and Sunday brunches." She grabs my hand and places it in her lap. "We like *you*, Raine Anders, and we've missed you more than you know. Now, if we could only convince you to open up to us so we could help you a bit, that'd be great."

And just like that, I tell her. I tell both of them. I tell Everett and my mom and my dad everything. When I'm finished, they wrap me in a hug, kiss the top of my head, and promise it's going to be okay. And for the first time in a long while, I really, truly believe they might be right.

CHAPTER FORTY-TWO

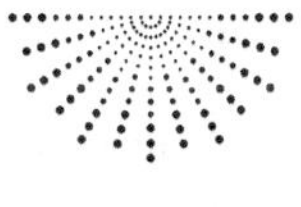

RAINE

"You still goin' to Dodger's performance?" my dad asks as I finish sweeping the front of Etch 'N' Ink. It's late, and we've already closed our doors for the night. Ever since my breakdown at his house last weekend, he's been...great. No kid gloves, though I know it's killing him. Only open, unfiltered conversations. They even went to Everett's home game yesterday and cheered him on like lifelong fans. If that isn't a miracle, I don't know what is. They also agreed to keep Drake's connection to Shorty a secret. No need to open old wounds, they told me. It was like music to my ears.

As for my phone? We picked it up from McDonnell a few days ago. They weren't able to connect it to Drake, though I'm not surprised. He received the restraining order the day after the video was sent. I have no idea how he took it, but I haven't heard from him since, so maybe there's some silver lining in this after all. I'm not holding my breath, but every passing day without interference from Drake makes me breathe a little easier.

One day at a time.

"Raine." My dad snaps his fingers a few inches from my nose. "Did you hear me?"

"Yup." I stop sweeping and look up at him. "I'm still going to Dodger's performance."

"Who's driving you?"

"Dodge," I answer.

"No Everett?"

"He didn't know what time he'd be back from the away game, so he parked his truck on campus and will meet me at SeaBird, which is why Dodge is picking me up." I check the clock on the wall. "He's probably already on his way since his concert is supposed to start in about thirty minutes."

Despite my dad handling the news of Drake surprisingly well, I can tell he doesn't want to leave me alone. He also doesn't have much choice. He's already late.

"You can go," I urge.

"I can wait until he picks you up."

"Dad," I tease. "I'll be fine, I promise. I'll even wait inside until he gets here. Sound good?"

"Fine," he grunts, tossing his arm around my shoulders and giving me a peck on the forehead. "Love you, Rainbow."

"Love you, too. Have fun babysitting!" My mom and dad would've definitely been at Dodger's last concert before leaving for London, but Penny asked them to watch her three kids so she could go on a date with her husband. And if there's one thing my parents will always cave to, it's babysitting their grandbabies.

"Yeah, yeah," my dad grumbles. "Wish your brother luck for me."

"I will. Love you!"

"See you, Bo." He lets me go and opens the front door but hesitates. With a pointed look, he adds, "Don't forget to lock up."

"I won't. Promise."

"That's my girl." He waves, then disappears, leaving me all alone in the middle of a quiet Etch 'N' Ink. Once I finish sweeping, I open my notebook and start drawing a new piece. It's bold and swirly and showcases a lion's head with a thick, full mane.

My phone buzzes on the counter.

DODGER

Having bike trouble. Gonna be late.

I roll my eyes. My brother's had an obsession with motorcycles ever since he was a kid. I blame my dad who's also a motorcycle junkie. Between the two of them? I don't even want to know how much they've spent on all the bells, whistles, and leather that—as my brother puts it—makes a girl's panties melt.

Gag.

The fact he's having bike trouble, however, is odd, considering how much time he spends babying the stupid thing. Curious, I type my response.

ME

Everything okay?

DODGER

The usual. Let me see if Judge can swing by and grab you.

ME

Don't you dare. Judge terrifies me.

DODGER

Judge terrifies everyone.

He isn't wrong.

Pretty sure I've only heard Judge say a dozen words in all the time I've known him. The idea of spending even two minutes in the same car with him sounds absolutely miserable.

ME

Seriously, don't send Judge. I'm good.

DODGER

Fine. I'll send Pax. Here's his number:
555.972.2234 He's on his way.

I check the time on my phone and frown.

ME

I don't want either of you missing your set.

DODGER

Don't give a shit about the set if you aren't
here to watch it.

Liar.

Don't get me wrong. My brother loves when his family is there to support him, but he doesn't play for me. He plays for him and only him.

ME

Mm-hmm. Sure.

DODGER

Stay put. He'll be there in five.

I check the time again. His concert is supposed to start in five.

With a huff, I grab my purse and tuck my phone inside, confirming the taser Dylan gave me is still there, too.

Yup. There she is. Good ol' Bertha.

Finley named it. Even decorated the side with neon puff paint during our girls' day. Peeking out the window, I search for Paxton's headlights, but the street is as dark as ever.

After fifteen minutes, I send Pax a text.

ME

Hey, Pax! This is Raine. Dodge said you were picking me up? Any idea how far away you are?

It's a stupid question. SeaBird is barely three blocks away from Etch 'N' Ink. If Pax left when Dodger said he did, he would've easily been here by now. Maybe something held him up? Anxiously, I pace the waiting area, rearranging the magazines sprawled on one of the coffee tables. When I check my phone again, another five minutes have passed and the message is still on delivered, never moving to read.

ME

Hey! No biggie if you can't come grab me. Just let me know.

Silence.

My phone buzzes, but Dodger's name pops up instead of Pax's.

DODGER

Tell me he's there.

ME

Uh…not yet? I tried texting but haven't heard back yet.

DODGER

Gonna kick his ass if he took a detour. He left twenty minutes ago.

Another message follows right after.

DODGER

That kid is on my last fucking nerve.

My nose scrunches, and I glance out the dark window again, checking for headlights or Pax's car in case I missed it. The idea of Pax getting in trouble all because he didn't want to run one of his bandmate's errands makes me feel...terrible. Besides, I already feel bad enough that my brother, dad, and boyfriend all have the need to babysit me twenty-four-seven. Adding Pax to the mix and having him on the opposite end of Dodger's wrath, all because he's super overprotective of his baby sister feels even more wrong. When headlights appear seconds later, I exhale a breath of relief. My phone buzzes in my hand, and Everett's picture flashes up at me. I bring my cell to my ear as I unlock the front door and open it. Juggling the keys, my cell, and my purse, I start locking up.

"Hey, you," I answer.

"Hey, we're almost to LAU."

Sliding the key into the lock, I twist it and close Etch 'N' Ink, keeping my phone pinned between my ear and shoulder. "Perfect. Pax just got here."

"Pax?"

"Yeah, something was wrong with Dodger's bike, so he sent Pax to pick me up." I pull the key from the lock and turn toward Pax's car, anxious to get out of the freezing cold. With a clatter, my keys slip from my fingers, and my body freezes. "Shit."

"Raine?" Everett prods.

It isn't Pax's car. It's Drake's.

"H-he's here," I breathe out.

"Storm—"

The creak of hinges cuts him off as Drake pushes the door open, and I swear he's moving in slow motion, but I'm frozen. I can't scream. I can't do anything. Like a deer in the headlights, I simply...stare.

"Raine, talk to me. Talk to me, baby." Everett sounds so far away. Like his words are spoken underwater, and I'm being dragged under. The cold glass hits my back. I lean into it, my mind reeling, while praying my legs don't give out.

"Tell your boyfriend good game." Drake slams his car door shut and slowly rounds the front of the hood toward me. "You're talking to him, right?"

His voice tugs on my spine, and my feet feel like they're glued to the concrete beneath my sneakers. He wants Everett to know I'm alone with him. That Everett's helpless. That I'm helpless. That, despite a stupid piece of paper and a police officer's promise, Drake's still here. And he isn't ready to let me go. If he was, he wouldn't have sent the video. He wouldn't be here now. And he sure as shit wouldn't be prowling closer. One. Step. At a time.

"Storm, the bus just pulled in," Everett says. "I'll be right there. I promise, I'll be right there."

My ears whoosh, making it hard to focus on his words as I face my stalker head-on. He's closing in. I want to run, but I'm afraid it'll only snap Drake's hunting instincts into over-drive. Part of me wonders if I could convince my body to move in the first place. Instead, I stay still and slowly slip my hand into my purse, blindly reaching for the taser I know is inside.

"Come on, baby." Drake closes the last bit of distance between us. "Tell him."

"D-Drake says good game tonight," I whisper.

"Is he talking to you?" Everett demands through my cell.

"Um..."

"Did he like the video?" Drake challenges. "I know the angle was a little fucked, but I was still impressed. You've always been a champ at deep-throating." He lifts his hand and drags it along the side of my face. "Glad he could experi-ence it once, so he'll know what he's missing."

"We're almost there." Everett takes a deep breath. "I'm almost there, Storm."

"Did he like the added audio?" Drake prods. "I took it from our video. So fucking good, baby. You know how to take me so fucking good. I was almost disappointed I had to film it from outside the cabin."

Bile floods my mouth and coats my throat, making me want to gag as I glare back at him. "H-how did you—"

"I put an AirTag on your boyfriend's car after we jumped him at the gas station. Why do you think I let him walk away in the first place?" His mouth lifts into a sneer, and my blood runs cold, leaving me shivering in the icy darkness. "You need to hang up the phone now, baby." Drake's friendliness from moments ago is now laced with a heavy dose of annoyance. Like I'm inconveniencing him or some shit by continuing my call with Everett. Covering my hand with his own, he lowers my arm, slips my cell from my fingers, and tucks it in his back pocket.

"There. That's better, isn't it?" he notes. "Wanna tell me why some dipshit handed me a restraining order last week?"

"Drake," I whisper. It's a plea.

He grabs my arm and moves even closer. "You promised you'd never leave me, remember?"

"You promised you'd never hit me," I reply. "Remember?"

His grip squeezes even tighter, and I wince.

"One fuckin' mistake, and you never let me live it down," he spits.

I squeeze my eyes shut and ignore the spittle as it hits my cheeks. "W-What do you want, Drake?"

"I've missed you."

My thumb fumbles with the taser's trigger in my purse as I try to get a good grip on the handle. "How did you find me?"

"Aw, come on. You forget how well I know you. You didn't think I wouldn't know you'd go right back to Daddy after quitting Lucian's shop?" Letting my arm go, he chuckles darkly. "Nepo baby through and through. And since your brother's been blasting all over his social media about his last performance in his hometown, I figured you'd want to be there with you being all chummy with your family lately.."

Understanding races down my spine. "Have you been following me?"

"It's a shame what happened to his bike."

My gaze cuts to his. "You touched his bike?"

"I knew your boy toy would be busy with the away game. Called the shop and asked for your dad's schedule, figuring he'd be gone, too. The receptionist is awfully chatty," he adds. "Didn't take a genius to figure out your brother would offer to give you a ride." Drake's fingers are strangely gentle as he tucks my hair behind my ear then tilts my head up, examining the storm cloud behind my ear. "This is new, though."

Stall him.

I tilt my head a little more, giving him a better view. "Do you like it?"

"I fucking love it." He drops his hand. "Makes you look hot."

Gross.

Praying he can't hear the trembling in my voice, I choke out, "Thanks."

Come on, Raine. Pull the trigger. Just drop the purse and pull the freaking trigger.

"Gonna need you to get in the car for me, though." His hand finds my waist, and he urges me like he actually believes I'll willingly go with him after everything we've been through. The man is fucking delusional.

I follow his lead, hoping it'll distract him as I start to pull the taser out, but before it's free from my purse, Drake snatches my wrist and yanks my purse away. "What you got here, baby?" He twists my hand around, making me wince. Then, he peeks inside my bag, and I already know what he sees. My only line of defense lying helplessly at the bottom. With a low laugh, he demands, "You really thought you could use this on me?" The sound grates on my senses, but I keep my lips gnashed together.

If he's surprised, he doesn't show it. Instead, he continues his assault on my arm, twisting it, making my muscles scream in protest as he yanks it behind my back and drags me into him until we're chest to chest. Face to face. I wait for the scent of alcohol to burn my nostrils, but it doesn't. His eyes are dilated, though. Angry and dilated. Is he on something? Those stupid pain pills he's always loved during the off-season when his precious hockey career isn't hanging in the balance of a drug test? Does it even matter?

He jerks me harder into him, making my bones rattle with his force. "Big fucking mistake, baby."

"Drake—"

"Shut the fuck up." He lets me go and shoves me toward his parked car. When I nearly lose my footing, the asshole laughs. "You good, baby?" His smile is kind, but his eyes? They ooze with condescension and anticipation. The combination leaves every inch of my skin feeling like it's painted with sticky tar. "Get in the car."

I gulp. "I'm sorry, Drake, but I…I can't do that."

"Nah, I'm pretty sure you can." His lifeless eyes scan me up and down. "Either that, or you can deep-throat me right here."

Terror shoots down my spine, and bile reappears in my throat with a vengeance. So this is what it's like. To be preyed upon. To be underestimated. Keeping my movements slow, I take a step to the side so it's easier for me to beeline it away from him.

I'm not sure why he's still playing this game. He's stolen my taser and my only line of communication with the outside world. Now he expects me to…play nice? I hold his stare, curious—and terrified—as to whether or not he's serious. He's never forced me to do anything sexually. Okay, maybe I'm giving him more credit than he deserves. I've agreed to things, hoping to keep his inevitable guilt-tripping at bay. I've given in when I wasn't in the mood because it felt easier, and we all know he recorded me without my consent. But physically forcing me to do something I'm not willing to do? This is new territory, and when all I find is hatred staring back at me in those dark brown eyes, I know he isn't bluffing, and he isn't afraid to take what he wants. Not when I've already pushed him away. Not when I've already left him, the same way his mom did by dying. It sounds so strange. Comparing myself to his mom. I almost feel sorry for him. For the life he's had and the challenges he's faced. But it doesn't justify anything he's done. It doesn't justify this. This moment. This betrayal. This line.

"Drake, let me go," I plead.

He shakes his head. "I can't live without you."

"You can—"

"I won't!" he bellows.

It's a promise.

A curse.

I bite the inside of my cheek and take a shallow breath as a million potential responses flutter through my mind, but none of them give me the outcome I need to get out of this. To walk away. Instead, I stay quiet and silently beg him with my eyes to let me go. To leave me alone.

"I need you, Raine." His voice is quieter now but just as unhinged. "I'll *always* need you."

Always.

Resignation settles deep in my bones, and I slowly take another step sideways, when his expression twists with rage. He lunges forward and snatches my arm, dragging me further away from the front door.

Instead of fighting him, I move in the same direction, lowering my shoulder and ramming it into his stomach. His arms are rigid around my body, and he squeezes. It's like a boa constrictor around my torso. We fall to the ground. With a thump, the hard surface steals my breath, and he rolls us both over, fumbling with my jeans.

No. No, no, no! This isn't supposed to happen. Not to me. Not to anyone, but especially not to me. You hear the stories. You hear the statistics. But it's so easy to brush it aside. To think it can't happen to you. That it won't.

Not because you're special, but because…because it *can't*. Because you're in a safe neighborhood, and you're smart and—

Fight, dammit!

Squirming beneath him, I kick and scream, clawing at his bare forearms until his skin cakes beneath my fingernails. He backhands me, his knuckles causing stars to blur my sight as my head snaps to one side.

Fight!

"Help!" The blood-curdling scream sounds like it's coming from an entirely different person. His hand finds my mouth, and he covers it with his palm while his weight on my chest makes it more and more difficult to breathe.

I'm going to be sick.

Or pass out.

Or both.

Hurried footsteps echo off the pavement as I squirm on the icy ground, attempting to get the asshole off me before I pass out from lack of oxygen. Digging my heels into the sidewalk, I buck up and down, left and right, while clawing at Drake's fingers against my mouth. In an instant, he's wrenched off me, and I scramble away on my ass, my adrenaline fueling me. The cold pavement digs into my palms as my vision starts returning, and my mind races to catch up with what's happening. Everett's on top of my ex. He's hitting him over and over again when a pair of arms wrap around me.

"No!" Another blood-curdling scream claws its way up my throat. I twist in the stranger's hold and gasp when I recognize Griffin. He brings me into his chest, rubbing his hand up and down my back as Everett and Drake go head-to-head. Jab, cross, hook, uppercut. Drake keeps his forearms up, attempting to protect himself from Everett's fists until he lifts a rock from the ground and slams it against Everett's temple. Everett's head swings to the side, and he tumbles to his left, rolling off Drake. Sensing his opening, Drake jumps to his feet, rushes to his car, and climbs inside, peeling out of the parking lot. The world feels like it's spinning because it all happens so fast.

I scramble across the ground, wrap my arms around Everett's neck, and sob. Fear. Exhaustion. Adrenaline. Relief. They all battle for the spotlight inside me, leaving me shredded and overwhelmed. So overwhelmed I feel like I can't breathe. Like Drake's hands are covering my mouth all over again. Like I can't get my lungs to work, let alone my legs or arms or even my thoughts. It's like a cloud hangs over me. Thick with thunder and lightning and rain and hail and—

"Sh..." The coo vibrates against the shell of my ear as Everett holds me close. "Sh...it's okay. It's okay, Stormie."

But honestly? I'm not so sure.

Brakes squeal seconds later, and I jerk in Everett's hold, searching the street as if the boogeyman might pop out at any second. Then again, he already has. When I spot a sleek black motorcycle stopping in front of us, it takes me a second to recognize it. When my brother cuts the engine and swings his leg over the side, my brain attempts to piece together what the hell is happening and why he's here.

He stalks toward me, still cradled in Everett's arms as we sit on the icy ground, his face twisted with fury. "What the fuck—"

Everett jumps to his feet and decks my brother in the face. "You told me you'd pick her up!"

"I was going to—"

Everett swings, but my brother dodges him, so Everett's busted-up knuckles only meet his forearms instead of Dodger's face like he intended.

"I had a flat, all right?" Dodger says, defending himself. "Then I sent Pax to come get her, but he showed up alone a few minutes ago. As soon as he did, I came as fast as I could!"

"Not." *Hit.* "Fucking." *Hit.* "Good enough." *Hit.*

The sound of flesh hitting flesh makes me flinch.

"He got to her!" Everett booms. "He was fucking waiting for her—"

"Stop!" I yell. Pushing to my feet, I stumble toward them. "Everett, stop!"

Blood trickles from his temple from the rock to the side of his head as he slowly turns to me, letting his balled-up fists fall to his sides. Like the fight has finally seeped out of him. Like the adrenaline has finally pumped through his system. His body sags slightly, and I move toward him, tucking myself against his side.

"Did he touch her?" Dodger demands.

"I'm fine," I whisper.

My brother's expression twists. "Where is he?"

"Ran," Everett answers.

"Fuckin' pussy." Dodger's molars grind. "Did you already call the cops?"

Everett nods. "They're on their way."

"Fuck." Dodger looks around the empty streets and stays quiet, listening for sirens. "Come on, if we hurry, we can get out of here before they arrive. Let's go." He starts to move past Everett, but Everett stops him by pressing his hand to my brother's chest.

"Wait."

"He's gonna get away with this if we don't get out of here and take care of him ourselves."

"Dodge," Everett warns.

My brother shakes his head. "You saw how he handled the restraining order—"

"Trust me," Everett grits out. "I'm aware the bullshit piece of paper didn't do a damn thing, but—"

"Do you know how many stories are like this?" Dodger sneers. "Without enough fucking evidence to actually do anything? It's gonna turn into a he said, she said contest, and he's gonna get off scot-free after she's forced to relive it a hundred fucking times." He slams his closed fist against his chest. "And that's if he doesn't already have an alibi in place. The guy might be an abusive prick, but it's clear he isn't stupid. And let's say the cops do believe her. Do you have any idea how long it'll take? He could make bail or press charges against you for assault."

"I was protecting her—"

"It doesn't. Fucking. Matter," Dodger spits until he's nose to nose with Everett in the dark parking lot. "He's gonna get away—"

"It won't happen. I won't let it."

"What will you do? Huh?" Dodger demands. "What are you gonna do, Ev?"

A vein in Everett's throat pulses as I stare up at him. It's like he's made of stone. But I know him better than this. Beneath the calm facade is a fucking hurricane, and it tears me to shreds.

"Ev," I whisper. Or maybe I don't. Maybe the name never slips past my lips because my brother only barrels on, his upper lip curling in disgust.

"Are you gonna man up and protect my sister, or do I need to do the honors?" he growls.

The muscles in Everett's hands flex as he glares at my brother. They're still nose to nose. Chest to chest. "Says the guy failed to pick her up."

"My bike had a fucking flat," Dodger spits back at him. "And Pax was supposed to—"

Pushing myself between them again, I face my older brother and rise onto my tiptoes, trying to close some of the distance between us. "Stay out of this, Dodge."

He glares down at me. "No."

"I'm serious," I push.

"I won't let—"

"Do you wanna know why I didn't tell you about all of this in the first place?" I ask. "Because of this. Because I knew you would be reckless and stupid and wind up sticking your nose where it doesn't belong."

"You're my sister!" he yells.

"And you're unhinged if you honestly believe taking the law into your own hands is a bright idea."

"Dodge." Everett's voice is low. Lethal. And manages to cut through the haze of fury clouding my brother's judgment.

His focus snaps to Everett and he snarls, "What?"

Everett moves closer and wraps his arms around my shoulders, tugging me into his side as he holds my brother's stare. "We'll be in touch."

There's something about him. The way he's looking at my brother. The way he's looking in general. Almost detached. Deranged. Like whatever restraint he's used to having has finally snapped, and if he was anyone else, I'd be terrified. "Ev," I breathe out.

But he doesn't look down at me. He only holds my brother's stare and repeats, "We'll be in touch."

"Ev." I tug on the collar of his bloodied shirt.

Tearing his attention from Dodge, he looks down at me, his expression softening. "Don't worry, Stormie. I'll keep you safe. Promise." He presses his hand to my lower back, and the man I've fallen for rises to the surface. "Come on. Let's get you inside and clean up before the police arrive."

CHAPTER FORTY-THREE

EVERETT

Fear. It's a funny thing. The way it encapsulates you. Making it impossible to breathe, let alone think straight. I can still see him on top of her. Hunched over Stormie as she kicked her legs beneath him. Fighting. Clawing. Screaming.

Fuck, her screams.

I close my eyes and pull her closer to me, breathing in the scent of shampoo clinging to her hair. Griffin was smart enough to call the police when we were on the bus. After they arrived, we gave our statements. It only confirmed Dodger's assumption. They'll open an investigation, but we shouldn't hold our breaths. It's bullshit. It's also the last fucking straw. I'm done. I'm done playing by the rules. Bending over backward to do this by the book when the book isn't fucking working.

The EMT took a look at Storm's injuries and insisted we go to the hospital. She'll have a bruised tailbone and some cuts and bruises on her palms. She also has a bruised cheek-bone from when he backhanded her, but otherwise? She should be okay...if you can call her long list of injuries the definition of *okay*. Regardless, since it could've been worse—so much worse—the prognosis was music to my fuckin' ears. As for me, I have a mild concussion and a nasty headache, thanks to Drake slamming a rock against my temple. They also looked at my hand, confirming what I already knew. A broken pinkie on my right hand and a few stitches from when Drake's tooth sliced me. It's worth it, though.

Officer McDonnell asked Raine if she wanted him to contact her parents. She agreed—surprising the shit out of me—and it took almost an hour of convincing until they finally let her out of their sight again. They wanted her to go with them instead of letting me drive her back to the cabin—to our place—but Raine wouldn't budge, insisting all she wanted was to take a hot shower and to let me hold her. I had no problem obliging.

It's strange. I never thought of the cabin as anything more than my childhood home. Now, though? Now, it's different. Those walls hold more than memories of me and my sisters and my parents. Now, they hold memories of Raine, too. The firelight dancing off her bare toes and along the walls of our makeshift fort. The way she hunkers down on the couch with her notepad in her lap for hours. The pieces of dark hair clinging to the shower wall. They used to drive me fucking nuts, but now I can't imagine a shower without them. Without finding one every time I step inside.

I tighten my arms around Raine, closing my eyes. Her hair is almost dry now. After we got home, I washed it in the shower and braided it, surprised the knowledge would come in handy. I make a mental note to text Hazel, my oldest sister, and thank her for teaching me how to do it. Honestly, I should thank all three of my sisters. And my dad. I should thank my dad, too. For teaching me how to take care of someone. How to look after and love someone. Because even though shit is far from over, my mind is clear. It's like I was made for this. For protecting the ones I love, and despite carrying it like it's a burden for so long, I can't imagine how quickly tonight could've taken a turn for the worse if I wasn't prepared. If I hadn't already played out a million scenarios like I've done with Finley and my mom and Dylan and Miley and Hazel and Ophelia and Tatum. It makes me want to take all of them and hide them in a safe house somewhere. Away from creeps and assholes and stalkers and every other motherfucker who preys on women. Who thinks they're owed anything for having a fucking penis instead of a vagina.

My stitches pull as I squeeze my hand into a fist while *Brooklyn 99* plays on the television.

I can't believe I almost lost her. Can't believe the police aren't protecting her. Can't believe Drake would get away with this without—

"You okay?" Raine whispers.

I shake my head, causing her flyaways to tickle the underside of my jaw. "What?"

With a quiet laugh, she wiggles in my grasp, stealing a bit more room but not moving away from me completely. I don't know if it's for her benefit or mine, but I'm grateful nonetheless.

Peeking up at me, she smiles. "I asked if you're okay."

"I've been better," I grunt. "How are you?"

"I'm okay, Ev. Promise."

"Not gonna let you out of my sight."

"Or arms, apparently," she teases.

"Not sure how you find this funny."

"I don't," she admits. "But when I have the option to laugh or cry, I'm gonna go with laugh." She sits up a little more and cups the side of my face. "Thanks for saving me today."

"Not sure tonight counts as saving," I mutter. "He got away, remember?"

"They're going to find him."

My muscles jump with the same fucking tension as before. "Not gonna leave this up to them."

Pushing herself away from me, she brings her knees to her chest and rests her chin on them. "What are you saying?"

"Do you trust me, Stormie?"

She hesitates, staring fucking through me as if she has the power to read my thoughts. My intentions. My plan and everything I have in store for Drake Haitt. It's better she doesn't know, though. If she did, there's not a chance in hell she'd let me out of her sight, let alone this house.

"Are you going to do something stupid, Everett?"

I don't want to lie to her, so I kiss the top of her head again and tug her into my side. "Get some rest."

"I don't want to rest."

"And what do you want?" I ask.

She sits up again, tosses her leg over my waist, and straddles me. "I want to erase..." Her fingers slide into my hair and frame both sides of my head, urging me to touch my chin to my chest. When I do, she presses her lips between my brows. "*This.*"

"This?" I ask.

Running her thumb above the bridge of my nose, she smiles. "*This.*" She kisses the spot again. "The little worry wrinkle you're sporting." Her lips find it again. "I want to erase it."

A gruff chuckle rumbles through my chest, and I wrap my arms around her waist. "Hate to burst your bubble, but I'm not sure it's going anywhere. Not any time soon."

"Not anytime soon, huh?" she challenges.

I sober and grab the outside of her thighs. "Not until I know you're safe."

"Well," her pink tongue darts out between her lips, "since we're here, and your arms are wrapped around me, *and* I'm straddling your very rigid cock, *and* there isn't anyone here but me and you, I'd say I'm pretty safe, don't you?" She slowly scrapes her fingertips against my scalp, massaging my head and making my dick jump at the attention. When she feels it, her mouth lifts. "I think you should kiss me now."

Lifting my chin, I move slowly and do exactly that, melding my mouth with hers. Tasting her. Convincing myself she's safe. She's here. He didn't break her. The reminder makes my hands dig into her silky skin, and I deepen the kiss. I'd give anything to erase every touch. Every minute they ever shared, knowing he didn't deserve any of them. Not one. Single. Moment.

She drags her fingers through my hair, tugging on the roots with enough force to bring me back to the present. To me and her. Without our ghosts or our demons. Only our hands and our mouths and our bodies.

When I pull away again, I rasp, "You sure you want this, Storm? It's been a long night. I can wait."

"You're not him, remember?" She slowly lowers her hands, letting them cradle my jaw instead of my temples and the back of my skull. "You're nothing like him." She bends forward and presses another soft kiss to me. "You call me the storm, Ev, but you? You calm my waters." Her lips find the edge of my mouth. "You make me whole."

I close my eyes, savoring the feel of her hands on me. Her mouth on me. Her weight pressing into my lap and the way her shampoo tickles my nostrils. The way she's completely inserted herself into my life, down to my very clothes, and I wouldn't change any of it. Nothing.

"I love you, Raine."

I can feel her smile against the edge of my mouth as she shifts on my lap. It isn't much. Just a tiny movement. But I can feel it. The heat of her core pressed against me. The stilted breathing as it fans across my face.

"I want to feel you, Ev," she whispers.

This girl. She could ask for the moon, and I'd find a way to lasso it. She wants to feel me? I can fulfill her request in an instant. But I don't want to pressure her. I don't want to hurt her. I don't want to do anything but worship her.

Opening my eyes, I lean my head against the couch and ask, "Where?"

Her smile widens, and she bites her bottom lip. "Everywhere."

The word is a plea, and I kiss her again, pouring all of my fear and tension and regret into it. I could've lost her tonight. I could've fucking lost her. My fingers dig into her thighs again as I kiss her harder. She meets it, though. Taking everything I have to give and throwing even more passion into it until I could come in my damn sweats, and I wouldn't even be surprised. A tiny mewl slips out of her as I drag my tongue along the seam of her lips, retreating ever so slightly, and she shifts against me again. It's less subtle this time, and my cock hardens beneath her even more. I shift on the couch, searching for a semblance of control when all I want to do is throw her on her back and mark every inch of her perfect skin, knowing he marked it first.

"Stay with me," she begs. "I need you."

"You need me, baby?" I challenge.

She nods and burrows her head into my neck, kissing my throat and grinding against me shamelessly. My arms are like steel as I wrap them around her slender waist. Then I stand, lay her on the couch, and kneel on the ground beside her. She's wearing my clothes. And fuck me, she's never looked prettier like this. Laid out before me. My white t-shirt riding up and showcasing her black, lacy underwear. Slowly, I draw a line along the black scrap of cloth, then press my hand right above her pubic bone and smile.

"What?" she asks.

"My fingers can reach both your hipbones."

"And that's amusing?"

My attention shifts from where I'm touching her to her pinched brows, and I laugh. Bending down again, I kiss the crook of her neck. "Just a reminder of how well we fit, I guess."

"Mm-hmm." She wraps her arms around my neck, refusing to let me leave now that I'm close to her again.

"Don't worry, Stormie. I'm not goin' anywhere." I breathe against her and drag my fingers along the waistband of lace again. Teasing her. Knowing exactly where she wants me and damn, if I don't want to be there, too.

With a slow exhale, she lets her legs fall open and murmurs, "Careful. If you keep teasing me, I might have to take matters into my own hands."

"Now, that's something I'd like to see one of these days." I kiss her neck again, then drag my lips down her throat and push her shirt up until her breasts are exposed. She isn't wearing a bra. The girl hates them and never wears one when we're home. The reminder makes me smile against her silky skin as I take a nipple into my mouth and draw a circle around the tiny bud. When it hardens against my lips, I suck it deeper into my mouth, and she gasps.

"Ev," she breathes.

Tangling her fingers in the hair at the nape of my neck, she holds me against her, squirming on the couch as I slowly move my hands down the outside of her thighs before finding her center. The fabric of her underwear is soaked, and I bite back my groan, playing with her folds through the lacy material.

"Finally," she whimpers. "I love you so much."

I'll never get used to it. Those words. Or my response to them. My chest tightens. I push her underwear to the side, then dip my finger into her. The girl's like silk. Wet. Hot. Silk.

Resting my head against her sternum, I look down, watching my fingers disappear inside of her as my cock weeps with need. "So fucking wet," I rasp. "You're so fucking—"

She tugs me up to her and kisses me, sucking my tongue into her mouth as she rides my hand. Fuck, I love her like this. Wild and carefree and desperate for me. Crooking my finger, I feel for the little rough patch of skin inside her channel, and she bucks against me, proving I hit the spot I was searching for.

"Need you," she breathes out. "Need you inside me."

"Patience," I whisper.

"I'm not patient." She laughs and shakes her head back and forth. "Not tonight."

I start to pull my hand away from her, but she closes her thighs, refusing to let me leave her soaking heat, and I laugh a little more.

"Gonna need my hand if you want me to undo my pants," I remind her.

Her bottom lip juts out, but I bend forward and suck the plump flesh into my mouth as her thighs fall open again and let me free. Hurrying, I shove my sweats down to my knees. She blindly reaches for my cock. It only feeds my need more. My need for her. To be inside her. To feel her. To know she's here and she's okay and she's safe. As she rubs me up and down, I grab her hips again and tug her to the edge of the couch, realizing her shirt is bunched beneath her armpits. Bruises from tonight pepper her sides. The reminder makes me see red, and when I hesitate, she shakes her head back and forth.

"Not tonight," she begs. "I'll deal with it tomorrow. Tonight, I want you."

Ripping my eyes away from the mottled purple and blue, I hold Raine's gaze, line myself up with her entrance, and move over her. On reflex, she wraps her legs around my waist while I stay kneeling in front of her, watching the way her breasts heave with every needy breath as she waits for me to push myself inside her. To stretch her and shove us both over the edge the way we both need. I could tease her more, and if it were another time, I would. But she isn't the only one craving this. This moment. This opportunity to prove we're okay. To take a mental picture and keep it with me forever.

Mine. She's fucking mine.

"I could worship you forever," I confide.

A sheen hits her eyes as she looks up at me and bites her bottom lip, sprawled out beneath me. "I think I'd be okay with that."

Reaching for the base of my cock, I drag the head against her wet folds, then slowly push into her, letting her tiny whimpers set the pace as her fingers slip under my shirt, creating sharp tiny crescents along my lower back. Sweat clings to my hairline, and I dive in for another kiss, leaning over her on the couch. When she arches into me, rubbing her bare chest against my shirt, I rip the thing off, desperate to feel her skin against mine. To shed the last of our barriers until there's nothing between us. Nothing but me and her. Forever. My shirt hits the ground at my feet, and, like a monkey, she loops her arms around my neck, bringing us chest to chest. Her heart pounds, matching my own racing rhythm, as I stand and carry her to the closest wall. Pressing her against it, I thrust into her over and over again. And I know she can take it. Know she's stronger than anyone gives her credit for. I also know she's hoping if we make love long enough, I'll forget about what happened tonight. I'll let it go and be grateful for what I have. That's the thing, though. I can't let this go *because* I'm grateful. I can't leave this to anyone else.

"You're mine," I growl.

"I'm yours."

"I love you."

She smiles, taking my cock like a good fucking girl. "I love you, too."

"Gonna marry you one day."

Her laugh cuts into a moan. "Just tell me where to be, and I'm there."

I keep one hand tucked under her ass and slip the other between our bodies, pressing my finger against her clit as my balls tighten. I'm close. Fuck, I'm close. Pressure builds at the base of my spine, and I'm not sure how much longer I can last. Drawing small circles against her sensitive bud, I press my forehead to hers and keep my rhythm steady.

"Come for me, Storm," I order.

Her jaw drops, and she tightens around me, milking my cock as I spurt into her.

Stars. Fucking stars.

We pant, resting our foreheads together and letting our heart rates find a slower pace.

"I trust you," she whispers. "I didn't say it before, but I do."

"I know you do." I kiss her forehead, pull out of her, and lower her feet to the ground. "Come on. Let's get you cleaned up."

It takes a while. For her breathing to steady, but once I know she's asleep, I lift my arm from around her on the couch and unlock my cell, dialing someone I never thought I would.

"What?" Dodger answers after the first ring.

Stepping closer to the window beside the kitchen table, I

watch the snow fall to the ground and ask, "Do you have access to a car with four-wheel drive?"

"Why?"

"Answer the question," I push.

"Yeah," he confirms. "Yeah, I can borrow my buddy's truck."

I glance at a sleeping Raine on the couch, the firelight flickering over her curves and highlighting her barely parted lips. "Gonna send you an address. Be here in thirty."

"Why?"

"I need you to watch Raine while I'm gone."

"And where are you going?" Dodge challenges.

After I met Dodger at SeaBird, I did some digging. Well… I asked Finley to do some digging. The man's into more shady shit than his sister knows. But even if he wasn't, there's something about being a big brother. The need to protect. To defend. To look after. And as I stared at him tonight, I saw myself. Saw exactly how far he'd go to keep his little sister safe. It doesn't matter how dirty his hands get or if he has to spend the rest of his life in prison. He'll do what needs to be done. And so will I. Which is why I already know he's aware of my intentions, even if I refuse to voice them out loud. Besides, the less anyone knows, the better. What I need from him is to keep Raine safe while I'm away. I'll handle the rest.

Growing impatient, I demand, "Are you coming or not?"

A long pause follows. "I'll be there in twenty."

I hang up the call, then dial Griff. I debated on whether or not to involve him in this. To involve any of them in this. But if the roles were reversed, I'd want to be there. I'd want to have their backs. And if I've learned anything from this, it's that doing shit alone isn't all it's cracked up to be.

The call rings twice before he picks up. "Hello?"

"Tell the guys we're going hunting in an hour. I'll meet you at the house."

Then, I click end.

CHAPTER FORTY-FOUR

EVERETT

It's risky being here again. In Cedar Springs. Last time, I had my ass kicked. It's also where Drake feels most confident, even if he is lying low after attacking Raine. I half expected police cars to be out in front of his apartment, but I should've known better. It was surprisingly easy to find him. He stole Raine's phone, and I still have her location, and now, *his* location.

There's no moon tonight. Nothing but black surrounds us in Griffin's car. I figured Drake would recognize mine, and we couldn't take Mav's bike. Reeves' car was also a no-go since I have no doubt the police would recognize it if someone was stupid enough to call them.

We won't, but Drake might when he realizes we're coming for him.

I glance down the street for the hundredth time. There's a bar, the tattoo shop, Drake's apartment, and about two blocks down, the Grizzlies' arena. They don't have a game tonight, but I wouldn't put it past Drake to go there in hopes of skating off his steam or solidifying his alibi.

Part of me wonders if I should've waited. If Raine will

ever forgive me for this. It doesn't matter. I promised to protect her. Even if it means handling it differently than she'd prefer. I check the GPS on my phone again, then look around the barren street. "He's close."

When a shadow appears around the side of the building in front of us, I study the figure, trying to pinpoint if it's the man of the hour. My veins buzz with anticipation as I stare at him. He's oblivious.

"Is it him?" Reeves asks beside me.

My eyes thin, and I slowly dip my chin.

Sliding a wolf mask into place, I reach for the door handle and wait until my friends give me the go-ahead. We bought the masks for a game night once, but they've been useful more times than I can count. And tonight? Tonight they're perfect. Hiding our identity while sinister enough to scare the shit out of the man in front of us. Crouching low, I slide out of the car and glance around the rear bumper, balancing the metal baseball bat across my bent knees as Drake inhales his cigarette. The bud lights up his fucked-up face, and I smile behind my mask.

"Fuck, man," Griffin whispers beside me. "Remind me not to get on your bad side."

"Don't mess with anyone I love, and you'll be fine," I reply.

Reeves' dark chuckle echoes beside me, and I lift two fingers into the air, motioning it's time for us to move. In silence, we cross the street, moving like ghosts until I swing the bat at the back of his head, and the asshole falls like a Redwood tree.

"Tiiiimber," Reeves jokes.

We let him crumple to the pavement. Reeves grabs Drake's ankles, and Griffin grips his hands. Then, together, we drag him back to the car and toss him in the trunk.

∾

I NEEDED A PLACE NO ONE WOULD RECOGNIZE. A PLACE WE could hide. A place not connected to me. Not easily, anyway. When Maverick suggested one of his dad's empty apartments, I figured it was a good bet. Mav already added black plastic to the walls, blocking out any potential tells as to where we are. It doesn't hurt that it'll make for an easy cleanup in case Drake decides he wants to play this the hard way. Now, here we are. Masks in place. Each of us dressed in black with gloves covering our hands. The man of the hour is tied to a wooden chair, his head lolled forward. The lights are dim, but I can still make out a stain on the front of his shirt where his drool mixed with the blood trickling from his face. Griffin brought a burner phone, suggesting we film his confession. But after giving it some thought, I realized a confession from a tied-up and bloodied asshole might not be the way to go. Not if we want it to stick.

"You ready?" Griff asks beside me.

"Let's do this."

We form a half circle around an unconscious Drake, but the clock is ticking, and the longer we have him, the more likely we are to be caught. With my gloved hands clasped in front of me, I cock my head and nod to Mav. He splashes a bucket of ice water into Drake's face, and the asshole sputters to life, gasping for air.

Griff was right. Drake's face is bloody and bruised. And with the way he's wheezing and the awkward angle of his nose? I'm gonna say I broke it during our fight. Poor bastard. I smile behind my mask.

"Morning, Sunshine," I growl.

"Who the fuck are you?" Drake slurs. His gaze shifts from left to right, and if I had to guess, he's sporting a massive headache and a possible concussion thanks to the baseball bat from earlier.

Good. Let him hurt.

"I think we both know who I am," I reply. "Not that it matters. What does matter is you understand a few things."

He laughs and tosses his head back, like I'm the funniest motherfucker in the world. "This is rich. You almost had me, Taylor. Almost. Let me go."

"Nah, I think you're gonna stay where you are," I decide.

"What are you gonna do?" He laughs even harder. "Murder me?"

"To protect the woman I love?" I join in his amusement. "Yeah."

He lifts his head again and looks me straight in the eye. And just like that, his humor evaporates. "You're not a murderer, Taylor." He says it like it's a fact, but the slight tremor in his voice hints that he might not believe his statement as much as he wants to.

That makes two of us.

"I think you'd be surprised what a wolf is willing to do to protect its mate." I let my words hang in the air, watching the way his hands tighten into fists and how he tugs at the ropes binding his arms behind his back.

"Look around," I add, motioning to the thick plastic covering every surface in the room. "Do you really think I'd go through all this work for a bluff?"

He stays quiet, but I don't miss how he takes in his surroundings or the way it's eerily quiet. No cars outside. No voices on the other side of the door. Just me and him and a few more wolves.

"Or maybe I am bluffing," I continue. "Maybe I don't have it in me to kill you. But do you really think I'd let you walk out of here without guaranteeing Raine's safety?"

His upper lip curls. "You can't guarantee shit, Taylor."

"You know, I think you have a good point. Nothing in life is guaranteed, is it? But I'll tell you what I do know." I step toward where he's tied and slowly circle him. "I know Raine's the best thing that ever happened to you. I know you had a shit life, and your only ticket out of it is..." I stop in front of him and bend closer. "Do you want to take a guess?"

He glares up at me. "Fuck—"

"Hockey. Hockey is your only ticket." Resting one hand on my knee while cradling a baseball bat with my opposite one, I crowd him even further. "You and I are more alike than either of us wants to admit. And I know how much you want it. Your career. The travel. The money. The puck bunnies. The recognition we both know you deserve after all the hard work you've put in. Am I right?"

His eyes flash with contempt, but he doesn't deny it.

"See?" I stand to my full height again and slowly circle him once more. "I told you we're similar. Here's the thing. There are benefits to analyzing our similarities. What makes us tick. And I have a feeling you'd really hate to lose your hockey career over a girl who doesn't want you anymore... even if you're delusional enough to believe she'd ever voluntarily pick you again. And sure, it's fun to terrorize her. Makes you feel powerful. Like you're in control, and fuckers like us love control, don't we?" I slap my hand against his shoulder. "But losing your hockey career over it?" I smirk behind my mask. "Yeah, I don't think it's part of the plan. Am I right?"

"Get to the point, Taylor."

I dig my fingers into his shoulder. "You're gonna go to the cops."

"And why"—he breathes through his wince—"would I do that?"

I scoop my fingers beneath his collarbone, squeezing the tender flesh until he shies away from my grasp, finally giving in and admitting he doesn't exactly have the upper hand right now. Good. It's time he understands how shitty his situation really is. Satisfied, I let him go, pat his sore shoulder, then stand to my full height. "Because whether or not we want to admit it, the sports industry cares more about what happens in the game with their players than what they do outside of it."

His eyes thin, but he stays quiet.

Yeah, the asshole knows I'm right. Not gonna lie, it's one of the things I hate most about the industry. The reminder of how much they're willing to sweep under the rug as long as they score wins in the process. And it isn't only the NHL. It's basketball and baseball and football. In fact, the last time I checked, it was almost five percent. Five percent of professional athletes had domestic violence charges against them.

"You're gonna go to the cops. And confess. And serve your time."

"Not a fucking—"

"Then," I continue, "you'll be released, and you'll play for the Springfield Titans, like you've dreamed of since you were a little kid. Who knows? Since it's your first offense, you might only be slapped with probation and community service."

Nostrils flaring, Drake grits out, "And why the fuck would I confess?"

"Because if you don't, I'll slam this baseball bat into both of your knees, and you'll never walk again. I considered only shattering one, but...why half-ass this, right?" I chuckle. "Goodbye, hockey career. Goodbye, gym. Goodbye, driving. Goodbye, life."

"You know, it's not a bad idea," Maverick interjects. "If he never walks again, he won't be able to chase Raine anymore. Maybe we should skip confession time and go straight to crippling."

"That's a good point," I muse dryly. "What do you think, Haitt?"

The bastard's Adam's apple bobs as his attention falls to the baseball bat in my hand. "Are you threatening me?"

"That's exactly what I'm doing."

"Try it," he dares me. "See what happens. My career won't be the only one up in flames, motherfucker. I'll tell the cops you attacked me and—"

"How?" I ask. "I'm at my cabin with my girlfriend. You see, she didn't want to be left alone after you attacked her, so I stayed up all night watching *Brooklyn 99* with her. In fact, her brother came up to the cabin, too, because he was so worried, and we wound up chatting all night after Raine fell asleep on my chest." I tap the edge of the bat against the outside of his left knee.

Tap. Tap. Tap.

"It's a shame you fell on the ice outside your apartment, though. Kind of ironic and all, but hey. Sometimes, karma's a bitch."

His shoulders heave as he glares up at me. "You really think this will work?"

I nod. "Yeah. I really do."

"What about your mess with the police?" he scoffs. "They're not gonna believe you over me."

Tucking my hands into my pockets, I shrug. "I'm willing to take my chances. I think the real question is…are you?" My head shifts to the baseball bat resting against his outer thigh, and he blanches.

"Look. I'll leave her alone, all right?"

"Yeah, but you really won't—"

"I will!"

"Nah, you won't. Not unless you face actual repercussions for once in your sorry existence." I click my tongue against the roof of my mouth. "Now, here's how it's gonna go." I stand to my full height and cock my arm back, hitting him in his already broken nose. My split knuckles scream in protest, but I revel in it, letting the pain beneath my gloves ground me as blood pours from Drake's wound. He curses in agony.

"Fuck!" His expression twists, and he spits in my face. The crimson dribble catches on my mask, and I smile wider beneath it.

Leaning closer, I whisper, "I'm gonna beat the shit out of you, so when you finally hobble your way to the police station, every twinge of pain will be a reminder of exactly how much restraint I showed. Because if you don't hold up your end of the deal—if you don't walk your sorry ass into the police station and confess to everything you were going to do Raine tonight if I hadn't intervened—I'll hunt you down and shatter both your knees so you never walk again. We clear?"

I don't wait for his response. Instead, I let the bat fall to our feet. As it rolls on the ground, I flex my hand, then grab his wet shirt collar.

Because this? This is between me and Drake, and I'm about to make shit very clear. Hell, by the time I'm done with him? It'll be fucking crystal, and he'll beg to confess.

If he's lucky, I just might let him.

CHAPTER FORTY-FIVE

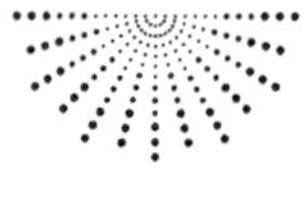

RAINE

I awake with a start, rolling over and feeling the cool covers against my palm. I fell asleep on the couch, didn't I? My brows crease as I sit up and search the empty room, then go to the bathroom, brush my teeth, and pad into the kitchen. A shirtless Everett is at the stove, and I breathe in deeply, smelling the bacon and coffee. My mouth waters.

When he notices me, he smiles. And it's full and genuine and, honestly, a little surprising considering last night's events.

"Who are you, and what have you done with my Everett?" I ask.

"They caught Drake."

I stop short. "What?"

"Yeah. He turned himself in. Gave a full confession."

My eyes widen, and I press the heel of my palm to my temple, convinced I'm hallucinating. "You're joking."

"Not joking," he replies. "McDonnell just called me."

"You're serious?" I ask.

He nods again. "Come eat."

I head toward the center island and grab a barstool as Everett places a heaping plate of pancakes and bacon in front of me.

"Thank you," I murmur.

"Of course." He rounds the edge of the granite while wiping his hands on a white dish towel slung over his shoulder and kisses my cheek. "You good?"

I nod, then notice his swollen hands. "What happened?" Reaching for him, I cradle his raw knuckles, dragging my thumbs across the crusted skin as I grimace. "I could've sworn they weren't this bad last night—"

"I'm good, Raine." He lets go of my grasp and cups the side of my face, tilting my head up and brushing a kiss against my lips. "Promise."

I peek up at him, searching his face for any hint as to what happened. What *really* happened.

"So what now?" I ask. "Now that he's behind bars?"

"Still not letting you out of my sight."

"Yeah, between you, my parents, and my brother, I don't see myself being alone too much for the foreseeable future other than to shower and pee."

"I'll let you pee in private, but shower time is now with me." He runs his lips against my cheek, then kisses the underside of my jaw, teasing a smile from me.

"How, uh, how accommodating of you."

"I'm very accommodating," he reminds me, stepping between my spread thighs and bringing us chest to chest.

"Mm-hmm. So, do you plan to...drive to wherever I live whenever I have to shower or—"

"Who says I'll have to drive anywhere?"

"Well,"—I pick at the edge of his basketball shorts before smoothing the fabric across his thighs—"since Drake isn't a problem anymore, we should probably figure it out, right? Our living arrangements and everything."

He leans away from me and frowns. "Tell me you're joking."

I press my lips together. "Not sure what there is to joke about. I was under the impression living here was always a short-term thing."

"Tell. Me. You're. Joking," he growls.

"Simmer down, big boy." I press my hand to his chest. "All I'm saying is we haven't had *the talk*, and I don't want to make any assumptions, especially when adding a thirty-minute commute to literally everything if we choose to stay here, let alone convince your parents to allow us to stay here. I want to make sure—"

"Do you honestly think I want you to move out?"

"No, but—"

"Then, what do you think?"

"I think you need to officially ask me to stay, considering the person who got us here in the first place is behind bars." I sit up a little straighter. "You know, for my own peace of mind. Either that, or I need to find out if Finley will have an extra room available at the duplex once their side is finished being renovated."

"You want to move in with my sister?"

"If you aren't ready to ask me to officially move in with you, then yes. I'm not above shimmying my way into your life by way of your little sister."

He scoffs. "She'd probably like that." Picking up a piece of my hair, he wraps it around his fingers. "I think she's been lonely since Dylan and Ophelia found boyfriends."

"Yeah, I think you're right."

"It's a shame I'm a selfish brother, huh?"

My brows bunch. "Oh?"

"Yeah. Sorry, Stormie, but I think I want to keep you for myself."

"Sounds a little controlling, if you ask me."

"Never claimed to be a saint."

"Just a well-hung, and sometimes grumpy, hockey player with a hero complex," I counter. "Who can cook."

He tilts his head and considers my description while trying to hold back his amusement. "Grumpy?"

"I mean…I also said well-hung."

He snorts. "At least I have something going for me."

"You have a lot going for you, Everett Taylor," I murmur. "And I mean like…a lot." My hands find his cheeks. "I love you."

"I love you too, Stormie."

"You want to know the crazy thing about last night?" A glassy sheen hits my eyes before I blink it away. "I was scared. I was," I admit, "I was scared. But…I don't know. I think a part of me knew you'd come. A part of me knew you'd fix it. Fix the situation. Fix whatever Drake managed to break while I was alone with him. Fix…me. I knew I'd be fine because I knew you'd be there." I suck my lips between my teeth and sniff. "Thank you. For always being here."

"You couldn't get rid of me, even if you tried, Raine Anders." He leans closer and kisses a tear away as it slips down my cheek. "Although, I do have a confession."

"What is it?"

"I had Dodger come stay with you last night."

I frown. "Was he the one who moved me to your bed, or were you?"

"Me."

I nod slowly, connecting the pieces. "I assume that's when the knuckle damage came into play. Am I right?"

"I went after Drake."

My stomach bottoms out, and I let my head fall forward, resting it against his sternum. "Ev—"

"I know you didn't want me to, but I also can't lie to you. I needed to make sure he never bothered you again."

"What did you do?"

"Beat the shit out of him until he promised to confess to everything he put you through." He reaches for me and cups the side of my face again, his expression sobering. "I want you to know I will never hurt you, but I will protect you no matter the cost. Even if you hate me for it. Do you understand?"

I nod.

"That's my girl." He rubs his thumb along my cheekbone. "The question is…do you hate me for it?"

It's a good question, and I'm not going to lie. Part of me wants to. To hate him for putting himself in a dangerous position like this. Drake could've hurt him. He could've been in trouble with the cops. He could still be in trouble with the cops. But I understand it. His need to keep me safe. It's the same way I'd walk through fire for him if the occasion called for it. And apparently, from his perspective, this occasion called for it. For him to walk through fire for me. And even though part of me wants to be pissed, I'm not. I can't be.

I shake my head. "I don't hate you, Ev. When I said I trust you, I meant it. If this was the best way for you to handle it, I believe you. You aren't stupid. Stubborn," I clarify, "but not stupid, unlike Dodge, who probably would've killed the guy."

As if my words are a balm to his soul, he bends forward and kisses me, making me melt against him.

"Fuck, I love you," he mutters against my lips.

I smile against him. "I love you, too."

Bending back a bit, he tucks my hair behind my ear and pins me with his icy blues. "Now, about our living arrangements. You might be onto something with the commute."

A quiet laugh escapes me.

"What if… What if we move in with Finley in the new place?" he offers. "We can take the top floor, and she can have the room by the kitchen. That way, Griff will have more space, Dylan can still stay with Reeves, and Fin won't be alone."

I smile. "You sure you want to move in with your little sister?"

"No, but my hero complex is kind of a stubborn bastard." He boops my nose. "You know this."

"And the idea of your sister sleeping under the same roof as us isn't more than you can stomach?" I challenge.

His nose wrinkles. "Call it the lesser of two evils until a house on the same street is put up for sale."

I snort. "Ever the protector."

"You know me too well." He tucks my hair behind my ear. "So, what do you say?"

I look around the place that's been ours, and even though I'll miss these four walls more than he'll ever understand, his suggestion feels right.

"I'm in," I whisper.

"Yeah?"

"Mm-hmm."

"Good. Me, too."

Then, he leans in to kiss me, and I lift my chin to meet him.

Damn, I love this boy.

CHAPTER FORTY-SIX

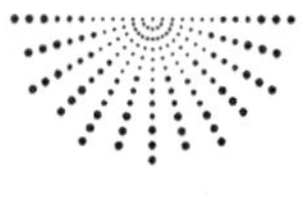

RAINE

So, splitting holidays is no joke. And I mean, no. Joke. Thankfully, my family was pretty great about letting us slip away after Christmas brunch. Now, we're on our way to meet up with our friends before heading up to the cabin with Finley and the rest of Everett's family.

Drake's sentencing should be pretty straightforward. My lawyer thinks Drake might be able to swing probation and a nasty fine since he willingly confessed to everything. But we won't know the full details for a while. For now, he made bail, and I haven't seen him since. The justice system can drag its feet sometimes, apparently, including my case against Drake Haitt. The only shining light at the end of the tunnel is that the Springfield Titans are a couple thousand miles away, so even if he doesn't spend any major time behind bars, I won't have to deal with him ever again.

The renovations should wrap up in the next week or two, but we won't move in until after winter break. Finley ordered noise-canceling headphones as soon as Everett suggested we move into one of the rooms on the top floor, but I think she's secretly excited to have someone to live with. Besides, with all the travel the boys are doing, we'll have plenty of time for girls' nights, and I can't wait.

As we pull up to the duplex, I notice Finley through the window. She's standing on the couch with her back pressed to the glass.

I lean closer to the windshield as if it'll give me a better view or explanation of what's happening.

"What's Fin doing?" I ask.

Everett hesitates before turning the car off. "Maybe she lost her last marble."

I laugh. "Once a softie, always a softie. Right, Ev?" I playfully shove his shoulder. "Way to be empathetic."

"Whatever got her there is her own doing," he argues with a laugh of his own. "But I am curious. Come on."

We head inside in time to catch a scream of horror.

Ophelia and Mav are in the kitchen, not even bothering to hide their cackles of amusement while they sip their coffee. Meanwhile, Reeves leans against the closest wall with his arms crossed and a shit-eating grin on his face. Dylan's beside him, her arms pulled close to her chest, and her hands cupped together.

"Reeves, I swear to all that is holy, if that thing is real—"

"What? You think I'd buy the love of my life a fake frog?" Reeves counters.

"Come on, he's really cute!" Dylan looks down at her hands and takes a step closer to Finley.

Another scream escapes her. "Don't you dare come one step closer Dylan Becca Thorne, or so help me—"

"You'll wake up with a frog in your bed?" Dylan offers ruefully.

Everett's hand slips from my lower back, and he covers his mouth with it.

"It's not funny!" Finley snaps at him.

Ignoring her, Everett glances at Reeves. "You actually went through with it?"

"Went through with what?" I ask.

"Fin's terrified of frogs," he explains. "And I mean, shit your pants level of terror."

"No one is shitting their pants!" Dylan interjects.

"Not yet, anyway," Reeves quips.

Finley's glare cuts to him. "I will neuter you!"

"There's no need for neutering," Dylan argues, though she steps in front of Reeves like she actually believes Finley might do it. "Besides, Frankie is a perfectly harmless gentleman."

"You *named* it?" Finley shrieks.

"Of course I did," Dylan says, defending herself. "He's part of the family now and is also your new roommate, so you might want to make friends with him."

"No deal." Finley shakes her head, her gaze glued to Dylan's cupped hands. "Nope, nope, nope. I'm good. Thanks, though."

Grimacing, Dylan steps closer but keeps her movements slow and controlled as if it might spook her best friend on the couch. "Seriously, Fin. I promise he's nice."

"I don't care if he's nice." She shakes her head back and forth all over again. "If that thing comes within ten feet of me, I swear I'll put it in a pot and—"

"Hey!" Dylan brings her hands even closer to her body like an overprotective mother. "You be nice. I already told you, Frankie's a perfectly harmless gentleman, remember?"

"Yeah, and if you threaten him again, Dylan will slip him into your bed," Reeves offers.

Her eyes narrow on Dylan's boyfriend. "I *will* get you back for this."

"For giving my girlfriend leverage against all your teasing?" he volleys back at her. "Try me."

"Okay, okay, people," Ophelia announces from the kitchen. "Dylan, put the frog back in it's cage—"

"Terrarium," Reeves corrects.

"Terrarium," Ophelia repeats. "Right. Then wash your hands, and we can finish..." Her nose wrinkles, and she sneaks a peek at Finley.

"Yeah, yeah. We all know you guys are ditching me for a week-long vacation in Cancun. Thanks for that," Fin pouts.

Striding into the room from the hallway, Griffin interjects, "Maybe you shouldn't have used up all your miles to go see Drew."

Finley glares at him, but instead of arguing like I know she would with anyone else, she stays quiet and jumps off the edge of the couch, sitting on the cushion with her mouth pressed into a thin slash of white.

It's been this way between them since the night I went out for drinks with the rest of the girls.

"Speaking of Cancun," Dylan offers carefully. Her gaze shifts from Griffin to Finley and back again. "Any chance you'd be willing to babysit Frankie while we're gone?"

The blood drains from Finley's face, and her attention snaps back to her best friend. "Tell me you're joking."

Stepping forward, Reeves rubs Dylan's shoulders and tugs her, pressing her back to his front. "I forgot about the trip when I brought Frankie home." He grimaces. "My bad."

"You're *bad*?" She scoffs. "Yeah, I'm definitely not frog-sitting, but good luck with that."

"Come on," Dylan begs. "Please? Pretty please? Pretty please with sugar on top?"

"Let her decide later," Everett suggests. "For now, let's iron out the trip details."

We've already planned the majority of it, but there are a couple possible activities we've been eyeing since Reeves first suggested a vacation. I do feel bad for Finley, though. It isn't entirely because of her lack of SkyMiles, thanks to visiting Drew, but there's only so much money to be made when you work part-time as a waitress while being a full time-student.

A small part of me wonders if she's also sitting out because the idea of going on a trip with Griffin after all the shit Drew's given her doesn't sound like it's worth the effort. If I was her, I'd probably feel the same way.

Does it make me feel like I'm having an eensy, teensy bit of deja vu, too? Yup. Do I say it to her? Honestly, I've thought about it, but other than Drew being a jerk on occasion, he isn't necessarily abusive. It's strange, though. Seeing the similarities. They're everywhere. Some are tiny. Some are pretty glaring. But that's from the outside looking in. And while sometimes it can give you a clearer view of what's going on, it can also do the opposite.

I don't know Drew. Not personally. I haven't even met him. Slapping him with a label when I'm so far removed from the relationship isn't fair. But it doesn't mean it's easy to watch Finley struggle the way she is. The way she has been since long before we met if what Dylan and Ophelia say is true.

Regardless, we all take our own path on our own time. I peek up at Everett and smile because I'm the perfect example of exactly this. And yes, I might regret staying with Drake for as long as I did, but if I hadn't, I wouldn't have tracked down Reeves. I wouldn't have been handed off to Everett. And I wouldn't have fallen so helplessly in love with the man of my dreams.

So, yeah. I think it's okay to wait and see how things play out for Fin instead of sticking my nose in it. Who knows? Maybe she'll figure her shit out all on her own and find her happily ever after.

A girl can hope, can't she?

~

IT'S SNOWING. CHRISTMAS PRESENTS HAVE BEEN UNWRAPPED. The fire is still blazing in the fireplace. And I learned Hazel and Miley definitely got their singing skills from their mom's side of the family. Not only are their voices beautiful, but their kids are also songbirds. Hazel is divorced but has a ten-year-old. Miley is happily married to a guy named Graham, and they have three kids.

Meanwhile, Everett and Finley sound more like seagulls than actual carolers, but today was still a blast. Things have finally settled down after the festivities. The kids are in the family room, sprawled out in sleeping bags. The parents are either catching the last few minutes of *It's a Wonderful Life* playing on the television or have disappeared into one of the bedrooms for a little peace and quiet.

Lifting the mug of hot cocoa to my lips, I stare out the large windows, watching the white flakes float from the dark sky. We're having a sleepover. Apparently, it's tradition. And even though the chaos is real, I've loved every minute of it. The hospitality. The playfulness. The Christmas cheer reminding me so much of my own family, yet it's different, too.

This hot chocolate, though? It's rich and thick, and when combined with Macklin's homemade marshmallows, I'm pretty sure I've died and gone to heaven.

A chair scrapes beside me, and I turn toward it, finding Everett in a reindeer hoodie Finley gave him. Somehow, he manages to ride the line between ridiculous and sexy in a way I'll never understand, but I really love it.

"You survived," he notes.

I grin up at him. "I survived."

Reaching for my cocoa, he steals it from my grasp and

takes a sip, holding my gaze over the rim of the mug. "Did you have fun?"

I nod. "Actually, yeah. I had a blast."

"Me, too." He hands me back my drink, then grabs the leg of my chair and drags it closer to him, pinning me between his spread thighs. "I love you. You know that, right?"

"Pretty sure you've told me a time or two."

"Just want to make sure you don't forget it."

He does this a lot. Stares at me, saying so much with a simple look. Half the time, it leaves me panting. The other half? I feel like I'm on cloud nine. This man. This freaking man. I thought I knew what it was like to be spoiled. To be cared for. Everett blew every single expectation out of the water. Doting on me. Loving me. Caring for me. And it isn't only the grand gestures like beating the shit out of my ex until prison looks like a walk in the park. It's moments like this. Sweet words. Gentle kisses.

His skin is slowly being littered with my art, and he's even stolen a few drawings from my notebook, had them framed, and hung them in our bedroom. His support? It's something I never even knew I needed. Seriously, I love this man.

"Don't worry. I'm not letting you go anywhere," I murmur.

"Good." He kisses my nose, then lifts my mug into the air. "To Christmas."

After he takes a sip, I grab it and do the same, adding, "To grumpy hockey players."

His chuckle is low and throaty as he watches me steal another taste of hot chocolate, then grabs the mug from my fingers. "To gorgeous tattoo artists."

Before he has a chance to sip it, I snatch it from him and give him a pointed look. "Tattoo *apprentices*."

"For now," he argues but outstretches his hand, waiting

for me to give it back. When I do, he swallows another mouthful and sets it on the table beside us. "To graduations and proposals and babies and every other curveball life can throw at us. As long as I'm with you, I say bring it on."

My mouth lifts as I lean closer, closing the space between us. "Bring it on."

Then he seals the promise with a kiss, and even though it's definitely PG, I know I'll still crave it for the rest of my life.

Bring it on, Everett.

We got this.

The End

HIJACKED EPILOGUE

GRIFFIN

Let's back up a bit, shall we?

"Hey, you good?" I ask.

My best friend's little sister freezes and looks down at my hand wrapped around her bicep. Fuck, I didn't even notice I grabbed her. Not roughly, mind you, but still. Forcing my fingers to relax, I lift them one at a time from forefinger to pinky, ignoring how soft her skin is, and let her go as the crowd moves around us. The bar is busy. To be fair, SeaBird's always busy. With reasonably priced drinks, kickass appetizers, a live band most nights, a laid-back bouncer, and the perfect location a few blocks from LAU's campus, it's the place to be. It's also why my friends and I shouldn't have been surprised when we found out the girls slipped away to hang out here tonight. Dylan, my little sister, has been best friend's with Ophelia and Finley since they were babies. It makes sense, since they were raised together, thanks to all of our parents being best friends in college. Raine, however, is new. She's also Everett's fake girlfriend and the reason we showed up to SeaBird tonight in the first place.

Everything was going fine until the girls were on the dance floor and a group of guys approached them. This isn't the first time it's happened, and I doubt it'll be the last. One after another, my buddies claimed their girls, and I stepped in to protect Finley from being hit on. Is she mine? Not even close. She's my best friend's little sister and has been dating a guy across the country for years now, but since attending LAU and moving into the place I share with the rest of the guys, I've offered a helping hand once or twice. Nah, fuck that. A hundred times. Maybe a thousand. We grew up together. She's one of my best friends. And even though we've never crossed that line, she's never been one to shy away from flirting or pretending we're together if the situation called for it.

So why the hell did she run away when I pretended to be her boyfriend in hopes of saving her from a handsy guy on the dance floor? She looked like she wanted nothing to do with me. Like I was a fucking pariah or some shit.

"You good?" I repeat.

"Yeah, I'm good," Finley whispers.

It's a lie, and we both know it. Or maybe we don't. Maybe I can read her better than she can even read herself. It's not surprising, considering the girl in front of me.

"Fin," I warn, then glance toward the crowded dance floor. "What the fuck was that out there?"

"It was nothing."

"I was only messing around," I argue.

"I know."

"Then why are you lookin' at me like this?"

"I'm not looking at you like anything," she whispers.

"You're right. You're not looking at me at all," I growl, moving closer until she's practically pinned between me and the rough brick wall. "What's going on? Did Drew do something again?"

Drew. The asshole boyfriend she's still with despite *literally* everyone telling her to dump his ass.

She rolls her eyes. "Griff—"

"What did he do, Fin?" I demand.

"He did nothing, all right?"

"Then what's wrong?"

"Nothing," she repeats. But her exasperation does me in. It taints her words and gives me way more information than she's probably comfortable with. It's always been this way with Fin and me, though. And maybe it's normal. Inevitable, even. To know someone so wholly after being raised together. Yeah, she might not admit it, but something is very wrong. I just don't know what.

Regret floods through me as I squeeze the back of my neck, hating how uncomfortable she looks. Like she wants to be anywhere but here. With me.

"Did I cross a line?" I rasp.

Her gaze flicks to mine, and the pain in them? The fucking indecision? It shoots straight to my chest.

Fuck. She's hurting.

I replay what went down a few minutes ago but come up empty. Again.

"What's goin' on, Fin?" I push.

"I, uh,"—she stares at the ground—"I don't want to do this here."

I step closer until her back hits the wall. "Do *what* here?"

"Griff—"

"Say it, Fin."

Her gaze darts up to mine. "I can't be friends with you anymore."

The words hit like a sucker punch, and I jerk back. "What?"

"I said,"—she takes a deep breath—"I can't be friends with you anymore."

"Why the hell not?"

Her tongue darts out between her pretty pink lips as she squares her shoulders. It'd be comical if her words weren't a knife to the ribcage. "Drew and I, we both think—"

A bark of laughter escapes me. "Are you serious right now?"

Mother. Fucker.

I knew he had something to do with this. I fucking knew it. That controlling asshole has been the bane of my existence since the moment Finley gave him her number. How does she not see it? How does she not realize how fucking toxic he is for her? The guy has made her cry more times than I can count, yet she still bends over backward at every. Fucking. Whim.

"Griff." She touches my arm, but I shift away from her.

"Of course, he has something to do with this." I scrub my hand over my face. "Of course he does."

"Look, you have to understand where he's coming from," she begs. "If you had a girlfriend who was really close with a guy—"

"We've been friends forever," I remind her. And I mean it. Literally. Since the day her brother and I were born, we've been inseparable. Then Finley, Ophelia, and my little sister came into the picture, and the saga continued. Some families are tight. Ours? Ours is steel. Not just woven together but hammered into one. One family. One unit. Unbreakable. Unwavering.

Her attention falls to her feet, and a glint of hope moves through me. Maybe. Maybe I can get to her. Maybe I can help her see how shitty he is for her. Now, he's asking her to give up relationships for him? It's bullshit. She has to see this.

Doesn't she?

Nostrils flaring, I exhale slowly, trying to keep my frustration in check as I repeat, "We've been friends *forever*, Fin."

"I know," she whispers. But she doesn't look at me.

Why won't you look at me?

"You think we can just...shut it off?" I squeeze my hand into a fist at my side. "We live under the same roof, Fin. We attend the same family functions. My best friend is your older brother, and your best friend is my little sister." I lean closer, letting my breath hit the side of her face as she stares blankly in front of her. "You really think you can avoid me? Write me off like I'm nothing? Like our relationship is nothing?"

"We can...we can keep our distance for a little while, you know? Nothing crazy—"

My scoff cuts her off. I drop my head back and stare at the ceiling, attempting to get a handle on shit, but the girl's making it difficult.

"I love him, Griff," she whispers.

The words scrape against my skin like sandpaper, and my head falls forward. How does she not. Fucking. See it?

"Have a good night, Fin." I push away from her, then head toward the exit, knowing she won't even bother to watch me walk away. Why would she? Her boyfriend forbade it.

Bullshit.

See what happens next in *A Little Secret* by Kelsie Rae

ALSO BY KELSIE RAE

Kelsie Rae tries to keep her books formatted with an updated list of her releases, but every once in a while she falls behind.

If you'd like to check out a complete list of her up-to-date published books, visit her website at www.shopauthorkelsierae.com/

Or you can join her newsletter to hear about her latest releases, get exclusive content, and participate in fun giveaways.

Interested in reading more by Kelsie Rae?

The Little Things Series

(Steamy Don't Let Me Next Generation Series)

(Steamy Contemporary Romance Standalone Series)

A Little Complicated - Maverick and Ophelia's Story

A Little Tempting - Reeves and Dylan's Story

A Little Jaded - Everett and Raine's Story

A Little Secret - Griffin's and Finley's Story

A Little Broken - Tatum and Paxton's Story

A Little Crush - Jaxon and Rory's Story

Harden Heights Series

(Steamy Contemporary Romance Standalone Series)

Coming Fall 2025

Jagger's Story

Ford's Story

Hawke's Story

Roman's Story

Don't Let Me Series

(Steamy Contemporary Romance Standalone Series)

Don't Let Me Fall - Colt and Ashlyn's Story

Don't Let Me Go - Blakely and Theo's Story

Don't Let Me Break - Kate and Macklin's Story

Let Me Love You - A Don't Let Me Sequel

Don't Let Me Down - Mia and Henry's Story

Wrecked Roommates Series

(Steamy Contemporary Romance Standalone Series)

Model Behavior - River and Reese's Story

Forbidden Lyrics - Gibson and Dove's Story

Messy Strokes - Milo and Maddie's Story

Risky Business - Jake and Evie's Story

Broken Instrument - Fender and Hadley's Story

Signature Sweethearts Series

(Sweet Contemporary Romance Standalone Series)

Taking the Chance

Taking the Backseat (novella)

Taking the Job

Taking the Leap

Get Baked Sweethearts Series

(Sweet Contemporary Romance Standalone Series)

Off Limits

Stand Off

Hands Off

Hired Hottie (A *Steamy* Get Baked Sweethearts Spin-Off)

Swenson Sweethearts Series

(Sweet Contemporary Romance Standalone Series)

Finding You

Fooling You

Hating You

Cruising with You (A *Steamy* Swenson Sweethearts Novella)

Crush (A *Steamy* Swenson Sweethearts Spin-Off)

Advantage Play Series

(Steamy Romantic Suspense/Mafia Series)

Wild Card

Little Bird

Bitter Queen

Black Jack

Royal Flush (novella)

Stand Alones

Fifty-Fifty

Dear Reader,

I want to thank you guys from the bottom of my heart for taking a chance on *A Little Jaded,* and for giving me the opportunity to share this story with you. I couldn't do this without you!

I would also be very grateful if you could take the time to leave a review. It's amazing how such a little thing like a review can be such a huge help to an author!

Thank you so much!!!

-Kelsie

ABOUT THE AUTHOR

Kelsie is a sucker for a love story with all the feels. When she's not chasing words for her next book, you will probably find her reading or, more likely, hanging out with her husband and playing with her three kiddos who love to drive her crazy.

She adores photography, baking, her two pups, and her cat who thinks she's a dog. Now that she's actively pursuing her writing dreams, she's set her sights on someday finding the self-discipline to not binge-watch an entire series on Netflix in one sitting.

If you'd like to connect with Kelsie, subscribe to her Patreon. Patrons receive a wide range of goodies including:

- Exclusive sneak peeks of works-in-progress
- ebook releases one week early
- Signed paperbacks on all new releases
- Exclusive special edition hardbacks
- So much more

You can also sign up for her <u>newsletter</u>, or join <u>Kelsie Rae's Reader Group</u> to stay up to date on new releases and her crazy publishing journey.